JAKUB ŻULCZYK

BLINDED
BY
THE
LIGHTS

Translated by Marek Kazmierski

Legend Press Ltd, 51 Gower Street, London, WC1E 6HJ
info@legend-paperbooks.co.uk | www.legendpress.co.uk

In agreement with Author's Syndicate Script & Lit Agency
Copyright © for the Polish translation by Marek Kazmierski 2018
First published in the Polish language under the title: *Ślepnąc od świateł* by ŚWIAT
KSIĄŻKI Publishing House in 2014
This English edition arranged via Red Rock Literary Agency Ltd.

Print ISBN 978-1-78955-9-859
Ebook ISBN 978-1-78955-9-842
Set in Times. Printing Managed by Jellyfish Solutions Ltd
Design by Gudrun Jobst | www.yotedesign.com

This publication has been supported by the ©POLAND Translation Program

BOOK INSTITUTE

©POLAND

Jakub Żulczyk is a rising star of the Eastern European literature scene.

His 2014 novel *Blinded by the Lights* was adapted into a TV series by HBO Europe and listed as one of the best TV shows made in Europe in 2018.

He is a successful screenwriter as well as the author of the bestselling Polish novels *Do Me Some Harm*, *Radio Armageddon*, *Hound Hill* and *Black Sun*.

Follow Jakub on IG
@jakubzulczyk

Marek Kazmierski is a writer, editor and translator, specialising in literary translations from Polish into English.

He founded OFF PRESS, an independent publishing house which has worked with the British Council, English PEN, the Southbank Centre, the Polish Cultural Institute and the Mayor of London.

DAY PAGE

FRIDAY

8:46pm

Warsaw, 19th of December. The radio is forecasting a truly cold Christmas. For the time being, the forecasts feel right.

At this hour, with all its retro-style neon lights outlining so much of its communist era architecture, the capital looks like a doodle knocked off by some giant, hyperactive baby armed with a sheet of black paper and broken bits of pastel crayon. Somewhere in the distance, I can hear a Christmassy melody creeping through the background noise of urban life – crackling voices and rhythmic steps, whirring engines, slamming doors. I can feel the song resonating throughout my whole body, like an advance warning of an impending toothache.

The city opens its eyes, eyes it keeps shut during the day, waking silently, heavily, like a professional drunk. The lids lift slowly, wasted, stuck together. Warsaw swells, as if its sidewalks, its gutters, its walls and windows, all of it was pumped full of dirty black water. We could use some rain, a storm, a mighty bolt of lightning to clear the air around here. Iron it all out, even if only for a moment. Then flood it smooth.

The city opens before me like the soiled pages of a battered paperback. My lips open too, as if I'm about to start silently mouthing its song. I close them again. If you were watching me from the back seat of my car, it might seem I was only yawning as I'm driving along. The city too opens its mouth. It is awake. And it wants to eat.

"Put out that cigarette," I say without turning my head, aiming the question at the back seat of my car. I exit Pilecki Street and make a turn down Puławska Avenue, heading straight downtown for Warsaw's crooked heart – a place they call the Centrum.

"What's your problem?" the guy they call Uncle spits back. I think that's what the others in his gang call him.

"No problem. Just don't fucking smoke in my car," I reply and lower the rear window, so he can toss the cigarette.

He flicks it loose and growls quietly, instinctively, like a dog that has just been reprimanded.

I can't think of any smell worse than tobacco worn into leather upholstery. The whole car ends up stinking like the skin of an old smoker. Like their hands. Their breath. We're in a graphite grey Audi RS4, 2009 series, its 305 horsepower, 2.2 litre motor running on regular gas. I bought it used, with hardly anything on the clock. The woman selling it probably only drove it back and forth between her villa and the nearest mall. Perhaps – in theory – it's a mistake for me to be seen in a car this beautiful, attracting the wrong kind of attention from both the law and the competition.

"Some fucker is tailgating you," says Uncle.

I switch lanes to the right to let the other guy pass, then watch him wildly overtake someone else, accelerate again and then jump a red light.

"What was that about?" asks Uncle. "You know them?"

I shrug my shoulders. It makes zero difference. If someone or something is going to jump you, they will do it, no matter how much stress you invest in glancing round, how quietly you learn to walk, how many locks you install on your front door. And whoever was driving that car has now been robbed of any element of surprise. I've clocked him. He's on my radar. I now know he exists.

I put on some music to drown out the noises the two on the back seat are emitting. A strange sort of wheezing, which may just be the way they actually breathe. It's all to do with their enlarged hearts, fluids in their joints, thinned out blood. One of them is constantly drumming his fingers on one knee. I'm not going to pay him any more attention. You can't do anything about people and their compulsions, their ticks. Especially not when one of those people spent a decade behind bars, while his pal looks like a bull terrier that's had its snout shoved in a blender.

"What the fuck is this music? We on our way to a wake or something?" asks the other, younger thug.

"You've never listened to the *Goldberg Variations*?" I ask him.

"Never heard of them," he shoots back.

"The *Goldberg Variations*," I repeat. "You never heard of Bach?"

"You music motherfucking muppet," Uncle snaps, but I don't take the bait.

"Where you from, by the way?" the other one asks, suddenly getting territorial like all the local gangsters, who measure men not by who they are or what they do, but by which part of Warsaw they were born in and which crew they run with. For so many of them, being born in this dark city is all that matters – if you're not from here, you're a nobody.

"Some place," I answer.

"What place?"

"I live in this town, just like you," I spit back, not letting him have the satisfaction of finding out whether I was born in his precious little capital or if I'm one of the countless aliens who came here, in search of something, poisoning what he thinks is his native ecosystem. He says nothing after that, all the way to Lublin Union Square, and as I get drawn in by the music my mind wanders. I got out of bed at 3pm, meaning I'm rested and focused. Before I got up, I felt a light cramp in my lower leg, but it's nothing. Just iron deficiency, lack of magnesium in the blood. I slept ten hours straight. After I woke, I did a hundred push-ups and took a cold shower. After that, I drank some freshly squeezed juice. Had some cornflakes, milk, then, before leaving, scrambled eggs and a slice of bread.

I try to avoid eating while out working. Unless there is a moment, a window of opportunity, when everyone has snorted what they were going to snort, but haven't started coming down yet – that's when I have a slot, before they start calling up again to place fresh orders. But when no gaps in my schedule appear – eating something, driving there, ordering, paying means half an hour, minimum, gone – even if it is just a shitty toasted cheese sandwich. Half an hour makes or loses me a grand. In your average desk job, the time of actual work done in relation to time paid for working is 30% / 70% max. The rest is Facebook, smoke breaks, eating lunch, shitting or playing with yourself in the staff toilet, daydreaming and all that. In my case, work means work, the whole day through, and then much of the night, minus sleep. I will probably get home just as it starts to get light, another 500 kilometres on the Audi's clock. Before sleep, I'll have to do some stretching, so I don't wake up as stiff as a dead man after all those hours behind the wheel.

But for now, I'm feeling fine. The city is breathing heavily, trying to clear its throat of mucus, air coming straight up from its guts and veins, stale and heavy, the Centrum heart around us beating like a drum. I can see them, all those dilated pupils scattered about our streets, hear the laughs and shouts as thin and tinny as old communist-era coins tossed about while we drive along a living wall of people, all of it shimmering in the darkness.

People. They keep on pouring outside, into the light and the darkness, into their own lives, their weekends, making a noise like marbles scattered by a giant hand. They're off to Basket Street and Saviour's Square, the epicentre of hip, the spot where everyone looks like psychopaths dressed by the latest fashion bible. On to Masovia Street, along Crane Lane, then down to the trendy Salt District. Today, I am going to visit every one of these places. I more or less know where I will be at each and any hour. The city has its day cycles. In different parts of town parties start at different points, peak and then wind down at specific times. And no matter what happens, the Centrum, the dead centre of town, will always fall last.

Both my cell phones are now ringing. I let them. They will ring until morning. I'm wasting time, driving these two thugs around, though I hope this won't be for much longer.

I waste ten more minutes looking for a parking place. It's only after a while that I realise those two in the back seat are still talking.

Strangely muted, though, as if they didn't want me to listen in. I turn off the music. They instantly start talking more loudly.

"I swear they were shooting a porn film. You know the fucking place, in that toilet down at the bottom of the stairs," the younger thug says.

"The ladies or the gents?" asks Uncle.

I can tell them apart now. Uncle sounds more gruff, as if something sharp was embedded in his throat, something which he's unable to cough up and spit out.

"In the ladies, two of them screwing some girl, a third guy filming it on his smartphone. They were riding her, both of them, loving it, gesturing at the camera that they were having a ball, but the girl, she was so out of it they could have been shitting on her head, she wouldn't have cared."

"And what did you do?"

"I told them to put their pricks away and get gone."

"And did they?"

"On the spot. Out of their fucking heads. Anyway..." He shuts up the moment I find a place to park, squeezing in by some miracle between a Range Rover and a brand new Mustang. Uncle taps me on the shoulder. I turn. He hands me some rubber gloves.

"You're coming up with us."

I notice, even in the dark, his head is the shape and texture of moss-covered stone. Millions of years ago, when this stone was still soft clay, someone stuck some eyes into it, drew a thin mouth, then carved a lot of scars across the cheeks.

"You need me to come along?" I ask.

"Yeah, I need you to come along. If I didn't, I'd have just called a cab," he answers. I say nothing back, grabbing the gloves and putting them on, then I pack all I have into my pockets. Documents, keys, phones.

"Piotrek said you're with us, so you're with us," Uncle huffs.

"And this is Piotrek's business?" I ask.

"Yes, fuck, it's Piotrek's business, that's why we're here and in it together," he says.

"Am I gonna have to smack someone around?" I ask.

"No, just try not to beat yourself up too much," Uncle spits back, trying to be funny.

I shrug, nod and follow them out of the car. Whatever they say, it's their business, not mine.

Uncle walks up to the intercom keypad of a nearby building, taps in the apartment number, then presses the button with a key on it, then enters the door code. We go inside an old stairwell. Somewhere up above, must be the third floor, I can hear the sounds of a house party. Glasses clinking quietly, muted squeals from teenage lips that sound like far-off air-raid sirens. Must be university students, first or second year undergrads. Meaning none of my clients are up there. If they're snorting anything, it'll be mephedrone ordered online. Listening to music on some ancient hi-fi wired up to a laptop, the playlist the same as any taxi cab in town, though I've learned to block that stuff out.

"Right," says the other guy.

The skin of the younger thug is dark enough to make him look like he's from somewhere in the Middle East and nowhere near Warsaw, so I nickname him Shady. He's wearing a sweatshirt and running pants. Uncle's got a blazer on, clearly made to order. His body shape is wrong for a human being. His arms are as thick as my waist, moving without grace, as if he can't quite find his balance, leaning slightly off to the side; he takes small, quick steps, as if moving all the time. Taken together, the two of them look like satiated predators, but that is only a momentary illusion. Their appetites could snap in an instant.

I stop half-way up the stairs, right by the door where the sound of the party is coming from, just to ask Uncle something.

"Why the fuck are you wearing that fancy blazer?"

"I'm going to work in a moment," he answers calmly.

"But what if you get blood on it?" asks Shady.

"I'll be taking it off in a mo, easy," Uncle assures us. The apartment we're about to enter is on the top floor. Door number 15. I stand behind them. The only one not panting. My phone rings again. I answer this time, just to tell whoever is ringing that I can't talk right now.

Uncle knocks calmly, as if he was a courier or a pizza guy. Someone asks me for a delivery to a rather fancy address in the Powisle district in twenty minutes.

"I'll call back, can't talk now," I tell them, listening to someone approach from the other side of the door. The party downstairs, as if by magic, suddenly becomes louder. I'm hoping they'll get things over and done with quickly. This is costing me time. My phone rings again. Right now, all across the crumpled map of this town, there are at least a dozen people thinking of nothing other than handing over their money. To me. Cash burning holes in their hands. Setting their pockets, their purses on fire. Desperate to get rid of it all as quickly as possible, as if their wages were clothes left behind by their dead loved ones.

There is this one room in Warsaw; I don't know why I'm thinking of it right this moment. Must be this stairwell has a similar shape. A room I know so well. Know each and every drawer. Which bit of it collects the most dust. I can name all the books lined up on each and every shelf. A room with a door leading to a small balcony, a high school on the opposite side of the street. A room which, at dawn, when the blinds are angled just so, looks like the inside of a messy pink aquarium. A room which is now off-limits to me.

I stop thinking about it when the guy on the other side of that door finally opens it, resigned to the idea that there is no other way out. We step inside, shutting the door instantly behind us.

I am the last one in, locking it behind me just to be sure. The hallway is covered, floor to ceiling, with fake wood panelling, a legacy of late communist interior design. It's a two-bed apartment, not an inch of it renovated or redecorated since the last millennium.

A bookshelf greets us with a stack of pulp fiction already half-pulped: Robert Ludlum, some Polish folklore fiction, scouting guidebooks, crossword annuals solved a century ago. The door to one of the rooms, to my right, is closed, the light behind its frosted window off. The guy, a kid really, is standing in the open door leading to the second room on the left. The space behind him is flooded with pale, blinding light. Behind him a table, covered with beer cans, an ashtray overfilled long ago, white smudges across the surface of the table, an empty bottle of one of the cheaper brands of vodka. Next to a wall, a small, kid-sized desk and a computer next to it. A thirty-inch plasma screen stuck to the wall, a PlayStation tailing from it. A folding bed, some clothes strewn across it, along with a bare duvet. No curtains in the window. A poster of Lionel Messi in a cheap glass frame, running, arms aloft. A dying pot plant next to the image and that stink – the stink of a thousand cigarettes, a thousand sweaty nights, unwashed clothes, uncountable hangovers.

Even so, the floor looks rather tidy. Somebody does the cleaning round here. Can't be the guy. Someone else must share this pit with him. He's standing there, slouching a little, wearing a tracksuit and flip flops, unshaved, his unwashed blond hair all over the place. He's a bit drunk, the beginnings of a beer belly starting to show, one measly tattoo of a local football team on his arm. He looks thirty, but I know he's much younger than that. Saying nothing.

Uncle takes his tailored blazer off and hangs it on the back of the door. The chase only lasts a moment. Uncle and the other guy get him cornered. He backs up, sideways, moving faster, but off-balance. They're on him in a flash. Uncle smashes a fist in his face, something made of soft bone collapses, like a pile of disposable plastic cups being crumpled up. The younger thug sweeps everything off the table, making a mess of that clean floor, while Uncle starts kicking the kid who at first only whines, before finally starting to scream, protest, something about the help he wants, about us stopping, all the usual requests.

"Where's the money?" Uncle barks. "You know I'll find it. Fucking right you do!"

The kid points.

"Wardrobe. Wallet," he croaks.

"Kuba, peek in there, count it up," Uncle says to me without turning.

I open the wardrobe. Hooded tops, T-shirts on hangers, a cheap suit. A cardboard box full of useless crap, broken headphones, phone chargers, old newspapers. A filthy shisha pipe. And a black wallet with the classic Legia Warsaw logo on it. I open it up. Inside, a wad of hundreds and a few fifties, thick enough to be what we need. I hear the kid get kicked again while I count it. Something crunches. A mouth which doesn't know whether to scream or just swallow air.

"Some thirty thou," I tell Uncle.

"Some?"

"More than some... thirty one thousand, two hundred and fifty."

"No more," the kid mumbles. "No, please."

I hear him spit heavily, something solid landing on the floor behind me. I turn around.

"Hold on to the cash for now," Uncle tells me.

"What next?" Shady asks the older gangster.

"Let's give him a souvenir to remember us by."

"Your hands," Shady orders the kid.

"No!"

"Face then," Shady croaks.

"Hands," Uncle repeats.

"Wait," I butt in, hearing a noise from the room next door, like something moved, ever so gently. A noise we weren't meant to notice.

"What?" Uncle asks. I wave my hand, letting him know he should mind his own business, and step out to the hallway. "Eh, Kuba seems a little too sensitive to be a coke dealer," he comments, but I don't know if he's talking to his partner, to me or to thin air.

The hallway is dark. I stand in front of the other door. Unable to see what those two are doing to the kid. It's enough I can hear it. First a howl, then weeping, then something clicks, as if a valve just broke inside an ill-defined, delicate mechanism. A split second later another howl, quickly muted with a pillow or a scrunched-up shirt.

"Fucker, be quiet," Shady rages.

I open the door to the other room. For a moment, I can hear a sort of squeal, mixed with sharp intakes of breath. I pull my phone out and turn on the torch app, to the sound of another crunch behind me, as if someone had stepped as hard as they could on a piece of unripened fruit, and again the kid's drawn-out scream.

I see a large mattress on the floor, a girl lying on it, wearing a man's T-shirt. She can't be more than twenty, clutching her duvet, staring at me with the bulging eyes of captured prey. A cheap silver ring on every finger. Highlights in her hair. A small tattoo of a bird beneath the ear. A swallow. She's breathing quickly, trying not to scream, trying to muffle her terror with the duvet, biting down on it, hard. Her spit is soaking the material. I look for a moment, see her shivering, petrified with fear, desperate to run, anywhere, to back down, but the only way out of the room now is the window, meaning her home has now become a dead end.

"Shh. Be quiet," I whisper, putting a finger to my lips. She nods a dozen times a second. "D'you understand me?"

My words are inaudible over the kid's screams, but she still manages to nod and finally take the corner of the duvet out of her mouth, trying to look beyond the light of the torch, trying to see my face. I can see her outline. Beneath the T-shirt she's clearly hiding a rotund belly. She must be seven, maybe eight months pregnant.

I step back and out the door, shutting it behind me. Uncle and the younger thug are already done, waiting for me in the hallway. Uncle is making sure his blazer hangs right again.

"What was that about? Anyone in there?" he asks.

"Nah," I shake my head.

We leave the apartment. Being last again, I shut the door. The staircase is full of the sound of drunken students, embarrassing Polish songs, all exploding upwards like a belch from a sick gullet.

"Will you drop me off on Holy Cross Street?" Uncle asks as we descend the cracked granite staircase.

"What about you?" I ask the other guy.

"Good for me," he nods. "I can walk from there."

We walk down the stairs and back out onto the street. I wipe my lips, the air creeping in beneath my jacket, as if a stranger was sliding their cold hands against my skin.

"Dough," Uncle says.

I hand over the wad of notes. Uncle nods and hides the money in his trouser pocket.

"That's it?" I ask.

"We make the call," Uncle shakes his head.

"Twenty past nine," I say, holding up my phone display. "An

hour. You've cost me an hour. I can tell you how much that is worth to me to the very last cent."

"You want a bonus, for fuck's sake, or what? How much is enough? Five thousand? Ten?" Uncle roars, pulling the banknotes back out of his pocket, taking one solid step towards me. I don't step back. "Really? You're skint? A big man like you broke?"

"Get in," I tell him as I drop into the driver's seat and lean over, opening the passenger-side door. The other thug gets into the back. I catch a brief glance of his eyes in the rear view mirror. He appears to be the smarter one, the one who can stop senseless situations from dragging on, save time from being wasted.

I plug the key into the ignition and the car fills with music. I turn it down, then look up at the windows in the flat we've just ravaged. The one which was dark remains so, and the one filled with blinding light is still blinding. One floor down, a few drunken girls are sitting on the window sill, trying to blow cigarette smoke outside. Finally, Uncle drops into the front passenger seat.

"Belt up," I tell him and fire up the engine.

"I bet you've never opened it up beyond city limits," he laughs. "You know, it's a nice enough car, but a bit flash, innit?"

I smile too. I've no idea if this car has ever seen roads outside of Warsaw, and I've had it a year.

"Yeah, well, I'm not gonna drive round in a Renault Clio."

I know I shouldn't be driving round in a car like this. But Uncle doesn't need to know everything I know.

"How much did you pay for it?" he asks again.

"Ninety grand."

"Cash?"

"No, I paid in Persian rugs."

"You what?"

"Course it was cash. What did you think I paid with?"

The city is now filling up with party people. They'll be walking along in groups, grinning through the next few hours of their lives, pouring out of underground subways, getting in and out of cabs. Erect yet swaying in the cold, as if attached to invisible strings. Playing for small stakes, and not caring if they win or lose. Running forward to forget, just for a while. Future managers, or managers already, in some middle, or assisting someone or other, students or slightly smarter mates. Trying to recognise each other in the dark streets, everyone confusing everyone with everyone else, kissing mwah-mwah, taking each other home for pre-drinkies, then on to clubs, crawling from their cabs. Some of them have need of my services already. Some only just starting to wonder.

Some might be kidding themselves, thinking the big prize is out there, waiting for them, but most of them don't even bother looking. All they want is food, sex, payments, tax rebates. Money, mostly. Thinking all the time that what they have is not enough. Those thinking of anything other than the riches waiting at the end of the rat race are lost, from the word go. Distracted. Their aim off. Trying to read the black sheet the city's scribbled onto makes no sense. That something, the real story this city's telling, can only be seen out of the corner of the human eye.

There's no point trying to tell them apart. They're identical. The trajectories of their movements, their thoughts, their fears are all the damn same. They only vary in terms of worthless details. Their uniforms. It's possible to judge, to describe people, group them in sub-sets, catalogue the bastards, pin them to their own networked maps. But here, we're all blurred points, aimlessly, ineffectively trying to return to a collective state of focus, to join back up into one blurred blot.

Me, Shady, Uncle, all those people – as if someone was keeping us condensed in one organic pile of coloured dust, spreading us across the city in wild, broad strokes. Covering the city with vivid, crazy colours. In seven hours, there will be less than half the crowd I see right now walking down these streets, only moving more slowly, wavering, louder and all the poorer for it. Failed seductions. Maxed out cards. Broken phones. Cave-boys calling out after cave-girls. Names. Nicknames. Insults.

The temperature outside creeps down another notch. Somewhere nearby, the lights of a passing ambulance cover everything in a heavenly blue light. Everything becomes more defined for a moment, visible in improved definition. I turn into Holy Cross Street and pull over.

"We'll see about later tonight," Uncle says, taking some chewing gum from his pocket and swallowing a stick. "For sure."

"For maybe," I answer.

I shake his hand, then turn to the back seat and shake hands with the younger thug. They both get out. I reverse, then drive on to New World Avenue. That kid whose bones they broke – it comes to my mind for a second – is like a fungus staining this city, dumber than moss. Human mistakes are just like human aspirations, fears, fantasies – there are only a few kinds. A list of them, if anyone could bother to make such a thing, would be as easy to understand as the rules of any childhood game. To fail to grasp this is to fail to grasp anything about life. That half-brained soon-to-be father broke his own hands, then lost his own money. We must never forget this. Excepting cancer, everything which happens to people is that which they bring upon themselves. I turn the music back on. That annoying sound, the heavy breathing, I can hear it again, though I'm as alone as can be in my car. It's this city, ejecting another breath from its hyper-inflated, steroid-addicted heart.

DREAM

I only ever have one kind of nightmare – a dream in which I have no idea where I am.

It is always a place right on the edge of civilisation, where wilderness takes over. A junction, a border – though I've no idea what lies either side of it. A narrow, asphalt lane in the middle of a forest. A dirty, empty beach dissolving on the edge of an oppressively grey horizon; only the appearance of a ship in the distance lets me know I'm in a world where anyone else is still seemingly alive. But then again, maybe there is no one on board. Maybe it's just a hollow shell, drifting along the waves. Or I see buildings, right on the edge of some anonymous town, grey shapes covered in tarpaulin, empty, abandoned, the street lamps stooping over them smashed, all outlines blurred, accompanied by the sound of cars passing by, somewhere very, very far off.

I don't have my phone, my documents, my money. Nothing. I only know my own name. Can't recall my date of birth, my address, my phone number, can't remember what my parents are called, what town I was born in. I'm nobody. Nowhere. Neither hungry nor thirsty. Just there, ghost-like.

I tend to then start walking, forward, trying to find someone, anyone, a road, a trail, and this lasts a long time, for hours. I know I'm not going to meet anyone. I know that even if I do, I won't ask for directions, too ashamed to speak.

This dream disturbs me on a regular basis. I wake from it, breathless, swallowing, gulping air, as if someone had punched me in the solar plexus. Such terror maintains its grip for a while yet, nestling in my mouth, slipping down the back of my throat, as if I was swallowing a fat, living larva. I then have to turn on a light, check that everything in my apartment is in its right place, is familiar. The wardrobe. The television set. Bookshelves. Dishes in the kitchen. My clothes, laid out on the sofa. I then sit on my bed and begin reciting my date of birth, my ID number, my phone number, my address. And then I lie in bed for another half hour or so, unmoving. Then rise, make coffee, shower, watch TV, all until someone finally rings.

Last night, I dreamt of a housing estate, of tower blocks.

As usual, I had no idea where I was. I didn't know if I was anywhere. That dream was, however, a little different, a variation on a theme; first of all, I was not alone. There was a teenage kid with me, a boy wearing a sports top and running trousers, his longish hair matted, greasy, falling in his eyes. I realised he was the same height as me, and that I too was a boy of his age. It was sunny, we were standing in the middle of a large, grassy playground. There were a lot of people about: kids, teens, their parents. Sitting around on benches, kicking balls about, looking around, killing time. Two older men were playing chess; a few others watching their game intently, a game that might have lasted minutes or days already. Someone was playing table tennis. It must have been a weekend, because groups of people in their Sunday best kept streaming back into the entrances of their houses, or else stood around outside the tower blocks, chatting.

Right in front of us, there were five such buildings, their grey-black outlines digging into the sky like dirty claws. Four of them, set close to each other, rose into the air like the barrels of some frozen asbestos artillery; the fifth was off to the side, at an angle which was different to the others. I knew that was where we were going to go and that we shouldn't be doing anything of the sort.

We walked towards the fifth block slowly, talking as we went along: it was a childish, playground plan, discussing what would happen next, as if we were about to go stealing apples, or go buying up all the bubblegum from the neighbourhood store with pocket money we had saved up. We wondered what time we would be getting back home, to make sure no one ever guessed where we had been. After 9pm, I guess, the other lad said. We have to be back by 9pm. He was walking slowly, dragging his feet, stopping time and time again to spit or to glance at something hidden in the grass, something only he could see. I had the impression he was somewhat deranged. I wasn't surprised. I had the impression his father was the violent kind. He spoke in a slur, filling his mouth full of cheap corn chips from a giant bag he was holding on to. He kept offering me the chips and the bag never seemed to empty. I refused, not feeling at all hungry.

The boy asked me if I had a torch. I realised I did, along with a penknife and pepper spray. We were nearing a place we should have been avoiding at all costs; the fifth tower block, set back from the others, was somewhere no one else on the housing estate ever went near.

The boy spoke to me with a familiarity which suggested he knew and liked me. That we were close friends. He talked a lot, but I couldn't really understand much of it, as if he was talking Russian. As we drew closer and closer to the dark grey building, I noticed its walls were covered in soot. As if someone had recently tried to set it on fire.

"And what if she is in there?" I asked the boy.

He bit his lip, but smiled a moment later.

"She's not there, you'll see," he replied. "They're all lying."

I turned around. There was not a soul in sight.

"All of them are lying," he repeated.

We kept walking.

With every step we took, I knew, I remembered more and more details. I knew that some people had lived in that crooked tower block once upon a time, but as time went by they'd all left, either moving to other tower blocks or to other towns. Some passed away. The entrances to all its staircases had been bricked up. All children on the estate had been expressly forbidden from going anywhere near it. All those who had the chance moved away from the estate – unable to stand living in proximity to the fifth building.

With every step I took I recalled another piece of the puzzle.

As we approached, I felt a stench, a fetor that crawled into our nostrils, sticking to our throats, a sour, sulphurous coating. A stink strong enough to taste.

Most of the windows had been smashed. There was graffiti all over the dusty, crumbling exterior, in a language I could not understand, scrawled in black tar; maybe the language was alien to me, or maybe I had simply never learnt to read.

"The entrance is round the back," the boy said.

"Who told you that?"

"I just know it. Come," he mumbled.

We circled the block, then he pointed to a smashed window which led to a basement, the only one that was not bricked up. It was at the bottom of a concrete well, covered over with an iron grating. The bottom of the well was littered with broken glass, cigarette butts, used condoms. All of it a decade or more old. Scraps of lives gone by.

We lifted the grating and tossed it aside. It turned out to be surprisingly light.

"I told you," the boy said.

"Why did they leave this one window open and not bricked up?"

"I don't know, maybe they forgot about it."

But I felt it, I knew it had been left like that for a purpose.

Something was ticking in the air around us, like a clock suspended far over our heads. I felt as if time was making little leaps, as if someone was skipping the day forward, as if with each second time was discarding another hour, which then flew down, fast and sudden like a brick tossed from a great height.

Once we'd crawled inside, it was already getting dark outside. The stench was indescribable, it filled the corridors like dirty cotton wool, attacking our mouths, filling our sinuses with sticky dampness. I'd never smelt anything like it in all my life. Something like mould, like fermenting fleshy tissue. Gangrene.

The room we were in was empty. The way out was barred with a door made of loosely nailed together planks. The boy pushed it gently, as if all the matter in this room was under his total control, as if he was able to move and erect walls, build staircases, change the arrangement of all the rooms.

The stink became even more intense, though this seemed impossible. It got under the skin, permeated our noses. I wanted to vomit, but there was nothing in my guts to bring up. The boy kept on crunching his corn chips. We walked up some stairs, lighting our way with my torch; I pointed it at the walls and noticed they were covered with a coat of thick, brown dust, something like a damp form of rust. We made our way up to the first floor, reached the entrance to a hallway, leading to more doors. I saw some elevators. Across their doors someone had sprayed the words: *BITCH, GIVE BACK WHAT YOU TOOK*. And next to that, another bit of graffiti: *CURSE YOU OLD WHORE WITCH*. These words I could read. Beneath that, I noticed lots of other scribbles, inscriptions, dates. Names. Lines. Something a kid might have drawn. Bits of old posters and announcements which had been stuck directly onto the wall and then half-scraped off. I tried to understand something of what they represented, but my friend said we had to move on. I followed; it now seemed he was no longer hesitant, walking along with confidence, picking up pace, not looking around every few seconds. I had the impression he knew where he was going. That he was home.

He stopped by the elevators and pressed the button to call one several times. The stink now filled my insides completely. It crawled around my guts like a worm. If I ever get out of here, I thought to myself, I will be taking that stink with me. Forever. I'll never wash it all away. I heard a noise reaching us from above, a buzzing, clanging, roaring – the agonised groans of an ancient, mighty machine.

"Can you hear that?" I asked my companion.

"No," he answered. "I can't hear a thing."

The lift awoke. I heard a dull, loud crunch and then the noise of a large, steel box descending towards us. I asked how this was possible, seeing as the building must have been cut off from any sort of power supply a long time ago.

"They say there's still some electric left on the 11th floor," the boy answered. "The other lift is also working, but that one will take us elsewhere."

We got inside. The lift was unlit. I could only hear my own breathing, sharp and sudden. The noise of a huge swarm of flies. Darkness. Warmth – it was warm inside that lift, hot even. My friend pushed a button marked '11', without the help of my torch. He knew exactly where it would be. The lift moved. Fear swamped me like water forcibly poured down my gullet: I couldn't swallow it, choking on the sensation.

The lift rose slowly, juddering, stopping every few seconds, as if it was being pulled not by machine, but by human hands.

I somehow realised I would never be leaving that building.

"I think I want to go back now," I said, but I knew it was too late.

"You'll see, she's not there," he said with flat assurance.

The lift seemed to be taking ages. Finally, it reached the 11th floor.

I realised that if I didn't make it home by 9pm, no one would even know to come looking for me in here. On the 11th floor, there was no graffiti, no litter on the floor. Only the walls were stained with the same rusty brown deposit as down below. It seemed alive to me, somehow, frothing, flowing, multiplying. My friend crushed something in his hands and threw it on the floor. It was the empty corn chip packet.

Something made a noise – something like a voice, a shapeless moan, a toothless call. The sound didn't ricochet off the walls, but seemed to crawl along them. The echo that followed sounded like hissing.

"There is no one here," my friend said. "Go."

I stared at him, his face lit up once I'd pointed my flashlight in his direction. He shook his head.

"Go on ahead," he insisted.

I nodded. There was no other way out. I knew I could not escape. I knew the lift would not work if I tried calling it, that he would be the only one who knew how to work it. Knew it had all been decided.

I started walking towards a door which had been wrenched off its hinges, into one of the apartments. It was filled with a deep darkness. Walking across the floor, I could sense my shoes sticking to it: it felt like it was covered with a thin layer of melted rubber.

"Where are you?" I called to my friend.

He didn't answer.

Something groaned again, right next to me. Croaked. I knew that the residents of our estate thought the thing that was hiding in this godawful building was some kind of a woman. I knew the writing on the wall on the lower floor was addressed to her. I knew that my friend had lied to me. I knew he was already down below. That he had probably already left the building.

I inhaled, knowing that along with air I was swallowing something which should not have been entering a human body. Thick streams of poison, mould, disease.

I took another step forward. Something began to emerge from the darkness, an outline. In the corner of an empty room, its windows covered over, something waited, by the wall, for me. It didn't have the shape of any living thing I could imagine, a shapeless lump of tissue which seemed to have slid from the ceiling, down to the floor where it now congealed.

I knew my friend had led me here for a reason. I knew he was serving me up as a sacrifice. That from time to time someone had to be delivered here, just so that the rest of our community could continue existing in peace.

Something shifted in that corner.

I could not move. My body felt as though it had been frozen solid, my mouth set in the shape of a scream. I waited.

I hadn't known about this when we'd started walking. Had I known, would I have tried to escape? Would I have run in the opposite direction, towards the people hanging around the entrance to their homes, the children on the playground? Would they not have vanished had I tried to reach them?

Or else maybe they would have captured me and led me here by force?

I woke on the floor of my bedroom at around 6am.

It was a few moments later that I realised I was asking myself those questions aloud.

10:15pm

I'm parked on Mokotowska Street, in front of another 'place' which opened recently. I don't know if it's a club or a café or a gallery – these things are just called 'places', trendy for about a week or so, rented thanks to someone's well-connected parents. Next door there's a boutique belonging to some local fashion designer, and a private gynaecological practice across the street. Inside, a fashion parade of some kind, I think, or a project presentation or the opening of an art show or a photo shoot or something of the kind, all involving ugly, skinny, dead-faced girls looking as lifeless in real life as they will do in their photographs. Art. Design. Aesthetics. A great number of the people who buy from me believe in this sort of nonsense.

The entrance to the joint is blocked by a crowd of young things, trying to be unique though all wearing asymmetrically mismatched rags, starved to near death, their phones glued to their palms or their ears. Someone pretending to know how to handle a set of DJ decks is spinning up a noise in the corner. Someone else nervously pouring drinks, mixing designer vodka with juice poured from cartons. People already ringing for taxis, the event dying down, everyone moving on somewhere else. The die is cast. This place is done.

An ambulance passes us by. The fifth I've seen this evening.

"I tell you, fifteen hundred people clicked to say they'd show, but as usual, only two, maybe three hundred turned up," my client tells me quickly, so quickly I'm worried about him spitting on the upholstery in the Audi. "This is, I tell you, 'virtual presence', or whatever they call it. If they click to say they're coming, it's as good as if they actually attend. But what's the point of that? These are new, Polish brands. Really fresh designers. Fucking classy shit. People forking out money to make the clothes, importing fabrics all the way from South America, just because they want to present their own unique vision, you get me? They don't give a damn what celebs will be photographed in their creations, if they make friends with some actress who'll attend the premiere of some shitty rom-com. No fucking way. People don't give a hoot about that sort of shit. They go in crowds. To see their mates. Not to where things are actually happening! Only to hang out with their own crowd. Can you get me just ten influencers who'll bring the whole of Warsaw out here? Then you'll see the true face of this town. Always the fucking same."

"I don't know," I answer.

"And I do. That's how it goes, I tell you. How many places went under because of these ignorant fucks," he says, blowing his nose. He's already done some lines today. I'd bet on it. "Friends are elsewhere," he adds, looking around, a little bit too nervously.

"I don't know. I'm not on Facebook," I tell him.

I open the glove compartment, dig in deeper, releasing the hidden compartment. Remove two baggies.

"My man," he tells me. "If you wanna be in the scene, you gotta put in the effort."

"Not everyone wants to be 'in'," I tell him.

"So how come you're not on Facebook?" he asks. "Things like that demand a philosophy."

"I don't even have a computer at home. I mean, I have one, in a special place, but I don't use it for all those, you know, internet things."

He looks at me for a second, as if I was covered in fish scales.

"I don't believe you. You're fucking making it up."

I can see his disbelief is honest, rising up from his fluttering, decent heart.

"Computers mess with memories," I tell him. "I have to look after my memories."

"I still don't fucking get it, mate," he says smiling. "Enlighten me."

His name is Lukasz, I think. He's only been buying from me for a year, but he rings often. Always picking up a whole bag, at least. He's pleasant, creates no problems. Gay, short, slim, his stubble neatly trimmed, always in suitably outlandish clothes, narrow pants, bowties, waistcoats. I like him. He's not from around here, just like me. Has a career going, works in some sort of journalism, writes for the internet, a blog of some kind, or so he says. He doesn't look the type who gets ahead by sitting on other people's dicks. He's cynical and has a talent for telling good jokes. Even if he gossips about someone, or says something nice about them, he has the gaze of a man who can see that the whole world is made of crap.

I like the guy. He's always got the right money for me. Is polite. Never too drunk. Never asks me to drive him to a cash machine. He likes to talk, and so I listen. A good client. A nice person.

"Eight hundred," I tell him.

He hands over the money, pulling each hundred zloty note out individually from his fancy wallet.

"What was it you were saying about memory?" he asks again.

"How many telephone numbers do you know off by heart?" I ask. "The dates of people's birthdays? Surnames? Can you recall all the meetings you've got scheduled for next week?"

He doesn't answer. Only his head is nodding.

"Do you have a favourite band?" I ask again. "Name me ten of their songs."

"You prefer having it all up here," he says, pointing to his head. "I get it."

"I don't prefer, Lukasz. It's you, like all the rest, that's taken everything from up here and downloaded it into a tablet or a computer or some cloud. External memories. But what happens when that external memory fails you?"

"That makes sense," he answers, then adds, "You know, I have to tell you something. I've always wanted to say it."

"No chance," I interrupt. "I'm into girls, Lukasz."

"I just wanted to say that you really dress well for a..." he doesn't finish the sentence, unable to decide what word to use.

"A dealer," I chip in.

"You really dress well. How much was that coat?"

"1,200 euros," I reply.

"Is it by Margiela?"

"Lanvin… Nothing doing, Lukasz. I don't love you."

He smiles. Hides the baggies in his pockets. For a moment, he keeps watching the group of people jostling about the entrance, as if they were an alien species, as if he was trying to fathom their minds. His face twists in a grimace, as if he'd swallowed something sour.

"Where are you off to next?" I ask him.

"That club, the Swimming Pool, will be packed. Some awards ceremony… I'm sure I'll see you round there soon enough."

"Maybe," I nod. "Maybe there, maybe elsewhere."

"Laters," he says, extending his hand. I shake it, watch him exiting the car.

As he slams the door, my phone rings. Pazina. I know where she'll be.

"I'll be with you in ten," I tell her.

"You know where to find me?" she asks, rhetorically.

"Yeah," I nod and cut the call.

I have the feeling that snow is on the way. Moments away. The sky is swelling, gathering. I open my mouth once again, no sound emerging. Nothing there. As if during the night someone had extracted something from me. An organ I had no idea was inside my torso. It will snow soon, I can feel it. Music. Debussy. Another ambulance. Watching Lukasz dissolving in the throng, I pull away.

11:10pm

There are three things everyone in Warsaw is guilty of doing.

The first thing is talking. People talk too much. Making no sense. Jabbering about each other, behind everyone's backs. About who owes who, who recently conned who out of whatever business. About who is weak, where their weaknesses are, where they came from. They talk about what others said about others. They talk about who is fucking whom. Who betrayed whom. Who was dumped.

They talk to talk. Talking, talking, talking. They drink to talk even more. Even more stupidly. Information seeping from them, pouring from their eyes, their ears, between their legs. Unimportant and important. The stuff that everyone knows and the stuff that's secret. Still talking. Talking until they drop. Talking just to say something else in a moment. Talking excites them, widens their pupils, speeds up their breathing, lubricates their throats. When talking comes with being listened to, it becomes more pleasant and more important than sex. Better and more essential, because it's more economical. Talking differs from sex in the vast difference between how much energy is put in and how much benefit is extracted.

The second thing everyone is up to is hustling. They either earn fucking shedloads or fuck all. If they know how to hustle, they earn lots. If they think they know but don't really, what they take home ain't worth the effort of getting up in the morning. They hustle what they know, what they have and don't have; they hustle when walking, when lying, when showing off, when counting, writing. They hustle ideas, marketing campaigns, the state of their joints, delivering pizzas or sticking flyers advertising whorehouses behind the windscreen wipers of cars all over town. They're like blind dogs, unleashed to sniff out a trail. They see nothing. Trying to hunt down all the money they can. Pulling it from the gaps in the sidewalks. Squeezing it out of thin air. Out of one another. But most of all, they hustle by talking.

And the third thing everyone does in Warsaw is snort coke. This is where I enter, all dressed in black. Everyone is on coke – those who can afford it and a large percentage of those who cannot. Lawyers. Politicians. Doctors. Entrepreneurs. Company directors. Middle management. Senior management. Television stars. Television crews. Advertising agency owners. Advertising agency staff. Financiers. Developers. Writers. Painters. Musicians. Journalists. Photographers. Producers. Publishers. Restaurateurs. Bandits. Barristers. Pimps. Whores.

Everyone, literally everyone without exception, is doing coke. It doesn't matter if it's crap, expensive, badly cut. Everyone treats it like a shared ritual. A gesture. Some sort of obvious emblem.

Taking coke is like wearing a fancy watch. Like going home by cab. Like talking and making money. It's the natural consequence of the former and the latter. It's the best help you can find to do one and the other.

In Warsaw, everyone has three important telephone numbers. These three numbers are always arranged in a hierarchy, set up on a specific podium. The gold medal goes to those who pay them. Bronze to those they're sleeping with. I get the silver. In all of the phones of all of the people I service, I am always second in line.

This is why it makes no sense asking why, after driving round the streets of this town with all this gear for eight years now, I've never been caught.

In respect of that there is one more interesting thing to note.

Everyone in Warsaw is hustling – I hustle coke. Which is special. Cocaine is something tangible, something you can touch, something that really does change reality, even if only for a short while. Coke is real. It's pure, white, hard; in large 100g bricks it resembles stones washed a perfectly smooth sort of white. It is more real than gold and diamonds – when did you last see a bar of real gold? Whereas coke – that went up your nose only last weekend.

Cocaine is subject to stock market fluctuations. People invest in it. It earns them real cash. Coke makes you take responsibility for your actions. Today, when everyone is peddling fictions, added values, different kinds of packaging, when the vast majority of the world's capital is a hollow vacuum, bubbles, invented zeros, when everyone is humbly glued to their computers awaiting the bursting of yet another bubble, I deal in real value.

I'm not particularly proud of the fact. I just know it's true. This is real trade. A profession in which little is said, little beyond what needs saying. The sums are real, the sentences substantial. There is no market forecasting, no advertising campaigns, no customer surveys. No need. The product is real. So is the money.

The money a certain guy nicknamed Tiny owes me is all too real. The club he owns is called Bethlehem. Noise travels along its poured concrete floor like thunder. Dozens of dancers touch or try to touch each other. The rest of the crowd round the bar, ordering whole trays of vodka shots, shouting at the bar staff, talking, talking, talking.

Bethlehem is a vast nightclub, occupying a small, pre-WWII block in the centre of town. Before communism fell, it was home to a hospital for children with infectious diseases. Word is, someone recently organised an orgy in the basement which used to serve as a morgue. Lots of people supposedly showed up, just no one fucked.

I am standing in the shadows, keeping out of sight, Pazina next to me. I'm holding a bottle of water, Pazina a double vodka on ice. Pazina is slightly built, skinny, her hair dyed black and pulled back in a bun, her hands constantly moving like two warring spiders. She's smoking a slim cigarette and is a little bit drunk. She's watching people with the calm gaze of someone who knows enough about them to feel a safe sort of disdain. She's probably the only friend I have in the world. Although I'm not actually all that sure what having a friend involves. Pazina is someone who devours secrets, who knows when to speak and when to be silent, who answers her phone and can show up at ungodly hours in places she should not be anywhere near, in order to handle something, take it to hers, hide and tell absolutely no one about it.

We've never slept with one another. The idea of sex has never been discussed, the same as it is never discussed between siblings or regular guys and the wives of their brothers.

"I'm sorry for you," she says. "To be sober in a place like this is worse than being hungover at work."

"We don't have jobs, Paz."

"I do. You do too."

"We don't," I repeat. "What we do is make money. But that's not the same thing at all."

"In that case, nobody in here has a job then."

Pazina is around thirty. I've never asked her actual age. She's been one of this city's top nightlife scene managers for about a decade: running nightclubs, organising concerts, finding new venues for rich kids to rent and turn into 'places'. She must know everyone, and everyone knows her. She should certainly know all there is to know about them. Her maths is great. Better than mine. I respect her for that most of all. What is surprising is that she never worries about where her next bit of income is coming from, a trait I can't get my head around. She spends or gives away everything she makes. Maxing her credit cards. Picking up strangers' tabs. Buying drinks, lending cash, helping folks. As if she knew that once the money she's got is gone, more will show up. I've never been able to explain to her that the world doesn't quite work like that.

She's tough and cool. She can stop a drunken thug from hurting anyone she's in the mood to protect. Drag people out of depressions, both the real thing as well as the imagined. Somehow, she's never been able to work the same trick for herself. She says she only resists. I know she'll never beat the inner darkness – for years, she's been living in a small, dark space without windows, with only a small slot in the door for meals. She's been through too much to ever leave it. This is another reason why I respect and can be straight with the girl. She's been cut up, torn down by people and by circumstances, but she keeps pushing on.

"Are you going to see him now?" she asks.

"In a sec. We'll let him party a little longer."

"Any longer and he's not gonna be able to understand anything you say to him."

"A good thing too."

"You gonna try and scare him?" she asks.

"Have I ever tried to scare anyone?" I ask back.

"I think that's your ex," Pazina says, pointing towards the corner of a corridor up ahead, and a crowd of people milling round, all holding drinks. I know them. And see her. The girl who lives in that pink room. The one I have no access to. The girl is called Beata. I should not be thinking about her. It really is a distraction, tearing me away from reality, blurring it. But I can see her, as clear as a coffee stain on a white shirt. Standing there, motionless, taller and more vivid than the rest, listening to someone, trying to raise a smile. I know she'll be leaving here in a moment. This isn't her kind of place. She only came here to check out what is happening. Rub up against it a little. To me, it looks like someone etched her outline into this scene with a razor blade.

The people surrounding her – I know them. One works in film, a young prick, jumpy as hell. The other, some director or other, back battling booze by the looks of things. Then a guy with an ordinary-looking girl, four dogs at home and a juvenile sense of humor. The fourth is a middle-aged DJ, as sad as only a middle-aged DJ can be. I know the rest of them too. My brain keeps tabs on half the people in this city. Pazina's mind works the same. We remember what people are called, who's been talking to whom, who earns what where, what their weaknesses are, what they like, what they're afraid of, what they are scared of, who should be left alone and who is worth talking to. Without such insider knowledge, doing anything in this city is just about as smart as weeding minefields.

And yet, I can still recall the people Pazina has no idea about and doesn't want to know either. She calls it 'the dark zone', and asks me if today I am in it. I nod. She asks no more questions. Just buys the fact. She doesn't want to know. This is another one of her attributes. She often doesn't want to know, whereas most of the people here, in this club, in this town, want to know everything. To know all there is to know about everyone is their biggest ambition.

"And?" she asks, staring at the crowd by the corridor.

"And what?" I respond.

"Something bugging you?"

"Nope."

"Liar."

"I don't think about it. Makes me lose focus," I add.

"So let me ask again – are you focused?"

"Always."

We knock our drinks together. I nod to let her know it's on. Without a word, I head out back, behind the scenes, and she knows enough not to ask any more than that. I like Paz. We don't have to waste our energies on pointless things such as greetings, farewells, kisses, handshakes, hugs. Neither one of us is troubled by what we have. Being around each other means a rest from all those other demands. Like a walk in the park.

Tiny is out the back. He calls it his office, maybe because he's painted the space all in white, and stuck an Ikea cupboard in there, along with a heavy table. I notice the cupboard is full of papers. By the wall, there are rows of cleaning products, cases of vodka, packs of toilet roll, empty ring binders. There's also a skinny blonde who looks almost thirty, but probably hasn't hit eighteen yet; she's wearing a flowery blouse, skintight leather trousers and has the absent look of someone who's seen it all, chewed it up and spat it out again, and is now thoroughly jaded. Tiny is cutting up lines on the heavy table. Outside the window, the Palace of Culture and Science is lit up in vivid purple.

"Long time no see, Kuba," he says, rising to greet me, trying to grab me in an embrace, just as I take a step back. "Take a seat."

I shake my head, still looking at the girl.

"I'm Marta," she says, her mouth moving as if she was chewing gum, although there's nothing at all in there.

"Marta, go," I answer curtly.

Tiny freezes, as if someone had just jabbed him with a paralysing shot. She doesn't react, just keeps looking at me, chewing her invisible gum.

"This is my girl," Tiny says, resting a hand on the table, cocking his head to one side like a dog trying to understand what its owner is trying to tell it.

Tiny's actual name is Dawid, but he got his nickname back in the 90s, when he was still a young and cute aspiring actor who starred in a film called *I Bet to Win*. It was some sort of crime caper, involving a group of young, sexy car thieves. His character didn't have an actual name – everyone called him Tiny because of the tiny Fiat 126 he drove round in – and the moniker stuck.

I can't remember what he looked like on that big screen. Today, he looks shit. His greasy hair is in need of a trim, he hasn't shaved in weeks, and his eyes seem to say that no one's home, along with the stupid grin pasted to his face. He's thirty-four years old and co-owns four clubs in Warsaw. He recently opened some shack with vegan street food – claiming that what matters to him most in life now is a healthy diet. In spite of said diet, he has brown, uneven teeth, except the front incisors, which were implanted recently. The originals were lost when he approached a group of bouncers somewhere on Sienkiewicza Street recently, thinking it would be funny if he asked them all whether they liked taking it up the ass. Afterwards, his front teeth were gone along with the recollection of what happened next – a typically cocky minor ex-celebrity with too much front and not enough money or guts to cover the bill.

He snorts tons of the good stuff. If only he paid for it, I'd think of him as an excellent client, but his debts have now mounted up to be a major problem. He also drinks more than he should – two years ago, he ruptured his spleen. They barely managed to save him. He now has a long and ugly scar all down his gut. Loves showing it off once he's had a few.

The boy has run up some debts. Some dangerous debts. No one knows how much he owes and who to. Not even Tiny. All I know is how much he owes me. And now I'm here to discuss what little I know.

"This is a waste of time. Especially my fucking time," I finally say.

"Do we have to get rude?" he asks.

"Facts ain't ever rude."

He pauses by his desk, then cocks his head to let the girl know she should leave. She does so slowly, dragging her feet like a surly kid. She leaves the door open. Tiny closes it behind her, returns to the long table and gestures with his hand for me to help myself to one of the lines he's just cut. I just stare back.

"You never get high on your own…" Tiny says.

"This is my powder?" I ask, intentionally sounding displeased.

He shrugs his shoulders. As he snorts, his back tightens, then the whole of him goes limp, as if getting over a cramp. Once satiated, he takes a bottle of water, pours a little into his palm and inhales it. His sinuses make an awful sound, as if he was slowly, repeatedly bringing up phlegm.

"I have an offer that you cannot…" I say, letting him finish the sentence in his head.

He sits down, smiles. I stay standing, my eyes still, watching his. There's something of the hyena about him, something sickly, ugly. He is, in a way, my mistake. Perhaps I should have been more careful, watched him more closely, cut his line of credit a long, long time ago.

I work the same way banks do – if a client is decent enough, if they buy regularly, and in substantial amounts, and they pay when payment's due, I then have certain deals to offer. Overdrafts, payment terms, promotional offers. If someone spends, say, ten thousand a week or more – and I have enough clients for whom such sums are little more than nothing – and then rings and asks me to extend a line of credit, for whatever reason, for say ninety grand, I agree. It's all about trust. In most cases, I'm mostly right. In Tiny's case, I was wrong. Though it was a question of favours to be done. He knows who I am, lets me into his clubs for free, no questions asked, lets me do my thing there without hassle. It's not necessary, but it is nice.

"I'm all ears," he kindly replies.

"I like this place."

"What is it you like about it?"

"I see more and more people coming here, and they're not the type to nurse one drink all night."

"That's why I like it too."

Slowly, his face shows signs that he's thinking. That he's actually listening to what I'm saying. Music from the basement rises up like a dirty mist. There are ghosts down there, dancing, not talking, not seeing each other, having a bad old time.

"I now consider your debt to have become my share of this joint. What you make here I get a cut of from now on," I tell him.

"Fuck me, I'll have thirty grand for you next week," he moans, jumping up from his seat. "Promise, guaranteed. We've done a deal with this whisky importer. The transfer is due any time, promise."

"Your debt is now my share of this place," I repeat. "I'm only the middle-man here. Let us say that my share of your income will be paid to someone who is a friend of mine, someone I like, someone who has experience of managing bars like this."

"Fucking hell, Kuba," he whines. "This ain't a scene from some shitty crime flick."

"You should know. All I need is a percentage of your income. And, from time to time, the opportunity to launder a little of mine through your tills."

"I can't do that, man, seriously, you know how it is. Tax brackets.

They kill profits. People are always bitching about how there's no good food in this town, but taxes eat up all the good people…"

He keeps talking, but my eyes are now on his trembling hands.

"Ninety thousand is a fair bit of money," I remind him. "Even for a roller like you."

"I can't do it, Kuba, please," he whines.

He's scared, the coke and the vodka amplifying the fear, heating his guts and his brain. I see he's turning a little red, a bit feverish. Still trying to smile, fighting to keep the grin pasted to his face, even as I see it fade like a wonky special effect. Still trying to kid his way out of this.

"Don't think of it as a choice," I tell him. "Just imagine I'm lending you a hand. I like you, Tiny. And I want to help. You fell in the street, a bit drunk, someone's taken your wallet, given you a few kicks to the kidneys, and here I am, helping you up, taking you home, making you tea."

Someone starts knocking on the door.

"Open it," I tell him. Another knock. Tiny isn't budging. "Let them in."

"What is it?!" he screams instead at the door.

Then he gets up, walks over to a shelving unit, pours himself a whisky. Takes a sip. Looks at me to see if I want some. I keep watching to see what he will do next.

"Get in here!" he shouts finally.

One of his security men walks in. I can tell he's an off-duty cop making extra money after hours. Broad shoulders, stocky build, and a face that will always look rough, no matter how many times a day it's shaved. He's wearing a fleece top, combat trousers, hiking boots. No neck. A moonlighting cop for sure. We stare at one another for longer than is necessary, though his eyes are as dull as an old spoon. He is followed in by two skinny boys: teens or twenties, tight jeans, baseball caps, ears pierced and skin inked in all the ways current trends dictate. They're followed by a girl, dressed and decorated in the same fashion. It's only by the length of her hair I can tell she's a girl – in all other aspects of her shape and appearance she's no different to boys.

"So what's up?" Tiny asks in a jolly tone, leaning on the shelving unit, smiling at the youthful trio.

The boys look at the concrete floor, glancing at each other, the girl too tries to come in on the shared eye contact, but they ignore her, as if ashamed of her presence.

"We should go now," one of them finally squeaks, sounding as if he's just hit puberty.

"Well, I don't really know about that," Tiny replies.

"Really. We've got nothing. This is all a mistake," the second chips in.

"They flushed the gear down the toilet," the security man reports.

"We could always perform a test," Tiny suggests.

I see the cop cracking a smile, then I glance at my watch. This is all costing time, but I'll spare Tiny a few more minutes. Let him feel he's still in control of things. Let him feel in charge. He's the kind of person whose guts and throat are constantly twisted by fear. When he's really scared, he falls silent, stops listening, stops thinking. I need to let him come back down to earth. To start processing again. Then, once again, I will make him the same offer he refused moments ago.

"You see this?" he asks me. "See how the battle over our future, over the soul of our youth is being waged? Look at them. How old are they? They should be playing football, going camping, anything, the little fuckers, writing poems and making records, but all they do is sit around on Insta, and if they ever move it's only to go to the toilets, in my club, and snort lines. If it wasn't for Johnny's intervention, they'd be making little amateur porn films in there, I bet. Can you see what is going on here? Don't you want to do something about it?"

"I'm not a fucking high school teacher," I reply.

"We really have to go now. Sorry," the girl says.

She has a quiet, soft voice that tells me that's all she ever does – apologise for everything.

"Hand over whatever you've got left," Tiny demands.

"There's nothing left," one of the boys says.

"So give me your wallets."

"No, wait, fucking hell," the other lad pipes up.

"Johnny, flash them a badge," Tiny demands.

The cop fumbles in his trouser pocket and pulls out a black leather pouch. He flips it open, shows its contents to them. They pull back, as if shown a picture of some horrific slaughter.

"Wallets, and whatever else you got left," Tiny repeats.

The girl once again wants the others to look at her, but once again they refuse. She reaches into her handbag, going through it haphazardly. Tiny takes the wallets and a baggie, pocketing the drugs and then going through the wallets. He pulls a couple of banknotes from one, then hands it all over to the cop. One of the lads nods once again. The girl starts to cry, quietly. The cop crunches up the money, stuffs it in his pocket and walks back towards the door. Before leaving, he turns to Tiny.

"That thing you asked about, I can get it for you. The piece," he says, looking once at me, once at Tiny.

"We'll chat later," his boss responds.

"Well, like I said. I can sort you out," the cop repeats, his voice stifled, as though he was trying to swallow a clump of bread. He then nods and leaves.

"This ain't a club any school kid can pop into and snort gear, you understand? This is my place, I have DJs flying in from all over the world, not some fucking end of year college disco," he says to the kids.

One of them nods, still evidently terrified, but now he's already thinking that it's all about to end, and end well. His stomach is churning relief with fear and the McDonalds Happy Meal he had earlier, washed down with five beers from the bar.

"If you understand me, get the fuck out of here," Tiny spits and begins cutting up more lines. I see out of the corner of my eyes that the trio are still hanging around, as if they hadn't got the message. "Fuck off out of here," Tiny repeats and only then do they leave, quickly, leaving the door open again. Tiny rises and shuts it behind them.

"Are you afraid of anything?" I ask, adding, "I don't think you've got anything to be afraid of."

"I ain't," he says, looking at me questioningly. Fear once again has tightened his lips, as soon as the word 'afraid' was mentioned.

"So why do you need to pay a cop to get you a gun?" I ask calmly.

"Don't you have one?"

I don't answer. Instead, I repeat my offer.

"Listen, I give you a week. Think it over. I know you're behind with the rent on this place. That the landlords have problems. That you owe the city money. That there's more than one person who would like you to settle your accounts. That in a while you might be losing your liquor licence…" Calmly, I tell him what he needs to hear.

He doesn't look up. Instead, still sat at his desk, he snorts a line and only then lifts his head.

"I can give you ten thou today. That's all I made this week," he offers.

He's pasted another one of those forced smiles back to his face, but the eyes are a puzzle of emotions. I walk over to the door.

"You have a week. Don't call me unless it's to say 'I have the lot'," I tell him.

I leave him frozen, stuck to his desk in his office, and exit. My phone tells me Pazina's messaged to say: *Had to run. Call you tomorrow.* I put the phone back in my pocket and go downstairs, in the direction of the bar. Looking around, my eyes seek Beata out, but she's gone, leaving her crowd of hangers-on distributed evenly round Bethlehem. I ask myself if she left because she saw me, but don't go as far as answering it. I blow out the question like a wasted match. Thinking such thoughts will mean I'll fail to spot someone's car, or talk to someone I shouldn't be talking to, or answer a call that should go unanswered.

For a second though, no more than a second, I wonder about where she went and who she might have gone with. Who she'll be sleeping with tonight. But that too vanishes. Very quickly. Then there is just the crowd at the door to clear, a few hands to shake – though the faces feel blank, transparent, nameless. Which is bad. I should be keeping count, a check on things, remembering who was there, who they were with, on their way in or already out. But I'm starting to feel tired. They're just people from a nightclub. Few of them count.

The only thing that counts now is the time I lost because of that fool Tiny tonight.

01:50am

"But the cash machine is just around the corner, man, for fuck's sake. Please. Please," he pleads.

"I'm not a cab service," I reply.

"Shit, so how am I gonna pay you?"

"You don't need to pay me, coz I haven't given you anything yet," I state. He says nothing. "Always the same story with you."

"I'll take two," he says.

My phone rings. A voice says: "We've been waiting here for half an hour."

"So wait some more, I'm coming," I reply and cut the call.

I drive him to the cash machine and wait. There's something about tonight I don't like. Nothing is fitting like it ought to, nothing going the way I planned. There's something troubling in the air, something that won't let me get the job done, something spooking my senses. As if someone was running the wrong version of reality, a version that wants things to run their course to the very bitter end. To complete shutdown.

My mouth opens, all by itself. No sound comes out, but I exhale those thoughts. I don't believe in sensations, in intuitions. "There's no such thing as intuition," I tell myself, taking another deep breath.

For a quarter of an hour, he couldn't actually find my car. I don't know who gave him my number. And I can't tell if he was born that stupid, or just got that way with advancing years. Everything about him is moronic and broke – he looks like a parody, a comedy version of your ordinary, household-variety, TV sitcom-style advertising exec or movie director, but a parody that's just not funny. He's trying to look sharp, but everything about him, his clothes, his haircut, the way he speaks, is blunt and bland. His chit chat might impress girls freshly arrived here from the sticks, the ones they call 'jam jars' for the home-cooked food they bring back from Przemyśl or Radom or some other godforsaken small town, food their mummies cook all week and then pack in old, recycled jam or sauerkraut or pickled gherkin jars, wrapped in plastic bags so they don't leak as their darlings get coaches or trains back to the big city.

"Shit, the machine took my card," I hear him say as he opens the passenger side door of my car. "Fuck, I swear. It took my card, the fucking monster."

"Get in," I tell him, though just for a second I toy with the idea of getting out myself, going round to the other side and smashing my fist into his solar plexus, just for the hell of it.

"What now?" he asks, looking nervously round.

"Precisely. What now? You were gonna buy two," I remind him.

"I have the cash at home," he says.

"So why didn't you just bring that with you?"

"I only just remembered. It's money I've put away for a deposit on an apartment," he explains.

"Eight hundred."

"I have it."

A little while later, we stop by a block of apartments near the Filtering District. He gets out of my car as if it was a taxi, slamming the door that bit too hard. I can see he's as high as a kite, his unfit body bouncing around like it's made of jelly, like it's that bit too heavy for the bones beneath its surface.

"Will you wait down here, or go up with me?" he asks.

"I'll wait."

"But it could take a while."

I sigh again, then pull the key from the ignition, get out and follow him. Just a few more hours to go before this night is over. I'm waiting for it to end, the way some people wait for payday or for a call from a clinic. He opens the front gate, we walk into a courtyard, he taps in the front door code, getting it wrong two or three times, then we go inside.

"Maybe you typed your PIN number wrong too into that cash machine?" I ask.

"You what?" he responds, turning around to look at me, eyes confused behind horn-rimmed glasses, the gaze of someone for whom the simplest correlations of cause and effect are always a problem.

"Forget it," I bark.

We go upstairs and end up in a large, airy apartment, littered with all sorts of crap, clothes and cartons all over the place. Two of his mates are sitting on the sofa. They seem half-conscious, drunk or high or likely both, but they're still capable of realising something is odd – a stranger is standing in front of them. I glance at the easel and canvases resting against one of the walls.

"My girl just moved out," our host explains, his arm sweeping across the mess of his home.

"She left all her things?"

"Well, no, actually," he answers, cryptically.

I grab a chair and sit, waiting for him to bring the money. His friends are sitting opposite me, staring with the sleepy gaze of farm animals. One of them is large, well-built, though turning chubby, the other stick thin, with no chest to speak of, his eyes dazed. Both dressed in similar Carhartt shirts, baseball caps, clean trainers. Adult rappers. I know one of them from some parties, where he plays other people's songs.

"How's it hanging?" the larger one asks flatly.

"Fine," I smirk.

"Fuck, it was here! It was right here!" I can hear our host screaming from the bedroom. "Where the fuck is my dough?! Where's the money?"

"Where's the money?" the skinny one repeats, laughing. "Where is the money?!"

They stop paying attention to us, get back to watching some YouTube films on a flat-screen TV fixed to the wall. A clip of a guy wandering round his apartment in just a pair of Calvin Klein underpants, mumbling something about wealth.

"And where will you get the money from?" asks the skinny guy.

"If it's not here, my old man will wire me the cash," our host shouts from one of the other rooms. "Fuck! He'll wire it tomorrow, goddamn it! Any time I call him and say 'Cough up', he coughs."

His old man will wire it. Yeah, I remember him saying something about his father once upon a time. That the guy has a furniture factory, somewhere near the German border. And when he turns thirty-five, there's a cool fifty million zlotys waiting for him in the way of a present. Yeah, he told me he drives a Jag, though he works in some gallery, or maybe sells tickets in a theatre, earning, like all the other plebs, two or three grand a week, max – peanuts.

There is a painting behind the sofa. On a white, primed canvas, someone has printed the letters: *WHO WOULD DARE SAY NO TO THE RICH?*

"Did your girl paint that?" I ask.

"She's no longer my girl," he replies, walking back into the lounge. He opens one of the drawers in an old sideboard, pulling socks and pants from it, some of them still in their original packaging, as if he went to H&M or Zara every week, just buying new underwear.

"Best look at this," the big guy says when a clip of a Polish rapper comes on the TV.

I don't know much about Polish hip hop and have no desire to increase that store of knowledge. I've heard a few songs, all of them composed with the aim of telling those who don't know how things really are, yeah, how they are really. If things are the way they are in those songs, then their authors live in a very different reality to mine. The song they're playing now is about a guy who smokes cigarettes, has no money and runs off from a gym to a friend's place to get high. The song describes how he gets high, looking out the window, and is having a little panic attack. Little and Large are laughing at the words, but know them off by heart, singing the ends of most lines.

It's 2am. Money is slipping right through my hands. This night is like being stuck in one hellish sort of traffic jam. On the other side of the river, there's four promising addicts waiting for me. They work as auditors for PwC, and must recently have got a bonus because they want two grand's worth of coke. I should have been with them twenty minutes ago. What the fuck do I care about some guy from the far east of Poland, shitting himself at his buddy's place and taking smack, when right now outside the window there are taxi drivers ferrying the bosses of utility companies to whorehouses, men who need my services.

"When did you split up?" I ask our host, watching as he turns another drawer inside out, looking for my cash.

"Two weeks ago," he says without looking up.

"Why?"

"She never cleaned up after herself," he says, then stops and looks at me with the gaze of someone who wakes each morning, stunned by the fact that the buildings in the street outside his window are still somehow fixed to the ground, and have not flown off into space in the middle of the night.

"Were you in love?" I ask.

"She was a great fuck," he shrugs. "But she was a little wrong in the head department."

"What does that mean?"

"What does what mean?"

"You said she was not right in the head."

"She'd burst out crying for no reason. And when she was younger, she cut herself. Shit like that."

"Did you talk a lot?" I pry.

He rummages through the last drawer and finally comes upon something that makes him pause – I think it's my money, because his jelly flesh starts trembling and he then claps his hands together.

"Fucking hell! I've got it!"

"I'm most pleased," I tell him.

He turns to me, holding a stash of hundreds of zloty bills, a couple of grand at least, pulls eight of them loose and hands them to me. I pocket the cash, take out two baggies and drop them in his palm. His fists clench around them, tight, paranoid tight.

"Maybe you two should talk," I tell him.

"She talks lots," he replies, looking around his apartment. "She's meant to come collect her stuff. She was meant to do it a week ago, for Christ's sake."

"Why don't you take it to her?"

"She's the one moving out," he spits back.

I now know why I can't stand looking at him. Not because he's stupid, and not because he's leaping up and down like some lump of aroused fat. I can't stand him because he's just like thousands of other men in this city. He has a cock, but he's no man. He doesn't respect women. Doesn't listen to them. He fucks them just to score another conquest, another notch on the bedpost, to rub his hands in glee, keeping count, twenty, thirty, losing count. He's a flake, a loser who needs his ass wiping, his meals cooking for him, his laundry doing. Everything he says sounds like a little kid pleading for his toys. That voice, superficially deep, but concealing a hidden squeal, which he uses to tell everyone everything. Sticking to people with hands he never washes, hands he keeps in his undies, confessing to all and sundry in some desperate attempt to earn their trust. He juggles secrets. Tidbits of personalised info he holds onto just long enough to spit them out like shameful little lies. He sucks up to everyone. A weasel. Soft. He's one of the sickly kind, those who never have original thoughts, whose palms are always sticky with sweat, whose dicks never really get hard.

"She can fuck off for all I care," he says, cutting up lines on a coffee table. "I'm not gonna run after her. She spent a year living off my money."

The other two stop paying attention to the laptop screen and sidle up to him, stretching as if before a gym session.

"Where is the money?" the skinny one says once again and giggles. Echoed by the big guy.

"That's right, where is the money?" I answer.

"See ya," says the lump of jelly.

Next to *WHO WOULD DARE SAY NO TO THE RICH?* there is another canvas, a picture of a small child perched atop a toboggan, ready to slide down a mountain. The kid is just an outline. The sky as red as fresh blood. At the foot of the mountain there is a rabid dog, sketched in rough brush strokes, as if ready to dissolve into the snow. I look at the picture and it takes me somewhere, but I'm not sure where yet, into some unclear memory, a strange place.

"You want to buy it?" our host asks.

"Buy it?" I answer, watching as he snorts a line off the coffee table, throws his head back and then downs a tumbler of whisky.

"Two grand and it's yours. That's how much she owes me for bills."

"I don't know. Maybe."

"You'd be doing her a favour," he says. "Fucking hell, I'll get the cash off her somehow. Pull it out her ass."

"Where is the money?" the skinny guy says once again, laughing and staring my way, but not at me, right through me, somewhere far off, into something invisible.

04:10am

"We need you to be at the Russians' place in ten minutes flat," Uncle says, calling me, and hangs up before I can say anything.

I was supposed to be heading home. Home and off to sleep. Popping a pill, sipping some tea, then leaping into a bath. Falling asleep there. Two hours later, crawling out and into bed, for another three hours. Listening to a bit of Debussy. Dreaming nothing. Resting.

I call him back. He picks up.

"What do you mean 'ten minutes'?" I ask. "I'm going home, for fuck's sake!"

"You're not going home," he tells me and cuts the line again.

'The Russians' place' is the old Soviet embassy building on Sobieski Street – there's a club there, a bar, hard to really know what to call the joint – a place not many people know about, the kind you have to know the right code to tap into the intercom keypad to get into. As a rule, they won't just let anyone in. They will sometimes hire the place out for parties, birthdays, christenings, that sort of thing, but most days it's where the Russians congregate. It's surrounded by some abandoned, ten-storey tall, hotel-like buildings which during the Cold War were home to an army of Soviet spies, keeping tabs on the whole Eastern Bloc and countries of the Warsaw Pact. Now, nobody lives there. The club does a decent trade, though. A range of imported luxury cars with Russian number plates on constant rotation in the street outside. Sometimes, they stop for a day or two. Meanwhile, nobody comes in and out. Only the guards at the door swap shifts.

I get there within a quarter of an hour. Angry and exhausted. It's fiercely cold outside, the wind sneaking in under my coat, cutting the skin. Snow slicing the air like tiny razors. I shut my car door. Parking on the pavement is not something I ever do for any extended period of time.

"What?" an old, heavy voice with a Russian accent barks when I push the intercom Call button.

"Kuba," I tell him. "Here to see Uncle."

A moment's silence. Then the gate buzzes. I go inside. There's a guard smoking a cigarette on a snow-covered courtyard, paying me not the slightest bit of attention. I can see some benches in the dark. Three old communist-era tower blocks look like dark, dead monoliths. When I look at them for any longer than a second or so, I feel like they're pressing down on my solar plexus, like they're starting to choke the life out of me.

I go inside the old embassy building. The place is empty. Its décor says 1987. Yellow lamps, wooden panelling, the smell of floor polish hanging heavily. A restaurant like they used to have all over the Soviet Bloc. A billiard table. Some people are sitting round, drinking in the next room. The lights dimmed. A massive flat-screen TV stuck to one of the walls is the only thing which reminds us the communists lost. That Poland is now part of NATO. Two men wearing pressed shirts, waistcoats and bowties are behind the bar, one of them way past sixty, the other much younger, no more than twenty. They look at each other without seeing, pretending to be doing something, polishing glasses or whatever. I approach the bar, order a coke. They don't even have a till, everything done via calculator and cash box.

"What you want with your coke?" the younger barman asks.

"I can't," I tell him. "I don't drink."

I don't drink because I have work to do, seven days a week. I don't drink while working. Driving drunk, in a car containing tens of thousands in cash, half a kilo of top-class drugs and a handgun could be considered an unwise thing. I don't take my own shit. I used to do it, to help me work longer hours. Then Barney, one of the lads who used to run around the Centrum, died of a heart attack. Barney was very ambitious. He was in his mid-twenties, lifted weights, did kickboxing in some fitness gym. He knew how to fight. Wanted to make as much as he could and did so: a week before he checked out he was negotiating the final details of the purchase agreement for a block of flats in Katowice. He wanted to make all he could, so he never slept. Always picked up the phone. Drove to where was necessary. Selling shit to people like communism had only collapsed a couple of days ago.

When his girlfriend found his body in their bed, I shrugged my shoulders. I never did like the guy, even if he was less of a dick than the rest of our crew. He never thought past what he was capable of delivering. Didn't hang around brothels, didn't strike up conversations with whores, didn't invest in relatively expensive watches so big you couldn't button your shirt sleeves around them. He wore no jewellery. Did not stand out. He was just hungry, and the hunger grew within him in some arrhythmic tempo. He fed on cash like it was protein – I had this impression he was freezing, marinating the stuff, eating sandwiches full of cash. He devoured money and grew fat with it. Swelled with it. I didn't go to his funeral. He came from a good home, his mother convinced – to this very day – that he made his living selling stocks and shares.

"Oi!" Uncle's voice calls out of the dark.

A TV hanging on one of the walls flickers on. A ripped Russian, his sculpted torso smothered in oil, barks some dire disco song that sounds like a metal bar being rammed into a wall.

I turn around.

Uncle looks like an exhausted animal, as if he'd been running a 100k since that moment I'd left them on the corner of Mazowiecka and Holy Cross. The sports top beneath his leather jacket is heavy with sweat. His eyes are wide open. He's out of it, rubbing his hands slowly, very slowly, looking about. Once he's done scanning the room, I see his hands are covered in blood. A lot of blood, already congealing. No one else seems to be bothered by this. The disco number on the TV ends. A busty Russian bimbo begins to sing some maudlin ballad, sitting on the porch of a luxury villa, wearing a flowing white dress. Pale silk on silicone tits, blood-stained hands – this night is not going the way I planned, not at all.

Uncle stumbles towards the bar, slowly, almost crawling. Puts two fingers up, signifying victory. The barman pours him two vodkas. Uncle swallows them both.

"What's up?" I ask.

"Wait here," he says. "A moment."

"I'm on my way home," I tell him, still scanning the room.

A fat, middle-aged bloke is sitting at a table by the wall, wearing an ill-fitting blazer, washing pickled herring down with vodka. His grey hair is slicked right back. A money launderer with a heart condition and a woman by his side. She's staring at him intently, as if trying to guess what is going through his mind. She's slim, a fine figure, but the rest of her looks worn out, her face blotched like someone had once put cigarettes out on her cheeks.

"Well, you're not home just yet," Uncle says to me without a trace of sympathy.

The dark-skinned thug appears, calm, unhurried, though he too looks tired. Shady's holding a small Adidas holdall, as if he'd just come in from the gym. He stands in the middle of the room, staring at us as if he hadn't been expecting to see us in here. Then Uncle nods at him. The barman lets us in behind his counter, we walk past him, not making eye contact, past a man who is absolutely unmoved by the presence of other human beings. As we go into a room at the back of the bar, he shuts the door behind us.

Uncle, Shady and I find ourselves in a small space full of freezers which in turn are full of bottles of Nemiroff vodka. No windows, no ventilation, the place as hot as a dry sauna.

"Show him," Shady says.

Uncle is still huffing and puffing; he places the bag on one of the chest freezers. Opens it. Inside it, there's coke, a kilogram, maybe less, some pills, MDMA crystals. Cash, euros, piles of it, tens upon tens of thousands. Uncle zips the bag back up again. Lights a cigarette. Chokes on it straight away.

"So what did you ask me to come here for?" I croak.

"That bag used to belong to Birdie," Shady says.

"Yeah, but so what?" I ask again, noticing that Uncle's hands are a lot more bloody than I realised.

Birdie. I know that name. A crooked gangster, so it's not surprising that he would eventually end up in Uncle's claws. Word is, he even dabbled in dealing heroin. Tried to get people into it. Set them up. Fed them bullshit. He smoked crack, in unhealthy amounts. But worst of all, he was a liar, an edgy, nervous lad with the smile of a con artist, the kind who would always try and cheat you out of every penny, even if you only sent him to the shop to get some cigarettes.

"He had a debt to settle," Shady said.

"Now, he'll have to borrow more money to cover the dental work," I reply.

"And more," Shady adds.

I lean against a freezer and look around the shelves, filled with bottles of booze and soft drinks.

"Fine, but what do you need me for?" I finally press.

"You'll look after this," Uncle says. I say nothing to that. "Nobody will think you've got anything to do with it. You know how to hide shit."

"Ten percent of what's in there is yours," says Shady.

"Screw the ten. This thing stinks," I tell him.

"Hold on to it, for fuck's sake," Uncle butts in, adding "There's fifty thousand euros in there. Exactly fifty k."

"Who's gonna claim it?" I ask.

"No one's gonna claim it," Uncle huffs.

"Someone always does."

"Just take it, no questions asked," he orders.

This scene will drag on a while longer. Standing around, looking at each other, breathing, Uncle coughing. There is a small sink and a piece of soap in the corner. Uncle notices it, walks over and begins scrubbing his hands. This makes the scene last even longer; more precious minutes when I could be sleeping, when benzodiazepines could be dissolving in my blood, dissolving me in sleep, dissolving dreams.

"I'll come claim it," says Uncle.

"You're not worried about where he got it from?" I ask.

"In a couple of weeks," is all I get in response.

He's the kind of man whose mind is not always up to the task of keeping up with rapid developments. Especially not in those moments when it's been busy making some sorry chump an invalid.

"What if what's in that bag is not actually his?" I press.

"So fucking what?" Shady answers with a question. "He had the stuff, so we took it."

"But what if he took it off someone else?"

I take another look inside the bag, check the cash, the gear, trying to estimate how much is in there, hard to tell in the dark, but adding up the drugs and the money there's the equivalent of a spacious apartment right in the heart of this city.

"Hide it where you hide other stuff," Shady tells me. "Piotr said he trusts you the most. Said to give it to you. And also you did well earlier."

I hear Uncle take another deep, ugly breath.

"Everybody knows he owed everybody. So where did he get all that from? The lottery?" I lift the bag up – thugs like these two are visual types, you have to show them things so they can understand. "Not a fucking chance..."

"You got a point," Uncle huffs. "What we need to do is watch what happens."

I don't want this. It's not mine. I've never touched anything that wasn't mine, anything I didn't know the source of. This is dangerous, moronic. This bag is not just full of gear and dough, it contains something like a mysterious mechanism I cannot unpick, something which stinks, something which could explode at any moment. A chemical weapon.

"Piotr said to give it to you," Uncle drones on.

"I'll talk to him about it next week," I reply, though seeing little choice I still zip the bag up and throw it over my shoulder.

It feels warm, and the warmth feels sickly. As if there was a dying animal inside.

I leave the back room, without waiting for the other two, exit from behind the bar. I can hear them walking behind me. Ambling along slowly. On the way back to their homes and the wives or girlfriends waiting for them there. I go outside. Old Soviet tower blocks stick up into the sky like giant ghost fingers, threatening violence.

"Hey!" Uncle calls out.

I turn around.

Shady is walking towards his car. Uncle is standing in front of me, his expression frozen by an unasked question. It's that odd mix of panic and shame, like a guy about to tell his doctor about prostate problems.

"What?" I whisper.

"I can't sleep," he says.

I wait for him to speak again. He still has blood under his fingernails. I see him looking at it, huffing with worry.

"Two months now. No fucking sleep," he complains.

"Go see a doctor."

"You mean shrinks, like some fucking mental case?"

"Hydroxyzinum," I tell him.

"Doesn't fucking help," he moans. "It's like something's got hold of me. Tossing me about. One end of the bed to the other. And my guts. Here. No fucking good. Nothing. I yawn. Can't open my eyes. But I can't sleep either. Like something was eating my guts out from inside. You know what I mean?"

"Rohypnol, try that."

"What is it?"

"The shit you spike girls' drinks with," I enlighten him. "You won't get it from a pharmacy. But I can ask around."

"I need loads."

"I know."

"Thanks," he sighs, extending his hand. Having parted, we

walk along side by side for a while longer. He doesn't look at me. Doesn't look back. We then split off to our separate cars. I don't look back either. It's even colder inside the Audi. I check my phone. Ten unanswered calls. Someone, somewhere still having fun, still waiting: needing more, wanting to get rid of something, to kill something inside. Someone wants to be wiser, more focused, wants to sober up, wants to fuck better, see that bit clearer. As of tomorrow, I'm back in the game. As of tomorrow, I'm back behind the wheel. All dressed in black.

The problem is – none of the people of this town will be seeing anything any more clearly any time soon. They're like caged animals – they pine, yearn for one another only to discard, unburden, to lose themselves in a day, a month, a year, in business, in sex, in friendships – cheating, extorting, lying. They cling to their personal freedoms as hard as they can, but there are no freedoms at all. Not because there's somebody out there pulling the strings. There's no freedom because everyone will always want something more than they're due. I deal in the illusion that some of them can make it. A fleeting bit of fakery. An untruth. A lie they're in desperate need of.

But as I've already said – the substance which delivers this illusion is the most real of things.

I head home. Put some music on just to turn it off moments later. I watch the road, but watch the cars rolling along it even more carefully, trying to read and memorise at least twenty number plates in a row. Little mental exercises.

I sometimes pray, though I've never thought about God for any longer than a minute. But I do pray. Opening my mouth, without making a sound.

I pray for rain.

Yeah, I pray.

Dear God Almighty, the one Godhead Trinity, send us rain. God Almighty, send a mighty rain, the sort we've never yet seen the likes of, raindrops like bombs, a deluge like napalm. Send your rains and drown this city. Do it fast, before anyone can react. Before alarms start ringing. May the waters of the mighty Vistula rise up, spill over both shorelines, flood Praga District to the east and the Riverside District to the west, let it drown Zoliborz and Targowek, Mokotow and Wawer. Let it just fall. Let everything be covered in water, black, dirty, cold. Let it flow. Let it cover town houses, streets, high rise flats, skyscrapers, crossroads, all the way to the spire atop the Palace of Culture and Science. Flood us, Lord, for if you don't, we'll just keep on running round in circles, bumping into one another, into walls we erected ourselves, furiously, rabidly tearing at the scenery, the dirty props everything's composed of, in order to get something out of it – love, money, our very selves, something which is not really there, and even if it is, then it's temporary, vanishing faster than it appears. It's like trying to catch a tiny bird with your bare hands. Pointless. End this, Lord, for whatever's left of us is dried up, died down, without point, or moral, or even punchline, sadder than the shittiest comedy. Let it rain and let it keep on raining. Dear Holiest of Holies, drown us.

Wash away restaurants and brothels, wash away office blocks and rented floors, homes and houses, wash away go-go bars, TV stations, advertising agencies, drown Toothy Street and Marshesall Street, Pulawska and Basket Streets, John Paul's and Sobieski Avenues. Let it submerge churches, Vietnamese street bars, shopping malls, bazaars, hospitals, the Presidential Palace, the University, the milk bars, the sushi joints, all the clubs on Saviour Square and on Mazowiecka Street, let it submerge all of Bethlehem, let it drown all of us and all those we know. Drown the decent and the losers and the whores. Drown those who speak the truth and those who spout lies. Mothers, fathers and kids. The loaded and the skint. The bosses and the bossed about. Drown us, Lord, kill us, in your holy name. Drown us, for we deserve nothing less. Let the waters rise, let the river take it all, leave nothing behind, the currents fast, relentless, resolute, all the way to the sea. Nothing else is going to happen here. Nothing to see. Maybe a long, long time ago, a very long time ago something worthwhile happened round here, but that was a momentary flash in the darkness, the credits rolling to a stop centuries back. Flood this city, else I'll just keep driving round and round its streets for millions of years. Drown this city so I can no longer hear its hum, its deaf scream. Drown us, for we know not how to think or to love. For we want none of it. For we are wandering, lost, in a dark wood, drunk on our own words. Drown me, because I want none of it. I only want money and the night. I only want to watch and count. There is nothing more I want or know how to do, and yet there is nothing here to look at, Lord, and nothing to count on, God, it's all the time, all the same clearly defined image, the same canvas covered in all the same possible details. Drown them all, for they know not what they do, they know not who they are, for they enter each day and leave every night just as thoughtlessly, just as falsely as little children, little babes running into a giant, brightly lit fairground and for a while longer they run on, carried by the music, by the spotlights, the echoes, the ringing and the jangling, the laughter of clowns, the melody of coins, but eventually they all come to rest and stand there, motionless, not sure of what is going on, deafened by the noise, blinded by the lights.

Listen to me, thou Holiest of Holies, listen though I have nothing to offer in return.

In the name of the Father and the Son and the Holy Spirit.

Flood us, Amen.

SATURDAY

2:10pm

"And what am I supposed to do?'" she asks, sounding like a drunk actress in some cable TV soap opera who, having just come off set and caught a glance of herself in the mirror, realises she's now well past sixty.

"I've no idea, Mum," I answer.

There's a bowl full of food perched atop an Ikea table in front of me. Something Indian, ordered over the phone from a restaurant a few streets from my front door, delivered by a sweaty, breathless guy who is just about the same age as my mother. I stare into the bowl, but I've no idea what any of it is. I ordered at random from their online menu. Scooping some up onto a spoon, I swallow. It's kind of fine, spicy and thick. Food fit for alcoholics. I swallow a few more mouthfuls, my throat burning.

"How do I explain to your father and Paulina that you're not coming home again this Christmas?"

"I've no idea what you'll tell them, but I know you'll think of something," I answer, trying to sound helpful.

"I just can't believe you have to work during this time of year," she moans. "I just can't. Nobody works during Christmas."

"Gas station attendants?" I mumble through a mouthful of burning food.

"What?"

"People need fuel to get about during Christmas," I repeat.

"Don't be facetious," she snaps.

My stomach feels tight. That's all I'll eat today. Maybe a bit more tonight. A snack, like a hot dog or a stir fry, if I have time.

I've no idea why I don't yet look like some sweaty Russian mafia don, the terrible diet I'm on. Always swallowing quickly, like I'm ashamed of the need to fuel up my flesh.

My eyes settle on the even piles of shirts, sweaters and trousers lying on the shelves in front of me. Arranged according to colour, from the darkest to the lightest. I put them all in order last night, when I couldn't sleep. I look at all those clothes, trying to work out how I'll go about making myself invisible tonight.

My mother begins to speak, telling me some story about her friend, a wife being cheated on by a husband who's found a younger woman, and seems to have got her pregnant, and she then seems to have poured a can of emulsion paint over his car, and smashed its windows in. I'm not listening. Bothered by the idea of invisibility. The absolute, essential aspect of what it is I do is invisibility.

"We're nailing the deal with the Taiwanese," I butt in. "Millions, mum. Euros. Tens of millions of euros, mum."

"But what will I tell your father?"

"Do you need money?"

I'm not from Warsaw – you could call me just another 'jam jar' who came here from another town in search of fortune. In Warsaw looking for something, something better, better than Radom, Tarnow, Koszalin, Ostrowiec Swietokrzyski and all those other cities dating back to medieval times: we were all the best in class, stars in our schools, topping all exam result charts. We've come here to get our degrees, our careers, our mortgages, deals signed in the suburbs, in the green belts, our cars leased, our cards maxed, our lives here and now. In some way, I'm one of them. Even more ridiculous. I came here from Olsztyn in order to become an artist.

And it is at this point I always hear the canned laughter, the same sort they used to use in TV studios all over the world.

"Grandma's really not well. She's in a bad way," I hear her say.

"I'm well aware of that," I tell her.

"I'm not sure that you are," my mother answers. "She really seems to be losing touch with reality. That Michal, he's been with Paulina for five years already, and recently gran asked who Michal was when they went to visit her. She's getting everything muddled up. She recently asked what it is you do. She's got it into her head that you have a wife, and her name is Marlena, but that's the name of her sister."

"She was never that good at putting two and two together," I tell her.

"Why do I even bother talking to you?"

"I've no idea."

I shovel up some more food, just to have something to chew on, and a bit so as not to have to talk. I look at the jumpers, the trousers, the trainers. All my footwear is black, even the sports shoes. Force of habit. I realise I must look like some sort of upper middle management type. An accounts manager who likes discussing imported wines over dinner. More canned laughter.

Invisibility. If you do what it is I do, you have to look so that nobody, on the street, on public transport, in shopping centres, would give you a second look. I've seen too many of my competitors, well-fed pigs who ended up jailed for their love of gold chains, pendants, watches, fancy shoes, slicked back hair, showy clothes, flashing bags of the stuff at their girls, saying loud enough for everyone to hear that they could go where there was plenty more of the stuff.

"Listen. Actually, Auntie Marlena wants one of your paintings," she says, and I finally hear her.

"She can have it," I tell her flatly.

That's right. One of my paintings.

Let's add a bit more canned laughter.

I came to Warsaw to become an artist. And I did actually finish art school. My parents still live in in a small city called Olsztyn, which was originally called Allenstein when it was Prussian territory hundreds of years ago. Our apartment is in a district called Jaroty, but which some still call Hamburg in honour of the Germans who once owned it. My mother worked as a school teacher, but is now retired. My father is the silent type, lips drawn tight all the time, all his free time spent pacing about our small apartment, stiff-backed, casting about nervous, panicked glances. He wanted to be a writer, a playwright, but only got as far as becoming the esteemed director of some government organisation for the promotion of local culture and education. He's never really got over the disappointment.

I rarely talk to the man. My sister tried, by screaming and slamming doors. I didn't even bother with that. It seems interesting to me now that my father never taught me a single thing: how to kick a ball about, how to hammer nails, how to drive cars. To this day, I'm not sure if the guy can do any of those things himself. I remember, rather unclearly, that whenever anything broke around the house, he'd panic. Whenever he got stressed, we could tell, because his face would grow even more tense, his movements even more robotic – jerky and sudden, like a machine that was going wrong.

My sister always wanted to paint. Like me, she would eventually graduate from the Warsaw School of Fine Arts. She then moved back to Olsztyn and now has a child with her as yet-unmarried fiancé, a kid I've only ever seen the once, and a shop which sells stationery that barely registers any sort of cashflow. I, on the other hand, stayed in Warsaw to deal top grade cocaine. I make between fifty and a hundred grand a month. Cash in hand. Depending on how late I feel like working some nights.

My mother is convinced I work for a branch of a multinational corporation.

"I'll come visit in the New Year," I promise her.

"Why only in the New Year?" she pleads.

"Because I'm off to Singapore."

"But you're working with Taiwanese clients," she corrects.

"Some in Taiwan, some in Singapore," I respond, remembering too late that she used to be a school teacher and that I should brush up on my geography before I tell her any more lies.

I'm not really going to have time to visit them in the New Year, even though that is when I have my holidays. It's a dead time for me. The worst in my line of work. People stick to their resolutions, making use of their newly purchased gym memberships, boozing only on Fridays and even then only half as hard, trying to finish reading all those books about harmony and meditation and being at one with the universe they got from Santa, forsaking the eating of white bread. And, of course, they swear blind they're gonna stop snorting shit. They get themselves checked out, detoxed, flush out their colons and their livers. They're usually told their hearts are fine. All they need is a bit more exercise. And so they go a few more times to the gym, the tennis court, the pool, and then February hits and everything goes back to normal. They go back to boozing, popping, snorting and whoring the same as before.

But before that happens, for the first time in a decade I've made plans to leave town for three whole weeks. No one knows that yet and they probably won't find out. I'm just going to turn my phone off, lose a whole load of cash, but that doesn't matter. I'm off to Argentina. I don't quite know why there; I once read an interview with the singer of some American rock outfit and he said something about what having money really means to him. It meant being able to go to any airport any time he liked, check the outgoing flights, grab the first one out of there and go anywhere in the world, check into a hotel and walk around the streets without anyone bothering him for a while.

I liked the sound of that. I want to see streets that don't look like the ones I work. Dirty and sticky, maybe, but in a way that's new to me. Besides, Argentina is a long way away, as far as it's possible to get.

My other phone rings. Uncle. I don't want to talk to him, but I want to keep talking to my mother even less, so I have the excuse to swap lines.

"I'm worried about you," she says.

Her voice is odd, as if her throat was swollen, tight. It means she's about to start crying, though she's still trying to hold back.

"What are you worried about?"

"I have bad... feelings," she says. "Feelings that something's going to happen."

"Like what, mum?"

"I don't know, Kuba," she says. "A plane crash, anything, I don't know."

"I don't have the energy to deal with your paranoia," I tell her, pulling a sweater gently from a neatly stacked pile of clothes.

"Look after yourself," she pleads.

"That's all I ever do in life, look after myself," I assure her without even trying to sound convincing.

"We'll see you," she says in parting.

"Yeah, see you," I tell her, then grab the other phone.

"So how's it going?" Uncle asks.

He sounds out of breath, like he's only just run a few miles. But maybe that's how he always sounds. His heart giving out because of steroids, or some lung condition.

"There's more money in that bag than you said there was," I tell him.

I hear something that sounds like a "Hmm..."

"About five thousand more," I add.

"I knew you were a good lad," he purrs.

"This isn't high school, for fuck's sake, to be putting me through tests," I bark.

"What's got into you? Go drink some green tea or something. Go knock one off."

"See you," I say, cutting the line.

A minute later, I put both phones into the pocket of my blazer.

I counted the cash earlier in the morning, once I'd driven it to my safekeeping place. I never bring anything illicit home. Not money, not drugs, not guns. It would be moronic of me to run the risk of being caught with any of that. A few years ago, I bought a tiny one-bedroom apartment on a shitty housing estate on the edge of town, a grim district called Goclaw, and this is where I now stash all the things I don't want to be caught with by the law. The tower block the apartment is in is mostly home to a lot of elderly pensioners. They only really care about their peace and quiet – nobody knows I keep all of my stock and a lot of my cash savings there. I sometimes pop in there in the daytime, put the radio on, just loud enough for it to be heard through the front door, and then return in the evening to turn it off and pull all the pizza leaflets out of the mailbox. Old people like to keep an eye on the neighbours, and so I do my best to give the appearance of actually living there.

Before stashing the bag, there was about half a kilo of coke there, which isn't much. Two sets of scales. Plastic wrap. A press. A replica handgun. A real handgun, loaded. Some two hundred thousand zlotys in cash, twenty grand in US dollars and about the same in euros, neatly wrapped and stacked in plastic bags. Along with additional door locks, there's also a remote controlled camera which constantly streams footage of the place to my cell phone, and is activated by motion sensors. If anyone were to break in there, my phone would instantly warn me, though it's never been tested.

I've never spent a single night there. From the day I bought the place, no one other than me has set foot in it.

I put my watch on, then my shoes. I slept very little, dreamt almost nothing. I suddenly remember what my mother said about having feelings about something tragic being about to happen, such as a plane crash. I think about it for a moment or two, flipping the thought like a coin in my hand.

But that's just a glitch in my mental programming. There's no such thing as 'bad feelings', nothing more than some paranoid tendencies manifesting themselves as bullshit talk over the phone.

I repeat in my mind, slowly: "Intuition is nothing more than paranoid tendencies manifesting themselves as bullshit."

5:00pm

"Hey,'" she says quietly, as if passing a coded message, while inside me something happens, something very wrong: there's a landmine planted in my stomach and someone's just stepped on it, while the fork I'm holding falls from my hand, jangling on the plate before me.

It takes a few seconds for my brain to register it's her. Standing by the shopping mall restaurant table I'm eating my snack in. It takes a painful moment for me to recognise her strong jawline, her small nose, glazed over eyes, the gap between her teeth. Blonde hair. She's tall, lithe. Standing over me, she looks like a prosecutor about to deliver a speech in court. Cutting the air before me like a blade.

Her face is calm, cold and still ever so beautiful. There's a world of difference between being cute and being beautiful and smart and graceful and all that glam stuff to boot. I once again feel what I recall feeling when we were together, those few memorable moments we allowed ourselves to be seen out on the town – that I was in some way proud to have her by my side. That she strengthened me somehow.

A very stupid mistake. She's not a star or anything, but people know she hangs out with celebrities, they associate her with certain crowds and with certain music videos, advertising campaigns, her face all over billboards, fitness magazine covers, all those sorts of places. People recognise her, even if they don't know her name. She's got those timeless looks, the sort of beauty which stops men and women in their tracks when they see her walking past. That kind of attention is highly unwelcome in my line of work. And then things between us got complicated. Some early mornings, makeup from the night before still smudged across her face, she'd tell me before falling asleep in her pink aquarium that her friends had started asking why she was going out with a coke dealer, seeing as she could have anyone she wanted.

I would then always tell her that dealers are people who sell cars – I was a retailer.

As I raise my fork again, someone turns, looks at me, a gaze I do not want, someone else coughs. That's all they are – looks and coughs – but they're still unwelcome.

"How are you? Don't you recognise me?" she asks.

"Sure I do," I nod. "I saw you in Bethlehem last night."

"Could be," she nods. "Could be you saw me somewhere sometime."

She sits at my table and I let her, though it makes no sense. But before she joins my table, before I recognise her, before she even gets near, something even more stupid happens. This is going to be another day when I lose control, miss things, lose things, get hung up, drop cutlery. Another day of nervous tics, unchecked impulses. Which is much worse.

4:20pm

I really can't ever stand by and watch when I see men getting violent with women. I don't know where I get that from. Maybe one of those things my mother managed to teach me. Or maybe some deep-seated memory of my dad hitting her when I was little, something registered deep in the subconscious. Something which is now a part of my most profound conditioning.

"When a man hits a woman, he deserves to be strung up," she always used to say.

Maybe it's true that women do have a soft spot for real bad guys, and just don't ever go for nice guys, no matter how tough they might be. Maybe, or maybe these are just the kinds of stupid things people say in cheap TV movies, the kinds of films Tiny used to get roles in when he was still young and slim and at least mildly charismatic.

Maybe. Wherever this thing in me comes from, I hate it when blokes put their hands anywhere near women, especially those who clearly think they can get away with it.

Anyway, forty minutes ago I happened to be in this shopping centre. Pushing through a crowd of people as they poured from shops, loaded down with their Christmas-coloured bags. I stopped to think about how many of them there are, how tightly packed into one indoor space, and began to realise that the holidays really are almost here, Christmas a week away.

I only came in here to buy myself some cologne and shoes. Maybe eat something. Coming into the restaurant I'm in now, sitting next to Beata, was unwise, but that fucker really shouldn't have spoken to his girl that way, and I did what I had to. And then had to hide somewhere afterwards.

They were standing at the entrance to a drug store – he looked like any old punk from some village disco, his hair gelled back, his broad chest wrapped so tight in a brightly coloured blazer that he looked like he was wearing a giant, fruit-flavoured condom. Stone-washed jeans and polished brogues. And that face, the face of someone born to a mother who never once stopped drinking during her pregnancy: broad, flat, without the indentation across the top lip. The girl with him looked like she'd just stepped out of a fake tanning salon – skinny jeans, jacket so short it exposed her pierced belly button, her hair a mess of multi-shaded strands, maybe in need of fresh colouring, maybe done to look that way. She might have been pretty, if not for the look of fear evident beneath all her make up. Her whole body, her posture was all fear. She looked like something which was just about to be crumpled up. I walked past, but stopped when I heard him open his mouth.

"Give me yer fuckin' phone, now," he growled, loudly enough for everyone to hear, though no one was reacting. His voice sounded like barking, like he was trying to shout through a mouthful of food. Swallowing the ends of his words. "Show me dat fuckin' phone."

"No," she squealed.

"Give it. I bet that bastard's been writing to you again."

"You're wrong in the head, you are," she countered.

He pulled at her arm, hard, then grabbed her handbag. There really was something likeable about her face, beneath all that vivid fear and cheap makeup.

"What the fuck are you doing?" she cried.

The security guard at the entrance to the store kept chewing his gum, hard at work looking elsewhere.

"What the fuck?" she appealed again.

"Shut your gob, bitch," he roared. "Shut it or else I'll shut it for you in front of all these fuckers!"

Someone turned around, an elderly woman who then walked on. That was when I spotted a large group of people, a whole family, generations of them, emerging from around a corner, slowly strolling past, right between the security guard and the couple. As the family moved along, that's when he hit her.

I instantly mixed in with the group, yeah, it was dumb, totally dumb, but I pushed through, quickly reached the thug and hit him in the solar plexus with all I had, right where all his nerve endings converged. I'm not much of a fighter, but I don't panic when things get rough either, and know how to land each punch so it counts. The effect was instant and predictable: his nervous system shut down for a second, his breathing paralysed, his body frozen as if someone had stabbed a knife into his belly, his mouth open, gasping for breath. The girl froze too and all would have been well if she hadn't suddenly started screaming.

I knew she was going to react in that way. I knew she loved him very much, though he beat her every other day, that she was his dogsbody, his thing to wipe floors with, that she didn't know how to free herself and, what's worse, wasn't sure that she wanted to know. It always goes that way. In every layer of society, people accept, even sometimes enjoy, being hurt, harmed, wounded, willingly walking into doors of pain. It can make them feel loved, though that's a mistake. It's not even sad, just banal, like the idea of the sun rising every day, just becomes something truly remarkable we're all used to.

When she started screaming, I was already slipping away, moving as fast as I could through those jolly Christmas crowds, turning the corner, but I could see out of the corner of my eye her taking a step back from the thug, just as he got his breath back and began to look for me in the crowd. I saw the security guard too, realising what just transpired, also starting to seek me out.

A moment later, I was in a randomly chosen restaurant. It's not the first time I've been in this position. Recently, around midnight a few weeks ago, coming home somewhere near Crossroads Square I saw a guy dragging a girl along the sidewalk by the hair, like some cartoon caveman. I pulled over, landed a blow with my elbow to the top of his skull, and then stood on his face long enough to hear his nose crack. The girl didn't scream that time, and I offered to drive her home. She accepted. We didn't say a word to each other the whole of the way there.

For a moment, I worried that the ape in that condom-coloured blazer would come after me – the last thing I need in my line of work is scuffles in public places, especially those covered by endless security cameras – but nothing of the sort happened. If he had somehow found me in that restaurant, if he had called the police – and he looked the type who liked to call the cops on other people – I would have had a problem.

"It's dumb," I thought to myself, turning off my phones, ordering a salad and water. That was when she appeared next to me, as vivid as a knife.

Conversations involving two parties who are both afraid of one other tend to be hard work.

She's definitely frightened, and as for me, I'm not so sure. I don't know, because I can't quite put my finger on what it is I am feeling. Moments like these, I feel like something is welling up in my guts, pushing out against the lining, twisting around its own axis; it's the same as those moments when I'm out driving and I think I see a car following me for more than a block or two. When I see there are two men in the car, and its wheels are cheap steel rather than fancy alloy, and the driver turns and stops whenever I turn and stop I know then it's a gang who is after me – I know they know that I know it too. But in amongst all that I don't know if it is fear or just concern. The thing inside my stomach feels alien, appearing and disappearing, never sticking around for long enough to make itself at home in me.

"How are you feeling?" she asks.

"Fine," I mumble.

Maybe we're both scared, or maybe we've simply got nothing at all left to say to each other.

"I'm not so good," she says.

She always talks about herself without being asked, and always speaks up first, a headstrong woman, a leader.

"Why not?" I ask. From what I remembered, her whole life revolved around not feeling particularly good.

"I'm having trouble sleeping... actually, I'm not sleeping at all."

I met her through one of my customers, a guy also trying to be my pal. He'd been the boss of a bank in London for a few years, and hid a rather miserable-looking wife at home, a woman he'd been with since high school, even though when he goes out on the town he always makes sure he's surrounded by a herd of long-limbed babes. She was one of this herd, though different. She stood out, her features classier, her voice more subtle, something alive in those glassy eyes, some strange nostalgia, something broken, soured.

She had the gaze of someone who'd had faith, doesn't matter what sort, though it had been taken from her a long while ago. That was how it seemed to me back then. Later on, I realised that I am able to assign elaborate interpretations to things which are plain, defined and clear as if projected in high-definition, nothing less, nothing more. But there I was, sensing vulnerability where there was none, arousing my defensive facilities, that tiresome desire to save women from things, as if they can't handle problems all by themselves. That desperate desire to be needed, to hold on to beauty.

"We're all struggling," I tell her.

"It doesn't matter if I'm alone or with someone else. I can't sleep. Maybe an hour or two, during the day."

"I sleep fine."

Listening to her voice rolling along slowly, her eyes dull, I guess she must be on some new prescription drugs, antidepressants.

"What are you up to?" she asks.

"Planning a getaway."

"For good?" she asks, seemingly spooked.

"Just a few weeks. Argentina."

"Sounds good. I always said you needed a holiday."

I can't recall her ever saying anything of the sort.

"We have to hook up, talk," she says after I finish checking my phone.

"Well, we're here, hooked up, and talking."

"Listen, things turned out..." she says, dropping her head, so as not to look me in the eye.

"Things turned out the way they turned out," I butt in. "It doesn't really matter now."

"It does to me."

"To me it doesn't," I lie.

I lie, because she smashed me over the head, stepped on my face, broke my nose. I lie, because there was something inside me, something I had no idea was there, and she took it. I lie, because when she split from a mate of mine, a banker, and I took her to a hotel and fucked her for two whole days straight, I knew then she was under my skin, deep inside my head, sneaking in through all the openings in my body, and that in time she would prove to be a distraction. Something she is amazingly good at proving to be, good at drawing a lot of focus onto herself. There is something sad in her eyes, something which pleads and appeals for attention. That which looks cheap on a TV screen can in real life be the best kind of manipulation. Her eyes cry and cost money.

Maybe I called her too often. Told her too much about who I was. Maybe I made a mistake, a terrible mistake, cuddling up to her in the middle of the night, listening to her breathing. Maybe I allowed myself to rest up next to her. Maybe, for the first time in my whole damn life, I allowed myself to become attached. Addicted even.

"You're not struggling with anything?" she asks.

"Struggling?" I ask back.

"You know what I mean."

"Nope. Everything's under control."

"Right..." she says, her head lifting, as if she had regained some sort of control over us. "I've never met anyone who has as much of a grip on things as you."

At some point in our relationship she started to run and tried shaking me off. Not answering her phone. Refusing to meet. Screaming down the line that I was crowding her in, just when I simply needed her by my side. I heard her drunk, wasted, other voices in the background, male, female, all sorts of music. Without any idea of where she was, without wanting to know where she was, just wanting her back. Even though when I did have her by my side it wasn't always all that meaningful.

Then Pazina told me she had seen her out with some other guy. Guys. One, two, three TV types. Those grinning fools, so carefully dressed, so finely equipped with production studios and media houses, often to be seen holding a free drink in one hand, the other making gestures of conviction, for emphasis, for show, unable to stop themselves telling crappy jokes and anecdotes, even in front of a firing squad. I tracked them down to some place, wanting to murder them , which was far from good. The need a man has to make love to a fine-looking woman, to possess her even for a short while, is no reason for one human being to murder another.

Eventually, I stopped paying attention to things I knew were priorities. Stopped managing risk effectively. And in my line of work, that risk is severe. It's not something to be trifled with. I began answering calls from numbers I did not know. Began getting my sums wrong, my sleeping pattern going haywire.

Any time I was ready to call it off completely, wipe her from my memory, whenever I felt I was really ready, she'd show up again, at my door in the morning, crumpled up like an old receipt, her mascara still running. She'd walk in and, saying not a word, begin to undress.

I didn't know how to shut the door before she made those entrances.

"I was just scared," she says. "Very scared."

"Of what?"

"Of getting into a guy who could be locked up at any time," she says, after a long wait, as if coughing up something stuck in her gullet.

"Sure, I can understand that," I say, kindly.

For a moment, she doesn't react. A waitress appears, asks if we need anything. She shakes her head, like a kid caught shoplifting, ready to deny everything.

"Let's just meet up, you know, so we're not scared, not surprised," she says, finally looking up.

"Maybe. One day," I answer, lifting some salad to my lips, chewing slowly and swallowing even slower, before suggesting, "Just call me."

"Which number?"

"You know which number."

Pazina told me about this one guy she saw with her more often than any of the others. I knew the one, had him down pat. He bought from me, all too often, and then stopped; I heard he was afraid I would do something to him. I've no idea what it is I might have done to him. Revenge is bullshit. Ten others would instantly take his place. Karma is justice stripped of satisfaction.

She had no intention of explaining anything. We met two, three times, in passing. Always in public places, always on the go. She didn't even bother making eye contact. Everything she said sounded like "Just let it go". I asked for nothing. I never ask anyone for anything, and with her it would be no different – I'd stand before her for a moment, and then turn and walk in the opposite direction. She'd then melt into whatever crowd. But then I felt like a young recruit on his first day in the army, like a battered child, like a prison piece of ass. That one time.

A few days later, I finally decided to forget her phone number. People sleep with each other, nothing exciting about that. Take your clothes off before someone, lie on top of them, that's no achievement, no adventure. The interesting stuff happens when you remove your skin, expose your muscles in front of someone and they can see your weak points, a little flame burning inside, a little light just below the heart, like kryptonite, they will then take it in their fingers and do something stupid with it: put it in their mouth, swallow, abandon, lose it. Then, much later, you'll be left alone with this hole, as if from a gunshot, and you can pour the bodies of so many strangers into this hole, so many substances and voices, but you'll never fill it, close it up, pave over it, no fucking way.

Every one of us has this little light inside, this kryptonite. I do too. And I should never have shown it to anyone.

She rises, grabs her coat, and I suddenly see how broken, grey and worn right through she seems these days. She's lost something, and loss always hurts, even if you lose something you didn't really want after all, something you only kept around for a rainy day.

"See you. I'll call," she says. "Unless you never want me to bother you again. If that's the case, just tell me."

I say nothing.

"Say it to me now," she repeats.

"I'll see you."

My eyes skip between my phone and the plate, still half-full of mashed-up salad. I watch as she walks away, going around a rushing waitress, then speeds up and vanishes in the crowd, without ever lifting her gaze from the floor. Maybe she'll bump into the guy in that fucking bright blazer. Maybe someone's waiting for her back home. Maybe she's just arranged to meet up with someone else. Maybe she'll then take them to bed, strip them of their skin.

I don't know.

I don't want to know.

I put some cash down on the table and get up to go.

I've deleted her number, but of course I fear it's still lodged somewhere deep in my memory.

9:30pm

He only answers on the fifth ring.

"Yeah?" I hear him say, sounding out of breath.

He's getting changed at the gym. I know where, I know what time he goes there and what time he finishes. The doctor recommended he go swimming and take regular exercise, because last spring he ended up in intensive care following a mild stroke – Piotrek is forty-four years old and probably about the same in kilos of excess fat, though not that long ago it was probably double that. Maybe because he loves to stuff his face, especially at night. Piotrek drives a brand new Range Rover and is my wholesaler. A very serious sort of gangster, but even serious gangsters can't fight off heart attacks.

"I have to see you," I tell him, which is the simple truth. I do have to see him – my stocks of the powder he supplies me with are running a little low.

"Sunday," he says.

"Sunday is tomorrow."

"So tomorrow it is," he confirms, then adds, "Fuck, I think I'm gonna cough up a kidney, bloody hell."

"You're pushing hard," I tell him.

"It's all I've got left, Kuba," he replies.

The line goes quiet. I'm parked on Jerusalem Avenue, right by the KFC. Looking out for a certain girl. Then I spot her, a little white dog in tow. She smiles and slowly approaches my car.

"What time?" I speak into the mouthpiece.

"Maybe 6pm, the same place as always," Piotrek answers. "My fitness instructor is a fucking Fuhrer, I tell you. He wants me dead. This is fucking inhumane. I'm not some kid who can afford to go bursting blood vessels, Kuba."

"Save your strength for tomorrow," I tell him.

"See you," he replies. "6pm, the usual spot."

The girl gets into the back seat of my car. I can hear the dog barking.

"Shush, Putin," she chides the beast.

"You really called it that?" I ask, turning towards her.

"Yes, but it wasn't my idea. How is your luck today?"

"My luck? That's a good one," I quip, shaking my head.

"Everyone has their own kind of luck, you just gotta know how to nurture it," she says, smiling broadly.

"I would very much like to believe that," I say, giving her my best smile. She's one of the few people I ever allow to see me smiling.

She buys from me every couple of weeks, always insisting that she's doing it on someone else's behalf. Her name is Anastasia. She has the prettiest face, stunning eyes, the solidly graceful movements of a body built for motherhood. Guys go soft around her like over-ripe fruit. There's just something about the way she sways that makes men want to become fathers all of a sudden.

"Just please ensure Putin doesn't crap in my car," I laugh.

"Have you been away?"

"Not yet, but soon enough I plan to go away somewhere, so don't panic if I don't answer my phone for a week or so," I tell her, preparing the same set she always orders: two bags of coke and one of MDMA. I hand the stuff over and in turn receive all the cash that's due.

"And a good thing too. You'll get some rest. Start breathing normally again. That's really important."

"And what does your luck look like today?" I ask, just to keep the conversation going. Whenever she gets into my car, it's like someone's just sprayed something pleasant on the upholstery, something which smells like home-made pie. Like Christmas come early.

Though this is, of course, no more than an illusion.

This one time she got into my car when I was driving someone else around, a pal. She instantly asked who my friend was, without hesitation. My female clients are way wiser and more sensible than men. They never raise their voices, never ask to be driven round for half an hour in search of a cash machine, never talk shit.

"I'm trying to sew my luck back together again." she says, smiling still.

"Did it rip?"

"In half. But, you know, that sort of thing can be salvaged. You just need to use tougher thread than before."

I know a bit about her, maybe more than a bit. She was Tiny's girl for a couple of years. That's how I got to know her – she'd be this wonderful bit of colour hanging around his places, like a fine piece of art hanging on a dirty old wall. Tiny messed her up the way only scumbags can mess up girls from nice homes who had, up until then, only worried about perfume and horse riding. He fucked other girls almost before her very eyes. Called her names, dumped her, then always came back as if for a piece of lost property. Those who feel the need to possess things will always tend to return for what was theirs, even if they never use that thing. Word was he hit her a few times. In public and in private. Did and said things which almost ensured she would never be the same again. Would never trust anyone the same as before.

Anastasia now likes to get her own back. I know she takes all her warmth and that glorious smile and uses them to possess and then destroy guy after guy, wipe the floor with them, any time any new idiot comes within range of her charms, drawing them in, and then dumping them as soon as she's good and ready. She takes them on a honeymoon ride, hinting between words at futures, families, kids, creating a safe, happy space for them to fall into, and then soon enough stops answering their calls. Or meets up and then says that she's not ready yet, after all. Or simply shows up with other men in tow, cuckolding them in the basest way possible. Always ending each relationship as if it was a meal and she was now full, the taste not all to her liking, and she certainly wasn't going to ask for any more helpings. Mild compliments to the chef and all that.

I know she's capable of sensitivity. Knows how to listen, how to truly be present. It's said she's an absolute goddess in bed. Two of her victims confessed to me, sitting in this very car, dejected, teary, holding their phones or wallets, as if they were talismans or good luck charms, hoping for a change of that luck. Chewed up and spat out and wishing they had the guts to get away or top themselves.

It's the most endearing thing about her, in a way. I like it when women have something dark and edgy about them. When they cheat, when they put on acts, when they explode. They have every right to do whatever it is they do to us men. I like her as she is, because there is nothing from her I want. Maybe, if she made me desperate to have her smell stick around the insides of my car for good, then things would be different. But I'm just a little bit too sensible, too cold, too sober for such seductions.

"I dreamt about you, you know," she confesses suddenly. "You were sailing somewhere, on a boat, the sea really stormy, rain coming down, water sloshing about, lightning slashing the sky, but you kept sailing on. Steady as anything. I was completely certain nothing would happen to you."

"That's a mighty fine dream. Unfortunately, I can't say I had the pleasure of being visited by you in any of my dreams. Sorry."

"You want to hustle everything, even dreams, Kuba?" she asks, smiling weakly. I smile too. She really is engaging, but my daily allowance of smiles is running low.

"Where will you be partying tonight?" I ask, changing the subject.

"At a friend's place. Something like a hen night, but not quite."

"Is she getting married?"

"In a sense. It's going to be some kind of a Buddhist ceremony. An imported guru is doing the nuptials. No idea where from."

"One way or another, she's getting hitched. Hold on, I'll give you something special. Give me back what I already gave you."

Intrigued, she hands me back the gear.

"I've something better right here," I say and hand over some fine Colombian, from a hundred grams Piotrek gave me as a gift in a momentary burst of generosity a few weeks back. I only share that with my special clients, at twice the regular price.

"How much extra?" she asks.

"Nothing. It's on the house. Have fun."

"Wow. Thanks a lot. Really, huge thanks," she answers, her eyes wide open, something doll-like about her now. She looks like someone's spent months sculpting her, polishing and perfecting, as if she was someone else's fantasy creation.

"Just be careful with it," I warn her. And mean it. That shit contains up to 30% pure coke. Which is a hell of a lot. "Start with small lines."

"Small lines," she repeats, then adds, "A Christmas gift from Kuba?"

"Take care of yourself," I advise her, in all seriousness, with all my heart. I don't want anyone else to get to her. I'd rather she got to them first.

"I will and you do too, Kuba. And be happy... Come, Putin," she says, climbing out of the car and vanishing into the night.

I sit there for a while longer, enjoying the special aroma she always leaves behind on that back seat. The warmth of holiday season. The smell of a fake Christmas tree.

11:10pm

They're all in here tonight – an ugly, large villa in the leafy Saxon Marshes District, two hundred or more people stuffed into it, the opening of some exhibition, photographs of misty forests, wine spilled on the floor, desperately malnourished girls looking miserable, sipping crap out of plastic cups, little groups of youths smoking weak-smelling cannabis, saying nothing. Chief editors of magazines relating to various lifestyles, hipster opinion-makers, photographers, DJs, gallery curators. There's a band playing, none of them capable of producing palatable sounds, the kid behind the drum kit unable to keep a regular beat, a charmless girl in a lace body suit straining into a microphone, emitting incomprehensible sounds from time to time.

I drove here from a bachelor party, hosted by the owner of a Middle Eastern restaurant somewhere near Novotel, dead in the heart of town. I'm only going to sell maybe half as much here as I did back there. The creative industries aren't doing all that well of late. Advertising spaces shrinking. Revenues declining. Crisis after crisis. Walls closing in, the world contracting, inevitably crushing those trapped inside.

Everyone in the villa is smiling, close to one another, chatty, but there's a palpable tension filling what little space is left around us – everyone is looking for a way out, or at least looking for a gap, an opening for some fresh air to come floating in. They're worried about their own exhibitions, magazines, jobs, projects, workshops, clothing markets. Though not many here will even think of having kids, they're there, inside their wallets, and those who have them worry about the little ones too. Worry about the babysitters who allow them to be here tonight. Worry about their private kindergartens, about the baby clothes on order from Berlin, about swimming lessons for infants which may not seem as carefree as they looked in the ads.

The same sorts of words circulate – project, edit, direct, deal. Today's show is sponsored by the letter C for 'Creative'. Or else 'Creation', everyone here busy putting on some kind of show, trying to be some kind of artist, everyone sending out the same kind of funky, trendy message, making whatever impression, not that any of them care about the others, only their own broadcasts, all of it vanishing the moment they disperse back to their urban lofts or suburban apartments. To cut more short films, produce more plays, put on more shows, events, launches, or just slave away at filling out applications for grants.

But for now, things are in some sort of order. People still capable of forcing smiles, coughing up responses, filtering information, hoping for some sort of change, for a better tomorrow, for money to come. Their blood not gone off the boil completely yet.

They're mostly harmless, cute even, working hard to make impressions. If they could, they'd claw each other's eyeballs out, but they were born with weak nails. They can only smile, like well-fed eunuchs. Stress gathers in their lymph nodes, which they flush out with wine and vodka.

I go up the stairs to the first floor. Someone is trying to get into a bathroom which is locked from the inside. Some sleepy-eyed girl is allowing a guy to manhandle her, unable to muster the energy to push him away. Someone is arguing about a film. I push past people, some of them nodding at me in recognition. I find the guy who called me to come. He's a nervous blond fella, in a tight-fitting bomber jacket, red boots, his hands flying about a little wildly, eyes flitting all over the place. It's clear the lad has problems. His breath fast and shallow, wiping his nose with a tissue a little too often to make it look good.

"It's not good news, man," he says in the way of a greeting. "I've just lost a load of cash."

"Happens," I nod.

"I really mean it, things have gone bad," he groans. "It's some kind of horror show, the end of this year. This one's been the worst."

"How much?"

"Two," he tells me without pausing for breath.

I hand him the baggies, collect the cash.

He buys a lot from me. Sometimes during the day as well as at night. He's a photographer, likes to get high during working hours, as well as after. He says he maintains better focus on his environment that way. Provides me with regular updates about his profession, about the bitchiness of it, the back stabbings, the cashflow problems, even though most of it is lines he's memorised from television shows.

"You know Gorecki?" he asks. "The son of that furniture magnate?"

"Not sure."

"He bought from you a few times. I talked to him about it."

"I don't remember those who buy just a few times," I snap back.

"A kid, really. Wears glasses. Drives a Jag."

"Maybe. What of him?" I say, not giving away the fact that I do remember. I paid him a visit last night. The guy who tried to sell me his ex-girlfriend's painting.

"They found him dead in his apartment this morning. His ex-girlfriend went round there to collect her stuff. She still had keys, went in and there he was, ice cold in his own bed," he says, visibly shaken, shifting his weight from one foot to the other, as if itching to dance.

"She found him?"

"Yeah, in bed," he nods vigorously. "Fully dressed. Called an ambulance. Must have been a heart attack."

I look around us. Everyone pretends they don't see us talking, their gazes skipping over us, as if not looking, but looking sure enough. The news must have gone round this crew like wildfire. Now that I know, I can see which ones are right now talking about it. More animated, excited, nodding their heads, eyes wide open, concerned, shocked. They'll be talking about little else for another week or so.

"A guy is twenty-something and dies of a heart attack?" he asks, a little too loud for my liking, then adds, "Was it the gear? Impossible. He must have had something wrong with him. Something concealed."

"What thing wrong?" I press.

"I don't know, something with his heart?"

"I've no idea. I'm not a doctor. Gonna have to go."

I sold that sorry guy what I sell everyone. There's no evidence that he got the stuff from me. They're sure to find it in his bloodstream, but the cops won't even go there, while his parents will try to swallow the facts in silence. If the old man is worth millions, he's not gonna be wanting the word 'coke fiend' etched on his son's gravestone. Anyone who ever made any sort of real money is able to stifle emotions and think above all of the reputation which seals deals.

When I saw him yesterday, he'd already done a few baggies. Breathing shallow, bloodshot eyes. But it was his decision to ring up and order more. It's always their choice. Big boys, with credit cards, tax numbers, PIN codes, brains and things uploaded into those brains. If they choose to ignore what those brains tell them sometimes, then that's their problem, not mine.

I think back to his bank card swallowed by a cash machine. Then

I stop thinking about it. I never liked the guy, and I never get to like people just because they've suddenly died.

"But on the other hand, if it was your product?" he asks. "You know, he took a hit and..."

"It's not gonna kill ya," I interrupt, pointing to the stuff held in his tightly clenched fist.

"I don't mean that. Let's assume that he had some kind of heart condition and, you know, it didn't exactly help."

"And so?"

"How do you feel about that?"

"What is this money you said you lost?" I ask instead of answering.

"Some shithead cut me out of a deal. Total prick."

He begins telling me a story about an online shop he was co-running with someone, health foods, supplements, that sort of thing. Hard to follow, as he's talking too fast, swallowing words, tossing in pointless "you know", "pal", "you get me" and "man". I stop listening, all out of curiosity.

"I really don't want to know that shit," I tell him. "Your shithead business partner buys from me too."

"We had eighty grand in our joint business account, man," he groans and I realise why listening to him fills me with such disgust – it's that soft, damp "r" which he pronounces with a lisp, as if his mouth produced too much saliva, his throat not keeping up with swallowing it down.

"Whatever – do you want me to stop supplying him or what?" I ask.

"That would be best."

"That's not how it will be though," I tell him calmly. "Your business affairs are no concern of mine. We all have tough choices to make."

"So, how do you feel about it? That kid dying?"

"Oh, I pity the poor lad," I lie.

The guy nods his head and I leave him to it, turning around and heading for the exit. My phone rings, stopping me in my tracks. It's my best customer. I knew he'd be ringing today. It's Saturday. There was no other option. I push on through the crowds, someone tries to stop me, ask something, buy something probably, but I don't have the time. Some are openly snorting stuff off flat, clear surfaces, like that black-haired, pale woman dressed like someone two decades younger, wrinkled from fags like a desiccated peach. A tall, skinny, short-haired kid she hands the rolled up banknote is not her partner, but her son. I know them both. They don't buy much. Money problems, connected with their work in colour magazines which are dying a death, filled with words not even their editors read. More people are arriving at the villa. I walk out to the car. Time to make some real money. My best client is ringing again. I answer.

"I need about thirty," he says.

"Why not fifty already?" I ask.

"Listen, make it fifty, whatever. I like it when shit is unlimited, when everyone is nice and calm about it."

"Well, your feeling of wellbeing and peace matters to me, of course."

"I'm always calm, but to give others the same sense of chill we need the right tools," he laughs.

Any time this guy opens his mouth it sounds like something pre-written, pre-rehearsed. He's made a fortune out of that attitude – the number one celebrity on all our televisions. I respect him for that.

"When will you get here?"

"Give me an hour," I ask.

"Fine. I'll be waiting."

I think for a moment about the girl who'd found her ex-boyfriend's dead body this morning. Maybe she hadn't come back to get her stuff. Maybe she'd wanted to talk. Maybe she still liked or even loved him for his loser status, for his inability to keep shit together, for his father's dough. Maybe. Not that it matters now.

00:50am

Money. It's always all about the money. Nothing else. You could try and argue that it's a fundamental motive. Which is not true. It's the only motive.

Let's assume you meet a girl and fall in love, and a while later she leaves you for another guy. Before you can begin asking questions about whether the other guy is more protective, manly, assertive, aggressive and all those other essential qualities, don't forget to notice one thing – he earns more money than you. He also has a better job, more power, better wheels, is more confident, but all that is just a result of that first factor – more money. You really can't blame the girl. When you are offered a job that pays better than your current boss, you too are lying to yourself when claiming that you're gonna stay loyal to what you've already got.

Let's assume that someone has shoved you aside, cheated and used you, betrayed you and beaten you up. Stripped you of what in theory was yours to have – in theory, because in reality none of us are owed a thing. You've been replaced. Lied to. Cut out of the deal. Brought to the brink of bankruptcy. Your apartment gone. Your family dejected. It's always all about the money. You have to keep in mind that, being in the other guy's shoes, you would have done the same to him, and the people who would not are few and far between. Heroes of schoolbooks and documentary films about self-sacrifice tend to come to sticky ends.

Human beings like to accumulate goods, wealth, back up their resources. Aggressive, territorial, stupid. We kill without thinking, especially when someone threatens our income and our integrity. Nothing more, nothing less. Atavisms. We're 99% atavisms, and the rest – language, culture, religion, ethics – are just accidents at work.

All I do is all about money. Nothing else. Making money, laundering it and then storing it safely. I only deal coke for the money. Not for the things I could buy with the proceeds, just for the cash alone. That is what matters. The sense money gives you, the awareness that you are present and capable of anything. There's nothing more valuable than that. It is a sort of superpower. Like the ability to walk through walls.

A million zlotys in laundered cash – that is how much money I used to have stored at my apartment in Goclaw. Ironed, wrapped in several layers of plastic film, shoved into the kind of sports holdall you carry your swimming cap and towel in when going to the swimming pool. A million is like a space suit – keeping you safe from everything, from all the dangerous rays. Allowing you to be away from the crowd, the mix, the masses.

And there is no better place to be than off to the side, away from the rest.

When you have no money, you're helpless, vulnerable to all sorts of harm – it's like being in the final stage of terminal illness, like the worst sort of disability, like living in someone's gun sights. It forces you to get in among people, throws you beneath their wheels, where you have to deal with their sweat, saliva, the soles of their boots, the hard ground. Some get used to it, lowering their heads, measuring time, extending it, occupying themselves with dubious entertainments, like the endless stream of TV shows downloaded from the internet. People can get used to anything. To loneliness, hunger, the cold, scum, shit, death. They survive by fantasising, visualising, denying. When we have nothing left, we can all close our eyes and use our imaginations to script endless variations of that one, Oscar-winning film – starring us – and then step up onto an invisible podium: beloved, accepted, triumphant.

To smile. To wave to your real self, hidden somewhere far away. To thank God and your family.

Maybe that's why I do what I do – I've never felt that way. I don't remember ever dreaming of anything. I just wanted things and knew I would get them, just in ways and timescales that were different to what I had expected.

I went to university to get my folks off my back, and to see for myself just what it was like. I moved to Warsaw because I no longer wanted to live in Olsztyn – a small, pretty, leafy town good for foreign students and retirees. I chose to study art for some unclear motive, shaped by indie music tapes I had copied from my sister's collection, from reading books about art, murky films watched on VHS: Lynch, Jarmusch, etc., the joints I smoked all the time on our housing estate, and some inherited talent for drawing. I liked drawing – a methodical, slow, scrupulous enterprise. Just like weighing and counting.

On top of all that, I was raised in an odd, impractical family which tended to favour the reading of books and pursuit of artistic careers. This is maybe why, once I had got into art college and moved to the capital, my parents sent me something around a thousand zlotys a month to live on. Which was nice of them.

I ended up renting a room in an apartment in the worst part of town. I still don't know how many other students lived at that one address. Six, maybe. Everyone busy snorting amphetamine, fucking any time and anywhere, dropping all their belongings, their food, their clothes all over the place. Eating instant noodles and tinned meat. Drinking the cheapest red wine you could lay your hands on. Listening to David fucking Bowie singing out of cheap laptop speakers. Rubbish everywhere, along with paints, cables, bottles of turps. My mother called every other day to ask how I was doing. Any time I came home for the weekend, she'd send me back with plastic containers full of meatballs, stuffed pancakes and cold cuts. Every time I got off the coach in Warsaw I'd toss them all into the nearest bin.

My friends from art school were as much of a laugh as any average Polish made-for-TV romantic comedy. Each and every one of them dreamt of making money, small amounts or whole heaps of it, though no one had what it took to say so. All those outsiders, the 'jam jars', crowded into rented apartments and student halls, hated the local kids from decent, urbanite, middle-class homes, driving their own cars, stuck-up wannabes dressed in all the latest fashions. Some of the girls who moved to Warsaw, the prettier ones, quickly found themselves local boys to move in with, playing 'home' in the apartments their parents had bought their boyfriends for their eighteenth.

All my peers were complete carbon copies of each other. They could all look forward to identical futures. Wading on their knees into a reality covered in barbed wire, mined to the max. Loans, debts, mortgages all earned in the process of trying to establish any sort of personal autonomy. Relationships and romances which, sooner or later, all went to hell. Deceit. Disasters. A soap opera with the enticing title *Grey Fantasies*. Two, three, four, five, eight thousand a month. Sums only slaves could live on. Taxes. Private health insurance or just state cover. In twenty years' time, they would all be down on their luck, dead end artists or middle class pawns trying desperately to pay off their credit card debts month on month.

I saw them, watched them trying to make it in this new Poland, post-communist freedoms going to their heads, but I saw through it all, right through them to the dirty, chipped walls and cracked tiles of the shit houses they were all living in. I saw kids living in their own home-made student short films, acting out cardboard cutout stereotypes. Overprotected or overloaded with expectation by their parents, stuffed full of false promises or outright lies – that life is for the taking, that the world they had been born into, unlike the worlds which had come before, shaping their parents, their grandparents, would allow them to become the selves they had always dreamt of becoming. They all starred in their own inner movie, like drunken actresses walking around their rundown apartments, practicing award ceremony speeches no one would ever ask them to recite. Abandoned by their men, for women who were younger, prettier and more stupid, fresh off the out-of-town coach. They were all like drunken kids, like lunatics, certain that it was enough to wait, that someone would eventually knock and offer them the lives of rock stars on silver plates.

They were all the same. Regardless of whether they had studied art or medicine or law or teaching or philosophy.

I knew in ten years' time each one of them would be asking the same two questions – Why the fuck? And who the fuck can I blame?

Nobody, darlings. That is how the system was set up – it will always work along those lines. I knew that the only way to solve the problem was to get out the building, rather than try finding the right room in it.

This is why I am where I am today. In this car. Driving towards Goclaw, Pazina in the passenger seat beside me.

That is why I sleep during the day and not at night. That is why my time is spent counting.

Even if they arrest and put me away, for a couple or even a five-year stretch, my money will still be out there somewhere. I will still be a free man behind those bars. More free than the rest of them.

How did it come to pass, that I have a car like this, though I'm not from around here, knowing almost no one when I got here? Being a skinny, weakling lad doing his first year of fine art – now, that's a whole other story, but let us just assume it is a question of certain pre-dispositions. I always liked activities which demanded a scrupulous, methodical approach. I always liked to weigh and to count. Always had a flawless memory. I never liked talking much, especially not repeating what others had uttered. It quickly turned out that I'm not much good at feelings either. Say, during a beating. Or an interrogation. Or when watching as someone cuts all the fingers off of someone else's hand. One by one.

I stop the car and get out to open the trunk. There is a bag inside, containing tea, coffee, sweets and pet food . Pazina is keeping quiet. I picked her up from some party where she was feeling lower than usual. She was grateful for the rescue, and we drove here without saying anything, which is another thing I appreciate about her: I don't have to speak when we're together, nor does she. There's no pressure for either one of us to talk. I know she finds this silence relaxing, inducing in her a sense of safety.

"Who is all that for?" she asks.

The tower block my secret apartment is in is dark and silent, as is the rest of this housing estate. Only a few lights are on inside the countless apartments overhead, like little watchtowers. I can hear a distant sound, as if someone had started up an air raid siren miles away. But everyone is in their homes. Dying in there. Watching TV. Drinking vodka. Applying hot irons to their wives' faces. Smacking their kids. Then those same kids sit out in the stairwells, crying. Soon after, they begin to take steroids. Or smoke smack, to help them dream. Because everyone here, both the kids and their folks, has trouble getting a good night's sleep.

I hear dogs barking not that far off as we leave the car and walk towards my stairwell.

"Who is all that for?" Pazina asks again.

"For my neighbour," I say. "The lady who lives next door," I explain as we climb the stairs to my floor. Her name is Halina, she's almost eighty, wears a wig and can barely hear. We reach my door, but I don't open that, ringing the neighbouring doorbell instead. When Halina opens, a smell emerges first, that of rotting teeth, mothballs and something intense, meaty, something which has been stewing on low heat for a long, long time. Even years.

"Good morning. Everything all right?" I ask.

"I haven't seen you for a long while, Mr Piotr," she croaks. That is the name she knows me by. I hand her the shopping. She grabs it, hard, like a mother grasping the hand of a child lost and then found. "You shouldn't have, dear me. Really..."

"I was away, on business," I tell her. "Soon, I'll be going on holiday."

"Where to now?"

"Argentina."

"Good evening, miss," she says to Pazina, only just noticing her standing behind me. Pazina returns the greeting, in a whisper. "Dear me, you do have the means these days, don't you?"

"Has anyone been round asking about me?" I ask, same as ever.

Same as ever, she says: "No, nobody, Mr Piotr. But if anybody did call round asking about you, I have that number you gave me..."

I nod, say "Good morning" and she shuts her door. The aroma of her apartment now permeates the stairwell. I let Pazina into my place.

"Smart of you," she says.

"No need to take your shoes off," I tell her.

I disable the camera mounted over the door via my phone, look around the apartment. Everything looks untouched, as it should be. Wardrobe. Table. Scales. Knife. Toilet paper, gloves, disinfectant, pure alcohol. Plastic jars containing creatine, supplements for bodybuilders, all stacked against the wall. Three bags: one with cash, the second with cocaine. The third is the one Uncle gave me last night.

I take the middle bag and place it on the table.

"What's smart of me?" I ask.

"Keeping that old lady working for you as lookout," Pazina quips. "Keeping her and her pets fed."

"She's a lonely old woman. No one ever visits her. Daughter

in Australia, son vanished long ago. She doesn't even know if he's alive. She's never seen her grandchildren," I explain.

"And that concerns you? Right..."

I grab a hundred grams of coke and weigh it just to be sure. That's all I have left. I have to meet Piotrek tomorrow. Reserves are running desperately low.

I do hope there's not going to be any problems. That nothing's been intercepted at the port in Gdansk, that no tyres have been cut into on a lorry coming in from Romania, loaded down with factory parts or wind farm propellers. That somewhere far, far from here nothing has happened recently which will fuck up my day.

"Do you ever ask yourself," Pazina muses, looking around the apartment, "Who might be above you?"

"What do you mean?"

"Who imports it, who keeps tabs, who allows all this stuff to enter the country?" she says, leaning on the wardrobe.

She knows she can ask me such questions. I cut a piece off of a large brick, smaller chunks breaking off. I scoop it all up into a plastic bag. I can hear a quiet, dull tapping noise coming from the apartment over our heads. One, two, three. I stop a moment. Then sweep up all the rest of the powder.

"No, I don't," I answer, turning to look at Pazina. "I never ask myself that question."

"You know already?"

"Nope."

"What do you cut it with? I always wanted to know."

"Why do you ask?" I put a foil wrap with fifty grams in my coat pocket. Pazina takes out her cigarettes and a lighter. "Paz, no smoking allowed in here."

She places the lighter on the table. I hear a knocking sound again. This time, it's the front door. Pazina looks at it. I zip up the bag with the coke, then move up to stand with my back against the wall. Slide over to the wardrobe, take out a handgun. Pazina looks a little fazed. I keep the Glock 19C around for such eventualities. A tool, like something from the kitchen, an external hard drive for your laptop. Necessary. For moments like this, involving unexpected visitors.

"Fucking hell, Kuba," Pazina whispers.

"Easy," I soothe the air between us, whispering also.

I slip the gun into the back of my trousers, then walk up to the door. Looking through the spyglass, I see it's Halina from next door.

"Mr Piotr, I forgot," she says after I open the door for her. "A postman brought this. He said it didn't fit inside your mailbox."

"Thank you," I say, taking the package.

"It's me who should be thanking you, so many things you bring me."

"Good night," I say, forcing a smile.

I think she wants to say something more, drawing out the moment of goodbye through lost silences, like all those who lack practice at talking to people. Those who keep salesmen talking when they call, feigning interest, the same with Jehovah's Witnesses or postmen or even phone-in radio shows.

"Good night, Mr Piotr. You're a nice boy," she murmurs.

I shut the door, take the gun out from my belt.

"Have you ever fired that thing?" Pazina asks.

"Something happened. Once. A certain... situation..." I tell her, concealing the gun again.

"What sort of situation?"

"Let's get out of here," I tell her instead of answering. Having put everything away, I turn on the security cameras again and double lock the front door. Then double check I did it all right. The gun still stuffed in my belt, I stop in the staircase, trying to listen out for any noises, but the tower block is completely silent. Everyone sound asleep. Done doing what it is they do for the night, ready to start all over again tomorrow.

"What sort of situation?" Pazina repeats her question once we're back in the car, seeing me remove the gun and hide it in the glove compartment.

"There was this one guy, locked me in his own apartment. He had a gun. Wanted to know something," I explain slowly as we drive out of the housing estate.

The streets are empty. For a moment, it seems that I see some people milling about the grocery store on the corner, but it's only an illusion, some branches casting shadows on walls.

"Did you know what it was he wanted to find out?" she asks.

"I kept repeating the same sentence over and over again for hours."

"What sentence?"

"That we're both just wasting time and money."

I drive towards Saxon Marshes, the villas near French Street, towards my best customer just as he rings me again.

"And did it work? Your explanation?" Pazina asks, ignoring the ringing phone.

"After ten hours on repeat, it did," I tell her. "Some people take a long time realising certain glaringly obvious facts."

"I thought maybe you disarmed him," she says.

"With patience, if anything," I quip and she chuckles, even though what I said was in no way funny.

"You're the most amusing person I know. Droll, but amusing."

We stop at the traffic lights. There is a car behind us, and I instinctively turn to look to see who is sitting inside. Two giggling girls driving to or from some party, in a small Alfa Romeo. One of them sees me staring. The other then checks her makeup in a small mirror. I turn back around.

"Will you wait for me downstairs?" I ask Pazina.

"I told you I would. Only what for?"

"Keep an eye out," I ask.

"What for?"

"For everything. Damn, in five minutes, you're gonna be texting me to ask what your name is. What's up with you?"

She's starting to get on my nerves, or else maybe I was unnerved earlier, but she doesn't normally ask this many questions. It's unlike her. Anyone who's seen and heard as much as Paz has shouldn't be going round asking stupid questions, just going with the flow, wherever that leads.

"I thought that our game was about enjoying the chance to talk to someone who really listens."

"Those who want to chat to strangers turn their cars into cabs,"

I snap back. She doesn't answer. "Sorry. All I need you to do is lock the car, hang around, move to keep warm and report if you see anything. Anything at all. Someone else watching the car. Checking number plates. I could be in there for a long while."

"Is something up?"

"No, nothing's up," I say, unconvincingly, then remember something. Grab my phone. Tiny. He still hasn't called. I'm not surprised, but my offer was not the kind to be refused. I call him, go straight through to answering machine.

I then know what I have to do. I dial Uncle's number. He doesn't answer, so I leave him a message.

"You sure?" Paz asks once more and I nod to keep her quiet.

Tonight is no different to any other night, everything will end the same as before. I'll get home. Go to sleep. Everything will be just as it was when I woke up. I tell myself this one too many times.

02:07am

My best customer. He opens his front door wearing a blazer with the sleeves rolled up, a crumpled up vest underneath that. That vest cost his personal stylist a whole afternoon of crumpling by hand to make. The same with the trainers he's wearing, seemingly ordinary, no socks. Plain black. The doorman who sits in reception recognised me straight away, nodded, handing over a pass card without a word, pointed me to the lifts. I am on the special list – the list of people who don't need to sign in, who don't need to give names.

I hear noise coming from inside his apartment. There must be one hell of a party going on inside.

"Kuba! You're very welcome, as usual," he says, waving me inside.

Standing next to me, he looks almost just the same as he does on the billboards, advertising another talent scouting show or some new deals from a cell phone network. It's only when you look more closely that a certain dryness around the eyes becomes apparent, tiredness, the skin blotchy. He's nearing fifty, not half that which is what he'd love the world to believe, though he does play the bumbling teen with some aplomb, something that goes deeper than his designer rags, some sort of sweetheart foolishness he wears well. Like school for him was never out, not really, the bell calling him back to class always ready to ring.

"Well, well," he says. "Will you have a drink?"

"Water," I say, smiling again.

His apartment is nicely decorated, though when I visited him the first time, I expected something a bit more loud and gaudy. Imported furniture, paintings too big for the walls they're on. Meanwhile, it is clean, sterile almost, black and white elements from some fine furniture catalogue, rather anonymously hollow. Everything's been minimised. There's nothing in his kitchen to suggest that anyone ever goes in there to do anything. His shelves don't groan under the weight of books he wants us to think he's read. The floors are dark polished concrete.

The place looks like it belongs to someone who doesn't need a home, who wants to feel like he's passing through, like a ghost, a temporary apparition.

In his company, I think about how nice it would be to have a face no one recognises: the face of a man who has never been born, who is not listed in any records, someone unassociated with anything at all. A person no one greets or says goodbye to, ignored by all; sometimes I'd like to have that kind of face, a different mask every day, every new day a new start. That would be the best form of camouflage. Know no one and be far from people, disappearing into transparency.

My best customer – I know he feels the same. That this is his ultimate fantasy, something he would give up all of his fortunes for – freedom from the slavery of celebrity.

"Listen up! Everything's gonna be alright now," he calls out to all his guests, pointing right at me. "The cavalry's arrived. The Allies have landed. No need to clap. All I ask for is a moment's attention."

For a second, everyone in the room freezes and looks his way. No one minds to give me a second glance, as if I wasn't worth the attention. A good thing, too. People are used to him taking all the space on screen, on stage, their whole field of vision. The silence, the interruption only lasts a second or two. Soon enough, everyone goes back to whatever they were doing before he butted in – fondling one another, chit chatting, guffawing, dancing to the very same David Bowie classics I used to be forced to listen to when studying art with all those impoverished artistes. I know some of the people in here, more or less. They sometimes flicker up on my TV screen when I'm trying to fall asleep, usually on early morning chat shows, breakfast telly, talking about homeopathy, about online hate, about legalising marijuana, molecular cooking, about speed cameras. All they ever do for me is help me fall asleep. In the evenings, just as I am waking, they go back to their jobs, starring in television ads or theatre runs. From time to time they might even land a real film role. The men swollen, their bodies surrendering to gravity, using the same set of smiles they save for work, their repertoire of genuineness, all the time thinking about money, about that restaurant they were going to open up in the coolest street in town, about how the opening might clash with some divorce hearings or other pre-arranged affairs. The women stand around, erect upon their high heels, constantly tense , their bodies long ago repaired from the damage done by addictions and abortions and births, ready to show up on more shows where they twirl and dance and grin, their movements restricted by clothes produced by young designers, movements which show just how much grace they truly lack, their ankles and wrists the colour of cheap ice cream. If anyone were to detonate a bomb in here right now, the whole of this country would have no one to read about the next day, in all the cheap gossip rags street-corner kiosks peddle all over Poland.

They're amusing. I don't mind their company. Above all, they're polite, genuinely polite, for a simple reason – they have no other choice. People trust them as much as they trusted old communist-era police officers. The public are only interested in them as a means of channelling their inner hate. And they know it too, though their awareness of what is going on in the world also comes from the same gutter tabloids that feature them on their covers. They exist in worlds utterly stripped of any points of reference. They're like trapped children floating round in transparent, ephemeral bubbles. Jigged about by shifts in air-conditioned air. Seeing little of the world other than brightly lit studios, the rest of reality projected onto wall-sized screens which flicker about behind them, beaming in images of real life from very far off.

There's a certain doctor in here I know all too well. They all know him too. A nice guy, past middle age, getting a divorce from his wife right about now – a wife who couldn't stand the fact that her hubby has to be at their beck and call any time of day or night, such as when there's a party on or some premiere, and they have to be back on set at 8am, or up for a photo shoot, some business breakfast or early morning rehearsals. He pays them quick visits, hooking them up to drips, serving up vitamin cocktails, calming pills, pseudoephedrine, averting his eyes when they line up those last lines to snort, the ones they'd saved up for a rainy hour. After a short while in his care, they reach a point at which they might or might not quite understand the things he is trying to say to them.

I know that he really is a rather lovely guy. I sell him stuff. He needs a lot of it, and I mean a lot: he sleeps only a couple of hours a day, holding down a full time job in a hospital.

There's a few others in here I know. Rock artists long past their use-by date – some of them used to fill stadiums back in the punk-rock heyday of the 1980s, but now they have to play the opening ceremonies of farming, country and western festivals in deepest rural Poland. But they still bring in the money, can't knock them for that. They pay their alimonies and cough up what's left for their addictions. Once a year, they can afford a bit of rehab, detox, some Tibetan bowl bullshit, vipaśyanā, maybe the effort of a guided tour round some Nepalese hills. One of the most enduring memories from my childhood is of my father singing their songs, after one too many vodkas. Now I see them huddled together, looking round, like a bunch of Halloween fancy dress party refugees – all leather jackets and straggly, greasy, thinning ponytails.

Sprinkled in among them are rock chicks, their lips artificially inflated, making sure they last the distance they need to blow their way to the top, every possible inch of their breasts on show, their skin flavoured with fake tan creams, bimbos from the less impoverished parts of rural nowheresville, ex-hostesses and party girls tired of being constantly shafted by ageing pricks, just to then get their fake gobs into magazines and from magazines spreading all over the internet like a rash. They float about the massive apartment, admiring my best customer's furniture and artworks, shining their sausage smiles, illiterate cunts who look older than their own mothers. When they looked that wee bit younger, they did blow jobs for coke at Bethlehem or whatever other club was cool that long ago. Two such ladies are now hovering about a film producer I know, who is dressed like a baddie from a second-rate sci-fi movie, his gob like something from a documentary about the KGB and the gait of a giant, plastic water sack.

There's a few other celebs hanging about, all looking like they want to be somewhere else right now – a TV newsreader checking out if there's anything left at the bottom of his third bottle of wine, desperate to unload another internet joke about Putin, still half-way through some anecdote he's been regaling his chums with that's louder than anything else in the house.

Everyone is smashed, shouty and stoned.

I am waiting to speak to my best customer, who is now moving among them, softly, slowly, without picking up on the nervousness the others emanate like body odour, the nervousness he cultivates on screen. Whenever he's live, he jumps up and down like a child, interrupting his guests, wagging his finger, correcting their mistakes, getting on everyone's nerves. Here, he's different. Taking in all the glamour, the fame, caressing all the egos, trying to embrace them somehow for later. They see him as their shaman, their authority figure. They owe him their latest fifteen minutes of fame, which is all he gives them on his chat show. They all know he's the smartest, the brightest, the most cunning of them all. The leader of their damned forsaken pack.

Though there's still something of the loser about him: the kid who was always the first to be picked on, sent on errands or picked for sports only so he'd be there to trip up. But I do like him. I like people who try so hard, stripping themselves of all dignity, sculpting their image like something out of heavy wood, just to sell themselves to the highest bidder, be their own billboards, their own sales pitches.

They've managed to break out.

I want to look through a window, but none of the ones in the room we're in looks out to the street. I keep standing by the wall, pretending to be checking my phone. My best customer is now lost in the crowd, but it's only momentary. I then see him slapping someone on the shoulder. Joking with someone, laughing with or at them, I can't tell from a distance. Only to eventually make his way back to me.

"Shall we go and have a chat, in private?" he suggests.

I nod and follow him, into his bedroom. He slides the door shut. The vast bed is covered with his guests' warm winter coats, along with blazers, shawls and handbags. A door leads to an en-suite bathroom. He stops a moment, suddenly aware that there is someone in there and they are clearly fucking.

"I'm sorry about this, Kuba," he says, a little flustered.

He's trying to be cool, but I can tell he's actually upset, not something he'd ever show to the cameras. I appreciate this little moment of frankness.

He knocks on the bathroom door, but whoever is inside would rather keep going than answer.

For ten years now, he's had his own prime time chat show. It doesn't have a title, nothing beyond his name – *The Mariusz Fajkowski Show*. In addition, he has gigs doing live radio and writing columns for a few papers and magazines. He's relentless. Ubiquitous. Omnipresent. There are young girls hanging around him all the time, desperate to be seen with him in one of his fleet of supercars. He's regularly photographed, supposedly off guard, only to then get into a scuffle with the odd paparazzi or two, though it's usually pre-arranged and always then settled out of court. I guess it's his way of getting his own back on all those bullies who made him bleed back in playschool.

I know he makes even more real money outside of showbiz. With ruthless effectiveness. He knows his Forex, the value of properties, stocks and shares. Uses business partners as tools, things to be discarded, unless they happen to have more money than him. Then he dances with them nicely, for a while. Almost everyone in Poland has heard his name, seen his face, and that impresses the hell out of his associates. Even if everyone knows how cunning, how slippery he is. Never pretending to be anything other than that. Never feigning noblesse. He's ruthless, effective, intelligent, and utterly loveless. Even friendless, even though he's great at playing everyone's pal. He never loses control over anything, the master at pre-programming every move, every angle, every take.

He's never tried to con me out of a deal. For four years now, since the first time his number flashed up on my phone screen, he's never asked for freebies or for credit. He's never owed me a penny – loves carrying cash around, big wads of it stuffed in the pockets of his perfectly ripped jeans. He sometimes loses it by the hundreds, just for show. Says he loves to find it afterwards, on the floor or in some shoe, the way the rest of us find coins. He laughs at this, says it's his only weakness, a little bit of small town boy silliness, proof that he's not lying when he tells the press he started out in some highland village in the deep Carpathians and made it out of there all by himself.

"We've both ended up here, now... and I'd say the transplants were successful," he said to me once.

I think we met through the same guy who first introduced me to Beata. He crept around after Mariusz, party after party, showbiz event after corporate gala, laughing like a rabid horse at his jokes, slapping him on his shoulders, lightly, for added effect. I quickly got to trust him. He was always thorough. I never saw him snort either.

I make some room on the bed to sit on, shoving the coats and bags aside. He tries the handle to his bathroom door, which happens to be unlocked. There's a girl and two blokes inside. A very young blonde, her face familiar, probably from some commercial or billboard. She's bent over the bath, arms outstretched, head down over it. I hear her moan very lightly as one of the men, clearly overweight and overindulged on wine, shoves himself inside, almost sleepily. The other guy is sitting on the toilet, struggling to light a crack pipe. The three of them only notice the door open after a while. The fat guy quickly drops the girl and pulls his pants up. The other hides the pipe in the pocket of his suit jacket. She's the last and the least hurried to straighten and tidy herself up. They all look at my best customer without a word, like a bunch of teenagers caught by a school cleaner doing something they shouldn't have been doing in the student toilets.

I watch the scene, mildly amused. Wondering why I can't hear a thing of the party outside the bedroom door. Must be soundproofed, I guess.

"I'm very sorry, guys, but I have to ask you to fuck right off now," he says in a matter of fact way.

"Mariusz, fucking hell, sorry about this," says the fatso who only moments ago was screwing that underage starlet, who is now moving past them all and, standing next to me, begins going through the pile on the bed, looking for her stuff.

"We're out of here," says the classy crackhead.

"Come darling," the other one says to the girl, "Let's get you something cool to wash that down with."

"Gents, we don't seem to have understood one another," Mariusz says, smiling sweetly. "Maybe I didn't make myself clear. You are to fuck the hell out of this room and then out of my home. Right the fucking fuck now."

The girl turns to look at them. She's a little dazed, but still can tell what the real score is. She's too thin for her height, bones jutting, telling the story of unnatural starvation, and still unused to wearing heels. She's not twenty yet. Surely not. She looks down at me from all that distance, our eyes meeting with all the potential intensity of strangers making eye contact on public transport, two people on two buses going in opposite directions. Going to work. Early morning. To hell. She's found her coat and her handbag. Walking towards the door, she trips over the shag pile carpet, but not so that she falls. Wise enough to hear what Mariusz said. Wise enough to do what she's told.

"I'm the only one allowed to fuck in this bathroom! I'll tell you why. It's my bathroom, in my bedroom," my best customer roars at the remaining couple. "Is that in any way clear?! You get the idea of personal space? Personal property? Or do you now need a little lecture on the fucking subject?!"

"Listen, wait, we didn't mean... spur of the moment, you know, eh..." says Crackhead, getting up off the toilet, his hands spread wide, so wide any child could tell he's trying to show he's sorry.

"She dragged us in here. We thought... we didn't think, sorry, mate," says the other guy.

"Do you two think I want to be cleaning up, personally cleaning up, anything you two leave behind in here?!" Mariusz is now screaming. To no answer. "You two realise if this was America, I would have the right just now to shoot you two?"

Instead of leaving, they just stay there, right in the line of his fire. Mariusz has no other option but to point towards the door.

"What the fuck are you two pricks waiting for?" he asks, a little more quietly now. Then he turns towards me. "Sorry about this, Kuba."

"Don't mention it, Mario," I answer, smiling sadly.

The other two approach the bed, rapidly looking for their coats. They find them, eventually, then leave so quickly they forget to close the door. Mariusz has to follow and do it for them. He's fuming, but knows how to act as if he's not. His lips drawn tight, his glasses slipping down his nose, he looks off to the side and I now recall seeing him on the cover of some political magazine, acting all angry, bitter, enraged even. Protesting against something or other, expressing opinions, taking sides. That's the kind of country we live in, where chat show hosts lead the way towards a healthy democracy. The truth is, this coke head isn't protesting shit. For him, it's just a game, a play on the way to making his own deals, a way to meet more people, gather more essential data, sign more lucrative contracts. Politicians like celebs like him, both sides of the left-and-right spectrum, because they know how much his backing is worth. He too knows the value of the association. When making public statements, he is true to those convictions.

He really is rather smart, as far as television personalities go. Knows which side his bread is buttered.

"There's never an end to human insolence. Where were their parents at when it came to feeding their kids some manners? Smuggling furs and fine carpets from Bulgaria? Marching for Solidarity? Too busy selling hot dogs to raise their own fucking kids right?" he rants, opening a cabinet next to the bed and pulling a bottle of whisky, with two glasses, from it.

"I don't drink, remember?"

"What, never?" he asks a little angrily, probably embarrassed to have forgotten this about me.

"Never when driving."

"Oh, that I understand," he nods approvingly. "You have to remind me of these things. I'm getting old. My memory ain't what it used to..."

Instead of finishing the sentence, he takes a big swig of the whisky. It's been a while since I've seen anyone shoot single malt like it was tequila. Come to think of it, I can't ever remember him drinking alcohol either – he's always got a glass of something in his hand, but I've never actually seen him drink from any of them. His face suggests his palate is not suited to the taste of fine spirits.

"Fifteen grand, to you," I say.

"Kuba, let me tell you something, just between us," he says, catching his breath from the booze and pouring himself another helping. "I'm a sucker for special offers. I'm too rich to ask for discounts. You get me? The things I really, really dislike the most is this goddamn semitic attitude to money. I hate people who have credit cards with no spending limits, yet still do their shopping in the cheapest fucking Romanian supermarkets. You're not recording this, I hope? The press would kill me if they heard that. 'Semitic attitude to money', 'Romanian supermarkets'. Dear me. But you know what I mean. You don't build fortunes out of piles of pennies. You don't fund wars from what you've got stashed in your mattress. Smart people know that."

"Stupid people haven't been told," I add.

"I know you agree with me, you know what money is all about," he says, waving his index finger in my direction. "You get it. Not many people do."

He takes one step back, another one forward, runs a hand through his thick, richly styled hair. Something's up. He looks tense, something I haven't observed before, as if his veins have been replaced with wires. He looks in pain, vulnerable. And it won't be those pricks who've been using his personal washroom for a brothel. He's forgotten all about that already. I can see how his shoulders are angled, his hands forming fists, trying to get at something.

"Make it twenty grand. What the hell. I never argue with customers," I tell him.

"For me? Kuba! A regular customer like me? Buddy!" he cries, waving his hands about like he was back live on air.

"Twenty large ones," I repeat.

"OK then, twenty it is."

He pulls a roll of banknotes from his pocket, starts counting, quickly, with grace I find attractive. I take out the tin foil wrap with his baggies, place it on the shelf, next to the single malt. Then check my phone. No news from Pazina, but there is a message – *The number you've been trying to contact is now available*. Meaning Tiny is now in my sights again.

Mariusz gulps the remains of the second glass of whisky.

"Is everything alright?" I enquire.

"Do you ever check exchange rates? The value of the dollar?" he asks, looking directly at me.

"I don't play those kinds of games."

"We're living in very interesting times. Very interesting indeed."

I say nothing to that, while he keeps staring at me, bored but not totally disinterested. Then he adds: "You look like you want to tell me something. Like you want to tell me I'm overdoing it. Which would be rich. Coming from my dealer. My supplier. Advice on moderation."

"I've no intention of telling you what to do. You're a big boy. With your big toys."

"There are times when things go wrong, though. You know? You know the feeling? The gut feeling? Something unplanned unravelling."

"I do," I admit. "Shit happens. There are ways of avoiding it, but not many."

He glances at his soundproofed doors, as if only just remembering that there are other people in the building besides the two of us.

"Not many indeed," he nods to himself.

"Listen, whatever it is, if I can help..."

He shuts me up by shoving the cash in my outreached hand. I hide the bundle in my trouser pocket.

"It's nothing," he says, waving the now empty palm. "Nothing's the matter. It might be raining outside, but I'm staying out of it. Got my brolly, you know? Got a solid roof over my head. In another life, I could have been an architect. An expert roof tiler, at least."

"I have to fly," I tell him.

"Wait. You've just made twenty large. That means you wait," he says, putting the crystal glass back on the shelf. "What was it you were thinking when you got here?"

"That it's Saturday night, and you should be having fun," I tell him.

"D'you honestly think I want those people in my house?" he asks, incredulous.

"Seeing as they're here..."

Somebody knocks on the bedroom door. Mariusz opens it, revealing an attractive blonde, thirty-something, wearing a flattering black dress. Her hair straight, her features sharp, her gaze too. I see muscle beneath the curves of that dress, and more of it in the way she looks at our host. The way people look at each other when they've slept together already and liked it, and not just the sex, but the actual sleeping too. Even if the whole world doesn't need to know about it.

"Am I interrupting?" she purrs.

"What is it?" Mariusz asks, words digging, but the smile playful.

"Hey," she says to me. I say the same back. She comes inside, he slides the door shut as she glances at the bottle, the glass and the gift I've deposited next to them.

"Are you two partying without us?" she asks.

"We're discussing some important stuff," he assures her, pointing at me. "My friend is a competitor. He is in some sense my informant. What's the phrase I'm looking for? Whistleblower?"

"And there was me thinking he was a dealer," she says, looking right at me, only the eyes smiling.

"You must have me confused with someone else, ma'am," I quip back, then get back to my phone and the message I've been wanting to send Tiny. It's not long: *What's up?*

The girl sighs, then looks at Mariusz with a special kind of familiar pity, as if he were her younger brother.

"What happened? Why did those three leave?"

"Nothing happened. They evidently had somewhere else they suddenly had to be," he lies without any attempt to make it stick.

"And the girl?"

"Oh, she must have had another appointment."

"She was crying."

"I've no idea why," Mariusz shrugs. "Marta, please, don't expect me to know why all the world's women weep sometimes. She found out today her father was running low in the polls. She's a young girl, you know. Unprepared for radical changes. Moving to Brussels, when all her male admirers are gathered here."

She smiles bitterly, shaking her head.

"For so many years now I've told you the same thing: Be careful where you stick that thing. I mean it."

"You're vulgar. Charmless," he jokes, pouring himself more whisky. "Go tell my guests I'll be with them in just a sec."

"See ya," she waves to me and I nod a response. Once the door is shut, the room falls silent again.

"You never saw that girl here," he insists. "I mean the girl from the toilet porn scene. We need to be clear on that."

"I've a terrible memory for faces," I sigh, shrugging.

"And there was me thinking it was rather photographic... What were we talking about before being so cutely interrupted?"

I spread my hands in a lazy gesture of ignorance. I can listen to his bullshit for another ten minutes, no more. In some sense, I've no choice, seeing as he's my best customer. He spends about 50,000 on coke each month. If he only asked, I could sell him shit on credit for up to half a mil, without flinching. He is, undoubtedly, a VIP kind of client.

"We were talking about how much you like having so many people piled into your home," I remind him.

"People. Do they bring me any joy?" he muses, lifting his hands a little. "Do you know the kind of people I value having around the most? People like you. People who really aren't all that interested in anything I might have to say."

"Well, I'm pleased."

"Now listen – ever since school, since that first fucking assembly and some shitty speech they told me to orate, I haven't said one thing to anyone just so they'd be pleased," he spits.

"Well, intentions and outcomes are two different things," I observe, unfazed. Which gets me a subtle smile.

"I should have you on my show. Now that would be something. Only we'd have to come up with some false identity. I would introduce you as a therapist to the stars! Now that would be good. That would be grand. Yeah, Kuba, there really is something of the listener about you. An assertive passivity. Or passive assertiveness... who the fuck cares which. You'd make the best kind of shrink."

Pazina texts: *How much longer?*

15mins, I reply.

"Do you understand any of it?" he asks, pointing at the bottle and the bag of drugs.

He then takes the bag, dips a finger in it and rubs it along his gums. Licking his lips like he's just swallowed a piece of chocolate.

"I don't, but do enlighten me," I respond.

"This," he says, pointing at the bottle, and then the bag, "And that, are things which love you. And it doesn't matter one jot to them whether you love them back."

I sigh. He must be both stoned and pissed, though it is always hard to tell with showmen this good. He's got incredible amounts of self-control, like an android, like something from a horrid sci-fi flick. He talks just as fluently, with the same pre-rehearsed certainty, moving almost as normal, only there is a tiny flicker, a glitch in the program, something you have to look very hard to notice. Then he becomes like rubber. His face stretched over something which doesn't appear to be bone. A different sort of narrative. A disappointed child. His eyes give it away, the look of someone who fears that everything around him – the walls, the floor, the furniture – beneath all the coats of polished veneer is made of purest shit.

"It's not that people love coke and booze," he says, getting back into a pose I recognise from his TV ads. "Not that you love them. It's that alcohol and drugs love you."

"Interesting, but does it make sense?" I test.

"I'll explain. Coke and booze love you most of all in the world. Unconditionally. Like a mother, like Jesus loves ya. Look at it this way – they're always there when you need them. Never moody, never absent, never failing. They always cost the same. Leaving aside minor stock market fluctuations, they're always priced the same. They always comfort, always soothe. Always make you feel better. Any time, day or night. How to name such a thing, if not as love? It's the definition of love. The purest sort of commitment. Who in your life is that generous with you? Who loves you that strongly, that steadily?"

"There's not many to choose from," I nod.

"And you think I'm any different?"

"You've a villa full of loving folks, no?" I ask, half-serious.

He pauses for a moment, as if he suddenly realised he was acting in a sketch, that he had just recited a rather trashy monologue about love and addiction or dependency or something else that's equally grim, in front of a stranger who hadn't touched a drop of drugs or drink all night. A shameful thing, like jokes about the size of your dick meant to cover up fears about its actual size.

"Get some rest. Some sleep," I tell him, watching his shoulders sag.

"I pay people to tell me such words of wisdom, Kuba," he spits back. "I keep you around for something completely different."

"I'm off then."

"No, stay a little," he entices.

"Your guests are waiting," I remind him.

"Let them."

He plonks himself on the bed next to me. Inches away, though the bed is huge. Takes one more sip of malt. Hunched over a little, as if recovering from a blow to the stomach. I'm really not in the mood for this, for any more words or outpourings of emotion or surprises hidden in bathrooms and cupboards, for any potential confessions, sob stories, family elegies. Not only because I don't have the time, or because Pazina's down there, out in the cold – I just don't want to start pitying someone I'd rather keep respecting. He should keep something back. From me especially.

"Is there someone? I mean, in your life? Women? Some need that. Attachment. Permanence. The sense that some things won't end overnight," he says.

"Nope," I state calmly.

"You're not going out with anyone?"

I give him a hard, disappointed look, but no answer.

"I have to go. Work to be done," I tell him instead.

"Listen. We're mates. There's things we can talk about," he says, rising to reach for the bag of coke.

"There's no one. No need. Not for me."

"So how do you do it? Fill the time? Brothels? Call girls? Are you paying for anyone to go through university?"

I shake my head, getting up.

"So what else? Are you gay? Sorry to ask. None of my business, but you know, I'm just curious. After all, we have a working relationship," he jokes, cutting up a line, then stops joking, snorts it, coughs, then throws his head back. "As a rule, I can normally read the people I meet. With you, there's more of a mystery."

"You shouldn't ask folks if they're gay. It's impolite," I tell him.

He jumps away from the night table, as if shot with adrenaline, his hands in the air again, higher this time.

"Oh yeah, I forgot! You're a man of the streets, of the night, a gangster, so to say. I have to watch my mouth. For you, mentioning sexuality's a taboo. Gay the worst sort of insult, right? What do you do to people who cross that line? Cut their fingers off? One by one? Drive them to the nearest woods? Sasha and Gregori taking us for one last ride? The shovel free of charge, plus a free text message – choose: mum or girlfriend to say goodbye to? Darling, I can't speak, there's a gun pointing at my head, because I just suggested my coke dealer might be gay. The one you met at that party one Christmas. I know I said he was an investor from Belgrade, but..."

"Something along those lines," I say, laughing in spite of myself.

"I was kidding about the gay thing. Really. Don't be mad. I know... I know one girl who was with you for a while," he confesses. At which point the smile fades from my lips.

"I don't understand," I tell him, honestly.

"Nothing, sorry. Forget I mentioned it," he backtracks. "Me and my infamous mouth."

"You discuss me with others?" I ask, sounding a little disappointed, but actually fuming inside. "I did ask, did tell you that was unwise."

"You know, you're an interesting guy. You have a remarkable job. I'm surrounded by actors, artists, you've no idea how boring that can be. Wankers wanking all the time, always trying to drag the conversation back towards themselves, always."

"You shouldn't have mentioned me to anyone. Not anyone," I tell him, my lips grimacing. My phone starts to buzz. Pazina. I answer.

"On my way," I tell her.

"Sorry, I didn't mean anything by it. I just met this girl, said she knew you," he explains, dejected.

"I know girls. Various girls. I've fucked some of them. Some of them were women even. So what?" I ask, getting up, instinctively checking if the roll of banknotes is still inside my pocket.

"Don't be mad," he pleads. "Take it easy, please. I've never been one for, you know, convention... My fault, I'm a dick. Big mouth. That's all I have. One fucking big mouth. Never know what's gonna come out of it."

"Get back to your guests."

"You know, it's been a long time since I said sorry to anyone. Think it must have been that time camping, holidays and that girl..."

"I'm not mad. We're good. All paid up," I assure, patting him on the shoulder and then I walk over to slide the door open.

As we leave the bedroom, all eyes are once again on him. The party's intensified since we saw it last, become louder, more chaotic.

More like some shitty business convention. His face is instantly back the way it was when he opened the front door for me, half an hour ago. A wicked half-smile. A mask from some billboard.

"See ya, Kuba. You're an interesting guy," he says, shaking my hand, then is once again swallowed up by the adoring crowd.

Some young starlet wraps her arms around his neck, her hips bouncing against his, almost knocking him off balance. I quickly retreat towards the door, his voice fading in the background, something about the bathroom, about how comfy it is to spend time in. The girl laughs. It sounds like the laughter of all the audiences who attend the recordings of all his shows. I shut the front door behind me to silence it all.

03:05am

"Thanks. And sorry about earlier," I say to Pazina.

I get out of the car for a moment. My back hurts. I stretch and something pops in my spine, in my shoulder blades, my chest. Sounds like the noises made by old wooden toys.

"Don't mention it," she says, getting out too. We walk over to the front door of her apartment block, dragging our feet like a couple who want to part, but are too embarrassed to admit it. Pazina lights one more cigarette. She gives me an odd look, and I don't really know if it is a concern or complaint.

I feel tired. It's too early in the night for me to feel that, but that's how it is: there's something pounding on the inside of my skull, a taste in my mouth as if I'd swallowed something toxic, acidic as hell. My head spinning a little, my knees soft. And the night is only just getting started.

"Maybe you want to fly with me?" I ask, Christ knows why.

"What?"

"Argentina. Three weeks, all expenses on me. You got a valid passport? Take off Friday."

"You're going to where?"

"Argentina. I have to go and see it for myself. Make sure it isn't all legends," I explain, smiling weakly. "The more time I spend here, the more I am starting to think that it's all a play of shadows out there."

I now have visions of nightmare scenarios – Pazina sitting beside me on a beach, watching a sunset, both of us clutching cheap drinks, made by barmen who don't speak any of our languages, both of us tense, too tense to relax, too tense to admit we miss home. The thought is so stupid, I burst out laughing. We're all the same – from here, yet from somewhere else, from nowhere. All our holiday photos looking like bad Photoshop. Lazy special effects.

It doesn't matter how we got here. What matters is we're here now, for better or worse.

"Do you honestly think you could manage to spend longer than an hour or two in the company of one person and not lose it?" she asks in all earnestness.

"If you could only see to it that you stop asking all these dumb questions, then yes," I answer, tiredness letting my annoyance show a little.

"You know what? When I think about the fact that I might just be the person in this town who's closest to you, it makes me... damned sad. Sad like old black and white British war movie sad. The kind of sad which makes your neck sore. Sadness as rheumatism."

"Gee, thanks."

"I sometimes ask stupid questions, because I really don't know you at all. I know who you say you are, that your parents live in Olsztyn. You told me about your sister Paulina, which is plenty, because it shows you have feelings after all."

"We don't get to know people by listening to them, but by watching them, watching what they do."

"Oh, I can recall seeing you in a few specific situations," Pazina says through a cloud of exhaled smoke.

"That's why I keep you around, kid," I say, trying to cover tracks.

"You're talking like a fake ass gangster," she snaps, disapprovingly.

There's plenty to recall. I met Pazina back when I was still a student at the art academy. We met at some party, though I think she tried to chat me up, ask why I was so silent, trying to get me to make eye contact. I think this was as much pity as anything else – she had a guy then, a friend of Tiny's, a musician, not a complete waste of time, though still capable of crawling into beds his ass did not belong in. We met for a coffee once, she spoke a lot, I listened a lot, and so it went on. A lot of cigarettes, a lot of tears, a lot of short commands from me: "Leave him!", "Dump now!", "Break his nose!" I had little idea I was acting like any good girlfriend. I didn't want to sleep with her. It would have forced something between us, not intimacy, the opposite of that. If we fucked, I knew the ease between us would have turned to tension.

It's true, though. She knows little about me. Through all the time we've known each other there was little about me she would have found interesting. The things in my life are filled with stink, like a passing hobo, and talking about them just makes the stink worse.

She's also partly responsible for the path I've taken since we met. It was her friend who dealt pills and MDMA. Bits and bobs, here and there. Popping more than selling. I first met him, then I met that other person. A guy with the tasty nickname of Pike, young, quick-witted, a young rapper from the rough side of the river. I knew how to talk like someone who grew up on the streets, remembered enough conversations from home, enough time killed together on the estates. Say little, only when necessary, and always make eye contact . Respect what's due, spit on that which stinks. I always found it easy to be around street folks. All about attitude, gestures, posture. It helped that I always respected gangsters more than I did anyone else. Teachers. Artists. Cops, clearly.

I always liked those who didn't live in line with norms, who wandered off-piste, taking what they needed, what was for the taking, never just what was offered. My respect for them real. My silence loaded.

One day, Pike asked if I didn't feel like making a little cash on the side. He had some good acid and MDMA to offload, and knowing I hung out with all these arty types from college, he thought I might find it easy to attract custom.

I went along. Everyone I knew was a potential taker. And so it began.

"I doubt I'd manage to stand you for three whole weeks. Even in paradise," she finally says, smiling, but meekly.

"You're just scared of changing scenery."

"Not as much as you are."

My phone buzzes once. Uncle. *I'm there. Where you?* Pazina gets the guilt trips.

"Sorry, bro, I'm just in a mood today, odd shit, please, don't read anything into it," she apologises, stomping on the butt of her cigarette.

I smile, writing back: *Need your help. Call me.*

I look up to see her staring over my shoulder, as if someone was there. I don't turn round.

"Have I told you I've started seeing someone?" she asks. Uncle writes back: *You mean the faggot?* I ping back: *Yes.* "You never ask about those things," she continues.

"Your life, your private affairs," I shrug. Another text: *I can bring a team.*

"Still, you could pretend to be a little bit interested. Anyway, sorry again. For today. Don't mean to offload."

"Onto me?" I ask, puzzled. Then type: *Four of you. Maybe five.*

"I don't know," she says, shaking her head. "I'm like all those other stupid bitches, aged twenty, thirty, thinking the beauty will last, the attraction, that the world contains decent men, just well hidden, that the shittier ones can be cast aside, used, a month or two, then swapped and discarded. I'm like all the other dumb cunts who have no idea what they really want."

Text: *20 mins.* I write back: *OK.*

"What's the matter with you tonight?" I ask.

"He's really in love with me," she confesses. "Can't stop that itching."

"In love?"

"Misses me. Needs me... not just for the sex, for the cuddling. The contact. You know how it is. When people are cold. They need warmth."

"Are you cold too?"

"He's a great guy," she shrugs. "A bit older than me. Divorced already. With a kid. Good. Good listener. Knows things. Reads, smart shit. Patient. Strong. Really strong. Though the ex let him have it with both barrels."

"You didn't answer my question."

"I think I am a little," she nods, lighting one more cigarette, taking a step back, suddenly looking round as if hallucinating, as if fearing apparitions.

Text: *Come to us. Mazowiecka St. Does Piotrek know?*

I write back: *Piotrek wants this.*

"I just don't know how to do it anymore. Kuba, I'm finished," she concludes. "But I'd like to. Everybody wants to. It's the only thing to live for, for fuck's sake."

"Don't lose yourself in all that longing," I tell her, kissing her cheek.

"I know I'll do it. I know I'll just screw myself up, and I can't have him being battered again. I can't. He's too good."

I nod.

"Our place is here, in the night, alone."

"In the fucking shit," she adds, getting teary, though only on the inside.

"We're gangsta, Paz," I add, barely half-joking.

"Yeah, right. Me gangsta. Your dad, maybe."

"You're here, middle of the night, outside your front door, listening to me. Not him. If you wanted to, you'd be elsewhere. You'd be with him."

"Will you fuck off? Now, fuck off out of here," she says, shoving me gently. Smiling, knowingly, though hiding it in the dark.

"I'm fucking off."

"To the dark side?"

"I gotta go get some mo' money."

"Just try and not kill anyone," she pleads.

"There's not gonna be a need. Much."

She types the release code into her intercom, vanishes inside. The heavy door slams shut, the automatic light inside not working.

Pazina vanishes into the dark and I go back to the door, rubbing my hands against the cold.

They struggle to answer the last text of the night. Uncle: *Need tools? Gas? Sticks?*

I write back: *Firepower.*

04:30am

"Conclusion is – people are fucked in the head," Uncle says, turning round to look at the back seat, at Shady and some other guy they've brought along. He's called Barracks and is younger and bigger than the other two. Looks like an inflatable teen, massive in every respect, barely fitting in the back of the car. He looks soft, but there's concrete underneath that baseball cap. Nothing but concrete. He keeps chewing power bars and thankfully saying nothing.

"I don't know," Uncle goes on. "Do please fucking enlighten me. What is it? Some fucking voodoo?" Shady and Barracks both chortle, and it sounds like sheets of metal falling down a well. "Did their mummy give them too many baths? Damaged their brains when washing their ears for them? Tell me, Barracks."

"Mother or father," Barracks mumbles.

"If you're not coming in, you're not coming in. Not in. That kid with the clipboard they got on the door now, he's alright, quick about it. Not on the list, not coming in. No debating, like with that last girl."

"But what the fuck are they thinking, going for the jugular, the monkeys?"

We're cruising past the intersection of Holy Cross and Marshesall. The city pretending to sleep. No one on the streets, nothing moving, but the action is now submerged, gone behind the curtains, gone down to the guts.

"Alcohol," Shady says. "Booze makes them brawny."

"That's not all," Uncle grimaces. "Not all. It's a lack of personal... values. No fucking manners."

"And the bigger you are, the easier to hit. Slower too," Shady adds.

Everyone bursts out laughing, my car trembling with reverb. Uncle takes the stick out from his pocket and starts hitting the side of his thigh with it, as if it was a drumstick. It's one of those spring-loaded metal batons, not too long, but heavy – hit someone across the back of the legs with enough conviction and they're going down, nerves giving way. Bladder too, all too often. Uncle toys with it like a pet, the heavy object, black paint peeling, dancing in his hands.

"Those three today, fucking hell, they just had to be kidding," he muses. "Fucking hell. You can take the boy off the farm, but you can't take the farm out of the boy. Fucking faggots. And that screaming bitch. Good thing I was too busy with the lads to waste time slapping her down. She was inches away from tasting some, the volume she was broadcasting at."

"They're always loud, their kind. Thinking they're screaming from the stands at some boxing gala. Like Pudzianowski's in their corner," Barracks chimes in.

His voice sounds artificially lowered, like it was being channelled through a modulator or some synth.

"Pudzianowski would be easy. Slow fucker," Shady laughs.

"They don't think. The bitches," Uncle philosophises, sighs, then adds, "Girls just like loud action."

"Find me a decent girl to take home," Shady says, shaking his head. "Nothing but whores, all around. Have you seen that film on YouTube?"

"Sure I have," says Uncle.

"Oh, forget it then."

Uncle shakes his head, eyes closing.

"Which fucking film, you idiot? How would I know if I have or haven't, if you don't say which one?"

"The one where this ordinary-looking guy is trying to pick some chick up in the street, and she says no so he walks away and gets into a Ferrari and she then runs up to him straight away," Shady mumbles quickly.

"Well, can't blame her for that," I chip in.

"What?" Uncle reacts. I look at him, hard.

"Can't blame someone for going after the money."

I stop the car not too far from Bethlehem, close to a taxi rank. We see coloured lights still flashing inside the building. Purple, red, yellow, green. I feel a flashback coming on, some deja vu, something I've seen in a dream, in another place, but I shut it off.

Instead, I put my hand to my forehead. I think it hurts. I blink a few times. It seems everything's becoming more blurry, day by day, almost imperceptibly so. As if dreams were sneaking through into reality, diffusing it, diluting. I have to do something about this. Sleep more. Get meds.

"We going in?" Uncle enquires. I nod, the first one out of the car.

The doormen almost pretend they don't see us enter. Nodding to each other, not us. The one who was on the door the last time is not here now. Good. The off-duty cop. I warned the other three he might be a problem, but we walk on upstairs uninterrupted.

This is the time this club really comes alive. The air is as thick as a rain cloud, the taps only running warm water, so no one saves money by drinking the cold water instead of buying bottles from the bar, everyone running back and forth, rubbing up against one another like wild dolls. No one is conscious any more, or aware that no one gets out of here alive. Dirty rhythms bounce off the walls, coming through without much effort, everyone trapped by them, partying to the same beat like some army of the future, an army designed to defeat itself. Hard to tell anyone apart, everyone uniform, bodies, clothes, dead eyes. Bethlehem at this hour is the last stop, the final destination.

Even at 4 am, the party goes on much the same in here. People dancing with the same abandon, regardless of what sounds are being played.

Tiny had the right idea. Transform this place, from a restaurant that attracted hardly anyone to its classy menu, into a hellish, sweaty, grim Eden – a black cave which will take in anyone unable to face the idea of finally going home. Warsaw has an endless supply of people like that.

It's an excellent place to offload crap-quality coke, MDMA,

ecstasy. And the demand just keeps going up. Higher and higher. I'm not even bothered much by the money Tiny owes me. That's only an excuse for me to get in on the money to be made on these dance floors, in these toilets. To ensure their powders and their pills come from me, from Piotrek, from my wholesaler. We need to be in, we need to control the flow, the quality, the access. We want to harvest this place. Harvest its passions. At the moment, it is fallow ground. Anyone can walk in and deal, like some village bazaar – anyone can set up a fucking stall. And it's wrong. It shouldn't be like this. Not here. Not in a town where even opening a fucking coffee shop needs permission from the right people.

The floor is a nasty mix of mud and shattered glass. I feel it as we walk through the dancing throng, no one paying us the least bit of attention. I see a couple by the wall, making out, eyes closed, but not closed in passion, rather exhaustion, minds gone, brains flooded with serotonin, not seeing, not hearing, not registering anything anymore. Tomorrow, they're not going to remember any of this. They're not even going to know they've forgotten.

We go up some stairs where the barmen finally notice us, whispering to each other, looking at us as we walk past. Uncle is still holding that steel stick, still tapping his thigh with it, like some band leader. Some skinny kid on his way to the bar almost bumps into him and Uncle grabs his elbow with his free hand and twists the kid around, pointing him in the right direction, as if the lad weighed no more than a coat stand.

"Gentlemen," Tiny greets us cordially as we enter his sparse office.

He's sitting at the long table, his face the colour of wet clay. His lips look dry. He's drinking something from a glass filled with ice, something which could be water or could be pure vodka. Seeing me, his lips twist into an ugly, unwelcoming smile. He doesn't seem to notice the other three. Uncle, Shady and Barracks stand behind me, watching Tiny not watching them. His eyes are blinking though, as if he was trying to clear them, to chase off some apparition. There's two other men in the room with us, a bearded hipster in a pressed lumberjack shirt and a heavy set type, his round head neatly shaved. I know them. The bearded guy is called Bully, used to run another place with Tiny on Saviour Square. Helps run a music agency, mostly hip hop, a nobody who knows a few key people. The other guy is also a face from the streets, but I can't even remember his name. If Tiny invited them here on purpose, then things have become even more comical than they were earlier.

I have the impression the room looks completely different from yesterday. Maybe it's a question of lighting. There's only one floor lamp on and all the ceiling lights off, trying to soothe Tiny's tired senses.

"Kuba, man, listen..." he starts mumbling, rises from his chair. "Maybe we could have that chat now? I have this thing I want to discuss."

"Sit," I order, politely.

"We were talking about Tuesday," Bully butts in. "Can you wait until then?"

"We've got work going on, building work. Man, it's gonna be fine, promise, hunky dory," Tiny says, his eyes not on mine though. "We can sort it all out. People sort people out, don't they?"

"You know how it is," says the bald lad, looking at me, then the three behind me, then shuts up.

Uncle bursts out laughing. I take a step back, make room for him at the front. Let him take it from here. Music rises up to a crescendo through the concrete floor , a thousand voices whooping.

And we haven't even made our first move yet.

"You two, fuck off, now," Uncle says, waving his baton in the direction of the door.

"You what?" Bully barks.

"Wait a minute, boys." Tiny tries to intercede, coming dangerously close to Uncle. Too close. I don't even see the blow striking the side of his leg, but he screams and goes down on to his knees. Now I see Uncle smiling. The other two haven't moved an inch. Bully wants to get up, but the other one holds him down with a steady hand.

Uncle bends down over Tiny.

"Now, did I ask you to move? No. I told the other two to fuck off."

"What the hell?!" Tiny complains.

"Do come back another day, gents," I say, staring at the other two, not moving a muscle.

"I don't get it," Bully says.

"There are pressing matters and less pressing matters. You two are the second category, so now clear off," I bark.

"This is place is being redone with my dough, man. I came here to get paid too, just like you. Ain't no difference between us, ain't no beef."

I keep staring him down. His voice is firm. He's not afraid. He's seen how this place works, and knows what needs doing. Knows how to handle the turbulence.

"Fuck on off!" Uncle roars so loudly they must hear him downstairs, in spite of the music. It even freaks me out a bit. "Am I talking Alien or something?! Are you two deaf?!"

"They hear you," I say, trying to ease things, then nod to them. They get up from the long table and move for the door. Once they're gone, I lock it behind them. Sit myself down on the same chair as before. Feeling more and more at home.

"Will you have a drink, lads?" I ask my colleagues, pointing to the row of whisky bottles lined up on one of the shelves. Tiny decides to get up, struggling with the delivery, but finally makes it back to his own chair.

"You too, kid, have a drink of something," I tell him. He shakes his head, sighing heavily.

Uncle grabs one of the bottles, unscrews the top, takes a swig right out of it. He passes the drink to Barracks, who refuses. Shady takes the bottle, holding it by the neck, not moving.

"Fuck me, Kuba. I have two kids. Alimony to pay. I've fucked up, fair enough, but you want your money? You'll get it, just give me some time to sort shit out." Tiny starts whining, unconvinced of whether it's the right thing to do. Chewing on words like they had shards of glass in them.

"Give me the documents," I tell Uncle.

Uncle does as he's told, pulling a half-folded piece of paper from his coat pocket. It's a contract relating to shares in the business, prepared by a friendly lawyer, so simple anyone could understand it. Even a kid. Piotrek had it done for me last week.

"I'll pay you back, every cent, I just need a bit more time," he pleads. "Fuck, look around you, we're changing shit around. Repairs. I got cashflow issues. You know how it is. A month from now, we'll all be eating caviar. I promise."

I open the top drawer in his desk. It contains lots of pens. I pull one out and throw it onto the long table in front of Tiny. The document is there already.

"You have two kids," I say. "Kids have mums."

"What the fuck are you doing? What are you saying to me? I thought everything was on track between us. Man! I thought we were cool!" he shouts, jumping up and down in his chair, rubbing his eyes.

"I'm not cool. Not cool at all," I reply, mouth set hard.

"What is this?" he asks, looking at the contract.

"Let me explain again. Your debts are gone. You can stay here and run the place. You can even consider yourself to be co-owner. But everything now goes through me. Me and Piotrek. It's not even about this damn bar, kid. We're more interested in the building."

He looks at me like I'd served him up his least favourite meal, his face making out he's not feeling well. Not well enough to eat what I'm dishing up. He says nothing though, so I continue,

"It's not just about the money you owe me. There are a lot of other debts that come with this place, with you, and we both know it... There is money to be recovered, and then money to be made. Your slate is clean. You're back from the dead, boy."

"No," he says slowly, rocking back and forth in his chair.

Uncle looks at me, the baton now still in his hand, slightly away from his thigh, suspended in mid-air.

"Did I not tell you I wasn't asking?" I ask.

"No," he repeats, this time a little more firmly. "No, fuck, no. I didn't slave, I didn't bleed for years, trying to make all this happen, for jokers like you to just waltz in, like it was Moscow, like I was some cunt, and..."

Barracks strolls up to Tiny, grabs him by both shoulders and tosses him aside, like he was a real child. As the body lands on concrete, I hear something pop, or crack, or snap. Hard to tell.

"Do you just want me to sign it myself?" I ask, staring at the prostrate body. "Just tell me."

Uncle approaches and lets the steel fly. Tiny lets out a scream, without moving off the floor. Uncle stands over him, arms pumping, ready for more, wishing for more.

"Pricks like you, boy," he says to Tiny. "I hate pricks like you."

He spits on the floor, inches away from Tiny's face.

"Put him back in his chair," I order.

Uncle does as he's told, Tiny not resisting, not helping either.

"We can keep this up for another five hours. Till it gets light. But what's the use?" I ask. "People tend not to respect the knowledge others possess. I have this impression about you. That you're one of those people, living blind, anonymous, disconnected. At risk of having all knowledge about them fade away."

I lean over the table. He looks me right in the face. Trembling a little. I see hate in the way his teeth are set, a fury which he's having to contain, unable to do anything with it other than keep it within, in check, show at least that much class.

"Meanwhile, everyone knows everything about everyone. In most cases though, they don't betray this information. But they know, they know and use this data. Are you keeping up or are you too fucked? Focus, Tiny. Try to focus."

He shakes his head, so I smile and keep talking,

"I know something about you. A lot of somethings. Like that girl. What's her name? Anastasia?"

"What are you trying to say?"

Someone knocks on the door. Nobody reacts.

"You really hit her with everybody around, watching?" I ask, truly curious. "What would such a pretty, cheery girl have to do to deserve violence?" Tiny doesn't offer any answers. "Your kids. Kajtek and Adas. Two different mothers though, right? A bar manager from Okna? The other a painter? The first is called Ewa Lutecka, if I'm not mistaken. Lives at no. 5 Rose Street, apartment number 20? The other mother is Barbara Mankiewicz, Zoliborz, no. 1 Henkel Square, lucky apartment number 13. Kajtek's school is not far. On Malewicza. Close enough for him to walk home alone. Right? While you're living with your girl on Tamka Street, number 20, door 6. Her parents' place, if memory serves right."

"Stop, for fuck's sake," he asks, turning away.

"Your parents. Irena Pieczewska and Krzysztof Pieczewski, still residing in Ursynow, which is where you grew up. Dereniowa Street. Your mum is an architect, they have the upper floor of a lovely villa. Like the one from that TV series, *Seven Wishes*, right?"

"You can't be doing this. This can't be happening." His head keeps on shaking.

"Your father works in Praga Hospital. Surgeon. Finishes his Monday shifts late, after 10pm, usually. Anything else we should know about you? Tiny?"

"This was meant to be a law abiding country. I've got cops working for me. I've got the law on my side," he mumbles on.

"But will they get to you before we do?" I ask, politely.

He says nothing, but I see, in time, tears running down his nose, into his warped lips. His thighs are jigging up and down, like he was impatient for something to happen. I see him, but not clearly, as if through a mist, as if he was dissolving. My fingers drum silently on the table top, as if I was trying to hurry this moment along. A formality.

Someone is now hammering on the locked door. Barracks, Shady and Uncle turn to look at it.

Once again, I see colours hanging in the air, as if there was a giant soap bubble and I was inside it, and outside of it there was a rainbow-coloured poison: the walls, the table, Uncle, Tiny, everything suddenly becoming either yellow, or red or green.

The loud knocking on the door continues.

That which has never happened before is here again. This has already happened and will happen many times over yet.

"The decision you have to make is whether you want to stay here and run this place for us, or if you'd rather not," I whisper to Tiny.

"Fuck off," he says.

"Open it," I say to Barracks.

"You sure?" he asks.

"What was that, Tiny? Can you repeat?" I ask.

"Fuck off."

Barracks opens the door. The off-duty cop enters, the one from last night, with another bouncer.

Green, yellow and red. Colours.

I nod to Uncle.

Barracks closes the door. The two new arrivals looking at us, trying to read the situation. Uncle moves towards Tiny, grabs his head by the scraggly hair and smashes it, quick and hard, on the table top. Producing a sound like a nut cracking.

"Time for choosing is over," I say. "The contract is drafted. Our representatives will soon be having a word with the owner of the building."

Shady takes out the gun and points it right at the cop's head. The other bouncer tries to grapple for something, something irrelevant, for Barracks makes a leap, smashes into him, then grabs him by the neck, draws the man to him and then uses his head as a battering ram against the wall. A dull, nasty sound. Thud, thud, thud. The man sinks to the floor. Barracks smacks the top of his head with his elbow for good measure, putting him to instant sleep.

The cop raises his helpless hands. Breathing quickly. Trying to keep calm. This could be the first time anyone's ever put a gun to his sorry head.

My eyes are starting to sting from within, as if someone was trying to scalpel away layers of retina. I now just see the one colour: red, red, red. Lack of sleep. Something dripping, something flowing, something falls upon the world.

The city outside this room has its mouth wide open. Wants something more, its guts endless, capable of swallowing and digesting everything.

Below our feet, hundreds of throats are screaming in joyful unison, stomping their feet, while another song reaches its peak.

"Do I need to repeat myself?" Uncle asks.

I shake my head and look at the cop.

"And what did you two come in here for?" Uncle asks him.

"In a moment, more of us will be here," the off-duty cop says weakly.

"Could be. Could be forty of you in here shortly," Uncle concurs.

"You don't know who we are. You think you do, but it seems you're wrong," I tell Tiny. "Your older boy is seven, and the younger five, right?"

He nods his bleeding head. I hand him the pen and he takes it, holding onto it like it was some alien tool, something he'd never used, never seen before in his life. Like a grenade pin or a cut off finger. He looks up at me, breathing heavily through his smashed, leaking nose. I move the unfolded contract towards him, but not so far as his chin might drip blood on it.

"Don't do anything stupid, gents," the cop says as his pal starts to move again on the floor next to him.

"Shut your fucking face," Shady growls, the gun still raised.

I get up. It's going to take a while before the document is signed. Tiny's hand is shaking, but he manages it in the end. I take the paper, hand it to Uncle.

"We're gonna have to have a word with your accountant, have a look at the figures. You know, standard procedure," I tell Tiny.

Shady lowers the gun. The cop steps back towards the wall. Barracks and Uncle look at me, waiting for further instructions. I turn to look out the window, but all I'm doing is buying time, not breathing, my lips wide open.

"Everything will be tip top," I finally say, to Tiny but not only to him. "Everything in order. Monopolies occur in nature. It's natural, right?"

I nod my head to the others that we are leaving. End of this business talk. All partners have arrived at a consensus, time to go on evolving the brand, to extend our reach, smiling into an exciting, challenging future. Consolidating, increasing incomes, letting a new management board do its thing.

I know I have to try getting some sleep. Turn the phone off. Do something easy, something pleasant tomorrow. Staring at a wall. Listening to a bath filling with hot water. Maybe listening to music.

Stravinsky. Stravinsky's alright. His music pulses with singular rhythm, has something of a swollen, shaking organ about it.

Colours, constant colours.

Tiny starts choking, as if he's about to throw up. Then does so, regurgitating everything he's eaten and drunk all over the table and the floor next to it.

Barracks opens the door. Shady turns and points the gun back at the cop.

"Be calm. No fucking about," he requests.

I'm about to walk out, but then I realise I've forgotten about something. A tiny thing, like a pebble in a shoe, annoying me ever so gently. Tiny looks at me without any sort of expression.

"Why did you hit your girl?" I ask him, speaking quickly, manically. "Tell me, explain. Why a piece of shit like you, a useless, pointless scumbag, deserving of fucking fuck all, ruining the world for us all, ugly as fucking sin, why was it that you managed to pull such a girl and then go about pounding her in public? Why these girls will even talk to you, smile, open their fucking legs for you and your filthy little prick is a whole other matter. Why that sweet little thing, that pretty woman let herself join that disappointing group of tasteless partners, a whole other matter. But to hit her? What is it you lack? What is it you lost? You've got a mother. She's an architect, not a whore. Not a drunk. You're from a good home. A piece of shit from a good home. A good Warsaw home."

He doesn't flinch. Then wipes the blood from his chin, his hand on his trousers. Now his gob is a bit cleaner, I see a look on it, some sort of heartless arrogance. I take a bottle and smash it on a wall. Glass flying about like scattered coins. He looks at me, still without expression. Lost in this whole wide sea of a situation. Catatonic.

I walk up to him and grab him by the hair. It's sticky, like old kebab wrapping, like soiled paper.

I put the bottle to his neck. Wondering what it would do to everything if I cut his jugular. I have no qualms about killing him, no more trouble in it than sweeping dog shit from the pavement outside my house.

"Kuba, for fuck's sake, don't you get carried away," Uncle barks.

"You should not hit women," I say.

Uncle walks up, quickly, grabs me by the arm.

"Here, he's had his bit of punishment tonight. You wanna kill him?"

"Tell me," I keep on talking to Tiny. "I know the girl."

"What are you talking about?" he finally coughs up.

This lasts a while longer. Me holding the bottle. Everyone watching. Tiny looks up timidly, the music dying down suddenly, something flashing outside the window, over the city, as if a giant camera had just taken a snapshot of us all.

"She was fucking a friend of mine, back from our school days. He runs one of my bars. In my own home. In my own bed. Spending my money," he says. "Not just him. She's not hard to convince. Not hard at all. You never...?"

I lower the arm holding the deadly bottle, look at him as he shrinks, shrivels, but keeps on looking at me, the eyes dead, the rest of him ready for more of the same. He says without smiling: "I thought you were smarter. But you Kuba... you think what? Someone has big round eyes that they're sweet and nice and light? And if they squint they're no good? Fuck me. You think women are wiser beings? Do you now?"

I throw the bottle into the corner of the room as Tiny keeps on preaching, "Seeing as you're taking my business, why not save me the lecture, about whores you know from somewhere, who you like smiling at you, just because they like the look of your fucking car."

"One day, I'll come back. Cut your heart out. One fine day," I say to him, firmly believing what I'm saying. He's in my way. Interfering. Making me gag, like the smell of burnt cooking oil, like something rotting at the back of my own fridge.

I walk out first, the other three follow. We stroll down the stairs, the noise on again, the fever, in three solid colours. Like the backdraft from some giant jet engine. That feeling persists as we go outside.

"What the fuck did you tell him all that for?" Uncle asks, pulling the document out of his pocket, stretching it straight. "You got wound up. Not cool. Over some fucking piece of ass? She one of yours or what?"

I shake my head without looking up.

"Easy now. We're done. Off duty," Shady intercedes.

"You ever offed anyone, talking like that?" Uncle presses. I say nothing, opening the door to my car. Knowing he's right. Bad scene.

Everyone piles inside, and I pull away, driving in the direction of Ursynow. Slowly, maybe a bit too slowly, but I'm so tired I just want the world outside the window to wash away, stop, for nothing to happen, ever again.

The city is asleep, but it's a restless kind of dream, tossing people round in their beds like a hurricane. A dream in which all our faces appear, as nightmares.

"Have you ever done anyone in? Ever pulled the damn trigger?" Uncle asks again.

He lights a cigarette, in my car, but other than opening the window for him, I do not reply. I don't have the strength to tell him off.

I look back at Bethlehem as we stop at the first set of traffic lights. The outside of the building is completely black. Colourless.

"Not yet," I say with all the honesty I can muster.

SUNDAY

DREAM

I'm at home, with my parents, sister, uncle, some other members of the family. I've no idea what time of day it is. Maybe early dawn, maybe dusk, it doesn't seem like any time of day exists any more. We're all huddled round in the kitchen. I know that if I look out the window, there'll be nothing there, no Olsztyn – instead, a space that is nameless, rootless, endless; covered in rubble, cracked asphalt, dust. Some kind of giant car park, stretching as far as the horizon.

It's dark. The only source of light is that coming from the small light in the extractor fan over the kitchen hob. The bulb keeps going on and off. No one seems bothered.

My father is the only one sitting at the dining table, the rest of us standing around. The table is covered with dishes, containing the remains of a meal, like a chessboard half-way through an unfinished game. Nobody's saying anything. Everyone's waiting for something which is meant to happen, something bad, evidently, something which is already very close.

The air in the room is thick, heavy, lifeless, like something taken from the back of the fridge. I've no idea what is due to happen next, who is going to be visiting us, I want to ask but know that no one wants me to ask, no one wants to talk, as if mere mention of the approaching evil would bring it here even quicker. We occupy ourselves with keeping still and quiet. The lightbulb going on and off. The room is stifling, but cold, as if it was freezing outside and the heating had been turned off.

Maybe it is freezing outside. Maybe we're on a different sort of planet, an evil sort of moon.

My parents' kitchen no longer looks the way it does in this dream. It was done up ten years ago, but now it's again full of this old, communist-era furniture, pistachio-coloured tiles, an old gas cooker. The fridge covered in stickers from Hanna-Barbera cartoons. And yet everyone – my mother, my uncle, my sister – are older. They look old, too old. Faces drawn out, ashen. Lips drawn tight. Eyes fixed on invisible points, everyone making small noises, coughing, scratching their heads, looking at each other, as if they needed to keep moving, keep gesticulating to prove to themselves that they're still alive.

Everyone is smoking, my father too – unmoving, staring at the table, even though he quit smoking fifteen years ago. My mother is by the kitchen, timid, pushing her back against a tall cupboard, as if trying to be absorbed by it.

"How are you?" I ask her.

She doesn't answer, merely shakes her head subtly, looking at me as if I was five years old, unable to understand the severity of the situation surrounding us. Then the knock on the door comes. Everyone jumps, as if jolted by electricity pumped through the carpet. My father stubs the cigarette out and rises up, moving like an old man, as if his back had been broken in two. He approaches the door. The rest of the family moves closer, barely perceptibly, but closer.

I try to see who it is my father is about to allow into our home, but I cannot see anything. Only some noise, the murmur of quiet greetings. The fear I should have felt from the very beginning is only now starting to explode within me, filling my guts as if I was drowning in salt water. I feel like vomiting. My head spinning. My mother's lips drawn so tight they vanish from her face. I support myself by leaning against the wall next to her.

Looking at the dishes on the table, I now realise what they represent – our last supper, the food gone, and there won't be any more where that came from. There is nothing to get and no one to get it from within miles, hundreds of miles. Everything has been checked and explored.

I also know we cannot leave the kitchen.

Two men enter the small space. One of them, wearing only a white vest, reminds me of a great, black stain. A single tattoo covers the whole of his body, all except the face. His hair is cut short, his trousers odd, hanging off of him like a light cotton track suit, though they appear to be made of leather. The other man, a little bit smaller, has a long beard and is wearing a long, shabby raincoat. I don't know which one of them arouses in me a greater fear. They are like two black, negatively charged objects. The spaces they enter seem full of them, so full the walls begin to cave in.

I don't know what they will do to us, but I come to think that we should ask them for a quick and painless death. To stop them having any thoughts about making this execution in any way more colourful.

My father makes room for them at the table. Then rises, and stands next to my mother. The men sit down. The tattooed guy says nothing. The bearded man picks a piece of cold meat off the plate and slowly puts it in his mouth. Chewing slowly, carefully, allowing the substance to dissolve on his tongue, as if it was chocolate.

After a painfully long silence, my father asks, "What can we do?"

"Only wait," the bearded man answers, his voice as dull and tired as his overcoat.

"How long?" my mother asks.

"No idea."

"How long?" she repeats.

"No idea. Do you have any more food?" he asks.

"Not anymore," she replies coldly.

The bearded man shakes his head, looking around the kitchen. Exhaling slowly.

I begin to understand and that is when I feel this powerful urge to start laughing.

"Can you help us?" asks my uncle.

"I've no idea," says the tattooed man. "You heard him. There's nothing to be done but wait."

I try to stifle laughter, like a child who's got the giggles in church after remembering a naughty joke. This suppressing of laughter actually hurts, and the pain brings tears to my eyes. Even so, I begin to laugh, the whole kitchen looking at me with growing disgust, shaking their heads, embarrassed, scared, only the two visitors sitting there expressionless, motionless, lifeless.

It now occurs to me that we aren't afraid of them: they are our last hope of help. I still can't help laughing.

Something's approaching. Something which will swallow everything, even this emptiness. Something which will delete it all. A magnetic reversal. Antimatter will overlap matter. Nothing is important, but the phrase "nothing is important" is also just a set of words, letters, substance. When that final something arrives, there will be no more words, no more letters.

I know it, I feel it more potently in my dream than I know anything else in reality.

I then remember what the solution is. Simple.

"I have some pills in the car," I suddenly announce, looking at everyone. "I really do. Enough for everyone. I have bags full of them. I can be back in a minute."

"What are you talking about, Kuba?" my mother asks.

"About pills, Mum. Everything will be fine. Nothing will matter anymore. You can't stop the inevitable. All you can do is hurry it up, bring it closer."

"Leszek, please tell him to calm down," she says to my father.

"Kuba, don't talk like that, son. Be still," he says, doing as he's told.

My father's never called me "son" in his life.

"Mum, we'll all just go to sleep, you'll see, all will be well. Don't worry. Don't be afraid," I plead, though I'm still choking back the laughter.

"Stop saying such nonsense, Kuba, please, quit now," she pleads.

"We're all together, that's what matters," I say, placating her. The tattooed man looks at me, carefully, then wipes his mouth, then gazes out the window, his eyes blinking. "We're not going to feel a thing. Our throats will swell, our hearts stop, but we're not going to feel any of it. At first, we'll lose consciousness. That's all. These pills are great," I say with my adult voice, though it sounds funny, like it belonged to someone else.

I can see they're terribly scared. More than me. Scared of what is yet to come. Of those who are on their way.

There is no hope of any rescue. We're people in the last stages of terminal disease. Each breath we take, each move we make, every touch is a prelude to dying, a terminal cramp, as if all our lives we've just been waiting for this, this descent. It's funny. I think it's all very amusing.

Death. Life is preparation for death. A mistake. A cut scene. The floor is cold, so I move, then sit down again. Who will bury the last person to die? Who will hear the bell toll?

I now realise the two visitors are a kind of police force, servants of the state. Their work has just lost its final bit of meaning, and they've come here to hide away for a second.

Nothing more. Nothing less. Finally, alone in the end.

"I have one last piece of chocolate, saved for you," my father says to me. "Do you want to have it now?"

"It's beginning," the tattooed man says.

"Do you want to have it now?" father repeats.

A gentle tremor goes through everything, the floor, the window sill, the ceiling, the lampshade.

I get up off the floor, approach the window and look out. Just as I thought – the car park and buildings are grey, endless, limitless, some kind of city, empty, abandoned, far off, vanishing already.

But the sky, the sky is turning brown, like shit, like wood polish.

My father puts the last piece of chocolate into his mouth.

"It's beginning," he says.

It's as if the sky was a roll of film, on fire, melting or being eaten away by acid. As if someone was torching it, torturing it. Great, white bubbles appear in the sky, like sick clouds. The purest white cuts through the brown overhead, a blinding white, too pure for human eyes.

It occurs to me, clearly, that this is not some abstract force – this is the coming of someone, that this entity will stop in a while, that it's conscious, an agent.

I start laughing again. Laughing so hard everything in me feels like it's rolling around.

"You have about five minutes," the bearded man says to me. "Go get the pills from your car. May God watch over you."

"We'll all just sleep," I say, smiling, excited. "We'll just be asleep."

My mother starts crying.

"Go," Beardy says. "Run."

08:50am

I've been lying in the bath for the past thirty minutes. Way beyond sleep again. No hope of that now.

I feel sick. Sleeplessness takes the breath away, like a plastic bag over the head.

The *Goldberg Variations*. Round and round, one starts in the middle and then ends. Something opens, something closes again. The flow of water. When I listen to this music, without noise in the background – the noise of water, noise of the city – they seem incomplete to me, somehow ripped out of context.

Sundays are never free for me. My phone is constantly connected with those who need to snort all week round, just to be able to function. Sunday is their day. They live their lives with both nostrils glued to a mirror. As a rule, they really make an awful lot of money, the bosses of investment funds, lobbyists, the sons and sons in law of those on Poland's Richest 100 list, restaurateurs, developers. Saturdays they tend to go wild, their supplies running low. Still, it's Sunday. Come the evening, they have to take their girls out to the cinema, visit the in-laws, or visit their own parents, go shopping, to the swimming pool, catch up on endless emails and calls. They'll never manage to do all that, to get through one day without a hit. They tend to ring around 11am. That's when the panic hits, the warning cracking of the ceiling over their heads, threatening to fall right on top of them and their dreams.

There are those who just can't stop partying – it's a permanent state of being, their element, the vinegar they have been pickled in. This endless tango is for them the norm, without side effects, apart from the fact that their faces seem to age twice as quickly as anyone around them. They're the ones who love to call me early Sunday mornings, well-known painters, cartoonists from serious newspapers, ageing Jews who made their fortunes on reclaiming lost family properties after the war and now insist on retiring as highly charged playboys. They sometimes call when I still haven't finished work.

I sink in the bath, my head submerged. I hear the music still, diffused now, sounding like it's coming in from far off, like a sonar. Emerging from the water, I catch my breath, grab my phone and turn off aeroplane mode. There's a message from Pazina, sent two minutes ago. Some kind of link. I don't know what she's up to. Her morning panic attacks. With every year, her panic grows worse. Her unhappiness seems to bother her more and more, as it begins to dawn on her that it's not going to go away. All she can hope for is to smooth it down a bit, like a stone or a piece of uncomfortable furniture; in time, we all end up smelling of mould, of rotting teeth, of dying flesh. Women have a harder time dealing with this, maybe because when they are little they have much greater hopes of being happy than men.

Let her send these links to her own man, as long as she hasn't just split up with him, via text message right after getting home. As long as whatever. It's all unimportant. In five days' time, I will be gone. Shut up shop. Out of order. Unavailable. It will be like a dream – I am only going there to get some sleep. Whatever happens while I am away, as soon as I get back I will reset everything, put it back the way it was to start with.

My entry phone doorbell rings.

I get out of the bath. 9am, Sunday. The person ringing must be lost, someone for a neighbour, a door to door salesman. I close my eyes. Seconds go by in silence. Then the doorbell rings again.

Another text from Pazina: *Open up*.

I wrap myself in a towel, press the button to open the downstairs entry door, then pull some trousers on. I start brushing my teeth, slowly, carefully. She knocks on the door so soon, she must have run up the stairs. When I open the door, I see she is exhausted, red-faced, eyes panicked as if on the run from someone. I step aside and let her in.

"Has something kicked off?" I ask, still brushing my teeth.

She doesn't answer, just walks into my lounge and starts looking for something.

"Have you seen the news yet?" she asks, breathless.

"No. What have you lost?"

She gives up looking, starts playing with her phone, then hands it to me to look at.

"See for yourself," she says.

I push the phone away.

"Calm down. Wait a minute. Do you want to drink something? Eat something?" I ask, walking into the kitchen.

The Indian food I ordered yesterday is still unfinished, set hard in a soup bowl, waiting to be cleared away. Besides that, I have little else to offer. Tea or coffee.

"Tea or coffee?" I ask.

"I couldn't sleep."

"Coffee it is then."

"You were round his last night, right?" she asks and mentions the name of my best customer. "When you told me to watch your car?"

"What about him?"

"Fuck," she says and starts searching the lounge again, finally comes up with the TV remote.

"They're bound to be talking about it. He's too big a fish not to fry. Unless they try to sweep it under the carpet, but that's just not possible. News is out already," she says, turning on the television and flicking through the channels, looking for a news station.

"Milk? Sugar?" I ask calmly. "Not that I have any milk."

I pour water into the kettle, turn it on. It instantly begins to hum.

"There," she says, without triumph.

A news report. A host with a face you could mistake for a million other middle-aged male faces, but behind him, projected onto a flat-screen TV set, is a picture of my best customer, his eyes pixellated in some lame attempt at concealing identity. I squint, approach the TV, stand next to Pazina.

"What happened?"

"Watch."

"Last night, the well-known journalist and television star Mariusz F. was detained by the police on suspicion of having caused a car accident which resulted in the death of a young woman and her unborn child. According to early toxicological reports, the driver's blood and breath samples contained excessive traces of alcohol and other substances."

"Did you pay him a visit last night or not?"

"Mariusz F. was bailed, pending further investigation into the incident. We have been unable to contact him for comment. His agent and the television station which employs him have also not issued any public statements at this time," the newsreader says flatly, though I can sense the underlying glee. This is the sort of news these people live and sometimes die for.

The kettle boils. I hear it click in the kitchen. From the kitchen, I then hear the TV talking.

"Unofficial sources say that large amounts of illegal drugs and prescription medicines were found in the suspect's car."

"Not good," I calmly shout towards Pazina.

"What will you do?" she asks.

"What do you have in mind?" I ask back.

I fill two mugs with water, dissolve some instant coffee, think about whether I have any sugar or not. I'm always meaning to buy a decent coffee machine, a grinder, a cafetiere, but never remember to shop for the bloody things.

"What can we do to cover ourselves? The first thing he's going to do is give them your name," she says, hurriedly.

"It's not about whether he gives them my name or number or not," I tell her.

"Are you still asleep?!" she shouts. Walking over and handing her the coffee, I'm convinced she hasn't slept at all. She could have taken something, snorted a line or two – her eyes bloodshot, the skin around them dark red, the rest of her face the colour and texture of papyrus.

"Sit down, will you?" I ask, politely. She does as told, reluctantly, eyes still fixed on the screen, hands clasping the hot mug.

"The mother-to-be died upon arrival at hospital," the news reader reports flatly. "Along with her unborn child."

"No one is going to forgive him for this," Pazina groans. "Pregnant, for fuck's sake. He must have been out of his mind. Well, he was, with all that shit he snorted. They're going to put him through the grinder and he'll spill everything. Just to save his own skin."

"He's got no idea where the stuff comes from. How could he?" I muse.

"What the fuck do you mean he doesn't know?!"

"He only knows my first name. Nothing else," I say, turning the TV off.

"You have no shared friends? No other connections?"

"None that matter. He could ask all the guests from his party last night to pop into the nearest police station and give statements about last night, but they know about me as much as he does. Next to nothing."

She shakes her head. I take a sip of the coffee. It's rank, tastes like old blood, like dissolved lead.

"Shall we go get breakfast?" I ask.

"Eat? I haven't slept a wink. The internet's been buzzing since early morning. Now you want to eat?"

"I've already told you it doesn't matter. Calm down."

"I haven't eaten since last night. We could go get something."

"I have to change sim cards," I tell her.

"You're still on the old number?"

"I've only just found out, haven't I?"

I put on a shirt and sweater, spray a bit of cologne on, turn off the music which is still playing in the background. Not going to get any sleep today either. Insomnia is starting to become a permanent fixture, an inevitable consequence of my professional life, like the stink which won't rub off a garbage collector.

"Not good," I say to Pazina, taking my phone apart to switch sim cards. "He was a very good customer, plus he knew a few of my other very good customers. Now, they're going to try keeping their noses clean for a while. Too scared to place orders. The fear will make them call me up eventually, of course, but it's going to be slim pickings for a while."

"Mother to be," Pazina moans. "What the fuck is wrong with people? What sort of state was he in when you left him?"

"He seemed to be standing straight, speaking complete sentences. Looked fine to me. I don't sell to people who can't count the money, who can't cut their own lines."

"I saw a gang nearby," she says.

"How do you know how to recognise them?"

"You taught me several times."

I take one more sip of the instant, then pour it down the kitchen sink.

"What will you do?" she asks.

I've no idea what I'm going to do. This is a bad, tense situation. My best customer will do his best to get out of it at all costs. Make all the deals they suggest. He'd kill to save his own skin, his career, his showbiz standings.

I have to talk to Piotrek, soon.

And not just him.

"Let's go get something to eat," I say to Paz, forcing the first smile of the day.

10:20am

Cafe Pomelo on Sienkiewicza is a safe harbour for all sorts of victims and castaways. A sort of horror show, displaying the kind of disastrous state people can bring themselves to, of their own volition. An all-day buffet of wonders, the last refuge of all those who managed to get into the best clubs and are still in need of something – they go to Pomelo to die down. This is where they begin to have the first proper thoughts of the day, about how much money they spent, how much stuff was snorted, who fucked who in which position in which cubicle. Who pulled who, who broke up with who, who got punched. This is where they are jumped by a sudden lack of serotonin. It is here they try to come back to some sort of life over freshly squeezed juices.

The waitresses here have old, tired faces, even though they're young kids, undergraduates, slim, sexy types. They've seen it all. No longer having to smile, to be nice, to notice anyone or anything other than who still hasn't paid their bill. Hundred zloty tips don't elicit smiles round here. Famous faces covered in scrambled egg or mayo don't raise grins. They patiently wait for nightclub refugees to make up their minds as to what they want to eat, and then wait for them to pronounce their orders.

Pazina is on her second coffee, immersed in her smartphone like a philosophy student immerses themselves in books the morning of an exam. I am looking for a certain number in my phone's memory, not sure if I saved it in the sim or the phone or if I can remember it off the top of my head still. It's been a long while since I've had to ring it, a number I really don't want to have, don't ever want to use.

But it's in there somewhere.

"You're thinking about it too much," I tell her.

"You're not thinking about it enough," she replies. "Do you really think no one is going to come looking for you? That they're just gonna try and bypass you and go higher? You'll be enough. Those higher up are safe, Kuba."

"If you know so much, perhaps you can advise me now of the best course of action?"

Her panic is starting to get to me. It shouldn't, and it wouldn't normally, but I lack sleep and like her too much not to be bothered.

"Think about the headlines," she says, lowering her voice at last. "The dealer who sold... it's like you bought him the car. It's no accident. They'll try to pin it on you."

"What's up?" I hear a familiar voice asking.

For a moment, I can't place the face. The rest of him disgusts me – oversized trainers, ridiculously tight jeans, some ragged blazer with its sleeves rolled up – typical styling of someone who has no personal sense of style. Then I remember him. A few years ago, he wore baseball caps, tracksuits, baggy T-shirts made by edgy designers no one now remembers. Today, his hair is slicked back, his beard perfectly groomed, his skin tanned a rabid shade of orange.

"Hey," I reply.

"Can I?" he asks, pointing at a free chair by our table.

"Sure."

"Xavery," he grins and offers a handshake to Pazina. She smiles, shakes his hand, but is too fazed to introduce herself. "Been a hard night, huh?"

A waitress approaches. Xavery looks up, still grinning, trying to make eye contact, his artificially white teeth too much for the morning light. Back in the day when I knew him in his previous incarnation, his teeth were equally straight and clean, only he was missing the two top incisors.

"Eggs Benedict and a tea," he orders, bouncing in his seat.

My eyes are drawn to his watch. A massive Rolex, costing as much as a small family car. Possibly the real thing. And totally unsuited to the wrist of this monkey.

He bought the watch with money earned selling heroin. He's probably still at it. Dealing brown is just as addictive as taking it, it's the fastest and easiest way to make money, completely different to dealing in coke – for very simple reasons. Each client is with you for life and will do all they can to buy from you. The first purchase involves the establishment of a life-long partnership. They will then buy whatever you're offering at whatever price. Shitty, dirty, contaminated, although it can't be too much of any of those things, because then the lifelong partnership will be quickly and irrevocably annulled.

Some think that heroin dealers are the worst scum on earth. That they're really dealing in death. That they actually help destroy human lives. There's a grain of truth in that belief system. Cocaine won't fuck with your work. Won't wreck your family. Won't have you leaving life via the back door, won't write your goodbye letters for you. Sure, it fires up your serotonin receptors, but not your very soul. It doesn't turn your body into a carcass, doesn't take your teeth, doesn't rot your veins. Some think heroin dealers are bad, evil kind of bad, Auschwitz camp attendant kind of bad. But I'm not one to instantly judge and ostracise people. I'm not one for marking anybody down.

Heroin dealers remind me of small reptiles. Fat, full of insects they've hunted down, drunk on their blood. Their burrows full of dirty money. Very calm – those who deal heroin are almost as calm as their clients.

I watch him pick up his cup of tea and I can just tell he's still in his old trade.

"I heard you're muscling nicely into the Centrum district," he quips.

"What do you mean 'muscling'?"

"All the hipster hangouts in the centre of town. I heard that you're all over them. You know, I'm not one for partying," he adds and winks at me.

Everything's quite clear. He looks at his watch, slowly, making sure I notice the toy.

"You've never complained before," I say.

Which is true. He's always been a happy-go-lucky kind of punk.

The waitress brings him the food. He takes a long hard look at the eggs Benedict, as if looking for some microscopic flaws.

"I was told they spit into the food here," he grimaces.

"Why come here then?" Pazina asks, a little testily.

"Coz it tastes good, even if they do spit into it," he replies, cutting the small portion in half and polishing that off with one bite. The way he chews turns my stomach. Not too much noise, but the mouth isn't completely closed. He's from a rough family, wrong end of the tracks – I try to forgive him.

"Anywhere you go they'll spit in our food," I tell him.

"Listen, brown is making a big comeback," he says, his mouth still almost half-full. "It's all about stress levels. People are cracking. They have to chill, else they'll blow. In corporations, in TV stations, the pressure is on. Everyone out to get everyone, before all the markets completely collapse. They don't know the hour or the day when the end will come, but they still have to be running at 300% revs. In the evening, they take your shit, and in the mornings they take mine. Or is it the other way round? Antidepressants no longer work for these monsters."

"There's always running. Triathlons," Pazina adds without looking up at us, still absorbed by her phone.

"That doesn't help," Xavery says, grinning. "It's like fucking. It stresses them out even more. Another competition to get lost in. More fucking, longer running. Better fucking, more running. And if you have a puff on something? I don't need to explain, do I? These are wonderful times for our wonderful trade."

"Have they ever been bad?" I ask, meeting his direct gaze.

"The economic crash didn't knock your profits?"

"Nope. My clients are not touched by the crises of others."

"True enough. Some people have always got enough. It's bread for them."

His breakfast all swallowed up, he closes his eyes, still chewing, evidently enjoying the process of digesting already. The little reptile. Pazina is still absorbed by her phone, I go back to mine. The number I was looking for is there.

We have to meet. Kuba. I press send. Xavery wipes his mouth with a serviette, gets up, looks at his watch.

"I recently opened a fitness gym. On Emilia Plater Street," he says, apropos of nothing. "All the best equipment, all the best instructors. Call me, I'll sort you out with free membership."

"Not that I have time for sporting activities," I tell him, "But thanks."

"You're too skinny. Some muscle would suit you. You know, it's like brands. People notice such things."

"Brands. Watches. Teeth. Yeah, people notice," I smile and then stop, as a way of goodbye. My phone pings.

3pm.

I know where, and I now know when.

Xavery finally gets up to move to a different table, waving his watch as he goes. So much early morning sunlight bounces off it, it looks as if he's wearing a torch not a watch.

"Who the fuck was that?" Paz asks.

"It doesn't matter in the least," I pacify her nerves.

"He's posted bail. They've released him from the cop shop," she says, showing me her smartphone screen.

"It's not about bail money. What it means is that he's done a deal with someone."

"I told you," Pazina confirms.

"You'll see, he'll come out of all this smelling of roses. He's the kind of guy who always comes out alright in the end."

I wave to a waitress and she comes over, hands us the bill. Without looking at us. Somebody in the corner bursts into song, a flashback from some highlight of the night before. No one pays him the least bit of attention.

"Are you not worried about that woman?" Pazina asks, carefully.

"Should the guy who runs Mariusz's local liquor store and sold him the whisky still running through his veins also worry? Find him, Paz. Find the store and ask his opinion." For a moment, she looks dumbfounded, as if I've just recited a particularly complicated poem. "Can I drop you off somewhere?"

"Home. Maybe I'll get some sleep."

She pockets her dying phone and gets up. I follow.

"Do something for me," she asks as we stand outside. "Talk to me and keep an eye out. I know you'll tell me that you always do, but please do it especially now."

"I always do, Paz," I tell her.

Don't be late, my phone screen tells me when another text message arrives.

As I stop to read it, Pazina grabs me by the arm, suddenly, just for a moment, as if she'd lost her balance and was about to fall.

3:00pm

The booths with Asian food sit there non-stop, morning till midnight, cooking in shifts. As if their clients' guts were no longer capable of digesting anything other than white rice lathered in super-sweet sauce and well past-it meats. This particular bar is near Metro Marymont, behind the shopping centre, between some apartment blocks. It's the size of an ordinary living room. The sign over the door says XIANG BAO, probably painted on by the owner. The

156

usual calendar with pictures of tigers for good luck, cheap vases with plastic flowers, even more plastic than the forks and knives. And chopsticks. Enough to launder serious income from heroin, mephedrone, brothels, gun running, all that and more. It stinks inside, stinks so bad I feel nauseous. Layers of horrid substances emitting their particles, battling mid-air, trying to assault my senses, overwhelm them. He's sitting inside already. Eating some spring rolls. Looks nothing like a cop should. He's got a beard, a hooded top, a baseball cap, designer jogging bottoms – a typical middle-class middle-aged daddy, on the run from his wife's designer cooking. Looks like he works in the media, or marketing, slumming it every Sunday, because for media marketing types places like this are way cool. He's eating slowly, sipping a coke. The stink doesn't appear to bother him, but cops working in serious crime don't ever seem bothered by sour odours.

"Sit," he says, calmly.

They always give orders in the form of requests, even when it's not necessary. It's in their blood now, their programming. On or off duty.

He's forty years old. His name is Marek. He lives close by, in very exclusive Old Zoliborz. Married well, a girl from a family of doctors. Works in the criminal division, is a deputy commissioner, and that's where he'll stay, it seems, hitting a glass ceiling. Drives his kids around in a ten-year-old Volvo estate. Smokes a lot, drinks a bit more, more than he tells the wife, less than the average cop. I know just about all there is to know about him. Otherwise, I would never agree to meet with him in a place like this.

The deal between us is simple. He knows what he knows and wants to exchange it for money. He has his secret little hobby, roulette, gaming machines, slots... things that require alternative sources of disposable income. Trying his best to keep his family out of it. Away from the debts he's accrued and the people who might be coming to collect. If she knew, I doubt she'd try borrowing the money from ma and pa – more likely he'd be out the door in a flash.

He's not a fool. Weak, but not stupid. He may drink, but not so as to beat his work colleagues at it. Keeps his head down, comfortable in the shadows. Knows his own place, and knows that being caught off side could prove costly, to his career, and much, much more.

"Will you eat something?" he asks, wiping his plate with the last piece of spring roll. I shake my head and start talking,

"One of my clients has a problem. I need to know just how much of a problem it might turn out to be for me."

He bursts out laughing, wipes his stained lips, looks at me, his gaze amused, which is what helps piss me off. He looks like a footballer who's just intercepted a ball and between him and the goal there's nothing but one incompetent keeper.

"How are the kids?" I ask.

"Fine. Doing real swell. A few weeks ago, my little one was not so cool. Hospital, fever, some sort of infection. But all's back to normal. Thank you for asking. You look rough."

"I'm not sleeping. Plus, the way this place stinks is turning my guts."

"It doesn't stink. It reeks. Of manure."

He takes a sip of cola, licks his lips. A thin, young Vietnamese girl walks up, clearing his plate. He keeps on licking his lips, as if intentionally trying to annoy me. Wipes his nose, then looks down at the plastic-covered table.

"There's not a lot I can tell you," he says. I reach into my pocket, and he adds, "This is the moment I get a present from you. And I say thank you. But this will not mean I can do anything else for you. Do we understand each other?"

"Infection, you say? Worse things can happen to a child."

I pull out a wad of notes, ten thousand zlotys, place it on the table between us and push it towards him. He coughs, pockets the cash, patting the suddenly bulging pocket of his hooded top.

"I told you, didn't I? Everything's in order," he tries to assure me. I look at him without saying anything. He's actually sweet, in a way. Thinking himself smarter and cuter than he really is, but that is understandable. He exists in a space where most people's brains gave up the ghost a long time ago. He has to manage them, be managed. Drink warm vodka at their tables. Type up reports no one will ever read into computers which are older than his kids.

No one knows we have this relationship.

"Let's go, sit in my car," he says and rises.

I nod and follow him outside, watching as he walks, one hand firmly stuck in the pocket with the money. Once we're in the car, he lets go of the cash and lights a cigarette. Hard to tell what smells worse – the car or the food hut, but the crap all over the floor and seats is unbelievable. Cassette tapes, energy drink cans, food packaging, like he was trying to prove to cons that he really lived undercover in there. The only thing which stands out is the dirty pink child seat in the back.

"We spend all our lives in cars, right?" he says.

"There is no 'we' that I can think of," I say to stop the small talk.

"Give me a break. We're in this together. Rolling along the same lanes, the same routes. The people who tell you what to do tell me what to do too. We all grew up on the same playgrounds, man," he says, sucking happily on his cigarette. "Our kids go to the same schools, play on the same swings."

I've no idea why he's telling me all this, or what to say in reply. I don't have the time, or the patience, for this today. I'm getting the feeling that all this money is only going to get me things I very much do not want to hear, things I know already. And know all too well.

"Problems start when there's a drought, for example. We've had no rain for a month or two already," he says, lighting another fag off the last one. "That's when a sacrifice is necessary. The slaughter of a virgin."

"What am I paying you for?" I ask without expecting an answer.

"Don't think that I see us as a team or anything," he answers. "But we are trying to be helpful, that bit is true."

"So help me."

He shoves a cassette into the dash tape deck, some ageing rock band, the Chillies I think. Then he turns his phone off, and looks serious for the first time today.

"I'm on this case," he tells me. "A lot of my boys are now on this. You can imagine why. What the press wants. Cameras like crowds. I don't know what he agreed to, what his lawyer advised. These are not questions for you or me. All I know is that the coke went into storage, and there will be some attempt to find out where it came from."

"I want to know if he gave you my name."

"You want to know if he knows where to look for you? Watching you, it seems you're smart enough. And if you are smart, then nothing you own is in your real name."

"I don't exist," I tell him, which happens to be mostly true.

My registered address is in Olsztyn, my grandmother's old apartment, which is rented out to a cousin from my mother's side. I am officially unemployed. The apartment which is my actual home was bought for cash, in the name of someone who never existed. The small apartment where I stash my wares I registered in the same name. The car I drive belongs to a company owned by my wholesaler, who also happens to trade telephone accessories online. All my phones are pay as you go sim cards. I have a few fake ID cards, a few identities. No one knows my real name, not that it matters any more. It's lost, dissolved. Money can make a man invisible. If you want, you can vanish. Something which has cost me a fair bit of cash, but which was also worth every penny.

"They'll need time to track you down," he says.

"The hunt is on?"

"Are you planning to leave town?" I nod. "So stay there a little longer than planned. They'll need a sacrificial lamb. The gods want blood. And I must say, this star boy really has his shit together. For now, nobody wants to go near him, but that's all for show. He has friends who owe him. Friends already pulling strings."

"So he tried to sell me out?"

"No one is going to be hung out to dry other than the dealer. You're the first and the last man seen with the gear. That's all anyone cares about. You know how it is. For TV audiences, you're the one who produced the stuff, distributed it, and then forced everyone to buy from you. This isn't a real life crime, remember. This is a televised bit of nasty showbiz."

"That's it?" I ask, impatient.

"You've got enough cash, right? Go, disappear for a while, let things blow over."

A couple of uniformed cops emerge from the bar we've just been in. They move slowly, wrapped in warm coats, as if carrying heavy backpacks. They don't notice us. A little sunlight seeps out from behind a cloud. Creeping all over everything, the melting snow, piles of it swept up off the pavement, stained black by pollution and dog shit, and the rubbish lying around, adding filthy colour to the proceedings.

"You have a little time before they track you down," he tells me. "See. I'm sitting beside you in my own car, and know nothing about you."

"There's nothing to know, not for the likes of you. Our next appointment will be free of charge."

"Listen, lad. You really have to get your head around this thing we're involved in. The power dynamic."

"Don't call me, don't write. The number I texted you from is already dead. If I need you, I know where and how to find you," I tell him.

"I'll send your love to the wife and kids," he quips.

I slide out of his filthy car, shaking in the cold, leaving him alone for a while to sit, stink and count his dirty money.

8:40pm

"I've lost too much weight. Fucking hell. My wife thinks I look unhealthy," he says, stabbing his fork into a pile of salad and scooping up a big mouthful.

He chews and swallows quickly, quicker than is healthy. Giving off the demeanour of someone who has lost a bet and now has to eat something as punishment: sand, rocks, mouldy paper. The waitress, a young brunette with an old face, is about to leave our table, but he gestures for her to wait.

"Darling, I did say to leave the dressing off, didn't I?"

She nods and takes his plate away.

"That's what I just said. You've lost weight," I say.

He shakes his head, mistrustful of everything. Piotrek doesn't even believe the things his most trusted friends tell him over dinner. Doesn't trust the sky to always be blue. His car to always obey his commands. Facts to be made of solid stuff.

It's hard to tell in this dimly lit restaurant, but it does seem he's looking a little healthier. His face less red, he's now looking his age, forty-four years old, and not ten years older. His gut no longer spills from his waistband, although his new clothes are as awful as the old – checked shirts, sports blazers, pointed shoes worn with jeans. Hair carelessly gelled, a thin silver chain on his thick neck. He is looking a little bit saner. One of his girls must have mentioned it to him, seeing as his wife never says a word.

He reminds me of a jovial brother in law, the one who's always got a cheap joke on the tip of his tongue, something about blondes and bachelorette parties and sexy brides. He looks like he owns a carwash, or a roofing business far out of town, although he claims to be a Warsovian through and through. Three generations back. He claims his grandmother was a radio operator during the Warsaw Uprising.

They're all like Piotrek. Nice. Calm. Smiling honest smiles. Built of weak bone and solid fat. His smile never leaves his face, a face shaped by all the fatty meats and potatoes he's consumed. He really is a likeable guy. He likes to be informal with everyone. Talking to women, he's all "darling", "baby", "teddy bear", and for guys he's always got a "buddy" or a "pal" or a "chap". Which is nice, but all it does is cover up the tumour growing within. It helps that he's actually funny, especially after he's had a few drinks and begins impersonating different personalities, toying with ideas. Pretending he's a priest, or a pimp, or a Russian oligarch.

That's when all his friends laugh as loud as if they were on television. Piotrek is a very nice guy, but he does command respect. Even for his jokes. We've never disagreed over anything. Never tried to cheat one another. Piotrek knows not to trust anyone or anything, but he knows who he can mistrust the least. Besides, all his friends know how it is. Know all about betrayals. They all remember the end of communism, the promises made by the suits, and the reality which followed. Like an old, Soviet-era comedy. So funny it hardly hurts any more.

If he ever learnt that I was trying to cheat him, I would soon enough find myself applying for disability allowance. Regardless of the fact that we just like each other's company.

"Have you eaten? You have to eat. Wait, I'll get you something," he says.

"I'm not hungry."

"Dearie!" he shouts at the waitress. "Sweetheart! Come on over."

The same young body with the same aged face comes back. He brushes her hand.

"Could you bring Kuba something delicious? Healthy and divine."

"But what would you like?" she asks, disinterestedly.

"All that is good and fine. Hummus maybe. Or curry, with a kick to it. A soup. Grilled cheese, the good stuff, with the nutty sauce. That is truly glorious!"

I see no point repeating myself. The waitress goes off and I see Piotrek smiling at me with a hint of pity in his eyes.

"You got to eat. Look at you. Thin as a pencil," he concludes.

Nobody, not the waitress, not me, not the manager would argue with him here. This place, a strange blend of nightclub, drinks bar and hookah joint, is his office, his palace, his property. His home. If anyone wanted to find him, for good or ill purpose, they know where they would have to storm. But he's not going to let that happen. His potato face, with suits and watches that cost a bomb but look fake, mean he will always look like a countryside playboy, all of it jolly and nice, concealing a hardness no bullet can pierce. There's titanium beneath those pressed shirts and that hairy skin. Piotrek knows how to live a long and prosperous existence.

The waitress sends the manager over. I still haven't asked Piotrek the question I came here with. He keeps chatting about diets, about sport, about dreams and squash, a game he once tried and which in turn tried to kill him.

I'm not at all interested in his sporting regime. I am interested in buying two kilograms of coke from him, thirty percent pure and costing me the wholesale amount of three hundred thousand zlotys.

"He's come back again," the manager tells him. The guy seems distressed, looking in the direction of the front door. I'm sitting with my back to the entrance and can't tell what it is he's looking at. I resist the urge to turn around.

"Let him come over, sit with me. I'll watch him," Piotrek orders.

"And if there's a repeat of yesterday?" the manager asks.

"There won't be. I wasn't here yesterday."

The manager disappears out of my line of sight, but I can hear raised voices. I blow my nose, the smell here barely any better than in that Asian fast food hut in Zoliborz, the air heavy with cigarette smoke, spices, spirits, artificially tanned skins, sweat, sauces. Mixed into one heavy soup, a sour cloud, intense, stifling.

"Fuck," Piotrek whispers. I stare right at his face. "A serious kind of guy. From out of town. Don't know what he's after. Haven't seen him for years. Tough. A tough, tough cookie."

"Must be looking to do a deal."

"If he wanted to deal with me, he'd just come out and say it," Piotrek barks. "Listen, it's a good thing you sorted things out with that Bethlehem joint. That is big money, that building, converted into apartments, I can smell the income now. We'll make a killing, you just wait, but patience. Yes, patience first. First, sell them drugs. Make some pocket change."

"How are things then? I've got a club, now I need drugs to sell in it. My supplies are down. I've got the cash in the car."

"The problem is..." Piotrek winces, smacking his lips. "I'll tell you what the problem is in a second. For now, I'm just glad you went over there, straightened out that Tiny fucker. It's sometimes good to show our faces out and about. You know what I mean? You did good."

I want to add something, but his attention is now elsewhere, his head raised. He gets up off his seat – since we've started talking, he's said hello to several people passing by our table, but he's never risen up off his seat once. Suddenly, next to me, there is a clearly pissed, bald fatso, his belly bulging next to my face, wearing a dark suit and dark glasses. His shirt is wide open, exposing some sort of exotic necklace and complex tattoos. He looks odd, as if pieced together from different constituent parts. His shades are prescription glasses, his eyes bulging behind them, big bright pools of keenness, of arousal, of wildness. Of the joy of seeing the fear in the eyes of others.

"This is Dario," Piotrek says to me. "And this is Kuba, a good friend."

"I'll join you," Dario says, shaking my hand.

I squeeze it without getting up. It is warm. I look into those hidden pools, calmly, trying not to show fear – it was like looking into the eyes of someone who's about to push you off a ten-storey rooftop.

"Join us. Do. We're just having a little chat about money," Piotrek says. "All in the family, no new secrets."

"We're all just always talking about the same thing – family and money," says Dario, the bald motherfucker. He smiles in a way which makes everyone else stare and think twice. I know guys like him. I don't want to do deals with them, don't want to share tables or shake hands. When they start getting rich, everyone around them goes crazy. Guys like him are like emotional napalm, setting everything that was calm before on fire.

I notice he is clutching a long raincoat in one hand, then hangs it on the back of his chair, smoothing it down with extraordinary care.

"Kuba, as I was saying, we've got a bit of a problem," Piotrek says, turning his attention back to me.

The waitress brings me my hummus and I push it to the centre of the table.

"Bring us a bottle of vodka," Dario orders, waving his finger to point at us all in turn. The gesture looks odd, his wrist limp, the movements of a sheikh, of someone in charge of everything the eye can see for hundreds of miles around. The hand might be bare, but it is covered in diamonds and gold. The invisible kind.

"The problem is that one of our transports was intercepted," Piotrek says, staring at the hummus. "I'm not drinking today, Dario, my lad. I can't. Gotta watch my sugar intake."

"Vodka. Litre bottle. Make sure it's not just chilled but frozen cold," Dario instructs the waitress with a grin which exposes the whitest, freshest, fakest set of implants around. "Screw your sugar intake," he says, presumably at Piotrek, but looking at me.

The waitress in turn is looking at Piotrek. He nods.

"Anything else?" she enquires.

"You know what else I'd like from you?" Dario asks, turning his big, fat, sweaty head towards the girl. His smile straightens into something of a grimace. "Do you know what I would do to you?"

The waitress tries to smile. Piotrek pats Dario on the arm. Dario leans back in his chair, trying to be still, but it's clear his body hates immobility. His hands keep moving, looking for things to stroke, to check out. He looks around, as if afraid of being spotted.

"How did the transport get intercepted?" I ask.

"Nothing about it online. The lawyers which service the long distance haulage firm in question deleted all mention of it from the internet. But it is lost, so... Four tons of bananas, on the German border."

"And what now?"

"For fuck's sake, Piotrek, are you done? Now, I have something to discuss with you," Dario butts in.

I notice he's watching me intently. I don't hold the gaze, but I don't avoid it either. He keeps staring and I stare back, trying to give nothing away.

"On Thursday, we'll have more," Piotrek tells me.

"I leave on Friday," I tell him.

"And that is a very good thing indeed. Men should get out and about, see the world," Dario interjects.

He's drunk. I can smell it without looking. He's drunk the way only someone who's been drinking nonstop for almost a week can be. Even when he's sitting down, he's dancing. When talking, he's dancing to the sound of his own words.

I can't tear my eyes away from those dark lenses and the enlarged, pale eyes hiding behind them.

"Don't you have any emergency stocks?" Piotrek asks.

I have back up plans, in the form of the bag presented to me by Uncle and Shady. But I have no intention of touching it. I could right now have a word about it with Piotrek, seeing as I'm sure the order for me to watch the bag came from him. Uncle's not quite the type to come up with such ideas alone. A little too guarded, though over time he's developed a bit of an imagination. He knows it's essential to allow someone in his position to survive past forty in our business.

I could agree to use the bag now with Piotrek, but I don't want to mention it around Dario.

"Listen, Dario, we can't have a repeat of last night. You wasn't playing nice," Piotrek says to him.

"Nice? And you calling thirty of your boys over to have me escorted off the premises is fucking nice? What the hell are you saying to me? Piotrek?"

The waitress brings over the chilled vodka, along with glasses.

"Pour," he says to me.

I look at Piotrek. He nods. I set the glasses up, pour two shots.

"Well, actually, you know, you're cute. You know you're cute?" Dario announces to me and adds, "You too. You're drinking with us."

"I'm driving."

"I don't give a fuck," he replies, pursing his lips as if to blow a kiss in my direction. As if I was his bitch.

"Is everything with you as it should be, Dario, or is something up?" Piotrek asks him.

I can hear something in his voice that was not there before, something odd. Dario's expression changes instantly. The smile is replaced by a look of complete disgust, his upper lip lifting, as if someone had shoved some dead meat under his nose.

"Kuba, drink with us," Piotrek says.

"We can't have that again, thirty gorillas showing up to drag me out of here," Dario whines on. "We can't have that. You know who I am. You know who I am? You know. What can they do? You know. They can't fucking do shit."

"Yeah, pal, I know who you are," Piotrek replies and lifts his glass. Looking right in his eyes, letting him know it's for his sake, I down the vodka. I haven't had a sip of booze for a year. It is cold, dull, biting. My throat feels like someone's just stuck their fingers down it.

I can't drink anything else. There's a whole night of driving still ahead of me.

Dario grins, rises up and kisses Piotrek on the forehead, then orders me: "Pour."

"Dario, listen, this is a calm place. You, on the other hand, raised your voice at the ladies, took your pants down," Piotrek says, his voice very level. "Waved your piece about. Jumping up and down on chairs, on the customers. I do understand the need to have a good time, you know I do."

Dario is smiling again, licking his lips. He leans over and pats Piotrek's hand. I pour the vodka.

"What is his name? The manager?" Dario asks.

"Hamim. He's been running this place like a trooper."

"Fuck him," Dario says.

"He's a good boy," Piotrek repeats.

"He's a goner. In a hole, in the ground. Fuck him."

"Listen, Dario, my man, there's no need. Let's have a drink."

"I love you. I do love you, Piotrek," Dario says and leans right over to kiss him on the head. "Thirty gangsters. You know how many boys I could have here at any moment? Do you know? Fifty. Fifty of my best boys! If I can find my phone, they'll be here," he laughs.

"We're having a nice time. A fine time. Let's sit. Let's talk," Piotrek says, forcing a smile. "There's money that's got to be made, you know."

"That manager," Dario repeats again. "Whatever his fucking name. He's fucked. He's gone. Dead. Fucking fucked."

I down another glass of the vodka. It tastes better than the first, but it will have to be my last. Still tasting shit. I hate drinking.

Dario unbuttons and takes off his shirt. Now, he's sitting with us, half-naked, his tattoos there for all the world to see. For a moment, he doesn't make a move, but then starts stroking one of his tattoos, prison made, rough as hell, a human skull wearing a hood, a swastika instead of a nose. It looks like it was drawn by a young child. Dario presses down on the swastika. Pressing it like he was ordering something, waiting for something to happen next.

"They will be here. Fifty of them. And I don't give a fuck about any of it. The guy who rang your boys, he's dead already. Now. Right now. Dead. Fucking fucked. Piotrek, I know you know. I know you wouldn't betray me. I know you understand whatever is meant to happen. I know you'll behave like a gent and not a prick," he says and then reaches behind him for his coat.

I see the gun appear, a second before it becomes apparent to everyone else in the restaurant. The waitresses are doing their best not to look. Piotrek remains still, only his lips move.

"Dario, you know we're all friends here. All friends. It's nice and pleasant and we all like each other," he drones, putting his hand on Dario's naked shoulder.

More colours. One after the other, for a moment. Something clicking in my ears, as if one of my ear drums just popped. I close my eyes, wait a moment, open them again. The sensation passes.

He's now up and dancing, dancing for real, the gun his partner, a devil, a drunken demon; he puts it on the table, starts clapping, then picks it up again. Kisses Piotrek, kisses the gun, kisses empty air.

"Call him over. Call him so I can fuck him over," Dario whoops.

He starts looking around the restaurant, now suddenly emptier than before, the gun held low by his hip, those still sitting at their tables trying not to look up, but he can smell their fear, their panic, smell it like a wild dog. His teeth bared, it's clear he's in his element, in his happy place. All he needs is a tail he could wag to show us how turned on he is by all this.

"I have to go," I say just as the waitress places a plate before me, full of something bright, steaming and wafting sharp spices to high heaven.

"Dario," Piotrek pleads. "Dario, let's not make a show of this. Not necessary. We can sort it all out. Sort it out like friends."

"You're not going anywhere," Dario says to me, teeth bared in a manic grin, and adds, "Or maybe, maybe we will now come with you."

"Come back Thursday, Kuba," Piotrek says, not smiling. "On Thursday we should have our supply problems sorted."

I raise two fingers in the classic victory sign, the palm of my hand held out to him. Two kilograms. He nods.

"Now, we're coming with you, pal. Going wherever you want, wherever you wish to take us," Dario drawls, smiling. He looks at Piotrek, at me, then sits down. Puts the gun on his thigh. Starts trying to put his shirt back on.

"I'm going to work," I tell him.

"Kuba works in retail," Piotrek explains, leaning towards Dario, but the fat drunk can't hear him, can't understand what is being said.

"To work? Sunday night? You're going to see some whore. Come, take us with you. Good whores? One you own? One you love? I'll show you how to fuck ass."

"Seems you've shown us yours," I spit back.

"Oh. We can't have that. Can't talk like that to me," he groans.

"Can't talk like that to me either."

"Kuba," Piotrek asks, firmly. "All is good, pal. We're all good here."

His face is set in some kind of hard grimace. Like something's ailing him. I get up, toss a hundred zloty bill on the table.

"Call me. I want to sort it before departure," I ask, smiling briefly.

"Where are you taking off for?" Piotrek asks.

"A faraway place. But not for long. It's all sorted."

"I don't like the look of you," Dario barks at me. "Don't like it at all."

"Let it go, Dario. He's our man. Fucking hell... Let it be. He's a stand-up guy," Piotrek says, voice lower now, duller.

"Standing up, sure. Sure he is," Dario once again grins, baring his godawful artificial dental perfection. "Let him walk. But I don't like the look of him. Don't like what I'm seeing. He's walking into trouble. Trouble I can see miles away. See it clear."

He lifts his shades up over his forehead. His eyes now small, black pools of damnation. I never want to look into them again, though I know all too well it will come to be. I know the time will come when I will have to have a conversation with him. Though I will not want to and may not be at all prepared.

"I see everything," he says. "But if you gotta go, you'd better get gone."

"You do look better, seriously," I say to Piotrek, putting on my coat. Piotrek shakes my hand. Dario does too. It's hot, as if he had

170

a fever. A waitress approaches slowly, stands before them with the terrified expression of a kid sent somewhere bad as punishment.

I turn and head for the exit.

"Bring me the manager, Piotrek. Please. Just bring him to me," I hear Dario mumble.

I know nothing will happen, nothing bad, Piotrek won't let it, but I also know he's going to be tied up babysitting that pissed psycho for the next few hours.

As I leave, my phone rings. The number of another good, wealthy, marginally well-known customer. But when I answer, instead of his voice I hear a woman, screaming and squealing down the line.

I stop in the door, still within sight of Piotrek and the other guy.

"Intercontinental, room 423. Come over, quickly, fucking hell, please" the woman shouts at me, sobbing in between words.

"This is a wrong number, I've no idea who you are," I reply.

"You sold it to him, so now you fucking come clean up, the feds are waiting downstairs, if you don't I'm going there to give them this number."

I glance back. Dario is still looking at me. His glasses back on his nose. His eyes the place where all of the matter, all of the mass of this room is focused, a second before they're swallowed up as if by a black hole.

"Now you got troubles," he says and points a finger at me. "Big troubles. I can see it. I see it because I see everything that happens in this city."

10:50pm

The lobby of the Hotel Intercontinental, decorated with plenty of glass and expensive woodwork, is as sterile as an unwrapped condom. I pass a group of Russians coming out of a lift, accompanied by some women, stuffed full of good coke and bad botox, ranging from the ages of twenty to fifty. We don't look at each other. Functioning in a kind of symbiosis. The receptionist knows who I am. I tell him the room number.

"What's going on?" he asks.

"A top up, I guess."

We're both whispering. In the lobby behind me, sunk into some deep sofas, there are two guys in tight suits, their faces as flat and grey as cardboard. Their coats are black, sucking in light. They're nibbling on nuts set on a low table before them with the expressions of men who are trying to understand what they are doing with their lives and what time it is anyway. Special service, feds protecting high-ranking government officials.

"He's up there with a girl," the receptionist says. He's a nice guy. Thirty, balding, wire-rimmed glasses.

"She a pro?" I ask. "Have you seen her before?"

"Not her. But she's wearing black stilettos with red heels. You know..."

I nod. The number she was calling from is ringing me again. I don't answer.

"And the shithead?" I ask.

"Been a while since he's paid us a visit," the receptionist answers with a smile. "A shame, really."

I nod. Shithead is another customer of mine, the owner of a large legal firm, around forty. In order to chill out, he'd rent a room for three days each month, just to drink and snort so hard he'd lose all touch with reality. His signature move was to take his own faeces and smear it all over the room, in various shapes, fractals or some such, only to then always leave shedloads of money behind just to pay for the clean-up.

"Do you remember that time he insisted on coming down to the lobby to meet you?" he says, grinning. "Fucking hell!"

"He must have left you a pretty penny that time, right?"

He nods, still smiling at the memory. I slip him a couple of hundred zloty bills, then go towards the lifts.

I don't like visiting hotels, but I sometimes have to. The guy downstairs always makes sure my face is wiped from the security camera footage, hence my payment to him. Hotels are just too damn cosy, like human asylum centres. Those who can afford them feel too good in their anonymous spaces – something's wrong with their heads as a result of this sense of safety. They become dangerously unpredictable. They fuck, snort and shit all over the place, feeling like no one is going to catch them, no one is going to care. They suffer nervous breakdowns, beat prostitutes, allow themselves to descend to the functioning level of a newborn child. The guys in reception are meant to keep them safe from their wives, especially the ones who find evidence of philandering, from their business partners, especially those who notice the company cards are maxed out. I can't stand hotels, but they pay too well for me to avoid them altogether.

Hotels smell of bad trips, of misadventures, a smell no amount of scrubbing and spraying of expensive fragrances can cover up.

Room 423. I knock and the door opens soon enough.

"Do something. Do something, for God's sake, or I call the cops or those guys from downstairs," she mumbles and pulls me inside, then slams the door shut.

She looks at me. Her makeup smudged. She's wearing some undies, a men's overcoat thrown over her shoulders. Even the state she's in I can tell she's fine-looking, a classy face, body sculpted by all sorts of gym activities. Her taut stomach trembling. She's terrified, furious, unable to tell which emotion will finally triumph.

"Who is it?!" I hear a man's voice screaming from somewhere inside the apartment. "Who the fuck is it?!"

"What is going on here?" I ask her through clenched teeth.

"You sold him the shit, you sort it," she spits back.

I push her aside and go through to the lounge. A two room apartment with a double king size bed, a vast TV, a not-so-mini bar. He's sitting in the corner of the room. Naked. Shivering. Holding a Swiss pen knife. His forearms are covered in scratches, maybe some cuts, the sort teens inflict upon themselves when they start dressing mostly in black. The floor is littered with sheets of A4 paper, stained with whisky from a bottle lying in the corner. There's a mirror on the table, lines cut up, along with a crack pipe. This little minx has conned me – I haven't sold him a fucking thing in at least a month.

"Who is this prick?" he mumbles. "Wait. I know who he is. From the Lityński camp. Lityński sent him. You let him in, you bloody whore, you did. And now give me those photographs. Give me those pictures, you fucking bitch! Give them, I'll fucking shoot you before you're buried, so they don't bury you alive!"

He's shaking like he was outside, in the snow and the cold. There's a fresh, wet patch on the carpet beneath him.

He must have started smoking a few days ago. A goner. Down a deep, black hole, the kind that takes weeks to crawl out of. Only his body left upon the surface.

I turn. Head for the door. She grabs me by the arm.

"Now you have to help me. Else you're fucked," she says. "Now you have to do something."

"Fuck you," I say, pushing her back on the bed.

"They know you're up here. They saw you. They're coming."

"That's your problem."

"If you go, he's going to fucking kill me."

Her voice is trembling, as if someone was clutching all the words and phrases in her head, and shaking them like a bag of bones.

"Not my fucking problem," I growl.

"I'll tell them you did, you sold him this shit, I will."

The man on the floor starts shouting. The sound is like an air raid siren. When I turn, I see he has the knife pointing towards his belly, his face a grimace of final desperation.

The knife plunges about an inch into his flesh, the skin compressing, blood seeping slowly but heavily. His eyes roll back in his head, as if he was coming. I watch him pull the knife out, then stand up, watching all this too slowly, while the girl behind me screams a second too late. I approach him quickly, hit him on the chin. He shoves the knife in my direction, and I struggle to pull it from his grip without cutting myself on the blade. He's strong – the crack has tightened his muscles, and I struggle to wrench the weapon from his grip. Finally, I kick him in the balls, and he groans harshly, then falls back down on the floor, right into a puddle of his own piss.

I throw the knife into the opposite corner of the room. My jumper now has blood on it. A stain as red and as vivid as freshly made borsht. Shit. He's a member of parliament, one of those wealthy liberals or neo-liberals... who cares. Secretary of state for transport. All of forty years old, a wife, two kids, the prime minister's right hand man. Studied law and international affairs at Oxford. I heard there will soon be elections for the Euro Parliament, and that he wants to join.

He likes press conferences. I often see him on morning television, talking into crowds of mikes in pretty, complex sentences. There's been a few times his steady voice helped me to fall asleep. Not sound sleep, by any stretch of the imagination, only for a short while, but it was still welcome.

But now, instead of announcing his running for things, boasting at conferences, making endless promises, he's down on his naked knees, swaying back and forth, blood from his belly dripping onto the light brown carpet.

"How long have you been here?" I ask the girl.

She's still lying back on the bed, as if it was a vessel which could sail her safely away from this whole mess.

"Only a few hours," she says.

"Did you give him anything?"

"He was already as high as a fucking jet. Wanted me to blow him. He couldn't come. Then he started to smoke crack, then he was on the floor, looking for something, and then..."

She starts to sob. Terrified. I try not to worry about her emotional state. Prostitutes are the worst people to confide in. They tell everyone everything, especially their friends from work. Or clients, when the work is done.

"Go the bathroom, bring me a towel," I tell her. "And get dressed."

I delete the most recent calls from my phone. Then ring Pazina.

He suddenly rushes up from the carpet, pushing against me, knocking the phone from my hand. Wants to rush for the knife, but I'm in the way. He grimaces like a heartbroken kid, trying to get at his favourite toy. I push him back against the wall. He rises and tries again: I hold him back, but he's stronger than me, even though – or maybe because – there's blood pouring from him.

"Tell them," he groans, teeth chattering, "Tell them that they're not gonna catch me. There's no way. Look, everything they had on me, it's all here, we'll burn it all. Get rid of everything."

I hold him. For a moment, until I feel his strength wane, and then I push him back gently and slap his face, hard, to make him stop and think, even if only for a second.

He drops down to the ground. In a state of shock. Trying to catch his breath.

"They planted something inside," he says, stabbing his wound with a finger. "Planted something here, only it's getting deeper and deeper. Those men from Gazprom. Russian agents. I'm fucking sure of it. They knew everything. Addresses, dates of birth. What books my kids like reading. Pippi fucking Longstocking. They knew my daughter loves them. Now I know. Fracking is fucking dirty. No one cares. Not even the commissions. Americans talked to me. About things. About sums. And now this fucking thing inside me. This implant. It's recording. Everything. You, me. But I'll get it out. You'll see, I'll get it out."

He tries to poke about inside the wound. Somebody knocks on the door. Before anything else can happen, before he can start howling, I jump towards him, pin his torso to the carpet with my knee, put my hand against his mouth.

"Sir," a voice can be heard through the door. "Sir, is everything OK?"

The girl is looking at the door, at me, at him, then back at the door, charged with manic energy. Her panicked hands shaking. I nod for her to approach.

"Sir, in an hour we have to be at that gala. The dinner dance," the voice informs us coolly.

I press down on his mouth harder. He tries to wrestle free, so I jab him in the stomach, though he doesn't seem to notice, his nervous system disabled by the crack. If all is well, he'll get some feeling back in an hour or two.

"Make some noise. Like you're being fucked," I tell her, quietly.

"What?!" she groans.

"Sir!" the voice followed by more knocking on the door.

"Make some fucking noise, moan, groan, for fuck's sake, just

176

distract them, will you?" I beg, while trying to stop my prisoner from escaping, pushing down on him with all my weight. He begins to shudder, like he's having an epileptic fit, but it's just him trying to break free.

"What are you on about?" she pleads.

"Go get an entry card," the voice outside the door orders someone else.

"I'll fucking kill you in a second," I tell her. "Get on the bed."

She finally does as told, evidently dazed. Fists are now hammering on the door.

"Make like you're loving it," I hiss, and she finally gets the message.

"Yeah... Oh yeah..." she starts moaning. "Fuck me. Fuck me, boy!"

I watch her going through the motions, instantly in her element, the whole thing sexy but fake. I think for a moment about all this, about what all this effort, all this expense is for. So much risked for so little, a bit of arousal, a monstrous high, all of it epically boring.

"Sir, are you OK?" The voice is now a little less panicked.

Unlike the voice of the politician, who lets out some kind of anguished howl, silenced by my hand pressing on his mouth. There are tears running from the corners of his eyes. He reminds me of the guy from *A Clockwork Orange*, being tortured again in the name of some stupid game.

"Fuck me, oh fuck me! Fuck me, fuck me hard!" the girl is now screaming, sure to be heard outside. The politician is groaning too, though muted, my hand covered in spit, my clothes in blood, and now I hear my phone ringing. And it's not even midnight yet.

"You're so fucking big, oh yeah! Do it, do it nasty!" she howls, and I can't help looking as she writhes on the bed, really acting now, really into it, eyes closed, her mind far from this room, really being fucked by someone, something she cares about. The security guys must be impressed. No one is knocking. "Yeah, yeah, yeah, oh yeah! You're so fucking big, so fuck me, boy, fuck!"

"We have an hour, sir," the voice outside the door says and then nothing. That's when the crazed fucker on the floor bites the inside of my hand. I lean back, he twists out from beneath me, rubbing blood into the carpet.

"Jesus Christ!" He screams with all his might. "Aargh!"

He screams, looking round the room at the mess, the crack pipe, the papers, me holding my hand, and I can hear the security guys departing, laughing at what they still think is a wild scene of debauchery.

Maybe the sound of them laughing reaches his ears. Maybe not. He twists and throws himself at me, but even though my hand stings, the bite deep, I clench my fist and smash it into his chin as hard as I can. It sends him flying against the wall, slumping to the ground.

"Christ!" the prostitute screams, and I say to her without turning around, "Get dressed, now!"

The man is down, trembling a little, like a fish straight out of an aquarium. I hear her jump off the bed and start rummaging round the room for her clothes.

I pick my phone up off the floor and dial Pazina again. She answers straight away.

"Hey!" she shouts.

"I need you to drive up to the Hotel Intercontinental, twenty minutes, with a package of lorazepam."

"Fucking hell, Kuba. I'm out working," she says coolly.

"I also need some elastic bandages and distilled water."

"Where am I going to get that at this time of night?"

"You can't get me a drop of lorazepam in the next twenty minutes? How the hell do you function then?"

"Fucker," she spits.

"Leave it for me at the reception. A young guy there, glasses. Balding. There are a couple of special services bodyguards waiting in the lobby, don't look at them. Fifteen minutes, starting now," I tell her, cutting the call.

The girl is now dressed, sitting on the edge of the bed like a discarded doll, sobbing still.

"Should I leave?"

"Stay there," I tell her and turn the television on.

I bend down over the guy, turn him over. Blood is still seeping from his wound, though not as fast as before. I hear a voice on TV, distant but familiar.

"Go get me a towel," I say to her, turning around. "Don't be staring at me like some dumb goat. Go get a fucking towel!"

"We're still investigating the incident," the television voice says. "Mariusz F. will remain under police supervision until we are done."

I glance at the screen. It's deputy commissioner Marek, hair nicely gelled now, wearing a cheap designer suit the same colour as a folding Ikea sofa, giving a press conference. At a certain point, he has to cover his mouth while burping silently. Must be that shitty food I watched him lap up earlier, paid for with my ten grand.

"And what about the death of Mr Górecki? Unofficial sources indicate drugs were also involved. Is there a connection?" a female journalist asks from the floor.

"Sorry, I can't comment," Marek replies, smiling sadly.

The girl comes out of the bathroom, holding about half a dozen towels, one of which I place gently against his stomach.

"You can't comment on whether there is a possible connection between two drug-related deaths, both taking place in the last twenty-four hours, both within your jurisdiction? Commissioner?"

"No comment," he says, stepping back from the microphones.

I press a towel to the politician's guts. Stemming the blood. He's breathing heavily, shallowly, eyes rising for the sky.

"You'll get rid of all that down the toilet," I tell her, pointing to all the paraphernalia on the table: smack, pipe, baggies.

She doesn't move. Doesn't respond. I rise to my feet, look at her closely. All she's capable of doing now is shaking her head.

My phone pings – Pazina: *30mins*.

"What do you think – are drugs now completely permeating the Polish showbusiness industry?" another journalist asks.

"I'm not paid to have such opinions," Marek answers. "Our operational capacities are now focused on trying to challenge the drug-dealing community and finding out the source of the substances allegedly found on the suspects."

I turn the TV off.

It's funny, thinking about it, how little people know. How much they don't know. How obvious facts seem to be surprising puzzles for them. Journalists are the funniest of the lot. Grown-ups who keep asking themselves – why is the air around us transparent?

Cocaine is everything. It's the blood which runs through life, through business, through money. It's not coke which killed the poor pregnant woman my best customer slammed into, and it's not coke which killed that furniture king's blobby kid. It was distraction. Disorientation. The inability to hold back.

I'm not responsible for any of that, nor is the stuff I sell. People tend to be dumb, and utterly careless – a simple fact the journalist asking all those questions refuses to accept. People mean well, they only want to make the odd deal, bury that which constantly keeps pushing them back into the ring, keeps knocking them down, and so they end up on the floors of hotel rooms, psychotic, shaking like kids before entering a dental surgery, covered in their own piss. They end up veering onto the soft shoulder, blocked in by patrol cars, wrists cuffed, staring down at their own shoes.

"He said, when I first came in here, that his daughter has cancer," she says.

I look down at his helpless body with disgust.

"When I bring you the meds, you have to force him to take five pills and wait half an hour. If those guys from downstairs want to get in here, tell them to wait. When the meds kick in, stick him under a cold shower, then help him dress," I instruct her slowly. She nods. "If you ever ring my number again, I will find you and do things to your face which will change the course of your life – do you understand me? If you tell the cops anything, a fucking word, I will find you and never let go."

"His daughter is five years old," she says, her eyes suddenly focused again, like the eyes of a fully conscious, sentient person.

"His daughter is little and has cancer and he's here smoking crack in a hotel room with a rented piece of ass?" I ask.

"Your crack," she answers. "You sold it to him."

"It's his crack, you fool. It became his the moment he bought it. And it wasn't from me."

She rises off the bed and walks into the bathroom. I sit on the sofa. Blood on my sweater – it's a cheap bit of Ralph Lauren, I'll have to get rid of it on the way home. The stain is the size and colour of an apple. Right in the same place where he stuck the knife into himself. Just beneath the belly button.

My phone pings. A text message from a number neither my phone nor I recognise.

What are you up to?

00:15am

"Two Big Mac Meals," Pazina says into the intercom.

"That's all?"

"Yeah, that's all!"

I drive up to the payment window. The night has become very cold. Ice and a slippery film of frost covering everything. I can hear again that melody, the dog tune, as if played by some bored kid on a toy instrument. It seems to be coming from within everything.

Pazina notices my mouth hanging open.

"Don't do that," she asks. "Any time I see you do that with your mouth, I get freaked out."

"Do what?" I ask, though I know damn well what.

"Your mouth. Hanging open. Makes me fear shit even more than I do already. You look mad then. Mad mad."

"Mad mad?"

"It's something bared, not mixed with anything else. Like it's separate in you, and you only turn it on for a moment."

I look at her like she's the mad one.

"Stop reading so many books, Paz. You're freaking yourself out."

"Should you not have that hand looked at? How do you know that fucker didn't have AIDS?"

"He's a member of parliament... Or at least he was when I saw him last."

"A member of parliament who smokes crack and fucks whores," she reminds me, distastefully.

After a short while of cold coming in through the open window, a sleepy-looking girl in a McD sun visor hands us a bag of food, forgetting to smile. I hand the bag to Pazina, drive towards the parking spaces. As she starts to unwrap the stinky shit, I try to ring Uncle. No answer. I've nothing left to sell. Not even a gram on me. Nothing other than the sports bag lying in my other apartment, safe there along with all my weapons and cash reserves. I pay, drive on towards the car park, stop and hand Pazina the hot paper bag.

"What's going to happen to him now?" she asks.

"If that girl turns out to have an ounce of brains behind that pretty ordinary face, nothing. He'll come to, take a shower, they'll drag him off to detox and personally apologise to the prime minister, blaming his sick kid. For everything. He'll be fine. And if he starts jabbering, then... Who knows?"

"She might have taken a few photos of him. Trying to sell them somewhere."

"She didn't seem in a frame of mind to do that when I saw her." I dismiss the idea, but now it begins to bother me. "She probably moved to Warsaw a year ago, fucking for twenty euros an hour. Studying something somewhere, just to qualify for the health insurance. Doesn't even know how to spend the money. Might go for a holiday one day, take a friend, be bored stiff. Though in the pics, they'll be having the time of their lives."

"I'm worried about you. You never used to have these sorts of problems. But now one's popped up, everything else is coming apart. Like some domino stack." She shuts up for a second, chewing her burger. "Anyway, it's good that you're leaving. A very good thing."

"I don't know if it is or isn't. Things like these can't be got away from. They'd best be sorted first. Once you start running, there's always someone in the mood to chase after you. Someone who likes the smell of fear on others."

"How do you want to play this? You want to go round Fajkowski's and threaten him? Take him to the woods?"

"Give me my burger," I say, ignoring the stupid question.

Uncle rings back before I have a chance to bite into my meal.

"What the fuck? It's Sunday, son. Give a man the chance to fuck around once in a while," he says, his voice unclear, as if he was chewing sandpaper. "If I have to go knock more heads together, you know the score. Two grand and I'm yours. Think about what time it is. Check the calendar. Your phone can help with that..."

"I need to borrow something of what you've given me to look after." I interrupt his sniping.

I hear him kiss his teeth on the other end.

"Alright, but you know... I can sell you a bit."

"Then sell. Just don't talk to me like I'm a prick."

My phone buzzes as we talk. Another text message.

"I can sell you the whole thing. Wholesale."

"Grand, but I don't need the whole thing."

"Alright, listen, I got a girl here, gonna get some shut eye, up in the morning, laters," he says and cuts the line.

"Can't you just shut up shop for the night?" Paz asks, chewing slowly.

Another text. I know the number. Of course I do. Off by heart. It's flown here all the way from that room with a window that looks out on the school playground, the one which at dawn looks like a dirty, pink aquarium.

I feel a stabbing pain, like I'd just bitten down on a sick tooth. That's all I need tonight.

Write me. Anything.

I knew it. Seeing her in that restaurant, I knew it would not be the last of it. It wasn't by accident that she appeared by my table. She must have sensed me around, followed the scent.

The distant sound of crooked music is turning my stomach. I eat half the burger and toss the rest back into the bag.

"She's a good customer," I explain to Pazina. "Always buys extra. And pays well. Can't pass on that."

"She?"

"One of those lonely dames. Bored. Bored without her candy."

"She's lonely?"

"Her husband is a board member of some corporation," I try to explain, but then give up. "We have to go to the other apartment. I have to change. Then I can drive you anywhere you like."

"Saxon Marshes, please."

Another text: *Please*.

"Busy night for text messages," Paz comments, reading my mind. "Your grimace tells me they're not good news."

"Toothache. Gotta go see a dentist before I fly. Why Saxon Marshes?"

"I got some breaking up to do. Like I told you, he's too good. I can't keep him hanging, he doesn't deserve that."

"You sure? You don't want this one going the way of the others. You're always beating yourself up afterwards, regretting shit. Usually after you see them on the town with some other girl. This one sounds... best."

"I can't keep doing it, Kuba. Kidding myself that I can make myself present. I've just got this permanent, mechanical fault. Can't connect. No warranty claim will fix that."

"Yeah, you're good at that. Saying pretty lines, pretty metaphors, looking all sad and cute doing it. Isn't that what everything comes down to in the end? That pose?" I press.

"Screw you. You know I'm not like that. I've had my unfair share of shit. So screw you."

"You think it's all over for you and love?"

"And you?"

"Yeah, sure. But it's not about saving you from that sorry fate. It's about those guys yet to come, the ones who will try to convince you that you were wrong about all that broken shit all along. Again."

"I won't. Screw you, I won't. You got me so fucking wrong, I swear."

"Half a year," I say, stretching out my hand. "The next one will also be sweet and good and have a kid or two. Shake on it. Five grand."

"Screw that and all. I'm serious. Fuck you."

Somewhere far off, I hear the despairing wail of one of those modern, digital ambulance sirens, the one which alternates with speed. Though it's far out of sight, everything around us begins to glow a subtle shade of blue. Cool, pale blue. Like the colour of the essential soul of this city.

I take a sip of coke – it's cold and flat. I think back to the two shots I had earlier. I think about Dario. The risk he presents. Fucking sizeable. Crazed motherfucker. His cold eyes are gonna swallow up the whole of this city soon enough. They're already feasting on it. He's miles away, but I feel him close. Sensing the stench of someone who wants what he knows he's owed.

"There are no good people in the world, Paz," I tell her, supping noisily on the coke. "Don't worry yourself. Doesn't matter either way."

Another text pings.

You always keep silent when I need you most.

"Fuck you," I think to myself. "Vanish, disappear, evaporate. Stop disturbing me and my fucking focus."

"Have you seen Beata lately?" Pazina asks, pretending to be busy with her own coke.

"Bumped into her."

"With your dick?"

"Not with that, Paz, we bumped into each other at a food court in a shopping mall," I tell her, not sure why I am suddenly on the defensive.

"So stop bumping into her. It's the last thing you need right now. That bump in the night. And don't you write back to her either. Why did you toss that burger? You're not gonna finish it?"

I hand her the bag containing the half-eaten burger.

"If that's not enough, I'll buy you another," I tell her and fire up the Audi.

01:40am

"I didn't think you'd come," she says.

"A hundred," I say, without entering the front door she's holding wide open. Instead, I point at my pocket. "As you asked."

"Won't you come in?"

At the very moment I'm trying to work out how to tell her "No", she pulls the door open wider, cocking her head to let me know I

185

shouldn't refuse. She lives in a villa in the fanciest part of Warsaw – Wilanow – Villa Nova, modified from Italian or Latin, I can never remember which. Tall, two-metre-high fencing, infra-red sensors all over the garden. There's a cute little Lambo in the driveway. Her husband splashed out. Making up for all the times he's not home. She hardly ever drives it. Not that he'd notice, seeing as he's constantly out, signing more deals to demolish communist-era buildings, on behalf of those who used to own the land before the last World War and are now living in New York or Toronto or Tel Aviv.

The money he makes on property portfolios he then invests in crude oil. Which in turn buys him more properties. He likes having things erected. Most recently, a large sports complex, with a golf course. I could recognise the face if I saw him – narrow lips, even narrower eyes, scanning everyone and everything to see how much his time with them was worth. Weighing them up, like they were meat, some soft substance which could be shaped and moulded and sold on.

"I don't drink," I pre-empt her coming in.

"I remember," she corrects me with a smile. "I'll make you some tea."

She buys plenty from me, storing the stuff for special occasions, like fine wines. I have to be nice in return. Making small talk now, catering to her fancies. She has no one to talk to, especially when Sunday turns to Monday and a new week that is not going to be in any way new looms. Her girlfriends, if she has any, have long ago drifted off into drugged sleep in their nearby fortresses. Her kids, off studying in England, are probably right now dancing their heads off in some overpriced nightclubs, but then again she'd never dream of calling them in the middle of a sleepless night.

The hubby's not home, but then again no one would think that he's ever around to deal with the question of her loneliness.

The interior of the villa feels strangely cramped, the furniture oversized, the paintings massive, antiques bought from auctions all over the place. Leather sofas that creak when you walk past. Everything a status symbol, a show of successful strength. All that's missing are Persian rugs and carvings brought back from African jaunts. They probably have them, but some interior designer has stored them in the basement, far out of sight. She probably paid them tens of thousands to rearrange shit to her liking, just for the sake of it.

"Sit down," she says.

"Green, if you have it," I say, in reference to the tea.

She's a shade over forty, at a guess. Slim, maybe even too slim, bones showing. Her hair is dyed black, pinned up in a high bob. Her dark dress matches the hair, light material, flowing. Her makeup is perfectly imperceptible. As transparently light as that tea will be in a second.

She's definitely fit, attractive, but it's hard not to be when you have nothing but time and money on your hands. Her husband constantly pumping cash into her, another one of his investments, sponsoring all sorts of treatments and regimens – his line of work won't allow him to have an unattractive partner. On the other hand, he can't swap her for a younger model. I suspect it would hit his profit margins too hard. Though this may be something she looks after and manages – she's smart, really quite smart for a woman who has spent the major part of her adult life doing little other than smelling good.

There can be no doubt her hubby fucks younger women. He fucks them for all sorts of reasons, not all of which make sense. She knows, and keeps herself busy pretending it makes no difference to her. That she's cool with it. The kind of woman who keeps on telling herself that marriage is like a fine business deal, one which needs maintenance and careful adjustment.

The armchair she chooses for me is comfortable, too comfortable. An armchair for those who are about to be disposed of, cheated out of something. A seat meant to send one's defensive senses to sleep.

She brings me my tea. That's when I notice she is seriously drunk. More than usual, come to think of it. Maybe it's because I took my time arriving. I hand her the baggie, a hundred, carefully weighed. Hard, solid chunks, cut from the gear I took from Uncle's bag earlier. She receives the goods, smiling. Hands over the required cash, bound with a silver clip.

"Thank you," I say, removing the clip and handing it back.

"No, thank you. Would you open the wine?"

"Sure," I reply, extracting myself from the trap chair and going over to the kitchen. She follows, takes a bottle of wine from the fridge and hands it to me, along with a corkscrew.

"Have you got a lot of... work left on tonight?" she asks.

"Same as ever."

"My son in his... how do you call those places, the students live..."

"Halls of residence," I help, trying not to look at the cleavage which has now come a little too close for comfort.

"His dorm. They found some drugs on him," she says, faking distress.

"And what now?" I ask, pulling the cork. "Trouble?"

"Probably. My husband doesn't know yet."

"Is it a good school?"

"Oxford."

"Then I wouldn't worry," I say. "Places like that, they're used to naughty rich kids and not keen on bad publicity."

She nods.

"I'll put some music on. Cheer myself up."

She walks over to a custom-designed hi-fi system, drops the needle on whatever piece of vinyl was already in place. Her body swaying imperceptibly, even though the music hasn't started yet. She waits for it, some jazz I've heard a million times before in a classier sort of hotel restaurant. She keeps her back turned to me. I see the muscles in it tense up, like her body is ready to spring, to launch into a run.

I have to go in a minute. I've never overstayed my welcome here. In the past, when sobriety let her speak more, half an hour was often enough for her to tell me lots about herself.

"I'm sure it'll be fine," I say, knowing what needs to be said.

"And so what?" she replies. "He only did it to spite me. Everyone there has something or other stashed away, but he's the one they catch? He's too smart for that. I trained him to be too smart for that. An appeal for help? Attention seeking?" She approaches and takes from me the glass of white I've poured for her, answering her own question. "It's not even to spite me or Adam. It's to spite himself, his own sense that everything he does will work out. I can understand that."

She then looks down at my chest and puts her hand out to touch it. Holds it there until I reach up and gently push it back.

"The son of some friends of ours is dead," she says, her voice dead too. "Overdose. Heart gave out. His girlfriend found the body. In their bed."

She goes over to the coffee table, grabs the bag I just sold her, then goes over to a set of shelves, reaching up to get something hidden out of sight.

"He must have been taking some awful shit," she says, back turned to me. "Why do they do that? They can afford the good stuff. The clean stuff. That's what confuses me. Terrifying." Then she turns, hands still empty, leans against the shelving unit and stares at me. "So forgive me for what I am about to say, but that kid was a fucking idiot."

"The son?"

"Yes. A cretin. If he'd lived, he'd have been no good to his father. Not in business. Not in anything. You know, the worst thing that can happen to a man, a father like Grzesiek, a self-made kind of guy, is to have an only son who is a dimwit," she states, then shuts up for a second, smiling to herself. "Don't you agree that just because someone is dead doesn't mean we don't have the right to speak ill of them?"

"Absolutely," I nod, watching as she turns again and starts rummaging around on those shelves. She finally finds whatever it was she was after.

"He was capable, like his father, of anything," she says, then shows me the prize she was looking for – a silver coke grinder. She dumps a rock into it, grinds it, then lines some up and snorts it, quickly, smoothly, to make it look good and sound OK. "Made to order. I also have this little silver spoon to go with it. But I take that with me whenever I go out with Adam. It's so pretty. I have to find it."

"I know what they look like."

I know what she wants from me. We're not kids. Were we ever? She's fine-looking, honed, maybe ten years ago effortlessly seductive. I don't even mind the fact that she's drunk. I mind the fact that she's simply in need. Like she's hungry. Like I'm a pizza delivery guy. She's desperate, determined someone should take her, shove her around, rip things, violate the terrible peace of her residence.

She gets up, aroused by the coke, walks over to me and makes eye contact, but whatever is hiding behind those pupils is alien to us both. Her perfume smells good though. I can't quite place the brand.

Another text pings in my pocket: *Come over.*

"Aren't you done for the night yet?" she asks again. "Or is there someone waiting? Someone else, like me? Another customer with bottles that need opening?"

I haven't replied to the text, but the phone burns in my hand, like something stolen, something loaded with guilt.

"I'm done for the night. And no, I can't tell you where I'm going next."

Another text: *Come over. Please.*

I haven't had sex for a few months, though I don't think about that every day. Thoughts like that just dispel focus, but the absence of bodies, of closeness, can be distracting. A soft, dull kind of pain which is hard to describe. An itch. An absence. A silent request. But I don't want her now. That would be awfully cheap. Inelegant. Weak, even. Staying here for longer than fifteen minutes is always a stupid mistake. Longer than thirty is worse. Is dangerous.

Every drug dealer fucks his clients, even those who sell heroin, but right here and now that would be a poor decision, and there is nothing worse than making poor decisions involving customers in the name of small itches, shallow longings.

Plus, she's married. And that always puts me off. The presence of that ring. That extra guy in the room with us. Not something I plan to make a habit of.

"Don't speak to me the way my husband does," she asks politely. "He's got nothing to say that I would want to hear. Never did. He's

190

not said anything of note since our wedding. Endless meetings, but he can't tell me anything about them. Endless deals, but he can't share any of the details with me, his wife. Call after call, during dinner, during our holidays, and he can't tell me shit. You know what I told him recently?"

I wait for the answer, backing away towards the front door in my mind already.

"I told him that if it is one of his young whores on the phone, and it is, of course, then he should stop making idiots of us both. He can just come out and admit how it is. How it's always been. 'Sorry darling, have to take this, one of my young sweethearts on the line'. I don't need to know the names. He can just give them numbers, Whore two on Tuesdays, Whore five on Fridays. Does it matter what their names are, what colour hair they have or what they like studying at school?"

"Sounds almost funny," I tell her, eyebrows raised. "You have a gift for comedy."

"Not many people appreciate the fact," she says, coming close again and putting her hand on my face.

"Wait a second," I ask, realising that beneath the delicate aroma of her perfume, there is something else, some other odour, sour, a whiff of rot.

Don't send any more messages I write to her, like a fucking idiot, asking myself at least ten times as I type whether to press Send. She's waiting. There. In that room. That pink aquarium. Like a dagger.

She has to fuck with my head one more time, shoot me down once more, because in her head everything is fine with me, because I've once more forgotten how our ending goes. Because I'm once again ready to surrender to that eerie assassination; every bit of cannibalism which can take place between a man and a woman is ridiculous, because I once again feel that real life human relations are no different than those in films, on television – the only difference being that those on screen often have better dialogue.

The woman I am actually with right now is now kissing me on

the mouth, her lips reeking of wine, of mouthwash, of meat and perfume.

"I can't," I tell her.

"You can," she counters.

I hold up my phone and tell her: "I have to go."

"Who to? See how much money you've made off me. You need more? Tonight? You sure?"

"I have to take care of something."

"Something you can't tell me anything about," she finishes my sentence, giving me a cold, hard look.

"Precisely," I tell her, without a hint of irony.

"Stay here," she asks. "You knew I would ask you this one day."

My phone pings.

What will you do to me?

Her hands slide down my chest, right down to my belt. She says nothing, doesn't have to speak, but she is smiling.

Will you kill me?

Using the phone as a shield, I push it against her, push her away from me. As gently as I can.

"You're married."

"In some sense..."

"Precisely."

She twists away from me, rests against the kitchen worktop. Still looking at me with that wide open, very drunk gaze. She's sure that one day, maybe in a second, it will happen. Besides, she's too proud, too insecure, to show me it hurts. To show me she knows she's becoming an ageing, sexless, rich bitch who takes far too many antidepressants, and most of all has far too much money and not enough ideas as to what to do with it.

Yes, I write and send. Not sure why.

"I didn't know criminals were so virtuous. Chivalrous even," she says, half-joking. "I only thought that happened in old noir movies."

"I'm just managing risk."

"You have someone?" she asks. "A girl?"

"That doesn't matter."

"We can fuck in the dark," she says suddenly, her voice cracking, a little lower in tone. As if someone was holding her by the throat, gently, but firmly. She glances at the coke, then at me again. "We can do it in the dark, and do it quickly, if you like."

"I'm sorry, I have to go. I'd love to stay, but... previous engagements."

She comes close again. Blocking my way. I put my phone away. She grabs my wrists, pulls herself close, tries to shove her tongue into my mouth.

"I've always thought you were cute. Yeah, I have, don't go blushing. There's something... cold about you. Delicate and cold." I push her away, gently, coolly and she doesn't resist. "Go on. Go."

As I walk across her massive lounge towards the front door, I hear her pouring more wine, then glance at the coke lined up on the coffee table. When I turn around, pressing the door handle, she's smiling, as if at a memory, a ghost. She's too proud to once again ask me to stay.

I look at her across all that distance and wonder how often she thinks about suicide. It's a given. These walls sometimes whisper to her. She's someone completely disconnected. From her husband, her kids. Perfectly distanced. Maybe that's why I like her. She's like me in that respect.

For all her money, all her treatments, all her little purchases, designed to kill time and boredom and disillusionment, she's like a newborn left on the doorstep for death to claim.

"You think you have time," she calls out to me. "Plenty of time. More than me. But you're wrong."

She's totally gone, her voice floundering, yet still proud enough to force whole sentences out of herself. Or maybe it's just years of pissed practice.

"Don't take this personally," I say, wondering why I'm saying anything at all, why I'm thinking of the balance between truth and lies. "It's as if you suddenly wanted to go out on a date with a pizza delivery guy. Just because you're lonely? It's a nice gesture, but not necessarily easy to accept. For the delivery boy."

"Stop talking crap," she says, waving me away disdainfully.

"What a shame to be so young and yet so arrogant. So fucking full of it."

She takes out a hair pin, lets her dark locks fall, and it works, looks lovely at a distance, looks youthful and ripe and graceful.

My phone pings.

And if I wanted to buy something from you? Would you come then?

"You're rejecting everything, everyone, leaving it all for later, because you think you've got decades left," she says.

"Nope. You're wrong about me."

"No, I'm not. You know how it is, don't kid yourself. You keep looking at that phone. There is a girl, right? Or girls. One day, that will all change."

"One day, I'll retire."

"What will you do then?"

"Not sure yet," I answer, honestly. I don't know. I don't have the time now to worry about such things.

"Of course you don't know. There will never be enough money in your pocket for you to stop. Such a sum doesn't fucking exist." *How much for 500zl? 1,000? How much do I have to buy for you to come? How soon?* She lights a cigarette. "You're just like my husband. And his friends. The same as they were in their thirties. Promising themselves to still find some time to retire, to live a little. After the first million. The first ten. Then twenty. Oh, how many times have I heard that target sum go up and up and up? Mouthing off about it, screaming about it, coked out of their heads, like football hooligans. There will be time! And you know where they are now? Their properties. Their whores. Their yachts. Still slaving away, still snorting, still swearing blind. Going so fast they can't stop, can't stop to think, just like you. Just like you, darling."

Listening, I write back: *Take something calming and go sleep*.

"Put that phone away," she demands. "You look... unnerved. It's unattractive."

"Well, I do apologise, but some things can't wait."

"None of my business, of course, not that you'll tell me what it's about," she chides, sitting down at the coffee table, picking up a bit of powder with the tip of the nail of her pinkie. "But you see? It's addictive, my white knight, my snowman, isn't it? You're so alone. Doesn't matter if the cash comes from property or currencies or this. I've seen it all. And then some."

"I'm on the outside. Counting. My lucky stars. They'll tell me when enough is enough," I tell her, trying to impress her with my erudition, Christ knows why.

I'm not begging just saying pls

I just want to talk.

Really need to talk to you

"My hubby said the same things. Ten? Ten years ago... There is nothing more important than your other half. Remember that. Nothing. Nothing beyond the milk of human kindness. In ten years' time, you'll be begging. Howling, honey. Begging strangers to sparc you some time. Sip some coffee with you. Play your PlayStation. You'll buy them a holiday. Maybe you're doing it already. Buying their time."

I write back, listening all along: *I'm not coming. Go sleep.* Then I look up, "What you say is interesting. But I really have to go now."

"No you don't. You want to listen. You are scared. You know I have a point," she says, her body taut again, expecting something to turn. "And remember, I just gave you forty thousand, for a bit of powder, so the least you can do is pay me some respect. Not that it's worth anything. My time, your time."

She's starting to act now, chaotically, badly, choking on the role. My phone pings, but it's an MMS this time, a photograph of Beata, naked, in front of a mirror. She's skinnier than I remember. Maybe it's the flash. Bones extending through the pale skin. Looks like something cut out of cardboard with a razor blade. Her breasts push forward, though, still vying for attention. Unnaturally large, as if photoshopped, pasted on from another body, a hyper-inflated joke.

I delete the message. I don't want to see it, hiding the phone in my pocket, walking over to the coffee table, grabbing her by the hair as she bends down to snort a line. With my other hand I stroke her neck. Her skin is damp. It smells sour. She trembles as I move closer, maybe from the coke, maybe from despair. I keep hold of her hair. Tight like a leash.

Don't know why I'm making these cheap, nasty moves. She belongs to someone else. Is paid for. Still, I'm tired, I'm hungry, desperate even. I have to do whatever is necessary to stop myself from driving over there, stop the text messages flowing, stop them scalding me.

My phone buzzes in my pocket.

She turns to me, and I remove my hand from her shoulder. There's a little bit of powder left on her top lip. She wipes it away with a sticky finger.

"You took up your own time," she mumbles. "And you'll never have it back. You drive that car of yours to fill a need none of us will ever manage. To get something you won't even know how to use."

"Smart talk," I hiss. "Smart, but you still don't know what to do with that."

"Same as some people don't know how to service women," she hisses back. The quieter she speaks, the more overpowering her aroma.

I kiss her, and she tastes the same: mint, sugar, sour grapes, bitterness, medicinal maybe. I try to get a taste for her, stop myself leaving, fuck and then go home, sleep, emptied out. Stop myself going mental.

"Wait a second," I say.

"You might not think so, but I am embarrassed," she says, sadly.

"Wait," I repeat.

"Now? Do you want me to turn down the lights?"

My pocket buzzes again.

02:54am

She opens her front door. Wearing an old, oversized black T-shirt. Her knees bent, her eyes looking sleepy, a little lost. A good act. Dear God, how good she is at that vulnerability shit.

"Hey," she says, eyes dropping to the ground.

Her hair is the colour of unripened lemons. The color she was born with. She brushes some strands behind her ear. I see her face, angled a little. Tilted. Another act, her eyes now on the floor, as if looking for a solution there, looking for a hint, but I know she knows. Knows perfectly. What comes next. What the outcome will be. Not that it matters. Not to the likes of her.

She's like a bayonet. The sharp tip of a rifle barrel. Pointed at me, same as it was back in that shopping mall, stood over me, silent or not. But she looked different then. Not quite herself. Something smudged about her, something otherworldly, maybe the clothes I hadn't seen before, maybe the light, or the time of day. Maybe my surprise at seeing here there, appearing out of the ether. She seemed less present. Less than now.

"Glad you changed your mind," she whispers, still not letting me past.

I wasn't going to come. I was going to bite my other hand, was going to get high with someone else's wife, was going to drive my car into some unborn child at a hundred and forty, at two hundred kilometres an hour, I was going to jump from the tallest bridge in town. All of that, any of it, would have been less obvious than this.

My mistake was thinking about it. Trying to choose. Pretending the film was over. The party done. The music no longer playing. This particular hole just cannot be filled. Cannot be lived without.

"I lost a good customer tonight," I tell her. "She'll never call again. I thought we could celebrate."

"I'm not sorry to hear that," she says, not smiling. "What do you want me to say now? That you shouldn't have?"

I know that look. Know that tone of voice. It all says – I should apologise, though I don't want to, don't know how. Make me. Force me. Explain it to me. Calm my nerves. Give me calm. Be calm, just for me.

She can hustle with the best of them. Crack men open and fry their guts in fifteen different ways. Make us hurt in a whole spectrum of styles. Make us mourn the kids we'll never have.

She's warped, wrong. A bad girl. A big, bad girl. Sculpted by some wicked witch like a swimwear model.

"Come in," she says, stepping back and pushing the door open a little more. She's just another one of the mistakes I've made today.

Maybe the biggest. A tall, shiny dagger of a mistake. Polished to a horrid, glaring shine. "Come on."

I don't move from the doormat. Looking her up and down. Falling. Falling into the inevitable, into a pit of godawful pain. I think back to the rich wife. Maybe she really will never call again. Find a different supplier of thrills. One she thinks less cute.

"Are we going to stand here till dawn?" she asks.

I've never ever been what people tend to term as 'in love'.

Never. Maybe I once wanted to be, but it didn't happen.

I go inside, closing the door quietly behind me. It's dark for a second, then she turns on the kitchen light. Leans against a wall. Becomes still.

"You said you wanted to talk," I remind her.

"Something's not right," she says. "Something is very much not right."

"Yep."

"You're here, in my place, at three in the morning."

"You extended the invite."

"I'm scared..." she says and I shrug. "In that restaurant, when you saw me, you looked like you wanted to kill me. And now you have the chance. No one saw you coming in or out. No cameras in my home."

"That's cute. And cheap. Awfully cheap."

"Because I am cheap. You had a cheap piece of ass, one that enjoyed the cheap things in life," she starts speaking more quickly, loudly. "I like handbags, shoes, high heels. As high as whores like them. Gold chains. Rings. All cheap and rough. You had a piece of ass who likes posting pictures of handbags and shoes on Insta. Who pouts for selfies. You wanted it and you had it. It suited you."

I say nothing, let her get the need to talk off her chest. I just wait for her to make eye contact. And wait some more while she carries on talking.

"You wanted to be seen with me. That's what it was about. I had more class, looked better than those whores, the ones your buddies actually paid for. I don't quite have their farmer daughter features.

Isn't that right? You wanted me because it gave you the feeling of luxury. Of achievement."

"Now why would you say such things?" I answer.

"So what was it about?" she asks, quieter again, wrapping her arms around herself.

I have never ever felt anything. Not once in my life. Apart from my first girlfriend, at art college. Before university. I remember her now, hell knows why. She had dark hair with a fringe and when she laughed her eyes squinted into two tight lines. She was sweet, too sweet to seem real. I felt something for her, for sure, some kind of attachment.

This doesn't apply to Beata. She has razor blades instead of skin, dangerous scales, cyanide instead of saliva. She's an addiction begging to be caught. Like a city full of vice compressed into a single person.

"I'm afraid," she whispers. "You look like you want to kill me again."

"It's dark in here. It's just a look."

I take my winter coat off and hang it up on the back of a kitchen chair. Knowing what's coming next.

"I felt alone."

"Coz you were alone. All your other beaus at home with their wives? Girlfriends? On business trips?"

She doesn't answer, just digests what I'm saying, letting it settle, feeling like she deserves it, or at least deserves to hear it.

"You know I am sorry. Things were supposed to be different."

"Different how?"

"I've no idea. I know I wanted to be happy, Kuba. Maybe there was something safe, in being your Russian trophy wife, for a while at least. And then..." I don't confirm or deny her theories. I can hear some cars racing past her windows, someone walking home from a party, singing quietly. Some other noise in the buildings, in the other apartments, a hive of human noises. People who will never know her, never know me, never even know we exist. "Or maybe I wanted to feel unhappy. Who knows?"

"Did you spend a long time rehearsing this gibberish before I came over? Is this what talking means to you?"

"Yeah. Insult me. Tonight, do it. Any way you like."

I take a step forward. She always smelt fine, finer than anything human had the right to smell. Maybe that was why. I can't stand the way most of the world smell, but I could inhale her. Especially the neck, the spot where her necklace is clasped together.

The girl from art college was called Maria. Then I got her pregnant. She didn't want to have an abortion. I remember how now – we'd had sex in her parents' bed. The same bed she'd been conceived in.

She got rid of it when I told her I would leave. It was blackmail. I left anyway, three months later. She tried to commit suicide. Didn't really know how. Hadn't prepared properly. She now lives in Scotland. With a husband and two kids. Sends me Christmas greetings, via text message, every Christmas. One of those things people send to all the contacts in their smartphones.

But now none of that matters.

"I've come to understand something," she says. "Maybe I wanted to simply tell you that I now understand." Something makes me take another step, ever closer. "This is so fucking hard."

She also takes a step forward, her bare feet audible on the kitchen tiles, toe nails painted a week ago.

"I'm tired of this," I tell her.

"I just understood that... and this is what I wanted to tell you, that when you do the kinds of things I do to others, you also do them to yourself."

"Who told you this? Some sort of guru? Coach?"

"Can you quit?"

"It's not the kind of complex theory you could have come up with by yourself."

"Stop it, asshole," she barks.

I keep looking at her, both of us motionless, forcing her eyes to focus on mine. Seconds go by that feel like hours, and then I approach, grab her by the waist, pull her to me, grab the bottom of her face, my fingers on her cheeks, pulling her face towards mine.

My other hand is already between her legs. She's not wearing anything beneath the T-shirt. I feel the stiff, stubbly hair, she hasn't shaved in a long while, maybe they all did indeed piss off back to their wives and girlfriends and whores...

Now I see where she is at. In what moment. The place she called me here from.

There's something honestly helpless about her. She's trying to catch her breath, like a fish washed up on a dry shore, someone who has lost their balance, but not quite fallen yet.

"Fuck me," she orders.

"Say it again."

"Fuck me now."

I once woke up in this very apartment, watching her dress in front of a mirror, for a moment, an utterly fleeting moment standing there completely naked, and then putting on her bra and panties. I remember saying to her: "How much do I need to fuck you, how much is it possible, and still not have my fill, not be complete. I would have to eat you whole. Kill and eat you. All of you."

She thought it was funny. Smiled out of the corner of her mouth, cocking her head a little. As if hearing a joke which was cute, but not funny.

"And?" she asks me. "Are we gonna fuck? Is that why you came here?"

I pull the T-shirt off her, the sweater and shirt off me, pull her close. Very close. She's trembling delicately, resonating, a broken clockwork mechanism inside her, keeping her going. She's wet, but I push her away, changing my mind when I turn and look towards her bed. The bedroom door is open, but I don't want to go there. I'm not going to lie down in that bed any more. It would be like being last in a long, long queue.

Even if she goes to see them, rather than having them here. It's a small apartment, a studio on Broniewskiego Street – helping them feel they are having sex with some teen student. Which is what she is, after all. Their 'call girl'. Just not one who studies or accepts hard cash for her services.

I pull off the rest of my clothing. Been losing control for a week now. I feel it now, tangibly, losing my grip. Slipping. Sliding away.

I drag her to the wardrobe, the full length mirror, so she can see herself. Then on my knees, I bury my face between her thighs, from behind. She moans. Quietly, then louder. I breathe deep into her. Grab her hips, pull her into my mouth. She begins to breathe quicker, to groan. I drink her in. Slowly. Too slowly. I've been thinking about this moment for too long. Couldn't help myself. I get up. Place her open hand on my belly, as if I wanted to grab her. I hold her like that for a moment. She stands up on the tips of her toes. Opens her legs and I enter her. She lowers herself onto me. I bury my nose between her shoulder blades. The skin there is cold, as cold as something taken straight from the fridge. She's dripping wet. She is now screaming, teeth clenched, as if in pain, as if wanting to run away. I put my fingers into her mouth. She bites down, convincingly. Her hand reaches behind, finds my hip. She scratches, and it hurts, and so I speed up, then slow down, many times over. Finally, I push so hard she screams the loudest, as if giving a loud burp. I pull out of her. Turn her towards me. Push her against the mirror. Her damp back sliding across the glass. She's breathing quickly. Smelling of fear and milk. She pinches my chest a couple of times, hard enough for it to hurt. Doesn't know what to do with her hands, with her whole body. Spits in my face. And again, but this time I open my mouth in time, swallowing her saliva, like a gift received. I then smack her face, as if in gratitude. Tell her not to do it again, but she does. Does the things she's not supposed to, the things no one gives her permission to do. She grabs my cock, starts moving her hand up and down, hard enough to hurt me, to strip me of pleasure. I slap her again, harder this time. With more conviction. My wounded palm hurts, but she doesn't stop. She's as cold and wet as a wild lake. I pull her down to the floor, her legs together, like in a coffin, lie down on top of her, with all my weight, enter her, first between the thighs, then inside her pussy. We're face to face, being the same height, and I put my bleeding hand over her mouth, not caring about consequences. About pain. She screams deep into the wound. Her eyes wide open. She always keeps her eyes open. I move my hand so the fingers cover them over. For a moment. She's slippery, wet all over, I have to push down on her even harder than before. As if I wanted to press and smash her into the carpet. I release. Climb off her. Lie on my back. She leaps upon me, puts me inside her, starts fucking herself with my body, her hands on my shoulders, my neck, round my throat, squeezing more from me, then she straightens, extends, looks like an evil tree, something growing new branches. She sings. Howls for a second. Sings. Without a voice. I grab her ass. This is her dog song. I clench my hands. Stopping her movements, lifting her up, then letting her head fall towards mine. This time she's the one to do it, to put a hand between our mouths. She looks and smells like an animal. A trapped animal, hunted and caught. I push inside her, again and again, fifty, two hundred strokes. Blocking her mouth. She tries to make a sound. Afraid I'm going to kill her. Rises a little, so I grab her breasts, as white as snow. She places her hands on mine, but then wrenches them free, as if holding hands was too nice, too sweet, even if mine are crushing her nipples right now. I throw her off me. Get up. Grab her by the hair. She kneels. I stand in front of the window, the one with the school outside. Dripping with our mixed up sweat. She takes my cock in her mouth and holds it there, paused, as if she knew I was recording this moment, saving it for later, for better or worse, and this is the worst, the very worst thing she can do, the least sensible act of all.

Nothing could be more stupid. Nothing at all.

After a while, she spits my cock out, slowly, kisses my stomach, places her cool cheek against it. I breathe deeply. Slowly. Short inhale, deep exhale. The way I do when I try to fall asleep.

She takes it in her mouth again, sucking on it, releasing saliva, lots of it, spitting it out, taking it in again, looking at what she is doing, then swallowing her spit again, her hands on my thighs. I can see a light, far off. And maybe, if I could last any longer, I would keep my eyes open, but everything takes as long as it takes. An addiction at a metabolic, a senseless level, costly, thieving time.

She says she loves my cock. Or something along those lines. I am no longer connecting.

A mistake. The worst of the worst.

Wanting someone. Flesh. The most base of mistakes. Wanting them so bad nothing could ever satisfy the hunger. No event, no touch, nothing that could happen. Wanting to be forever hard. To sleep forever.

I am thinking all these thoughts, but they mean nothing.

When I finally come, I try to scream quietly, to reduce my losses. For a second, I think she is not who she is.

She forces me to look down. Swallowing. Brushing her hair aside. Then she rises. I pull her close. She's breathing hard. Unevenly. She puts her hands around my back, awkwardly, the way one embraces an uncle at a family gathering.

I use her to cover up the view from her window.

In fact, I've used her to cover up everything.

"None of this matters," I think to myself. Then wonder why I'm making such excuses, even now. Awkward discipline. I only came over to fuck a babe, someone I used to know, someone who turned out to be worthless. Nothing other than a fine fuck's happened. Nothing's gone wrong. I'll be gone in a minute. We're done talking.

I should reach for my wallet now. Maybe.

"Come to bed," she whispers, kissing my shoulder.

I want to hit her again. Right through that window.

"That bed? That crowded bed?" I ask, fuming.

"Nobody else's been in it. Nobody comes here," she says.

"Liar."

She won't argue. Breathing calmly. Gripping me properly now.

Though it is winter, and far too early for dawn – it seems I see a sickly kind of pink beginning to glow over the playground outside, slowly seeping into her home.

08:50am

The blinds are drawn, in order to hold back as much of the light as possible.

"I've never been inside your home," she says for some reason.

204

"I don't see why you should have been."

"Well... men do ask their women to visit from time to time. You only ever came to my place, like visiting a call girl."

"Men. Women. I know what lifestyle mags say about all that. I read them waiting to see my dentist. You don't need to recite them back to me now."

"You live in Mokotow? Same place as before?"

"How do you know I live in Mokotow?"

"I remember. You once drove me there and made me wait outside. I asked if I could go in. It was after you took me out for supper."

"You couldn't go inside. You're not going to be able to go inside."

"I remember the address. Just not the door number."

"So what if you do? What the fuck is that supposed to mean?"

"Stop it. Stop being so mean. I should be the angry one. I know nothing about you. I knew nothing about you. You think that was easy? To be seeing someone you know as well as you do your local shopkeeper?"

"You know too much as it is."

"I know next to nothing. Just like everyone else. You're a terrible sort of person. But you know what's strange?"

"I shouldn't be here any more."

"Do you know what's odd?" she asks.

"What is odd?"

"I feel feminine when I'm with you."

"You shouldn't."

"I shouldn't. That's why it's odd. I don't know why this is. You make me feel... damaged. Used. All women feel this way."

"Seriously? Is someone paying you to punish me with this psychoanalytical bullshit? I've had too much. Going now. Bye."

"Then go. Get up and go. Go on."

I don't answer.

"Exactly. You're not gonna go because you want to fuck again."

I say nothing.

"Did you never think about going away? Starting over?

Somewhere warm, somewhere disconnected? Serving people coffee? Renting boats?"

"Everyone does that. Homeless people have such dreams. The boss of the national petrochemical works dreams them too."

"But not you? Not ever?"

"You're an idiot."

"It's as if you always thought that the only world which exists is this one, right here and now. Just this fucking terrible town."

"And what if it is?"

"What do you mean?"

"The things which do not concern us do not exist."

"You, on the other hand, are cheap. A cheap shot."

"It's all a cheap shot. Absolutely everything. In the end, it all stops existing, all vanishes. It's all shoddy and crap."

"You're shoddy and crap. Like some fucking philosophy undergraduate."

"Have you ever even once met a philosophy undergraduate? Seen one with your own eyes?"

"I know nothing about you."

"Why would you want to?"

"Because you're here, lying in my bed."

"You need to know everything there is to know about everybody who happens to find themselves lying in your bed?"

"I told you already. Insult me all you want tonight. I don't mind."

"I'm not."

"But you can. Do it."

"You're an idiot. An actress, reciting lines recycled from fashion magazines, marketed at women who live in big cities, women who end up thinking those lines are their very own thoughts. Their personal reflections."

"I don't know what I want. To see your ID. To know what your real name is."

"Why?"

"Maybe because we all look ridiculous in those photos. I would like to see you looking silly. To know I'm dealing with someone who is a human being."

"You are."

"I'm not so sure."

"I should go. Bye."

"Show me your driver's licence."

"Laters."

"It's the least you could do. Do something to prove to me I've had someone inside my home, inside me who is not a robot. Just a picture. I send you photos of my ass, tits, my pussy."

"I have to go."

"That's all I ask."

TUESDAY

6:20pm

I remember those two.

When you haven't slept for seventy-two hours, everything begins to change. Sounds vanish beneath the skin of your surroundings, beneath the floors, the paint on the walls. Colours take on odd shades, paler, weaker. Everything moves more slowly. It's necessary to adapt, adjust to these new circumstances. To change tempo.

A food joint, Riverside District. I have the impression that if I close my eyes, then open them after a moment or two, I will find myself elsewhere. The place is absolutely full of people. They're all making noises. The most noise is made by a group of kids, some kind of party. A birthday or something. I'm trying to swallow whatever it was I ordered. Some of my customers are in here, making eye contact. Making it meaningful, but brief. A business transaction. They're off duty now, not dealing with me on that level, having conversations, after work, talking with or about their kids, their wives, friends, longing to look at their phones instead.

I find kids odd. Like they're not quite human. Or human, but modified, shrunken, insane. I couldn't function as a father. It's like having a pet that talks. A unique sort of hostage situation.

Besides, what on earth is the point in having more kids? We're all so hideously imperfect.

I look at those two, certain I know them from somewhere.

My mother rang again, half an hour ago. Asking what the weather was like in Hong Kong. Singapore, Mum, I corrected her. I'm in Singapore. She apologised, but then instantly excused the mistake by moaning about how much travelling I do. I told her it was sunny, though overcast. Right. That's what she said... Right. She said Dad had eaten something, takeaway, and caught food poisoning. Right. That my sister was still trying and failing to get pregnant. Right. OK. Fine, Mum. Gotta go. Yeah.

I remember those two.

Today is a special day. I look down at the phone on the table next to my plate and realise what it is. The 23rd of December. Tomorrow is Christmas Eve. She said something about that. The streets choked, like sick arteries, people like diseased cells, the city choking on itself. Waiting for the evening. Waiting to catch its breath. For those who litter it during the day to go to bed. Warsaw does not like itself in the daytime. It looks naked and ashamed, like an old, faded woman.

The melody which has been haunting me for days has risen to the surface. Pounding my head like a migraine. I try to eat, but whatever it was I ordered is already cold. I try to think back to the last Christmas I spent with someone other than myself, the last time I received any gifts, just to keep my brain occupied.

I can remember their faces. They're sitting in a booth with two very young-looking girls, their hair unnaturally straight, their shoulders slumped, their looks downloaded from the internet. The girls are talking and the two of them are absorbed by listening to them. Eating slowly, though taking big bites. Without taking their eyes off me. I now know where I know them from.

They're the two who were in that chubby fucker's apartment. Playing Polish hip hop, watching funny films on YouTube, waiting for their best friend to find the money to pay for the stuff that they were all so very much looking forward to sharing.

I look away. Let them stare. My food's gone cold. A kid has gone off like a fire alarm, howling to high heaven. Three nights without sleep feel like the world has been covered with an odd sort of blanket, one that doesn't quite cut down on sounds, just modifies them, distorts them somewhat. Too tight to move, too hot to lose consciousness.

Pazina enters. Walks into a kid who bounces off her skinny legs, falls under a table and starts crying. Pazina apologises. Comes over. Sits. Takes my plate and starts finishing whatever it was I ordered.

"It's gone cold," I tell her. She doesn't seem to notice. "Don't look in the direction of those two idiots sitting over there, with the girls."

"Why did you do it? What the hell for?" she asks, chewing slowly. I shrug, helpless.

"Did we arrange to meet here for personal therapy reasons? Paz. We're grown-ups. We can handle mistakes."

"Fucking hell. You do what you do, only to then call me up, for no reason other than I'm the only person you can actually have a conversation with?"

"What?" I ask, trying to process what she's saying. "People talk. People need to talk, Paz."

"What is so special about the bitch? So many others like her around. Cute, educated, hungry for cash, for fucking, for making tiny, insignificant scenes. What makes her different, Kuba? A birthmark? Is she clairvoyant? Does she shit amber?"

"Nope. The sex is alright though," I smile.

"Sex is easy. Everyone can fuck fine. We start young and learn from the internet. It's not hard."

"Why are we here?" I ask, wondering that myself. "To discuss social habits?"

"Normal people meet for normal reasons. To talk, about anything. Talk about the things that matter."

"Normal people. Normal things. Indeed," I say, leaving that hanging.

She's making a mess of things. I know it. I can sense it already.

Paz takes a sip of my coke. A heavily tattooed waiter comes over, ears pierced with big, plastic things, his gaze dull, his voice thin.

"What can I get you, miss?"

"Wine. Red. And don't make me wait half an hour, like the last time," she says and then looks at me, wide eyed. "Christ, you look like you've just come out of hospital."

"Me?"

"Pale as fuck. Christ, I told you to keep away from her. Told you

213

she spelled trouble. You need someone you can trust. Trust to do what is wise. Or at least sanc."

I'm not looking at their table, but I can feel them looking at ours. Looking, just because they have nothing better to do. Their girls chattering away, about shopping, about who went where at the weekend, who screwed who and why and where, or talking about shoes, or about which girlfriend is getting the most action right now, and whether any of them need saving from themselves, etc., etc., etc.

The youth of today – posting and reposting, endlessly, posturing, painting themselves all sorts of vile colours. They are the living, talking forecasts of the coming fall of western civilisation. Kids who have no idea how to invest and multiply their parents' monies. Like our recently deceased furniture fatso. Unable to do anything other than dream, and dream in poor taste. One of the girls at their table, wearing a backwards baseball cap and a black hoodie, turns to look in my direction. She freezes for a second, only her mouth, chewing relentlessly, in motion. Her eyes are large, pretty, hollowed out.

"Tiny's vanished," Pazina tells me. "No one's seen him since Sunday. His phone's dead. They say the club will keep opening, but for how long?"

"It's doing fine. Why are you telling me this?"

She looks at me very carefully, without concealing it, but I'm too tired to go playing hide and seek, feeling overwhelmed with boredom and actual worry.

"Did you do anything to him?" she asks, evidently fearing my reply.

The waiter brings her wine. Walks away, also tripping on a kid. The kid starts howling and the waiter apologises profusely.

"Do what to him?"

"I don't fucking know what it is you do to people you think are not doing what you want them to do. You know I never normally ask."

"You've been making up for lost time in that respect of late."

"I know this girl, Ewa, a friend of mine, the mother of his child. Just tell me he's not buried in some forest or floating downriver to the Baltic, cut up in bits and packed into carrier bags. That's all I want to know."

"You think we do such things?" I ask, trying to act incredulous.

214

For a moment, we sit in silence, like a couple trying to avert an argument. She pokes about the remains of my food with a dirty fork, thinking.

"Maybe that's what it was about, that he has a child," she says, looking at all the kids running about the place. I respect Paz for a number of things, and her ability to change the subject is one of them.

"It's just an excuse," I tell her.

The two guys and their girls get up to go. They walk past my table. Trying their best to pretend like we haven't noticed each other.

"Maybe you're right," Pazina says. "But normal people need normal relationships. Need to have others close. Skin needs skin. All animals are soothed by touch, being stroked. Cuddled."

"Where did you get such notions from? 'Normal people'? You want to suddenly assimilate? Breed? Establish family units? Cook oatmeal? Go on. I double and triple dare you. Plenty of men will buy into this experiment. Some farmer or such."

"Yeah, I'd like to try living a normal life. I think about it. Before going to sleep. Is that a bad thing? Uncool? Falling in love with a whore, is that good, is that cool?"

"Who's in love with a whore?" I ask, lost.

"You didn't touch Tiny? Is that right?"

"Let's get out of here."

No, I haven't touched him. If someone else has, though, it would be worth finding out. But not yet. In a moment. There are more important things I need to take care of. A few customers to call on before my flight leaves. I have to satisfy their needs, let them have their fill, so that they don't go looking for other suppliers while I'm away. They have little or no idea how many others would love to step into my shoes. With wares that are cheaper and almost as good as mine. I'm bound to lose a few. But I have to go.

I think I can sell on all the stuff Uncle gave me for safekeeping. It's not going to be a problem. I'll pay him off. Then wait for Thursday.

I wouldn't have such problems if I cut my stuff the way all others do. In 90% of cases, you have no idea what you're putting up your nose, shoving up your sinuses, absorbing into your blood. Cocaine, the actual stuff you're paying for, the substance made of coca leaves grown somewhere on the other side of the world, picked by terrorised, starved locals, crushed into a paste and baked in microwave ovens, is at most 10% of what you get. The rest is crap. Lidocaine, to help numb your gums. Nitroglycerin to make your heart beat faster. Amphetamines or mephedrone to help you feel the kick you're after, to stop you sleeping, to turn that beating heart of yours into a hard, alien-feeling fist. Crushed lightbulbs to sting your sinuses, to help the shit enter your bloodstream quicker. Glucose or creatinine for the colour, the consistency, the weight.

You never know what you're gonna get. If you started snorting more than five years ago, you've never ever had a taste of anything near real fine cocaine. Poland is a country where advertising agencies sell roof tiles and fencing to villagers, a country of motorways lined with litter, a kingdom of sandals, moustaches and amphetamines. All drugs in Central Europe are substandard, faked, fucked. Even the expensive shit is still shit.

The fact that I sell the purest coke you can get in this godforsaken town is a question of taste. Of good manners. Something you're raised with, maybe even bred with. A certain sense of decorum, even when it comes to illegal substances.

Not that it's somehow shockingly pure. Otherwise, I'd never make a profit. But I don't cut it with speed, nitroglycerin, wall plaster, crushed sleeping pills.

"Hey!" Pazina shouts, clicking her fingers right in front of my face. For a second, she appears as a smudge, blending into the background, but now she's back in focus. "Go home. Please."

I won't, I'm sure of that. I might just faint instead.

I have to keep going though. My holidays are coming up, my chance to finally get some sleep. Any sleep. It will be indescribable relief. I keep looking at photos of the hotel room reserved for me. Imagining that the bedsheets will smell of nothing. No one. That the air con will be noiseless, though it will be turned up high, a little too high, the room cool instead of comfortable. That the heavy curtains will be drawn, saving me from questions of whether it is day or night, here or there.

We go outside. I approach the car, pull leaflets for local go-go bars and saunas from behind its windscreen wipers, holding them like playing cards for a second.

It is dark, but the city knows evening hasn't begun yet. It's angry, tired, from working all day, all year.

"We're not good friends, you know," Pazina states, once we are both inside. "We're actually bad friends."

"Maybe you have a point."

"We're the worst kind of friends."

"Maybe..."

"You fail to grasp even the most basic of principles," she says, putting her hand on the door handle. "You don't have to drive me anywhere, I need the walk."

"I grasp them alright. I know what normal people are like. What they want. I just don't get them. They're nothing to do with me. I wouldn't know what to do with them, even if I tried."

"Exactly. This is where we misunderstand each other, Kuba. Where we will always differ."

"Maybe so," I answer, exhausted by this exchange.

She looks at me for another moment, with something which feels like patronising pity, like she was my older sister. Now I remember where it was I celebrated Christmas the last time. Four years ago, with my sister and her husband, in their apartment. The guy is a slightly overweight manager, partial to pastel shirts, convinced he's on a decent salary. We watched a bit of TV, saying nothing. Their kid burnt his hand. No need to go looking for a doctor. I spent the night on their couch, watching the tree lights twinkling, unable to sleep. Something I ate disagreed with me. Or maybe I was allergic to their dog. I left in the middle of the night without waking anyone. She hasn't called me since.

"You do know he's been released?" she says, then opens the door. "They mentioned it on the news. Be careful."

"I'm going far, far from here, remember?"

I look in the rear-view mirror and see them standing there,

smoking, looking at my car. One of them checks his phone. They look like they're not right in the head, like they're slightly deranged. One of the girls waves her hand in protest, saying something, but the two of them do not seem to be paying her any attention.

9:15pm

"Don't worry yourself, buddy," he says. "All is grand."

He's perspiring like a racing pig. Soaked with sweat. Must have started on the hard stuff days ago. His eyes like smashed windows, jagged and empty. And that harsh Polish gob, a face which looks like some computer simulation representing a modern farmer, thirty years old and already past it, sick, sweaty, gone. He's breathing, hard, fast, loud, like all his life he's been on the run, like he's already fought off two heart attacks. He keeps throwing his big, fat hands up, trying to say something with them, though not sure what, not sure if he actually wants to have anything to say with them, or if he just wants to wave at invisible enemies.

He's a totally gone coke addict. Beyond rescuing. He has to top up every day. If his home was on fire and he had to think of what to save first – his kid or his stash of powder – there would be no competition. It has to be said, the most committed coke heads don't make for good customers. They're annoying. Lost. Chaotic. Usually heavily in debt. And never with any cash actually on them.

"It's grand, motherfucker, grand all the way down, it's just that I, you know, am in waiting, in flow, process, got some boys owing me dough, heavy dough, wholesalers, days away, hours maybe, they're coming, bringing cash, cold, hard, pure cash, sonny, so you know, it's a bit tense, at the last hour, but you know... Selling fashions. Fashions always sell."

I can tell just from the way his tongue races that things are far from well. Someone showed me his music videos on YouTube. I don't know which ones, don't remember how many I sat through. They've uploaded dozens. The coke fuelling productivity. All hard-man poses, T-shirts and baseball caps proclaiming "Informants Die" and "Don't talk to cops". Waving warning fingers at the camera, reminding listeners to remember those who, behind bars, are waiting for deliveries of instant coffee and *Men's Fitness*. They're just pawns in a giant crowd, wannabes, small time hoodlums, bad boys from half-decent homes, or from hoods where no one has a full set of teeth or all their wits about them. A few decent rappers, but only as guests, not actually keen on showing their asses to millions of Polish schoolkids who watch their vids. I thought the titles of their songs mildly amusing: *Rules to remember, Brother to brother, Street testimony, Silence when the time comes*.

This particular sweating piece of pork is called Sebastian, though they call him Percent – for all the profits he makes from his various deals. He used to be an athlete, but then switched to garment manufacturing and the music which was meant to sell his wares. Half the kids in my home town wear his garments. They make serious money, but most of it goes on drugs and parties in places such as the one we find ourselves in now.

His art is meant to educate. To develop moral fibre, teach set rules, helping the needy, maximising personal potential. For kids who only know real life through their broadband connections, he's all the guru they need. They see him in those clips, working out, lifting up kids who belong to his friends, the ones behind bars. He's the one who inspires youth all over Poland to use prison slang, as they stand around waiting to buy bubblegum from school vending machines.

"Two tens on credit and all will be hunky dory, coz it always is, my man," he says grinning at something just to the side of my right ear.

Some guy comes near, a small, awkwardly moving trouble-maker, face the colour and texture of fresh clay, the eyes permanently surprised at the state the world around him is in. His small, roughly shaved head contains a few ideas and a few more words to go with them. It's all he needs to move, eat and function. There are street guys like Uncle, with some substance to them, some drive, people who deserve respect, because that's the last thing they want from you or anyone else. And then there are people like this monkey, people who must not be trusted, unable to ever repeat correctly what is said to them, much less do what is expected.

"How you doing, bro?" Percent says to him. The guy mumbles something in response, barely audible, much less comprehensible. Then he turns to me. "So, how's it gonna be?"

"Your last lot was on credit too," I remind him.

"Yeah, and, what, you think this is some permanent state of affairs, some kind of glitch of epic proportions, come on!"

Maybe it ain't. Maybe he wants it to be cool. But here we are, in a shitty go-go bar of his choosing, and I know he's not left it for three days, blowing all his money, and some of mine, on drinks for the dancers, vodka for his buddies, the food they have delivered in, on ganja. Something stinks here, something in and around him, something reeks. Of rotting puke, of dirt. Him. After three days of not washing, everyone smells the same.

I don't know what people see in places like this. Some of my competitors are hanging around, idiots, gold dripping from them, watches on show, girls on each arm, smoking their own profits. This place is just loaded with idiots. Only the girls, treating all men like cash-cows, seem to have any sense – women the punks in here treat the same as or worse than the luncheon meat they had for breakfast, like old plastic supermarket bags – only they understand anything of what is going on, know you have to get what's yours and smile, looking people right in the eyes.

Places like these are already museums. A show of traps. I could lead guided tours of how to avoid them, what to do, what not to, and how I navigate them.

People do what I do in order to earn substantial incomes. For most people, money helps them shine for others. A bauble. A cause for joy. They want to plate their lives in gold, cover up their pasts, the times when they had nothing, when they were dead meat. They make money to burn money. To show disdain. They make money to get their revenge on those who said "No" to them in the past. There is nothing more colourful and at the same time pathetic than a barbarian with a platinum credit card.

And this club, these sofas covered in easy-wipe plastic, these women with their upgraded tits and painted-over cellulite, these watered down drinks that cost a hundred each, this stench rising up from bodies that feel nothing and want everything, impoverished bodies covered in overpriced perfumes – this club is a cave of barbarians. An ogre's paradise.

The first thing I learnt when I started dealing was never to leave a cent of my own money in their tills.

Another guy approaches Percent. A huge, lumbering caricature, pumped full of steroids and cheap beer.

"Yo, yo, yo, sit down, how you doing?" Percent howls.

"I need to get paid for that thing," the monster says.

"This is Kuba, a good pal of mine," Percent says, pointing at me enthusiastically.

"Listen, the others, they're putting pressure on," the monster mumbles.

"Sit, sit, have a drink, guy, relax. I'll order you something, take the weight off your feet, brother."

The ogre sits. Perched on the edge of one of the sofas, hands on his knees, looking at me as if considering whether to kill and grill me or not.

"So, right then, what will it be? Tomorrow, sunshine. Tomorrow. You see, Gobby is a good guy, but he's behind bars, so we're trying to collect some dough for him and the kids. Been put away now for a stretch, needs representation, got caught manning the scales. Red handed. Had previous on top, you know how it is. You know, you know, you know, right? I don't need to explain to you!"

"If they caught him with his scales, that means he's a fucking idiot," I comment.

A waitress approaches. I ask for a water. He'll pick up the tab. Meanwhile, he's digesting what I've just said, how that affects the dynamics with the ogres, how the game will pan out now.

"I know some solid faces got your back," he says to me, straight-to-video gangsta style. "I understand everything, but for fuck's sake, g's gotta talk! Tomorrow? Coz I need the stuff tonight. The party's on, you get me. Our last record went platinum. Tomorrow, I will get all the dosh. And then I'll call you."

"See ya," I smile and rise, turning towards the exit. The DJ starts playing some 80s hit, which is all they have in places like this. I walk past a girl taking her bra off on top of a podium. She's not here, her mind on the nail-polishing business she wants to open in some shopping mall or what she's going to wear to her sister's kid's christening.

"Wait, wait!" Percent races after me. "Come back."

"You got the eight thou you owe me?"

Not tonight. I don't have it in me. It's not even about the fact that this punk has nothing on him other than attitude and clothes he had designed by someone with actual taste. It's that he thinks everything can be skated over, everything sorted by sheer force of his personality. That anything's possible, just as long as he wills it, as long as he is resilient, determined, a champion. Meanwhile, he's not even the coolest overgrown kid on his bit of the block. He's a fucking clown. I'm too tired not to want to tell him straight. Even though he's a customer, and the customer is always... I'm sure his card is marked and that if he keeps throwing money that is not his around, someone will have his knee caps for souvenirs. Me, for example. A fact which really does appear to be beyond his ability to comprehend.

"We work in the same business, buddy," he pleads.

"News to me, punk."

"Yeah, alright, I know. I know, just sit down, come on. Listen."

His pleading is making me want to faint. Vomit, then faint. I have the impression that everyone else has already told him to scram. I look around the club, a few faces I don't know make eye contact, then quit, like they're watching us but don't want me to know that. I look into his eyes now and know for sure. He's empty. Out. Past the point of no return.

When I started selling, I saw dozens of pricks like him. I see his eyes wander, then he looks down at his phone, scratching his head. Then looks at me again, then back at his enormous pal, then back at the phone.

"Alright, we'll work something out. Wait a second."

"What for?" I growl.

"Wait a second, please," he says, dropping the showbiz gangsta act.

After three sleepless nights, closing the eyes is like falling into a well. Things are audible, but they sound far off. The air turns ice cold. Shapes lose all definition.

She sent me a few more messages. *I don't know if we did the right thing... we should talk, I think... Worst thing is I want more... we're the same, I know it, the same spirit.*

Fool. We're not the same. Not a single cell of what constitutes me is anything like the cells which constitute her. It's a complete accident that we both have ears, lips, heads set at the same height. An accident of cosmic design.

I never wrote back. No more pathetic fuck-ups. Maybe we all have our addictions, our Achilles heels. That we can never be complete if we don't identify and battle those vulnerable spots. It's as natural as breathing. This pursuit. This war against weakness.

Still, it's annoying that I can't just delete the messages, can't wipe her completely. I feel ashamed, indecent, as if I was unable to stop picking my nose in public or biting my nails.

Indecent, completely. I turn my phone to silent, though she hasn't written at all today. Argentina. That is where I will quit thinking about her. Find someone else to fuck silly. Stop thinking – full stop. Bedsheets, air con, curtains. I will finally get some sleep.

"Come," he suddenly instructs me and rises. "Come with me."

"Where the fuck to now?"

"What do you mean – where? To get the readies!"

He gets up without looking at his mates, and I follow. We go past a stage, some girls up on it, then along a bar holding up a couple of bored, lazy-looking guys sporting leather jackets and white running shoes. Now the music has shifted gear, from the 1980s to the 1990s. We go outside. Percent looks around, as if trying to recover his bearings. Finally, he takes a deep breath and his face takes on focus, sharp and present – for a second I have the impression that he's not that much of a prick after all, that he has something going for him, that the words he keeps spitting, the lyrics, are actually a dream he is living for real.

It's the city which is sick. I can feel it, wanting to vomit, sensing the pulsing of a dark, destructive narrative beneath the sidewalks, just waiting to seep out, to poison the water table, to crack all the roads, melt the asphalt, cover everything in a thick layer of dung.

I follow him. There's another club next door, empty for now, but at weekends it's always full of screaming teens, in from out of town via trains or borrowed cars, awkward-looking idiots in shirts too tight for their skinny chests, their hair gelled to hell. He walks in, greeting the bouncer, whispering something, then walking on. He's now looking round, nervously, I can sense it in the way his spine seems to tense up. He glances all over the place, like a dog sniffing enemy territory.

I spot them straight away. Huddled over a small table, smoking a hookah pipe, drinking vodka, a bottle in an ice bucket between them. Four of them. Faces from a local gang who used to keep it simple: extortion, smuggling. Now they're running brothels, gambling machines, poker tournaments. Guys like Percent are next to nothing to them – toys, dancing teddy bears. Dressed in shirts and suits, they'd look like any other middle-aged guys, having a drink after work, if it wasn't for the way their eyes pierce, like butchering knives, like sabres. He walks up to them, his steps semi faltering, a mistake. A major mistake.

"Hiya," he announces.

The greeting is half-formed. He's spooked. Out of his element, a new employee on his first day at work, unsure which desk may or may not be his.

"Where did you fucking pop up out of?" one of them says.

"Easy, easy now, all is well," Percent says, pointing to me. "This is Kuba."

They don't look up. Not one of them. A round of vodka shots is poured, none for us.

"Listen, there's this thing, you know Gobby is behind bars, trying to sort him out, the legals," he says, awkwardly. "We want to send him some help, you know, he's in there for the sake of the firm."

"And?" a voice asks from within the huddle.

"And Gobby is a fine kid, and...." He pauses, looks back at me

224

and winks. I now see I had starting giving him too much credit. He's just a broken bit player, and would be even if he didn't stick so much blow up his fucking nose.

"Screw Gobby," one of the gang says, stretching, his joints cracking like an old toy. Percent catches a breath. He wasn't expecting this turn of events. Wasn't expecting shit.

"Where you from?" a fat bald fucker asks me, his chest wrapped in a worn jumper, a heavy diving watch wrapped round a trunk-like wrist.

"Mokotow," I reply.

"You're also on this charity drive for... what's his name?"

Percent looks at me, eyes scared again. I look at him, without flinching. Time is being wasted again. My phone buzzes, and keeps buzzing. I check it, wondering why it always interrupts at the worst possible moment. Pazina. I told her not to bother me.

"Kuba's my guy, sorted, known him for years," Percent mumbles over my silence, putting his arm on my shoulder. Then he pulls it back, as if embarrassed. Coughs. I look around, tiredness gripping me instead – flames done graffiti-style up the black walls, a couple of barmen busy behind the glass bar, getting ready for later. Seats upholstered in fake black leather, surrounding tables made of glass tops and legs of plaster, shaped like naked women. The floor is slippery, black, looks like it is ready to be washed clear of blood or sperm or other such fluids.

"I asked if you too are begging for your prison boy?" I hear again.

"I know him," someone else says, nodding my way. "Bielany crew."

A typical village warthog, getting rich off city punks, tourists and students . His neck as thick as my waist, his wallet, once he pulls it out, just as impressive. He looks up at Percent.

"My kids say your fashion line is doing a roaring fucking trade. How much do you need?"

"Wait," says the guy in the worn sweater. "You didn't answer, Mr Biclany. Are you part of this charity run?"

"No," I say, my head perfectly still. "I don't give a hoot about Gobby."

The guy smiles, in spite of himself.

"You came here for the crack? Boring round your neck of the woods? Why don't you two join us?"

I see Percent's neck flinch, like someone stabbed him in the ribs. Not a good sign. Not for a coke head like him. I sense him looking at me to take the lead.

"Thanks for the offer, gents. Percent, I gotta go."

He looks at me, unable to comprehend what it is I've just said and done. The bald guy is still holding his open wallet out.

"Two grand. For the lawyer, and some good, coffee, mags, you know... And the kid. There's a kid."

"See ya," the bald guy says to me, his hand gripping the wallet tight.

I turn to walk away, a smile playing on my face, and then see what I do not want to see. Not now. Not ever. Not that I ever had a choice.

"Lads, good evening!" Dario howls, strolling right towards us.

I smile too. Nothing else to be done. He is swaying, as fucked as he was last week. He's wearing a clean white shirt, hanging out of his designer blue jeans. His glasses are different. Less dark. He walks towards me and now I realise I was wrong. He's not drunk. Not one bit. His gait steady, his purpose clear and I remember now. Remember what I felt like back in Piotrek's restaurant. A cold and sure sort of terror.

He stops next to me, not even noticing Percent, looks down at the wallet the bald guy is holding out. I think I remember the guy's nickname now. Finger. That's what they call him. A known face. The name nothing to do with his bald head, as bald as any thumb. He was one of those who, not that long ago, enjoyed unleashing a trend for cutting off people's fingers. Fingers of fuckers who didn't pay, like Tiny, like Percent, like all the other kids that people the world of adults. Dario's smile vanishes, replaced by a thin grimace. The eyes are the same though. Swallowing everything whole. Eyes that swallow and then incinerate everything with a white hot fire. Dario smells like winter, like the coldest sort of night. Then those eyes turn on me, "Kuba!"

I hold my hand out, still smiling.

"Sit down," he says.

"I was going. Gone, actually."

"You weren't. Again?" he asks. "You were staying."

"Gobby. You've heard of the bust, right, we're collecting funds, to help..." Percent butts in, unhelpfully, but Dario gives him a look, the glasses making his eyes bigger and bigger as he stares and stares until Percent shuts the hell up.

"Funds, funds," Dario says, shaking his head, but Percent is getting the shakes, and has to try his luck one more time.

"Well, you gotta help a brother in need," he shrugs, trying on a weak smile.

"You gotta shit," Dario says, sitting down with the others. The bald guy slides a glass towards him, fills it with vodka. Dario puts a hand out to indicate he is on duty today and cannot indulge. Then looks up at me.

"Kuba, so good to see you in here tonight, of all the bars in Warsaw. Very good. Reminded me of something. A man has to come home and clean up. Nobody can do that for us. I have a little question to pose to you," he says, not looking at me but at Percent. "Kuba, is this boy with you?"

I don't answer, wondering what the hell Dario is doing here, hanging out with this particular crew. On Sunday, I saw him with Piotrek, who is not exactly on cordial terms with this lot. I'm trying to scan the situation, fathom possible plans. Looking down at Dario, I nod in answer to his question.

"Actually, we're trying to work out what the fuck both of you are doing here," the bald guy says, his wallet long gone back in his pocket, his free finger waving in my general direction.

"That's clear to me," Dario says, smiling. "But first, I'd like a tea. Tea with heaps of lovely sugar."

Percent is doing a subtle jig next to me. I can't help looking as a big, thick vein, as thick as a power cable, emerges on the side of his temple.

"Sweet tea," Dario says, looking up directly at Percent. His face is the colour of granite. Finally, one of the others gets up and waddles over to the bar. Dario then pulls out his phone and starts flicking his fat finger across its screen, as if looking for something.

Then looks back up at Percent. The gaze of a predator studying a piece of living, breathing supper. Then, once his hollow eyes are done feasting, he turns to me, "Kuba, have you ever lost anything? I bet you have. Keys. Phone. Your way in this world."

"Nope," I cut him short. "Not once. Others do the losing."

"Indeed," he counters, unimpressed with my answer. "We'll come back to that, though. Give me a minute. Let me catch my breath, and I'll explain everything."

The blond guy who wandered off in search of tea actually comes back with a thin-walled glass of the stuff. Sets it down in front of Dario. Lights a cigarette.

"They call me Percent. Mokotow," Percent says, extending a hand towards Dario.

"He's collecting for a boy behind bars," Finger adds. "I just don't know if it's one of our boys. Adam knows him."

"Indeed," Dario nods, sipping his drink.

If Percent was just a wee bit smarter, if my stuff hadn't turned his shitty brains to total mush, he would have got the message. Would have taken a few steps back, smiled and backed the fuck out of there slowly. Having apologised for the mistake. When it still wasn't too late to back out.

Unfortunately, Percent is now living inside a rap music video. Something none of the gentlemen round the table we are still standing and staring down at have ever seen. His fantasy has just come crashing into their reality and come right apart, into tiny pieces. A fantasy Percent was riding in without wearing a seat-belt.

"Gobby..." he says once again, like a magic password.

Dario takes out his automatic, cocks the hammer, aims it at Percent's head, his elbow resting next to the glass of sweetened tea. Nobody else moves. Percent's eyes widen. But nothing other than that.

"You had something, lad, but now you don't," Dario hisses.

"Fucking hell... hey... but everything here..." Percent tries to find the right scrap of sentence, but he can't, his brain is like a broken drum inside a washing machine, tumbling bits of broken language, the simplest gestures, blurred instincts.

"You had it and now it's gone, you little prick," Dario says, sweetly. "You had it and now it is mine. You will have to pay dues. You will have to thank me, boy, that I don't put a hole in your fucking head. You will now say: 'Thank you very much, Mr Dario, thank you.' Say it, you shit."

"Dario, wait," Finger interjects.

He wants to extend a hand and lower the pointed weapon, but Dario shoots his free hand out, grabbing Finger's face, hard, then shoves it back. Finger falls.

"You come in here, trying to squeeze serious fellows for silly money, you fucking smack head, you come here with some runaround, interrupting serious folks," Dario seethes. "Now I should get rid of you. I really should. Nobody would mind. Nobody would care. You know why? People don't talk about what it is I do. People know."

Percent is not used to having guns pointed at him. To being talked to this way. Talked into an early grave. Dario lowers the hammer on his pistol.

"Tomorrow, someone will pay you a visit. Will ask something. In your offices. And you know what the answer will be. Now, fuck off, you fucking fashion victim."

Percent doesn't seem to be breathing. I take a step back. Dario is not looking at me, his focus still on Percent, but he notices.

"Kuba, sit. Sit still. You're not going anyfuckingwhere. While you, you punk, you can fuck right off. You fuck off to wait for my friends to arrive. And then you know what to tell them?" Percent has no idea. Frozen stiff with ignorance. "You tell them – 'Dear sirs, of course, dear sirs. Twenty percent, dear sirs. Maybe even thirty. Of course, of course. Will you have a drink of vodka, gents?' That is what you will tell them, bastard. You will ask them if they are thirsty for your vodka."

Percent is still baffled, but his head is nodding in agreement. Trying to get this over and done with. Which it will never ever be.

Dario rises and his gun rises with him. Glowing black. He stands there, the gun held steady. Nobody says a thing. Those who can, don't need to. The rest no one cares about. Percent forgets all about me, starts walking back, trying not to bump into the fine furniture. Dario doesn't have to do a thing. Whatever he chooses it will be right. And even if it ain't, nobody would want to correct him. Nobody would bother trying. This city is his doormat. Bent over backwards for him, while he does what he does, without even thinking if he still cares about it.

"Right," I hear Percent say, still backing away while I look at the gun pointed in his direction. "All good. All is good."

"Say one more word, you fuck, and I will pull this fucking trigger. Do it."

I hear Percent's footsteps fading. Then I smile. The world dissolving, my sleepless brain unable to keep up. Even Dario, his gun soft and cartoon-like for a moment. I decide I need to sit down. Dario lowers the pistol, places it on the table next to his phone. Takes a sip of the tea. Lowers that too. His giant eyes pinned to mine.

"How was it all not meant to go to hell, Kuba? Tell me. How is it all meant to work when tiny pricks like that are able to walk around, unchecked, turning this world into a fucking circus?"

I watch his mouth warp into a grimace, but I don't quit smiling.

"Nothing to do with me," I tell him.

"Did I say that it was?" Silence. It takes its time. Something flashes before my eyes, bouncing off those flames on the walls, off the lenses in Dario's glasses. I watch him put the tea down. "Shall we have a chat?"

"Why not," I say without asking.

I want to hear what he thinks he's got to say. I want to know what it is he expects from me. I have no other choice, so I might as well listen.

"I've heard good things about you. I heard you're really just in it for the money."

"Everyone is in it for the money."

Finger is looking at me. I understand now that they are his people. He could send them to McDonald's for burgers, if he wanted to.

"Well, yeah. You know some things, hear others," he says, cryptically, looking at me. My reality is now limited to his face.

I try not to get sucked in by those oversized eyes, focusing on his skin. It's as smooth as latex.

"Where from?" I press.

"Piotrek. He said you can be trusted. And if people think that about you, it means they tell you things. They tell you because they trust you to keep your trap shut."

"You hear, and then you forget... Actually, I'm feeling rather thirsty."

"Seba, bring Kuba a tea from me."

Seba looks at Finger, who looks back without making any moves at all. Seba instantly gets up and heads back for the bar.

"Things get lost. People get lost. Vanish. But then sometimes they can be found again," Dario says. "I was once, I can reveal, in the town of Czorsztyn. It is a very pretty little town. Have you ever had the pleasure of visiting Czorsztyn?" I look at him, hoping my smile will speak for itself. "I like mountains. And I like water too. Together, they're a fine thing. And so I'm there, you see, in this town, with a friend. And the friend came prepared. He had a bag. A suitcase. Full of documents. And money. You see? A nice piece of luggage. Heavy. So we are in this gondola. The sun shining. Some girls along for the ride. And beers. This year, I'm going back. This little town is something, I tell you."

Seba hurries back with the tea. I take a sip. It's hot, bitter and unpleasant. Dario places his hand on the handgun, gently, as if it was a woman's hand.

"And you know how it goes," he continues. "One beer, and another, and another. Hot. Jokes, laughs, as it goes. When there's ladies onboard. We get off the gondola, Kuba, walking along back to our car, time to hit the hotel. Do something to those girls of ours. And then, just before we drive back, my friend remembers that our little suitcase, our bag, was left behind on the gondola. And it wasn't a trifle either. A hundred thousand euros. Enough reason to go back to get it, right? A hundred thousand little reasons."

He bares his teeth in an attempt at a smile. A beastly grin.

"Indeed. Reason enough to rush back," I nod.

"Our mood a little soured, we went back. To find that gondola. And you know what? It was getting dark."

"You left half a million zlotys on a fucking boat?" Finger asks, visibly shaken, but Dario isn't paying him the slightest bit of attention.

"We went back and the boy working there, the one who had that gondola, a young kid, twenty maybe, a fine kid, plenty of muscle on him, smiling and all – we don't have his like round here anymore, brave, strong boys, not at all fucking camp – gave that bag right back. He even apologised for not noticing it earlier. Swearing that he didn't open it, didn't look inside. So we gave him a tip. A thousand euros for his trouble. And his decency. Let the boy have some fun. Young boys, they need to let off steam. You get the point of this story? This crazy story, Kuba? You see what carelessness can do? You're not stupid."

"Enlighten me," I tell him.

Dario takes his hand off the gun, just to draw attention to it. His hands go up in a gesture of helpless confusion.

"Things don't get lost. Don't vanish. It is people who lose them. And then they end up in the wrong hands. Not lost. Do you understand now?"

"You've lost something. You want me to find it."

He's grinning again. I preferred him when he was drunk. He was straight with the world then, not this smoke and mirrors shit. And maybe I was less tired.

"A lot of things changed. I was away, you see, Kuba. Got my hands on a little bit of a certain substance. Banks froze my accounts, took my house, and the rest, well the wife took that, fuck her, Kuba, fuck her till she's dead. I did have this thing hidden though, this little back up plan. An apartment here, a little gold there. And cash. And a bit of blow, which now appears to be lost, because some nasty person from this nasty little town decided to help themselves to it. The blow, the cash, a little bonus. I quickly found out who that naughty party was. Despair has a certain... aroma, Kuba. Easy to track. And so I tracked him down. A fella known as Birdie. You ever heard of him?"

"I have," Finger butts in. "A homo."

I too have heard of Birdie. I saw him recently, in a Russian bar. I saw a part of him. A fragment. All over Uncle's hands. Being washed down a dirty old sink.

I can feel it, even though my expression hasn't changed, I haven't flinched, the pause, the light in my eyes – I look at Dario and can see he knows I know. Knows I checked myself, tensed up, trying not to give shit away. Fucking shit. I knew it. More than sense – I damn well knew it was his. From the very beginning. Saw it in Uncle's eyes. The way he was washing those hands.

"You know, we tracked Birdie down. To his apartment. Though we found it hard to talk to him about the missing items. He was... not in a fit state to talk to anyone. Ever again. I suspect someone must have taken that lost property of mine. And then shut his trap for him. Shut it good. Very good. But I suspect you know. I know, Kuba, that you're a well-informed kind of operator. Two kilos of powder. Some dough. Pills too."

I take another sip of tea. Look up to see Finger looking at me.

"Maybe you heard something," he says, helpfully. "You come over to our table with some dickhead campaign. Sit at our table, trying to pull something. You and your jukebox pal."

"He's not a pal. He's a customer. He came here to get my money."

"Well, now you'll have to wait some more," Finger says, coldly.

I have to get out of here. Before I faint. Call Uncle. Things are starting to spin. Inside my head and all around. I close my eyes. Forcing myself to stay sober, clear-headed. My brain will listen to what my will wants. It won't fade. I'm not going to doze off. Something is ticking though. The world around me spinning. Something deep down in my guts crawling upwards, acid in the throat, dryness in the mouth.

Bad decisions. A whole heap of bad decisions. Argentina. The one good solution to it all. Where I can think clearly. A good hotel. Clean sheets. Clean every day. No people. Phone off. A swimming pool. Its surface as flat as a mirror. As smooth as frozen skin. Maybe the ocean. I've never looked out at an ocean. Dove into one. I could do that, travel the world, see all its oceans, from different angles.

A couple more days. Survival. I need to survive, need not to be swallowed up by this dark little town, not fall beneath its wheels, disappear beneath its floor, inside its guts.

"Nothing, Dario. Finger. Nothing comes to mind. I've heard of Birdie. Yeah. Who hasn't?" I tell them.

"But you will," Dario promises, menacingly. "You will for sure."

He grins again, those plastic teeth. They are so funny I grin back.

"Perhaps. As soon as I do, I will share."

"You're going away," Dario states.

"That's the plan."

"That's a good thing, Kuba. People need distance. Without rest, there can be no harvest. No life. Sunshine. Beers. Vodka. Ladies on order. Far from the maddening crew. When you return, you will share. Right? So much to share. So much for us to discuss."

I rise. My legs feel weak, and I try to keep them straight, rooted, trying to make my swaying appear relaxed, not weak. I shake Finger's hand. Then the others. They look up, faces showing nothing. No interest in me at all.

"I'll be in touch," I say to Dario. He also stands up, reaches out a hand, grabs mine, pulling me towards him. Patting me on the back. Embracing me. Mumbling in my ear, pleased with himself.

"I'll be in touch, don't you worry. I'll find you, Kuba. You have my number?"

"I do not."

He pulls his phone out, touches the screen, unlocking it, then pushes it about some more. My phone buzzes. I look down at it – an unknown number.

"You do now," Dario says, putting his phone away.

I nod, do the same with mine. Then I turn and head towards the doors, trying to make a more graceful exit than Percent. I know his eyes are buried in my back, and I also know he is smiling. I know his thoughts are on the gun. He has me. Can see everything I do. Even with his eyes shut. That is when he sees me the clearest.

Which is not good. Very bad in fact.

I leave the club. The street stinks.

I am now just a piece of his giant, ugly puzzle.

I should have spotted them earlier. Driving behind me. I was talking to Pazina on the phone. It's not her fault, she simply has to talk. The fault is mine. We're parked by the side of the road, and one of them places a reflective plastic triangle on the asphalt behind us. They mean to be here for a while. I feel thirsty. I forgot to hydrate.

The cars going past make a soothing, whooshing sound. And so I wonder what they would do if I just collapsed and fell into a coma right now. Or at least a very deep sleep.

Standing by the side of the road, it looks like my car has broken down, and they are preparing to give me a tow. They're driving a beige Renault, rolling on cheap winter tyres. Undercover cops always ride round in shitty cars. These three look alike, Siamese triplets separated at birth, a freak of inbred nature. Their faces do not speak of intelligence. Quite the opposite. They seem irritated, tired, crumpled up, permanently hung over.

"You know you have no due cause," I tell the one leaning against my car, wrapped in a thin leather blazer, hair done in a severe army issue crew cut.

"If I wasn't at the end of a shift and on my last legs, I'd laugh at that," he replies humourlessly.

"Me too," says another over the noise of a passing truck. "I too would laugh. If it was funny."

"We have no reason?" Crewcut repeats. "Fucking hell, do we need reasons?"

"Due cause, not reason," I correct him. "You need due cause."

I was talking with Pazina, but it's not her fault. She insisted on talking, and I didn't turn on the hands-free system in time, but she meant well. Paz always means well. I am to blame.

"What is it you want?" I asked her.

"Bethlehem's online profiles – Facebook and all that, you know what it is – said it would be shut tonight. Warning people to keep away."

"That place is always open."

"Yeah, but it was Tiny. He posted about it being shut."

"Fine, maybe today twenty less idiots will go there to waste their money, why do I care? Get someone to change the password on their Facebook account, get Tiny off it, that's all. You know the score."

Tiny must have got drunk and posted shit without thinking, or thinking he'd get sympathy, or that he'd gather up support for his punk cause. How his club, his little club has been taken over. No one cares. No one trusts the fucker.

"I don't know, Kuba, I'm getting a bad feeling about all this. Tiny wants to pull something, I can feel it. I just know. I can just tell such things, so don't give me lectures now about superstitions. Did you talk to Dawid?"

I talked to Dawid, the manager we installed at Bethlehem, earlier on the phone. Paz recommended his services, said he'd run some clubs for trusted people, could be counted on to run a tight ship without too much hassle. I told him to do what was needed to keep the place running smoothly, keep an eye on the stock, the cash, but soon enough realised he knew what needed doing better than I did. That Paz chose wisely.

"Paz, please, thanks for stressing, but go get some sleep, will ya? Stop worrying about everyone. Bad for the heart."

"Fuck off," she countered.

"And I'm the one who's meant to be aggressive when confronted with feelings? Listen to yourself," I joked.

That was when I saw them overtake and slow down in front of me, indicating I should pull over. Just as I was saying to her "I don't have time for..."

I saw one of them get out and knock on my window.

"What's going on?" I ask.

"Get out," comes the reply.

I got out.

"Hands on the hood."

I did as I was told, the hood nice and warm, comforting, while he went through my pockets, while the others started on the Audi. They found fuck all. Maybe they're detectives, supposed to know hiding places, secret compartments, fake CD players, that sort of thing. They know various tricks, but not mine – they'd have to hand my car over to someone far more clever than these dicks. So they poked about the insides, putting on a show of professionalism. Nothing doing. They moaned and groaned and all they managed to do is stink up the interior, smudge the upholstery.

I waited patiently for them to finish, even though they were touching everything with their dirty, unwashed, smokers' hands. Hands I would love to disinfect. Unhygienic fuckers.

"Anything crop up? Is Mikolaj on the way?" the one who frisked me shouts now.

I stretch my back, rubbing my hands, jumping sprightly on the spot. It's a good thing it's so cold out. It's keeping me awake. Aware.

"Nothing so far," comes the reply, then I hear the trunk lid pop.

I go round to watch as he fumbles around the bottom, like a teenager at the end of a third date.

It's not that they don't know anything. They know, hence this whole scene. Not often, once a month maybe, but it is inevitable. They stop me to go through the car, check my documents, wanting to show off, put me down, set me on edge, make sure I don't ever feel totally safe. Ask me questions they know I won't answer. Detain me from time to time, the standard twelve hours of cell time, nothing worse than visiting Olsztyn, sleeping in my old bed, answering my mother's equally pointless questions. Yeah. Nothing. No. Not now. Maybe. How are you? All good? No idea. Can't help you, sorry.

I do hope they're not in the mood for all that tonight. It's cold, and frozen fingers are no good at frisking.

"It's cold," one of them says through a nose which looks like it's been broken more than once.

It is cold, well below zero. Last time I looked at the dashboard, it was minus fifteen Celsius. The kind of cold that won't let you forget it's there. One of them pulls a thermos flask from his car, pours himself a drink of something. More cars float by. I feel a little cramped, like being stuck in a lift with strangers you don't like the look of.

"We do really have to fucking talk."

"Are the three of you bored? You should think up a game. So many interesting games. Associations?"

"This guy really wants to be a comedian for the night," he says to the guy with the hot flask.

"We'll have a joke or two in a second," says the guy who went through the trunk. "I know one. What do smart asses say when they've been locked up and are about to be fucked in the ass? You know what? Nothing, coz they've had their front teeth knocked out so they can suck better cock."

"One of yours? Or did you download it from a film?" I ask politely.

"Call base, tell them we're bringing someone in," hot flask says.

"I'll do a bit of poking around now," says the one with the flattened nose.

He dives inside the car, lights a cigarette. His awkward fumbles last a good few minutes.

"Empty."

"Maybe we should drag it in for a strip down?" says the third, but I don't panic – to do that, they need a warrant, and if they had a warrant, they would have flashed it by now. Instead, I decide to play the decent citizen.

"Can you please not smoke inside my car?" I ask. "My girlfriend's allergic."

"You're starting to get on my fucking nerves. Christmas is coming, party season, and you're worried about allergies."

"Let's all go visit the nearest church. People deposit things this time of year, for the needy. Maybe we can find something that fits your neediness, gentlemen."

We could be here, hanging around, for all eternity. I don't have a record. A perfect example of a decent citizen. I don't even have an unpaid parking ticket. Nothing they can pin on me. I've no idea who put them onto me, but they know. All about me. One of them once said they were surprised I was still on the loose. The answer was simple. I think before I act. I just didn't tell him that. Not many people think in this line of work. The same is true of them, but I didn't tell him that either.

Some think if you go long enough without going down, then you've made a deal with the law. Paid the right people. There are those who play it like that, of course. Selling out the smaller dealers, the ones running around schools and cheap gyms, setting the law on the competition, trying to win that way. A symbiotic arrangement, especially as cops have their stats, their targets to hit. But for me, it's unsavoury. The one still smoking inside my car has doubts about my manners, but for me it's just bad form, talking to cops. Like paying a prostitute for dinner before hitting a hotel.

"We'd better go. It's cold," says the third guy.

"What is it you wanted to talk to me about?" I ask.

"Oh, various things. Such as dead bodies," says flat nose.

"Now what would I know about any such things?"

"A little birdie sang. Sang us your name, pal."

"Dead bodies don't dead themselves. Someone always knows something. But not me."

"Then why are you dancing on the spot?" thermos flask cop asks. "You need the toilet?"

"I'm cold and I want to go home," I answer. "Just waiting for you to finish hassling little old me."

He doesn't answer. I look at them – in another life, under different circumstances, I might feel a twinge of pity. They're all the same. Struggling to make ends meet, struggling with their addictions, frustrated, dysfunctional, too far from cop school to retrain, too close to retirement to quit. Hating everything and everyone, because the world they work in is fuelled by hate. Piotrek, for example, has a soft spot for the enemy. Speaks of them like they were disabled, or exiled or some other tragic story. But not me.

They are where they are because they choose to be. It's their wish to be fucked by everyone, higher or lower than them, fuckers climbing ladders, climbing just to fall – into loneliness, into drink, into a hail of bullets, or just that one, that self-inflicted wound. Some of them last, hold on to that top rung, but there they get fucked the hardest, forced to smile for the cameras, for the whole of Poland, fucked in style by the courts and the politicians and the secret services. By the process of natural selection, because everyone knows that their bosses and my bosses talk to each other regularly, through a carefully balanced network of connections, favours and deals. The problem is that my bosses treat the likes of me a little better than their bosses treat the likes of them. I can earn a ridiculous amount more money, and never have to take work and stress home with me. Cops, on the other hand, they grow to hate it all, especially money. They want to rip me to shreds to get at it. If only they could, they would most like to torture me for hours, stripping me of skin, covering me in acid, just because I have so much more, enough to not give a flying fuck about any of them, my lawyers ensuring that. They can dream of locking me up for a year, or three or five, but when I get out the same blessings will still be waiting for me – prestige, respect, riches. All the things their bonuses and their promotions and their successes will never nail. Luxury in their book is a clean whore, blended whisky from a supermarket, alimony paid on time most months of the year.

I will never understand what drives them. Did they go to cop school just because? Like those guys from school who decided to become priests? For no reason other than to have all their choices made for them? Could they not come up with a more sensible way of wasting the best years of their lives? Chasing criminals no one wants them to catch, because everyone wants what the criminals sell, including the highest authorities in the land? Is it just that they watched too many cop shows when young and terribly impressionable?

"I've told you what I know. Which is not much," I finally say, feeling tired. Very, very tired. Time to get back behind the wheel again.

"Maybe when we take you in you'll recall something you forgot to tell us," smashed nose says.

He stares at my car as if trying to work out which bit would look best with his spit frozen to it.

"Wait a minute," says the third, plain one.

Someone is ringing. The guy with the thermos flask sees me looking longingly at the container, then drains the last of what was in it. Steam seeping from his clenched teeth.

"Hello," I hear one of the other two saying into his phone. "Yeah. We are. But... No, nothing here... I get it. Yeah, fucking hell. We

240

have... Yeah, a buddy, oh yeah, and he wants to talk... What do you mean he can't? Is he drunk or what? Right. Fucking hell. Right on."

The others wait in silence. I turn to look.

"Fuck," says smashed nose. "We have to be in Ochota in ten minutes. Something going down in a brothel."

Their eyes turn to me. The three of them poised, like cartoon characters, waiting for someone to say something. Like something from an old black and white movie.

"Must be your lucky day, motherfucker," says smashed nose.

"I'm sorry to hear that," I say.

My phone rings. I look at the display. Uncle. Just when I need him the most. I cut the call and pocket the phone again.

"We'll be back," says thermos. "And have a proper chat then."

A text pings. I struggle to pull the phone out again with my frozen hands. Uncle, of course: *Come to Bethlehem. Sharpish.*

"If you're feeling lonesome, I recommend the internet. They tell me it's a gold mine of information and valuable contacts."

"He's a barrel of laughs, this one," says plain cop. "A little lazy though. Must try harder..."

I send just the one character to Uncle: *?*

All three of them slam the doors of their beige Clio. One of them rolls down a window, his breath exploding from the car.

"People are dying, you fucker. A young kid is gone. A young mother-to-be. People like what they like, I get that, but I always thought dealers were murderers. Fuck all that talk about free will. There is such a thing as responsibility for the lives of others. Right and fucking wrong."

"I really would take great care making such moral judgements, considering your line of work," I reply. "Easy to mix things up if you lack the necessary training."

"We're gonna squeeze," flat nose shouts from behind the wheel. "Holiday season is over. Hunting season begins here. Zero tolerance, motherfucker."

"Best get the cuffs, then," I bite back as my phone buzzes. Uncle: *Fire. Fucking inferno.*

Fuck the cop, I think, enraged. I want to walk up to them and say something else, but they race off, wheels spinning the gravel by the side of the road, the plastic warning triangle left on the asphalt.

I jog over and get inside my car, just to warm up. I have to compose myself. Sew myself back together again. Things are splitting, tearing, my sight fading, faltering. My movements jagged, and they saw it, they know, ready to pounce. Dario sensed it and Beata sensed it, especially in the morning. In that vile, pink aquarium. Fire – what fire? What on earth can I fuck up next?

For the first time ever, I am starting to think that if I don't stop, if I don't get out of this town, even for a short while, it will win. It will triumph. I will die. This city is like a concrete rainforest, everything rots quicker here; mould, gangrene, toxins all raging, in the blood, the guts, over and under the skin. I feel like the beginnings of a terminal illness are eating away at me, getting purchase. I need to change settings. Or this setting. Clean my organism of Warsaw. Otherwise I will dissolve, turn into dirty foam.

This city is killing me, not so slowly after all, but the process is hurting us both. Killers feel the suffering of their victims, but unlike their victims, they cannot die. Warsaw. A vast, decomposing mass. I can hear it squealing, quietly, far off, like a dog locked in the trunk of an abandoned car.

The car stinks of cigarettes, of dirty skin, hair, sweat-soaked fabrics. I have to get it cleaned before I leave. Then buy a new car.

Uncle, ringing again. I don't answer. I can't, my hands seemingly glued to the top of the steering wheel. Another ping from him: *Where the fuck are you!?!*

00:20am

"Technically speaking, he's the owner still, and the contract for this place is between the city and him. He didn't sign away those rights to us," Uncle growls, trying to clear his throat of the smoke which hangs in the air, as if bursting from the massive campfire, the furnace that is the heart of this city. I am holding a tissue up to my mouth and nose. Swallowing something that has been through everything, all the rooms, the lungs, the air con pipes of this building.

I am trying to keep calm, but it's working less and less well. I'm starting to forget what it means to be calm. How it's done. I want to hit someone. Even Uncle, though he's done nothing wrong. I feel like I've overdosed on steroids, desperate to smash someone's face in, hear bones cracking, unleash violence, a terrible itch.

"He signed something the lawyers gave us, but it wasn't confirmed by the authorities." Shady tries to explain something he knows not all of us are capable of understanding.

He's standing next to me. Chewing gum. He's calm, the calm of an old shepherd dog. He smokes more weed a day than I do in a month. Couldn't function without it. I envy him that particular addiction.

"Where is that Dawid, for fuck's sake?" I ask.

"I don't think he showed up for work today," Uncle says.

The shapes around me are turning all shades of blue, like there was a police car outside, its lights spinning, making everyone in here look half-dead already. We're inside a huddle of people, standing on the sidewalk, looking up at the upper floors of a town house, at the windows billowing huge clouds of black smoke, clouds bursting upwards towards an already black sky.

More colours. Lots of them. Wild now, like they only happen to me here, at this address. I lean against a car involuntarily.

"She was right," I say to myself.

"Who was?" Uncle asks.

"Doesn't matter. Is there anyone here who works for us? A barman, a waitress, any fucker?!" I shout.

Those in uniform are standing around, visibly angry. They want to be at home, dressing Christmas trees, wrapping presents, arguing with the wife about this year's spending. Meanwhile, they're here, like me, pressing tissues up against their mouths, gaping helplessly. In a moment, when everyone gets the message that the fire had been started deliberately, they will come, maybe even the same guys driving that beige Clio, even more furious than before. Those unlucky enough to have been residents of flats above the club are shivering in the cold, covered in emergency blankets, smoking fag after soothing fag, like there wasn't enough smoke in the air already. We watch firemen in full emergency outfits emerging slowly, tiredly from the ashes.

"Do you think I can tell who is who among all these fucking hipsters?" Uncle asks.

"And Tiny? Did anyone see him? He had to get in somehow," I spit back.

"Look at these trendy fuckers, they haven't washed in a week, just look at them," Uncle groans.

"Fucking dope heads," Shady adds and spits on the ground.

A young, ugly woman wearing high-heeled winter boots, a short-sleeved shirt, seemingly impervious to the cold, face covered in soot, starts crying after a skinny, balding guy wearing a track suit whispers something in her ear. The crying is hysterical, bottomless, tears which force her to crouch down, arms wrapped round her belly.

"Someone said there was a kid. Teenager. In one of our bathrooms," Uncle tells me, lighting another cigarette. "Underage."

"Fuck. They're going to want to speak to everybody."

I spot one girl, leaning against an ambulance, wrapped in a thermal blanket. I recognise her awkward stance, her tattoos, her unusual height – she's one of the bar staff.

"Dawid," I say to her. "Where is Dawid?"

She looks at me with complete disdain, a dullness which suggests she's shell shocked. I could be anyone, her dead grandmother, and she still wouldn't speak.

More and more smoke pours forth from the club. Colours still surround me. Mainly blue, but a different kind of shade now, darker. I close my eyes. Open them again. Then I open my mouth, silently. I have to focus. Help others focus too.

I snap my fingers right in front of her nose, and she seems to notice.

"Dawid's on the way. Someone rang him."

"Have you seen Tiny?"

"Tiny doesn't work here anymore. He's been barred. The door staff won't let him in."

The girl seems to be sniffling, crying maybe. I hand her a tissue.

"He had to have been inside there. Tiny had to have got in," I press.

"Christ! I told you I haven't seen him. Talk to the bouncers." She nods towards two stocky, tattooed guys, all in black, sipping from a bottle of mineral water by the fire engine. "They'll just tell you they've been told to call Dawid as soon as we see Tiny."

I leave her to it, see Uncle and Shady looking up, trying to read things in the smoke signals over the city.

"The fire started on the first floor, where the office is. They still don't know what it was though, some are saying it might have been a wiring short-circuit," Uncle says, shaking his head.

"Fuck the wiring," I tell him. "On Facebook today Tiny posted that Bethlehem would be shut up and that people should keep away."

Dario is right. Despair has a certain smell. Like vinegar. Like piss. It's here, beneath the burning, beneath the thousands of smells, the plastics, the melting metals, the fried sound systems and cameras.

We could have done this differently. Paralysed the fucker properly. I should have known he'd panic, should have noticed the craziness. His mind ticking like a bomb. Once they investigate, the stink will last a lot longer than the smoke. The city will think it was extortion. That we burnt the place down to get the insurance and the permission to put up flats here. Days after we used force to get Tiny to sign the place away. Ugly.

"What we gonna do?" Uncle asks.

"We have to track him down," I say.

"What the fuck is up with the bastard?" Shady asks, shaking his head.

"Compensation. He wants to get paid. And wants us to get lost."

"There he is," Uncle points. "The wimp you were asking about."

Pazina's boy, the manager. Walking towards us, quickly, almost trotting along. Dawid looks honestly terrified, trying to take it all in – the people, the ambulances, the fire fighters, the stink, the smoke – but it's too much, too wrong. He stops, looks round, blinking, trying to compose something of a stable image.

I close my eyes again. Too much. Colours. Pieces of a puzzle.

The stink of vinegar and ice. I could have focused earlier. I could have predicted this would happen. Should have done. But now is no time or place to go reviewing catalogues of big, bad mistakes. Now I have to wrench my eyes open again and look – Dawid is in front of me, saying nothing. Too frightened, too disoriented.

"Dawid? Listen." He tries to focus on me. "How did Tiny get in so that the doormen wouldn't see?"

"Sorry, I was... I hadn't slept for two nights, turned off my phone, man, sorry," he mumbles.

"Call Piotrek," I tell Uncle.

"Really sorry," Dawid says. "What the fuck happened here? Is everyone OK?"

"No, everyone is not OK," I assure him. "How did Tiny get in there?"

He seems to be hearing me, his brain turning the question over and over in the confusing darkness. He runs a hand through his hair, rubbing the shaved bits over his ears.

He gives the impression of being an ordinary, dumb-ass hipster, someone absorbed by looking good in online pics, busy crashing bicycles without brakes and poking his cocks into all the latest barmaids, but Paz says he's quick, and can handle the work. Well, we're about to discover if she was right.

"Oh fuck!" he suddenly groans, like he's remembered something, his eyes wide, his mouth poised open as he stares at the carnage before us.

"What?" I bark.

"Cops been inside yet?" he asks.

"What now, for fuck's sake?" Uncle chips in.

His phone rings.

"Piotrek," he says to me, waving the phone. I nod.

"There is... A guy arrived today. Left a package inside. And cash..." Dawid slowly announces.

I turn to look for any cops I recognise, see one of them talking to a senior fire fighter. They're both pointing at the building. The awkward barmaid is talking to another plain clothes cop, who then nods at Dawid.

"What was in the package?" I ask him.

"MDMA. A big batch. And cash. If they find that in the office, I'm gonna cop all the blame," he says, trying not to look at the cops.

"You better pray all those goodies went up in smoke," Shady says, hiding a smirk.

"Can't be sure. Fuck! They're gonna inspect in a minute. Come, I need to check something."

"Stay here," I tell Uncle and Shady and follow Dawid.

He enters the crowd, bumps into someone, but on purpose, to cause a bit of a distraction; we go round the corner, turn into a side street, then right, towards the back of the building. He's walking quickly, without looking round. Between some shops, there is a side entrance, a courtyard to another building. He types in the entry code on the digital panel. A pleasant-sounding ping indicates the code was correct. We cross a concrete covered courtyard, lit only by an altar to the Virgin Mary, the same you'll find in all of Warsaw's ancient doorways and private parks.

"This is the back entrance," he whispers in the dark. "The residential section."

"Of what?" I ask.

"Of the club. There are apartments round the back. Tiny wanted to rent them out to artists. Have residencies. Some kind of vision, Pazina told me. To create a commune. But then people started to move out. Shit went missing. Equipment, furniture. Weird shit started to happen."

"What weird shit?"

"Back during communism, there used to be a hospice here. Terminally ill kids. Before that, just after the war, some kind of prison. Don't know. Political police used to hold suspects here. Bad vibes."

"How do you know all this?"

"If I'm gonna work somewhere, I want to know all there is to know about it," he says, gesturing for me to follow him up some steps. He's looking for something in his pockets, then pulls out a small set of keys. A steel door leads to a boiler room, hidden out of sight. "The manager's entrance."

We stop by the door, and before putting a key in, Dawid turns to me.

"He could still be in there. Could have been there for a week or more. He knows you'll come looking for him."

I nod. We go inside. The place is completely dark, and smells – rust, mouldy paper, and of course smoke. We try to move quickly, but the floor is uneven, rubbish, broken glass, the corridor low, narrow, bare brick walls rough to the touch. Using the torch in his phone, Dawid leads the way.

"If that room didn't go up in smoke, we have to grab the shit and get out. Can't afford to be nailed for a bag of happy pills."

He looks like a fool, but doesn't work like one. I sniff the air, trying to work out if I can now smell people, smell Tiny, if he is here, panicked, hiding. If he is, I hope he knows I'm thinking about him. Let him feel fear. All the easier for me to track him down.

Then the smell of smouldering building is gone, replaced by something else. The smell from my dream. Rising up from below, familiar, evil. A sweet, heady smell. The smell of the abandoned block of flats. I pause a second, my heart beating faster all of a sudden.

We go through various dark rooms. I look around, listening.

"He's not in here," Dawid says. "The offices are further on."

Some lifts, stairs. I can feel the cold again. And that smell. The smell of that other building. We turn right, a corridor that is lower than those before it, like a canal. I have the impression that the floor is now angled downwards.

Flashbacks. The kid from that building. The smell of those corn chips he was eating. Blue colours.

Dawid stops, starts going through the bunch of keys. I look over his shoulder to see a large, steel door. Someone has painted the word HERE onto it in big, dripping letters.

"What's up?" he turns and asks.

"What do you mean what's up?" I ask back.

"You alright?"

"Why wouldn't I be?"

"You're trembling."

"Need sleep."

He unlocks the door. It squeals in the darkness. More of the smell, like fresh vomit. Cut. Room, floor, presence, a body in the corner, huge, irregular, dissolving, turning liquid. Cut.

"Are you coming?" he asks.

I didn't take the gun from my car. I should have. Too late now.

"Doormen," I say to him.

"What about them? I told you he came in through here."

"Did you fire the old door staff like I told you to?"

"It was the first thing I did."

I nod. Everything is slowing down, his steps, mine, the sound of the door closing behind us, the thud. The thick darkness.

"I forgot to charge my phone," he says.

His voice now sounds very far off. Cut. Sound. Noise, loud, like a tornado, like a jet engine, at first far off, beneath the belly of this town, I hear its hiss, drumming, digesting.

I turn on the flashlight in my phone.

"You sure you're alright?" Dawid asks again.

Bright colours. Like being slammed in the head. Red. Yellow, green, red again.

Cut. The boy there, instead of Dawid. The boy is back. He didn't take the lift down. Returned. Everything red, until it dies down, less tense, turning pink, vanishing. I stand with my back to the lift. *Give back what you took, bitch...* I'm breathing heavily.

"I doubt he's in here," Dawid says, his voice trailing.

Cut. Very intense redness, very close. Cut.

I have to sit down. On the floor. Sitting down, I turn into a child. Once I am on the floor, the corridor turns into a dead room.

Jump cuts, flashes, disruptions. Uncle, Dario, Pazina. Cut. Noise. She, naked, mirror, sees herself, sees me. Cut. Furniture kid. Noise. Hotel, prostitute, politician. Cut. Mariusz, celebrity, girl, the prime minister's daughter, leaving his bathroom. Cut. Cops. Cut. Cash. Packed in bags. Cut. Head hurting, as if being drilled, through the temple. Cut. She's there, naked, piercing the world like a blade. Cut.

I want to vomit, for a moment, like everything I've ever eaten is suddenly coming up, wanting to be free of me.

Cut. Boy. The boy from the dream. The twelve-year-old boy from my dream, his long, matted hair, the one who led me there, to serve as sacrifice. He's next to me.

"Look," he says.

I'm standing right before her. Sitting down, I have turned into a child who is standing up. I look at her. In her body, the pinkish, grey, shimmering body which looks like it is made of glittering wax, reeking of a million undigested meals, a body which can devour, can swallow up anything it wants, tiny mouths showing, appearing all across its surface, mouths without teeth, a body which has seeped out of the ventilation system and is now taking up the whole room, still rising, growing.

"Look," the boy says again.

"I'm looking," I answer.

"She's the one making you see all these colours."

"I know."

The first time I went to get a kilo of coke, eight years ago, at night, I was nervous, I recall, nervous in the way anyone would be on their first day of work. The guy who sold me the stuff, wearing a hooded top, his teeth rotting, hair all over the place, opened the trunk of his Volkswagen Golf and said to me: "You're going to do this for the rest of your life. You, as it happens, will keep doing this till the end of your life."

I asked if he was trying to tell me that they were going to kill me soon, but he didn't answer.

I recall it was in a forest north of Warsaw. I gave him the cash, took the sports bag from him, slinging it over my shoulder like it was full of running gear. There was a girl nearby, in the car park, watching us, but we only noticed her later.

"It will eat you up, slowly. At first, you're not going to feel it at all. It will feed and eat you at the same time. To keep you alive that bit longer. At first, you'll feel no pain," the boy explains.

"I know."

"It will eat each one of us. Digesting forever."

He approaches the mass. Extends a hand, stopping a little way before it, where a giant, toothless mouth opens up. The boy smiles. Pulls his hand back.

"She's just like that. We all live right next to her guts," he says. "She's breeding us. Breeding to have something to eat."

It must have been the car park behind the McDonald's. The girl stood near our cars, by the sign with the parking rules and regulations. Her eyes wide open, her mouth shut tight. She was crying, shaking. Arms wrapped round her torso. The guy selling me the stuff stopped me when I tried to approach her, spat on the ground as if she was a bad sign.

"We all live right next to her guts," he said then, it was definitely him, the guy with the rotting teeth, with the silver chain round his neck. He said the words and then got into his car.

Once he was gone, we stood there, me and the girl, which is when I decided to go up to her.

"Your turn," the boy says to me.

"What should I do?" I ask.

The mouths are appearing and disappearing all over the fleshy mound, quicker and quicker.

"Get up," he says.

I wanted to approach her, that girl, at night, behind the McDonald's, but she escaped in the direction of the motorway, dissolving in the darkness.

"Rise," the boy asks again.

Red, all over the place, squealing, unbearable noise, two metal objects rubbing up against each other. Cut. A live conference on TV. *For example, was the cocaine found in Mariusz F.'s blood from the same source as that found in the blood samples from Antoni Gorecki, could it have come from the same supply?* Cut. Pazina in Bethlehem, leaning against a wall. Cut. Car park, the inside of my car. Far off music. The city as if painted with broken crayons by a kid across a black surface. Pazina's voice: *We're all bandits*. Cut.

I approach her. The body rises and falls, dark pink, glistening like rotting meat, like puddles of petrol in the sun.

"Don't be scared," the boy says. "Now, it's your turn." I bring my hand close to the monster. "This could last for months. The real pain comes at the end."

"Get up, for fuck's sake!" Dawid is shouting.

Cut. Colour. Cut. Smouldering, choking, exhausting, blocking my nasal passages. Cut. Light. The dim glow of a mobile phone.

"Fucking hell, Kuba. I thought you were going to cough up both lungs," he says, panicked.

I inhale deeply. We're in a room, painted all white, a mattress rolled up and dumped in the corner, a windowless space, Dawid opposite me, a bag hanging over his shoulder. A sweet, sickly taste of everything I ingested over the last few days fermented into one caustic liquid is gluing my mouth shut.

"How long was I out?" I ask.

He shakes his head.

"It's the fumes. We'll choke to death in a second. Monoxide," he explains.

"Is that the stuff?" I ask, looking at the bag.

"Your phone was ringing and ringing."

"Ringing for how long?" I ask, angrily.

"I don't know, all the time we were wandering around here, and you kept stopping to throw up."

I open my mouth, not to speak, but to inhale as much air as I can, as if rising up from a deep dive.

I get up, but need to prop myself up against something. The nearest wall. I check the phone. Three unanswered calls and a text message. Two minutes ago. Uncle.

We're outside I know where that fucker went.

"You should rest, man," Dawid says. "When did you last sleep?"

Cut. Dario. Colour, for a moment longer. Fading. More and more greyness. Cut.

It will pass once I'm out of this hell hole. Uncle rings again. I spit out whatever is left lingering in my mouth. Dawid hands me a bottle of water.

Things are rotten. I am rotten. I need servicing, replacing. The state I'm in it's gonna be hard to escape, to say anything to anyone.

I should go to hospital. Go on a drip, on serious meds. Feeling abysmal.

"When did you sleep last?" he asks again and starts walking towards the exit. I follow.

I don't remember this corridor. Don't remember how we got here.

"A few days," I mumble at his back.

"You're sick, man. Go see a doctor," he says, sounding honestly concerned.

I spit again.

We keep moving. Towards the exit. I inhale more air, but all I can taste is tar and vinegar.

02:10am

"Wait, wait, I thought we knew each other, that everything was cool," she says. I can see she's honestly frightened. Speaking in a slightly raised, childlike voice. "I thought we were cool."

She's trying her best to keep everyone calm. Us, myself, the guests. It's not working. She's trembling, slightly, a tension rising up from her solar plexus, all the way to her top lip. I like her, it's not about that, but right now it's not even remotely about who I might like or not.

I am standing here, my feet glued to the floor, my eyesight clear and true. It's better. Better being here, because driving over I snorted a line. Something I've managed to avoid doing for five long years.

"Silence that dog, else I'll throw it through this window," I tell her for the third time.

Louder this time. Before, I said the words quietly. Shady and Uncle are saying nothing.

Her eyes open even wider. The rest of the guests' eyes too. There are about a dozen of them gathered in this small apartment, between the centre and the start of the suburbs. A moment ago, they were still drinking wine, smoking spliffs, snorting lines, nibbling on healthy, fresh snacks, their remains visible all around us on plates and serving bowls. Unrecognisable music is coming from a set of laptop speakers.

We've already visited both mothers of Tiny's children. His parents. No one's seen him. I was polite, introduced myself as a friend. We couldn't get into his current girlfriend's place, and then we had to drive all the way here, after Pazina got me the address.

"Silence the fucking dog!" Uncle roars and then another girl, sitting on a sofa, slight, red-haired, as sad as can be in a large, black sweatshirt, jumps up from the sofa.

"Putin, be quiet," she pleads. "Putin, come here."

She locks the dog up in the toilet, and returns instead of staying in there with it.

I look around the room. Whitewashed walls, dirty at knee-height, from the dog. A mix of old, communist-era furniture and matching Ikea crap. Vintage cinema posters. A few books, though not many. Clothes hanging on a freestanding rail. Flowers. Some real, some plastic. A small Christmas tree, decorated with identical baubles. Must be her place. A sweet warren, good enough for a final year undergraduate, where apart from polygamy and colourful alcoholism something else shoots through, something she thinks is good taste. It's the apartment belonging to someone who rides a vintage bike imported from Amsterdam, and thinks that Berlin is the prettiest town in the world, and playing with herself in the tiny bath imagines being squeezed into it with Ryan Gosling.

Outside the window, along a busy road, cars are roaring past even at this late hour. The first thing I did when I came in here was open it to let some air in.

"Where is he?" I ask everyone, but most of all Bubbles, the one with the beard, the one who tried to act tough back in Bethlehem, trying to get Tiny's back, but who got up and left when told to do so. Without a squeak.

"I know you from somewhere," said the other prick when we came in. Then his memory really caught up with him and he shut up.

Uncle reaches out to the nearest food tray, grabs a handful of pasta and stuffs it into his mouth.

"We're sort of having a pre-Christmas party," Anastasia says, trying to act assertive and determined. "Maybe you want to sit and eat with us, and then calmly tell us what you need to know."

I lean back against the door frame. My gums are itching, as is the roof of my mouth, my nose tingling, my eyes too, as if I had drunk fizzy water that bit too quickly. I run my tongue along my teeth, but these are only side effects. What really matters is that all the pieces of the surrounding puzzle are now lined up, and making some sort of bearable sense.

I haven't snorted shit in five years. I don't ever touch my own stuff. Cocaine without booze is odd, giving a sense of fake reality, a simulation of what should be here, a cheap knock-off. Without booze, I can feel its pathetic softness, soft in all its glory. Like a piece of plastic fruit.

I had to do it. Cars run along only so far, and then they fall apart during the ride, first the wheel arches, then number plates, the bumpers, then mirrors, then the windows crack, doors fall off, the car stripped naked, a caricature, then it rolls, turning along its own axis, leaving the road and, what is worst of all, moving still, as if it was being pushed by some giant, invisible hand. The hand of a monstrous child.

I am falling apart. Me. I had to. Now, I can go. Managing to get along by sniffing superglue from a local kiosk. By getting high on my own scarce supply.

"Do you want to drink anything?" she asks, frightened by my silence. In this setting, this light, she looks like the prettiest girl in the village, Miss Country Bumpkin. A cat runs between Shady's legs, and he grabs it before it can sneak off. Watching him, she takes a step back.

The moment she moves, though, there's something simple, something ordinary about her looks.

"Merry Christmas," Uncle says and starts laughing, all alone.

I approach Bubbles, who is sitting between two girls on a cheap, fold-out sofa. As we came in, he was sitting up proudly, legs splayed out, laughing at his own jokes. Now, he's tense, gripped by something, folded into himself, into the sofa, into their protective threesome. Keeping completely quiet. The girls too. The one on the right, the one who got rid of the dog, is still red-haired and still sad. The other girl is tall, heavy set, hair cut short, a cute bob on a decidedly cute face, the kind magazine editors are always on the lookout for. I approach Bubbles and drive my fist right into his silent mouth, the girls falling back, screaming, the dog howling, the street outside howling too. I stretch, something snapping in my upper back, as if something clicked, loosened up, as if I was now losing my mirrors, my doors, then I repeat the treatment with my other fist, this time feeling something crack beneath that funky beard, a tooth maybe, the nose definitely in on the action, now pouring blood like a broken tap. I look behind me at the gathered crowd as the impact of what I've done settles. Uncle is still chewing pasta, Shady stroking the cat.

"Stop it!" the redhead screams.

I crouch in front of the three of them. Take out my gun. Then put it away again. The tall, heavy girl on Bubble's right starts moaning horribly.

"You did this together. You set the club alight, so as to then divvy up the insurance money. Sneaky fuckers. Now talk. Where the fuck is he?"

"Christ, I've no idea!" Bubbles mumbles through the blood and bones. "I haven't seen him. Don't know nothing! He owes me a hundred and fifty k! I've no idea where the fucker's hiding."

"Nice try. Nice alibi," I compliment him, my hand reaching for the gun again.

"You've gone mental," he says, crying into his beard now. "You're mad..."

"Not really, pilgrim. Quite the opposite."

I lift him up and shove him towards Uncle, who catches the flake, grabs him by the head, a head which is now screaming something incomprehensible. The head is next shoved against one of the whitewashed walls, the body slumping, the wall now marked with fresh blood, the plaster chipped by teeth. There is still some quiet music seeping out of those laptop speakers, and I think I recognise the tune.

"Fucking hell, stop it!" the redhead screams.

"I'm calling the police," one of the crowd says, and I turn to instantly spot him – a chubby twenty-something, cheap fringe, looks round at me and Uncle but Uncle gives him a look which stops his feet walking and fingers dialling.

This takes some time, and I feel something pleasant, something that feels like we're playing a game. It's like when you go to a nightclub with a girl desperate to party on a Friday night – then spend five hours looking for somewhere cool to party – the dog keeps on barking behind the bathroom door – looking for five hours for someplace decent, circling round people, moving back and forth, drinking and smoking and killing time until, in the end, in the very end, once everyone is more or less fucked, or vomiting or fucking in the toilets, the bar shut, suddenly your favourite tune comes on, and you start moving, start dancing. I sweep everything off the table before me – plates, bowls, glasses, bottles. Colourful bits of food flying everywhere. Scattered across the cheap carpet. Glass breaking, the cat escaping Shady's embrace. Anastasia starts to cry, she knows. I push her gently forward.

"Where is he?" I ask. She doesn't answer, shaking her head, tears running down her cheeks. I touch them, the soft surface, the tiny hairs, like the skin of a young peach. "But you do. You know. Bonds develop between people. Connections."

"What do you mean?" she asks, voice trembling.

"People fuck, people connect. The longer they fuck, the stronger the connection. Right?"

I need a top up. This is going to last a fair while.

There is a plastic bottle in my pocket, along with a small spoon. I got it as a present from someone, a while ago. In my hand right now there is a plastic bottle with a small spoon.

"Telepathic connections. That's what I've been told," I tell her.

I've also been told she's great in bed. That many men want to have babies with her. A real fine, homely Polish yummy mummy to be. Though they also say Tiny hit her, in public, more than once.

I would never hit a woman. The silver spoon goes up my nose and I feel better already. Swallowing the spice. Licking my lips. Looking for something to drink. Most of the bottles now on the floor.

"I haven't talked to him for months," she says.

"You're fucking lying," I reply. "I don't like dogs."

Uncle starts walking about the apartment, looking at the people, the furnishings, like a curious guest. He too has had a line. He too wants to act. I can feel his hands itching all the way from here.

"I will send your dog flying in a minute," I tell her. "And then I will kill one of your Christmas guests."

She starts to shake now, not just tremble. I would very much like for her not to do anything stupid. Like piss herself. I would like to have fine and sweet memories of her. I point to the sofa.

"Him, for example," I say, looking at bleeding Beardy. "But you'll be fine. No need to worry. Take a deep breath. Ten deep, steady breaths. You know the technique? Good. Anastasia, proud of you. Hold it together. You and me are fine. You just have to tell me where he is."

"I don't know... Have you been to see Basia? Or Ewa? You have to go see them."

"We've been everywhere," I say, touching her cheek again, so soft and warm.

"Basia and Ewa," she repeats.

"A holiday home by the lake? A favourite camping spot? Where do you think he might be hiding? Lisbon? I know he's been there a few times. Just give me an address. Nothing more I ask."

The car, cobbled back together again, is once more moving down the road, though it is raining and the visibility is poor. Warsaw. Where it's always raining, even when it's not.

"Leave her alone!" the redhead screams.

She jumps up and runs at me. At the last moment, Uncle lashes out and hits her in the face.

The dog goes quiet. The redhead falling to the floor makes a dull sound – I see a knife in her hand.

"Stay down, bitch!" Uncle roars.

He makes to kick her hand.

"Leave her," I bark.

His leg freezes in mid air. I hear something from the street outside, a signal. Anastasia slides to the floor, collapsing onto the scattered food, the broken glass. The cat runs up to her, curious. Everything stops. Everything fallen.

The music coming from the laptop, I now recognise what it is – the *Goldberg Variations*.

"Let's go," I say to the other two.

"What?" Uncle is surprised.

"We're off."

The redhead lifts herself off the floor. Wiping her face. Uncle pushes her back down onto the sofa.

"Don't touch her," I tell him.

"Listen, you," Uncle stares at me, something mean in his eyes meant only for me.

"We're going," I repeat.

Shady looks at the both of us, as Uncle stares straight at me, then bends down to pick up the knife.

"We have to find him. Tonight," he says, weighing the weapon in his thick hand.

Music comes floating in via the open window from another apartment. I can taste blood. Must have bitten through my own lip. I wipe it with the back of my hand. Look down at the red. The redhead crawls along the floor towards Anastasia, trying to wake her up, slapping her face ever so gently. I step over both of them and head for the door, trying not to touch anything, leave any marks behind, like everything is charged with electricity, anything could shock me to death.

"Let's go," I say one last time.

02:38am

Uncle and Shady follow me to the car. It is very cold out now. All I have on me is a shirt and a blazer. The sky is clear, stars all up there, something refreshing about that, like freshly laundered clothes, the air new as I breathe it in. Uncle and Shady are following me, I hear their footsteps, then feel someone's hand grab the back of my neck, shoving me against my own car.

"You're not the one giving orders round here!" Uncle screams.

I get up off the cold ground. Uncle approaches and kicks me in the stomach. Something inside me twists. Lying down, I turn on my side, then vomit. Then I try taking out the gun, but I'm too slow. He kicks my wrist before I have a chance to reach for it, the pain almost audible.

"You don't give no fucking orders round here, pal," he repeats. "Someone else is in charge, you fuck. And the order is to find Tiny."

I get up, covered in dirty snow. The air is sterile, I breathe it all in like medicine, coke mixed with mucus running down the back of my throat. I open my mouth wide, as if to sing something.

"Don't hit women," I tell him, gently. "You mustn't, you fuck."

He punches me, the side of the stomach, the kidneys, I think, and I spit something out, something salty. I take out the gun, very slowly, but he smacks my hand so hard, the pistol flies off and lands next to my left boot.

"Do it again," I ask.

"You're not here to give orders, you piece of shit. Remember that. You're a fuck-all nobody. You're making people mad. The wrong sorts of people. Piotrek will have to be told. You're making all sorts of problems for us all, you little shit!"

"Do it again," I repeat. "Then I will tell Piotrek that you stole from the Pruszkow gang and forced me to hide your loot for you. Piotrek needs to know... That the problems come from you."

He takes a step back. Needs a moment in which to put together what it is I've just said and what it is he should be saying in return. His face is now the snout of a fat, stupid dog. I look past his shoulder – lights are still on inside the apartment we've just left.

"I'm quite capable of returning the drugs to the guy they belong to. Capable of not telling him who gave them to me for safekeeping. Of keeping Piotrek in the dark. About your lack of loyalty. But kick me again, you fucking moron, do it, and I will handle things my way."

He's thinking. Looking at me, focusing all his energies into thought. I smile and repeat: "You hit a girl. And that too is wrong." He takes out a cigarette, lights it, though I can see he's not enjoying the smoke one bit. "Everything will be fine and dandy, but go on, kick me again and it will all turn bad. Your bed will be in the trunk, motherfucker. Right fucking quick."

"You're a fucking piece of shit," he mumbles.

"Don't say that," I ask.

"Fucking homo fuck."

He takes the cigarette out of his mouth, exhales smoke, approaches and punches me in the guts again. Then headbutts me, awkwardly, and though I see it coming, it hurts. I manage to absorb much of the impact, but it still drops me back down into the snow.

He starts kicking me again. The stomach, the back, the head too, then spits at me. Another kick, to the thigh. He's breathing heavily with the effort.

"You're a fucking dead man. Fucking bitch, you," he growls. "You don't tell me what to do. Your job is to be fucking silent, cunt, and come along when told, and keep your trap shut, and give no orders. No one tells me what to do. I did ten years, you fuck, straight up, and no one's ever gonna tell me what to do, no fucking orders, not some prick like you."

I compose myself, slowly, and say: "I asked you something."

He kicks me again, then turns to Shady.

"Let's get out of here before they call the fucking cops."

They walk off together, the snow crunching beneath their feet, then they get into the car.

I stay down. Resting in the snow. It's soothing. The sky clear. Everything in its correct place, along with pain, pain that keeps radiating like a dark sun. Everything clean, bathed in some sort of grace. Baptised. A uniquely pretty night, as far as this city goes. Someone gave it a bath, conducted a purification ceremony, cleaned up all the stinking meat and the devoured people it's littered with. Today feels like a special day, like a wedding or something. I turn and lie on my back, stretching my legs, raising my hands to touch the face. More blood.

Cut. The boy points a finger upwards. There is something written on the ceiling. With soot. Hard to decipher. Cut.

I hear a dog barking. My dog song. My mouth falls open. I start laughing. Mouth open, I start to sing.

WEDNESDAY

"Open up, for fuck's sake!" someone is shouting, using my voice, and it could be me.

"Today is going to be a wonderful, blessed day," someone said on the radio. It was only when I heard the word 'day' that I realised what the weather was up to. "*We do have a glorious day, Christmas Eve, sunny as hell, but drivers should watch out for black ice on the roads, let's hurry to meet up with our families nice and slow. Our lives and our health are what really count. Christmas suppers can always be reheated. The family will wait by the tree, the wishes will keep. The presents too. Meanwhile, here is caller number one. Kuba, how will you be spending your Christmas?*"

I hear a door open a floor below, and a voice rising up the staircase, "What the fuck is going on? Quiet or I'll call the fucking cops!"

I stop kicking the door and listen. Then put my ear to it, though there are no sounds coming from within... "I know you're home", I want to whisper. "I know what time you got back. Get up..." *Kuba, how will you be spending your Christmas? Will you be eating with your whole family?* Alas, I won't have the opportunity. Things to do. *What sorts of things could take precedence over the family on a day like this? Kuba?* Oh, more and more things. And they just keep piling up. We're dealing with something of a domino effect, a negative development which is like an active program, once it's initiated it has to run its course. Unsuccessful.exe, moronic.exe. It's kind of a geeky, computer metaphor, normally these things are not my bag, seeing as I hardly ever use computers. It could be said I am not a man of my time. *Actually, all things being said, Kuba, you're an original kind of person.* Thank you, it's not like I'm trying to be original. *Fine, Kuba, but what are these things you're hinting at? Me and the rest of our listeners are now very curious to find out.*

"Will you fucking stop?!" the voice from below comes up again, male, young, deep.

I lean over the bannister to take a look at him. Thick-set, hair cut short, wearing a pair of tight running shorts and a polo shirt.

"Go home," I order politely.

"Listen, you fuck," he says and starts walking up the stairs.

Soon enough, however, he changes his mind. And knows what it was he was supposed to do all along. He turns back, walks down those few steps without turning around, opens his front door and vanishes. I hear the locks clicking, one after the other.

Kuba, are you still on the line? I am. And so? And so, for example, in order to get into someone's apartment you sometimes have to knock on the door very loudly, because people aren't always keen to open up. In such cases, as one waits for a response, neighbours might become annoyed and involved, and so it might be necessary to point a gun in their general direction. Yes, flashing firearms about is sometimes highly useful. *And Kuba, has this always been true? That it is always necessary to resort to such measures?* I don't know. Hard to say anything about firearms until one has fired one. *And have you, Kuba, ever done so? Have you ever shot anyone?*

Someone's leg kicks the door, though it's not mine.

"Open up, for fuck's sake, else I'll set this door on fire!" And once again. And another kick. "Open up!"

I know she's inside. There is no other possibility. Unless she's not inside.

I've had some practice at a shooting range. *And beyond that? Have you ever shot anyone? This is a fascinating question. Our listeners would surely love to know.*

I finally hear some footsteps. I then remember, not sure why now, that I haven't eaten anything in the last twenty-four hours. I've done plenty of throwing up, but no eating. My stomach hurts a little, as if it was starting to digest itself, the taste of bile rising up my gullet.

The sound of pouring water, this sometimes really helps, because there must be sound, something suspended in the air, and music is too complex, helps overheat the brain, a thing which needs soothing. *OK, Kuba, but let's get back to the gun. Have you ever fired at anyone?* No, not yet. *So you only threaten people with the thing?* It happens, though rarely. *Only when absolutely necessary?* Yes, only when there are no other avenues. I've shot the thing at a firing range a hell of a lot.

Pazina finally opens up. She's got a bathrobe on, hair all over the place, eyes sunken, absence of make up making her look older than usual. Any other time, I might have thought it cute. All those tiny wrinkles, the reddened eyes, the naturalness. It suits her. But then again, as I said, any other time.

"Are you completely gone in the head?" she asks.

What other time, Kuba? It doesn't matter. *Fine. But is there anyone out there you would like to send Christmas greetings to?*

I push Paz right into the apartment, mistiming it just as she moves herself, and she falls to the polished wooden floor.

"Fuck!" she screams.

I close the door behind me, step over her and go down the hallway. This is the first time I have ever been in here.

Kuba, are you still with us? Is there anyone you would like to send Christmas greetings to?

"Where is it?" I ask. No, there is no one I want to send greetings to. *Not even our listeners? There must be someone out there who wishes you well.* "Where is it?"

I pull the pistol out again. She looks at me in a way I have not seen before. Maybe it's the setting. The scenario. The night.

"You've lost it completely," she says, softly, her eyes cold, furious, ashamed of me. "Completely."

"Tell me, Paz, else I'll shoot you in the guts. For starters," someone says, coldly, calmly too. And I think it might now be me.

Fixing. I like this word. Very much. To fix, repair, restore. The process should be quick and precise. It should be done without too much thought, intuitively. To be good at repairs, you need to have imagination, the ability to foresee the consequences of one's movements.

I turn the phrase over in my mind – to fix. In order to fix something the person doing the fixing has to know the thing being fixed inside and out.

The weather is really rather fine. I only noticed when the guy on the radio said it was a lovely day. I was listening to the radio, because I had to listen to something and it couldn't be music. Music is too absorbing.

I've crossed the river now. The badlands. Goclaw. Gang upon gang. And my little apartment. My secret sanctuary. Pocket. Keys to the apartment. I still haven't slept, just lay in the bath, three hours, half-awake, or rather a quarter awake. Conscious, but I let my brain float off a little and disappear into a comfortable hole. I remembered something, though I don't recall what. It helped. The noise of the water. And some more coke. A tiny little bit. One or two spoonfuls. Maybe three.

Argentina. My bed to come. I will get there, lie down and sleep for sixteen hours straight. The sleep of the dead, or at least the innocent. And then I will wake and never take any drugs again. I've been a fool. A cretin. Tasteless. Shameful. I could just as well now be working a cab, driving a fifteen-year-old Opel Omega, brakes squealing, head not much better, taking the odd bit of speed only to keep going, to keep earning those few extra coins.

"Unfortunately" is another word I am turning over in my head. Unfortunately, it's unwise to pander to morons who are like little kids, unable to connect effects with causes, fire with burns. Especially those who let others get burnt. I don't give a fuck how many years Uncle spent behind bars, reading old paperbacks and even older copies of *Playboy*.

Repairs. Unfortunately. I will give Dario his bag back. Tell

Piotrek everything. Find Tiny and pull our cash right out of his dead guts. Sort things out with the cops, rent a different apartment under a different name, move everything, vanish. Change my numbers, get back in touch with my finest customers. Fix it all. Tidy up. Before I depart for the tropics.

I stop the car by the block of flats. It's bright, too bright. I put on a pair of sunglasses. The estate is almost empty. Someone dragging a last minute Christmas tree through the melting snow. I look up to notice coloured lights twinkling in many of the windows that belong to my pretend neighbours.

She sent me a text message in the morning, a long, begging thing, not worthy of quoting. I didn't write back. People ruin other people's lives, but only because they're allowed to. Allowed in. They're irrational, psychotic, only because they're allowed to be all that.

I only felt a tiny twinge of desire to drive over there, an itch beneath the skin, a hunger to fuck her one more time, a Christmas present to me, to fuck her up, walk in and out. But then I would want to do it again and again, I would hang around, I would linger, and that is deadly. She's not even a person, but a stage or an exam I have to pass, a test of maturity. She's a seductress, a siren, something from scary old fairytales. In a decade or two, she'll be a wasted madwoman, with a kid here and there, a daughter probably, doing her high school finals, in need of deep therapy, of all sorts of fixing, repairs, things I cannot manage, not in her mother or her. The door to the stairwell is open. I feel a tiny, tiny bit of a chill creeping under my shirt. Climbing the stairs, avoiding the lift, I look out down the hallway of my floor – my ancient neighbour's door is shut. Mine is slightly ajar.

The ice comes crashing down the back of my shirt. I go back to the car for my gun, problems focusing my eyes as I race down and back up again.

I push the door to my tiny apartment gently. Someone has

forced it open. The whole building must have heard. I stand in the doorway, pointing the gun forward. Breaths, ten deep breaths.

Dario's bag is gone. My bag, the one with all my savings, is gone. My face mask, documents, gloves and scales are all scattered across the floor. The scales are smashed. Bits of carpet pulled up. All the furniture upside down. A thorough job.

Good fucking God, fucking Christ, fucking Christmas, for fuck's sake.

The camera over the door – I turn to look, but it's gone, ripped from its mounting. Someone noticed it. Or knew about it beforehand. Somebody was told. The ice keeps on falling along my skin, like a melting glacier.

Ten deep breaths, again, calm down. Be cool. Look around. The bag with the money is gone. Uncle's bag, which was now no longer Uncle's bag, but was now Dario's bag. That is gone too.

Calm down. Someone's robbed you of 200,000 zlotys in cash, along with half that in euros and some kilos of coke, plus all the MDMA. Calm down. You have another hundred grand at your other place. Whoever did this can be found. And quick. twenty-four hours. Max. Keep cool.

There must have been at least two of them. Could have been anyone. Could have been undercover cops. Probably cops. But then there'd be tape all over the place, the media, Commissioner Marek on national TV talking about a successful bust. No one knew about this place. I've never brought anyone here. They had to have been tailing me. But I always know when I'm being watched. No one knew about this place. No one knew.

On the other hand, if it was the drug squad, they could have waltzed in, grabbed the cash and the coke, split it between themselves, taken photos, interviewed neighbours, and now be waiting for me, one floor up, on the staircase, monitoring everything.

I rest against a wall. Looking around. At the kitchenette. Walk into the bathroom, open the toilet lid. Boot marks on the clean floor. A fag butt floating in the toilet, like a business card, a thank you note – THANK YOU AND GOOD BYE. Not that long ago.

No one has ever been in here before. Never ever.

"Merry Christmas, Mr Piotr."

I put the gun on the floor of the bathroom, exit and close the door behind me.

"Merry Christmas," I hear again. Mrs Halina. Forgot all about her. I have a bag of Christmas goodies for her in the trunk of the Audi. Coffee, sweets, herbs for her heart condition and several crosswords and puzzle magazines. She stands in the smashed doorway, wrapped in layers of sweaters, fiddling with the broken reading glasses perched on the end of her wrinkled nose.

"Merry Christmas to you too," I reply.

"Are you spending Christmas in Warsaw? I thought you were leaving."

"My flight is tomorrow," I say, struggling to get the words out. "By the way, did you not hear anything? Any noises?"

I walk towards her. She looks at me strangely, as if with each step she was less and less sure she knew who I was.

"What noises?" she asks.

"I don't know. This morning. Last night. They broke into my home."

"Oh Christ! Oh, no! We have to call the police."

"You heard nothing?" I ask, calmly, I think.

"No, I sleep like a log. I just came out, thought I heard you moving about. Not that there was any noise before this. How could I miss that?" she says, looking at the smashed doorframe around her.

"I've lost something."

"Then we must, we must call the police. Right this second."

"No, we don't need to ring the police. Please, go back inside. I'll come to you in a moment."

"No, we have to report this. And to the housing association. Oh, my dear God!"

"Don't call anyone!" I bark.

She takes a step back and I shut the door in her face. Looking around, I find some shoes, trainers, several pairs. That's all. Apart from the cigarette butt in the bathroom, not a trace of them.

"We have to call the authorities, Mr Piotr, please. We can't leave it like this," she pleads through the door. Once again. Focus.

Details. Objects. Smudges. Marks. Focus, Kuba, focus for fuck's sake. "Maybe I did hear something, earlier, but you know me – I have a hearing problem, deaf in one ear..."

The table. A lighter. I know that lighter. A plastic, disposable thing, with the word Kreuzberg written upon it. On the table, right before me. What do you mean there was no one here? You fucking idiot. You stupid, stupid shit!

You did tell her she couldn't smoke in here, didn't you? You did.

"I heard people on the staircase, but there's always someone moving about, you know how people are," she goes on and on.

It's not possible. Not possible? Everything is possible, every little thing, all life is one great pack of cards to be dealt and picked and shuffled, all of them alike, all of them just as likely to happen. One has to be ready for anything, predict all avenues of possibility, accept nothing as firmly true or untrue. Trust no one and nothing. You fucking, fucking pathetic idiot.

Calm down. Standing here and trying to keep the breath steady will produce nothing. Calm down. Right now. Right now, get a hold of yourself, get to the point you were at a while back. A state when things were fixable. Not yet beyond repair.

I open the front door. She's still outside her own, staring through those cheap reading glasses.

"No one came to ask about me?"

"I will call right now, Mr Piotr. Just a moment," she says.

"No one was here? No one asked?"

"Who? Who would have asked me anything?" she asks, genuinely puzzled.

"No idea. Anyone."

"No, nobody, honestly. The guys from the gas board asked, of course. Wanted to take a reading. When you come back, we have to send them the meter readings. Gas. Electric. Water."

"What did they look like?" I ask.

"Who? The utilities men?"

Asking her makes no sense. I'm just wasting energy I can't spare trying not to scream at the crone. I can't bring myself to do it. Her world is gone, a broken kaleidoscope. Dates, events, hours are beyond her now. Her apartment a museum of post-war crap, communist-era baubles and broken furniture and dusty shelves and empty cupboards.

"I can't recall. They always look the same. There were two of them, they said they needed our readings."

"Goodbye, Mrs Halina," I say, maybe forcing a smile, I can't tell, walking down the hallway, down the stairs, out the wide open door. I can't be talking to anyone right now. A word wrong, a look, and I'll wring their neck in a flash.

It really is a pretty day. A day of blessings.

I aim for the car, but then I see them appear from behind a kiosk, suddenly, not wasting time, three detectives and four armed response guys, armed with rifles, sweating with delight, screaming at me like we were back in the playground again, playing at war. It's a glorious day, so they are running, ready to claim their prize: we have him, the bad guy, the bogeyman, Kuba G., the name which will be all over the news, if not tomorrow, then the day after Christmas. What a gift. A major coke dealer, supplier to the stars, caught red-handed, caught, cuffed, disarmed. Their eyes are shooting fire. I recognise one of the three who stopped me last night, the one with the twisted nose. And then the other guy, the plain one, he's got me pinned to the ground, the cuffs out, the knee in my back, spitting, "We told you, fucker, we'd be back. You fucking loser, you fucking homo, why keep all that shit in your own home?"

Someone kicks me in the side of the head, bruised already, and I look up and see people in those twinkling windows, looking down, pointing.

"Merry Christmas," I think to myself. "Merry fucking Christmas, you fuckers, you shits, this is for you, for being such good little citizens. Santa is proud. Come, sit on my lap. Listen to my story. You might even get a bonus, buy a few extra bottles of cheap sherry, cheap whisky, cheap wine."

Cut. They're all gone all of a sudden. All the cops. All the guns. Just my imagination.

The estate is empty. Piles of snow and me. I approach the car, unlock the door. Deep breath.

Inside, I try to fix the flaws in my own thinking. Someone stole something of mine. For the first time ever. Now you have to find them and you know where to start looking. You made a mistake and now you're being punished. And have to do some punishing of your own. A simple deal. Push, pull. Action, reaction. Friendships come, friendships go.

Forgive yourself. Forgive yourself and quick – nothing is as damaging, as maddening as anger aimed at the self.

1:55pm

"What the fuck are you talking about?" Paz whispers.

She's fuming, but not just that. There's something else there. A deep pain.

"You're the only one who was ever there," I say. "You and only you. Nobody else, Paz, not a soul. No one else even knew the place existed."

"Can I get up?"

I gesture with the gun for her to rise. She does awkwardly, as if already tired of my shit.

"Can you lower the fucking gun?" she asks. "You have one, I don't. Enough for you? You don't have to point it at me, for God's sake."

"You knew about the camera. You knew where it was concealed."

"Please. Lower the fucking pistol." I let my hand drop, then look around her apartment. It's nicely decorated. The floor tiled in dark wood. The walls bare, except for a few tasteful paintings. "You have to get a hold of yourself, Kuba."

Her words are like someone tiptoeing backwards.

"You were there. You told someone. Told someone about the cash and the stash. Told them the place was mine."

She looks at me like I'd just spat in her face.

"Who do you take me for? Who the fuck do you take me for?" she asks, looking convincingly puzzled.

A guy emerges from one of the other doorways. Must be the

274

bedroom. He's wearing trousers, but his chest is bare. An ordinary looking guy, nothing special, middle aged and all that. He looks at me with deep concern, wondering what to say now that he sees what I'm holding. He wavers, takes a step back. Touches his well-exercised six pack, holding onto his own reality, the reality that existed before I introduced mine in here.

"I'll be with you in a second," Paz sighs.

"Is everything..."

"Paz will be with you in a second," I sigh too.

"Pazina?" the guy says, weakly, knowing full well he's pushing his luck, which ran out long before he got into that bed. I wonder if he's the nice guy, the one with the kid, the one already too broken inside to toy with.

"How can you suspect me, Kuba? Tell me that. How can you come in here, brandishing that, Christmas, daytime, attack me, then say I betrayed you. How?"

She approaches and smashes both open palms into my chest, shoving me backwards. Almost tossing me down to her floor.

"You were the only one who knew about that place."

"Fuck off out of here!"

"Only you, dear. You know I'll find them. And quick. If it was you, I'll be back."

"Get out and don't ever dare come back. Ever."

We stand there, facing each other. Wordless. I then realise, as soon as I am gone, she'll start crying. She won't do it now, won't give me the satisfaction, but she will cry. As soon as that door is shut.

"Oh, I'll be back," I say, smiling as I push the gun back behind my belt, feeling awkward, as if I had said or done something out of turn, constantly repeating to myself that it must have been her. I always knew she was a good actress, but not when it came to me. She could fool others, but not lie to those she cared about. Then again, maybe she was leading me on from the start, keeping me around for the dark glamour, one of her collection of dysfunctional men, all the faces in this town hers. Maybe she decided to cash our association in when it became worth her while. Paz, my mate. My only mate. I believed it too, like a kid in playschool. Meanwhile, this is Warsaw, a city where every fucker wants to do every other fucker over, where people would sell you dust and tell you it's flour, where not that long ago there were wars, uprisings, partitions, all of them lost. All of them tragic. Things like friendships were chased out of this town a long time ago. Burnt to hell and gone.

We look at each other as if in slo-mo, as if this was a scene from a shitty old western. I exhale, realising I was holding the breath in for too long. Pazina changes colours, red and white, shimmering. Her mouth drawn tight, her fists clenched tighter.

I know plenty. I know it all. I know she recently had cashflow problems, had to keep going from loan to petty loan, that her credit cards are maxed out, that she's never asked me for money, and when I offered, she always said no, but people will do anything to cover up their plans, right?

"What are you waiting for?" she asks, exasperated.

I turn around and open the door. Step outside into the stairwell. I hear as she turns too and walks barefoot back to her boyfriend. "So she never broke up with him after all," I think to myself. "Liar. She wants to be normal. Wants to disappear, be like all the others. At any price."

Maybe she wants to grab hold of that child of his and treat it as her own, and smile at it, and have it smile at her, the innocent, the plan almost complete.

50,000 euros and a kilo of coke, worth at least that much again, will surely help pay for her ticket into that dream prison.

Kuba, now, one more question from our listeners. The last one, really. Do you really think no one can be trusted? How did you realise this? Do you not believe that some motives, some intentions are pure? No. 'Innocent intentions' is an oxymoron. *Pardon?* Oxymoron, a rhetorical term. *We know what that phrase means, but perhaps you could elaborate for our listeners.*

All intentions are dirty. We always think solely of ourselves. We always want to get rich, then richer, to get a cut of something, a bite, to keep it safe, to win at whatever cost. Nothing is pure. Nothing. Even the idea stinks. Stinks of death. No one has ever experienced death, the same as no one has ever touched purity. Even kids scream for their mother's breast, not out of love, but out of hunger.

Says a man, holding a gun, all alone every Christmas.

No, so says a man holding a gun who is right now going to have some Christmas Eve supper.

This is a sad, sad story, Kuba. Very depressing.

I don't think so. I just think of it as another chess problem to be solved.

3:10pm

It's like a whole life spent in the shadows, the back of the house. Like circling the city down backstreets only, seeing but not being seen. A good feeling. Empowering. Problems, however, begin when it comes to emerging from the shadows. When in order to sort certain problems one has to step out of the shadows, into the light, while still trying to remain invisible.

People with kids, the elderly, teens, women selling flowers by the local all-night mini market on Wilson Square. Cab drivers, cops, salespeople. All their flesh, their muscles making a mark on reality. That sense of being unable to access their reality, of being in a completely different sector, separate dimension. The sense of separation, of going unnoticed. Nobody knows anything. My mouth hangs open. No one sees. I close it. No one notices. Except maybe those who have my money.

Uncle is not answering his phone. Maybe he did it? But how would he know how to find the place? Would someone tell him?

It's starting to get grey, the day ending suddenly, as if it had made a mistake, as if the world was saying sorry for it. I know where he lives. I know he'll be home. Old Zoliborz, the boy from the hood done good, dirty money buying a way out to a clean district with clean streets leading to clean parks for clean kids to play in. Retired artists. Young families. I sell a lot of coke there. Architects, doctors, actors, kids belonging to millionaires. Upper middle class.

Marek lives on Wieniawski Street. I mentioned already that he married well.

I stand outside his house for a little while. It's a semi-detached villa, solid, unadorned by any fancy crap. The garden empty. I look through the windows of one of the few buildings left standing after the Nazis and the Soviets were done bombing this town. When I was a kid, back in Olsztyn, taking walks with my parents around our district in the evenings, I loved looking inside people's homes, all the different coloured lights, curtains, lampshades. Thousands of bright little aquariums. I was always under the impression that fascinating things had to be happening inside those rooms, that they were portals into different worlds. I dreamt of having the power to turn invisible, to watch people, listen to them, watch how they behaved, study their inner lives.

I always wanted access to the greatest number of worlds, while myself remaining unseen. A rather cute aspiration. The only one I can ever remember having.

I ring the doorbell attached to the gate. Several times. Nobody answers. I stick my hand through the railings and open the gate from the inside, looking around. The light of day fading rapidly.

I walk up to the front door, knock on it, then wait. Counting to twenty. Then I knock again, looking for a doorbell. It's there, but I don't use it. I wait some more. Finally, I see the light go on through a stained glass panel in the front door. It opens and I see his eyes open too, very wide. He's wearing a suit. Hugo Boss, maybe. Nice. Navy. The shirt open down to his chest, a little uncouth, like an 80s Italian crooner. His shock really is sweet. The stupid, stupid pig.

"Christmas fucking Eve. Have you gone mad?" he asks through gritted teeth.

"Who is it, Dad? Is it the unannounced guest?" a small kid calls out from inside.

"No, darling. Wait," he says, turning round, then back to me.

"We have to talk, and yeah, right now," I say, telling not asking.

He closes the door behind him, shakes his head in disgust when I lift my blazer to show him the gun I've poked into the front of my belt.

"You fucking moron. You come to the house of a police commissioner, on Christmas Eve? Go fuck off out of here before something really crazy happens. Fifteen minutes from now, you can kiss a decade of your life goodbye. No problem, pal. Christmas present from you to me."

"I want to show you something, wait here. And relax. For the time being, we're all good. We're just talking."

I pull my phone out, hands shaking with the cold. Since the sun set, the temperature's gone with it. It takes me a while to find the right recording, but then it's there and pressing play is the easiest thing in the world.

It's muffled, the speaker shit, but he knows his own voice when he hears it. After I press Stop and put the phone away, he looks away, but his eyes are filled with fury. His body tense, muscles desperate to stomp my head into week-old snow. Someone opens his front door from the inside. It's his fancy wife. She looks at us questioningly, but is wise enough to know not to ask a thing. She might have been considered pretty once, her unnaturally coloured hair is pulled back in an extreme ponytail, stretching her skin and accentuating the harshness of her jawline even more. Her sleeveless dress suggests she's a gym-goer. Skinny, muscular arms, forearms veined, unnaturally so. She'd have no trouble shooting up, that's for sure. Maybe she does too – a little doctor's treat from herself to herself, from time to time, clean needles, quality shit. Keeps her slim. Saves the body from changing shape, becoming like her mother's, heavy, misshapen, sculpted by processed fats and starchy foods. I can smell the wine on her breath from a distance, which suggests she started boozing early on this lovely family Christian holiday.

"Someone from work?" she finally asks.

"Go in. It's cold," he says without looking at her.

"Merry Christmas," I add.

"Would you like to come in?" she asks, seeing the cut of my blazer, the shape of my jeans, my shoes. In this light though, she can't see the bruises on my face, the dirt dried into my sleeves, the blood on my hands. My own blood. The blood of others.

"Hon, it's work. Couldn't wait, sorry. Go in," Marek says, voice trembling, the cold doing its thing to us all.

"It's Christmas though. Damn it," she says, suddenly not so inviting. How alcohol can throw people off balance.

"It is," I say, smiling. "Would love to."

His teeth grate, I think. I think I hear them in the dusk.

"Welcome. Agnieszka Cewińska," she says, holding out her tiny hand.

"Piotr Bałczyk," I say, returning the greeting as gently as I can.

I do it to punish him. To shock him out of his comfort zone. His cop-like sense of sacred order. His wife must believe it too. Must think I am another cop. Maybe even his superior.

Which makes the whole thing even more fun.

I step inside, trying to beat the dirt from my blazer, my jeans. Going inside, I follow, without taking off my shoes, as is the tradition. Fuck him, he's not going to have the satisfaction. The house must have been left to her by family. Old books, old pre-war paintings, crystal chandeliers, lampshades, other goodies on the shelves they could never afford on his regular salary. Not what you imagine the house of a mid-career detective looks like on the inside, that's for sure. The Christmas tree is massive, dominating the already large salon – unnatural, monstrous, like it shot up from the ground and pierced the foundations, penetrating their familial abode. Two little kids sit at the large oak table, a boy and a girl. They look at me, but don't seem pleased. I'm no musician, here to sing carols. No priest offering blessings and pretty little cards with pictures of gilded angels on them. Definitely no Santa. In the light of all the candles and the mirrors and the fairy lights, the dirt and the blood on me becomes visible. Dried black.

I stand before them, trying to smile, but failing and knowing I'm failing, thus failing even more.

"You forgot to take your shoes off," the girl says. She seems to be the more assertive sibling.

"Yeah, it's winter," the boy adds.

"No need," the mother says from behind me, sensing something is not as she first thought. Sensing she needs to take action. Take charge. She rushes up to the table, which is covered in Christmassy baubles, bits of fir twig, fancy napkins. She finds the special seasonal wafer, the one all Poles snap bits off when wishing each other the impossible each year, and holds it out to me.

"There you go. Merry Christmas," she says.

I snap a piece off, waiting for her reaction, for what her face will look like after she's noticed the damage all over me. Eating the wafer, trying to remember if it tastes the same as I remember from childhood, I forget that the tradition is for me to offer her back a piece, so we can all have a bit of each other's wafer and then come up with original sounding wishes afterwards.

"All the best," she says, looking paralysed as I chew, then swallow the tasteless pulp.

"Same to you," I say, once my mouth is empty.

"Go break the communion wafer with Mr Piotr," he orders the kids, Christ knows why.

They run up to me, holding out bits of already snapped wafer, looking up at me.

"So you're the unwanted guest?" asks the boy.

"Unannounced," the girl corrects him.

"Yes. That's me," I say. "Now, can I have a minute with your daddy? We need to chat about something."

"Do you have any presents?" the girl asks.

"He's not Father Christmas. That comes later," my deputy commissioner interrupts.

I look back at him, his face frozen, expressionless, but his skin the colour of blueberry ice cream. He keeps stretching his hands, extending the fingers, trying to keep calm, failing miserably. Everywhere and anywhere, he thinks to himself. He could manage to keep cool any time, any place on earth – but not here. Not with a gun about to be pointed at his kids. In his own lounge. In his own house.

"Please, sit." Agnieszka points with her hand at a clean plate set up already. Polish tradition – always expect the uninvited guest at Christmas, as it could be Jesus, back to announce the end of days. The kingdom of God. The Good News. The table is loaded with food. Spiced, fatty. Home-cooked dishes, traditional delights, fish, cabbage, poppy seed pasta, dumplings, rice, salads and sweet things.

"You look hungry. Come eat," the boy says, and smiles, even though I don't move.

"Can I have a word?" Agnieszka asks her husband, and they depart for the kitchen. I smile, watching his head turned, his eyes on me, promising all sorts of vengeance. Once they are out of sight, I look back at the table, delighting in the sights, happy to have a gun in my belt and a phone in my pocket, both containing things that ensure I am in charge here, for a while. He's taken so much of my money, the fuck owes me. Looking down at his wife's culinary efforts, I think he owes me more than this.

"Don't you have a family of your own?" the girl asks.

I sit at the table and select from the dishes in front of me. I chew very slowly. I haven't eaten in a day or two. I think maybe it's not a good idea to be sampling all twelve dishes, as is the tradition. The carp, smelling of mud, that cabbage smelling of shit, borscht smelling of sweet blood.

"I do. Everyone does," I tell her.

"Then why are you not there now? Are you angry?" she asks.

"Do you need money?" the boy adds, and I laugh.

"I do. And I don't," I say, trying not to speak with my mouth full. "It's... complicated."

"Did you have a fight?" the girl asks, gently broaching the subject of my severely beaten up and kicked in face.

"No, nothing like that. I just need to talk to your dad."

Taking my eyes off the kids, looking back to the kitchen door, I notice all the antiques sprinkled tastefully about the place. Oak-panelled floor. White walls. A fireplace, unlit. Some tastefully selected books, their thick, gold-lettered spines looking dignified on the shelves. Outside the window there must be a balcony, or a patio, and then a large, classy garden beyond it. But it's dark now, and none of that can be seen. All of it is hers. And he knows it. If she kicks him out, his debts will catch up with him, his addictions, his corruptions too. He'll end up sleeping on a mattress in a crappy one-room apartment, not far from here, next to some Vietnamese and

Ukrainian students, a picture of the kids the only sign of identity, of him in the place. An old, heavy flat-screen TV dumped on the floor. She'll let him take that with him, dragged out from the attic. He knows all he makes will be lost, in casinos, cheap brothels, and that I am his only way towards freedom, redemption, regaining control.

"Work? This time of year?" I hear from the kitchen, a subdued yet raised voice, Agnieszka losing the last bit of hospitality and goodwill this Christmas season.

"Keep it down!" he barks back.

I smile.

Something smashes on the floor. The boy frowns. The girl keeps looking at me, like she knows I'm making this happen, controlling the objects in that other room, breaking things in her kitchen.

"Phone calls... nights... your fucking buddies, coming round here pissed... leaving their bloody cigarette stubs in my garden... fucking whores... Christmas? Christmas?!"

I listen to Agnieszka's rising voice as if I was listening to an aria. A Christmas special by Debussy or Bach.

"Do they often argue?" I ask the kids, gently. The boy is frozen, but the girl nods. "Do you two go to school?"

The boy starts crying, subtle tears running down both cheeks. His sister starts stroking her arm. She looks at me and says, "I started this year, but I don't want to go."

"When you go to pre-school, do you cross the river?" I ask, then hear Marek shout: "Calm the hell down!"

I lay my cutlery across the plate. I think I've had three or four bites, but my stomach is ready to explode.

"How did you know?" the boy asks, tears drying. "Saxon. It's called Saxon Marshes."

"And the street?"

I don't know if I'd ever hurt a child. It wouldn't ever occur to me to have to do it. I'm just asking questions. Besides, I'm trying to get the kid to think about something other than what's going on in his kitchen. If he starts crying, howling, I don't know how I will react. What I might do. I don't want to do anything unexpected. Unwelcome.

"It's got a funny name, like a country," the boy says.

"French Street?" I ask.

"I'll sort it!" Marek roars and I hear footsteps behind me.

"No, Mexican Street."

The footsteps were hers.

"Marek is waiting for you in the kitchen. Mr..." she says, confused by the names all of a sudden.

"When can we open our presents?" the girl asks, sensing opportunity.

I don't wait for that particular ceremony, going through to the kitchen as quick as I can. As I pass her, I stop to put my arm on her son's head. It is smooth and very warm, as if he had been sunbathing all day.

"You've got guts," I whisper to him.

My eyes are on his mother, a woman who sees me touching her child, in her own home, and then it seems she gets it, or begins to get it, something dawning, that I am not from work, or rather that I am something to do with work, but the dark side of it, not the light. I did not come here to solve problems, but to cause them. Not to take work off his hands, but to add to an already merciless caseload.

"Mum, please... Can we open our presents now?" the girl pleads, looking at her paralysed brother.

"What are their names?" I ask, smiling kindly.

"Marek is waiting in the kitchen," she repeats.

He is indeed. He's all there. Breathing heavily, smoking a cigarette, trying to keep the smoke blowing out the open window. The small dining table between us is old, but the fridge is very modern, with an ice-making machine and everything.

"Yesterday, some of your colleagues stopped me. Without due cause, I might add. Bothersome. They were all up for making love, but they're not my type, if you know what I mean. I had to give them the slip."

"I can't do a thing," he says without looking at me, so I can't tell if he's lying or not.

"And then this morning, someone broke into my home, would you believe. Damaged things, everything, smoked indoors without opening the windows, the scum. They took things. Things that did not belong to them. Small things, but they meant a lot. A fucking kilo of coke. Plus pills. Plus tons of cash. Didn't even wipe their feet when they came in."

"I can't help you," he says again.

I come up close to him. Very close. He knows. Can tell just by smelling me that I'm not being my usual careful self. A realisation which, at least for him, right now, is definitely not good news.

"Did I bring mud into your house?" I ask, coldly, looking down at my own boots.

He looks down too.

"You're not the only one," he says.

"Your kid," I tell him, "A very tough little lad."

"You're not alone. They're coming for us all, trying to shut us down, orders from above, I told you before."

"I swear I wiped my feet before I entered your home."

I can hear the girl sobbing in the other room.

"If a kilogram of coke was taken as evidence," he tells me, trying to sound determined. "If any money had come into their possession, banked or not, I would know about it. I'd get my cut. I'd be here, at home, in a much better fucking mood than now."

I can feel something drawing over me, like a heavy blanket, again, my head clouded, the day far from over. I have to keep going, then pack, then make it to the airport. Plenty of time yet to kill. Forty-eight hours may not sound like much, though something tells me this Christmas is not going to be like all the others. Nowhere near as forgettable.

My phone pings: *Kuba, let's meet*. I don't recognise the number.

"We're all screwed for now," he says, hopefully. Without forcing anything, without acting, as I look around his kitchen, the expensive Swiss carving knives, the marble kitchen top, the restored cupboards. Once she finally cuts loose of him, he'll be eating out of that Asian food kiosk until he dies.

"The fucker from the TV show, he caused an explosion. That's our problem. All eyes on our hands. Even the prime minister spoke out. That dead woman, driving around that private estate, she was connected. Someone wants blood in return. Someone high, high up. The fucking TV star will vanish, then reappear, better than new, doing charity work, adopting other little orphans. But a sacrifice has to be found. I can't stop them. Even if they come for me, much less you."

"That's honest of you. That's kind. Wait a second," I say, typing back *Who is this?* "Do they know his supply came from me?"

He looks at me without nodding. Shit.

"What else do they know?" I ask, though I'd rather not know.

"You're a ghost. Can't lock up someone who never existed. But ghosts can be trapped. Punished in other ways," he says, cryptically, too cryptically for my mood right now.

"What else do the fuckers know?" I ask, a little louder than intended.

He seems a little more relaxed, looking past me in the direction of his family, of his old life, but then the look of hope is gone. I take out the bottle and the little spoon and feed myself. Straight away feeling much cleaner, cooler, refreshed. I spoon up a bit more powder and hold it up towards him, a peace offering. He is frozen with panic, but certain hungers are not interested in logic. He takes the spoon and the powder is gone. The beginning of a very, very long night for him and his troubled brood.

"I don't know what else they might know," he says, sniffing as if troubled by hay fever. "I don't fucking know anything else. Not that I haven't tried to ask. But my boys didn't take your shit. I would know about that."

"Have they interviewed anyone?"

"Like who?"

"Don't fucking play fucking games. Answer straight, while I'm still being nice," I growl through gritted teeth, the coke buzzing in my mouth.

He tries to think, his eyes flickering, eyelashes trembling, tongue licking the lips. His son must have the same expression on his face when stressed, when unsure of what to do, to say, what excuses to cling to when shit is fucked up. People are like kids, so easy to read. Transparent. Especially when surrendered to substances, to simple addictions.

"He gave your name," Marek says. "Whatever name you gave them, he coughed up straight away. In a heartbeat. His fucking lovely Bentley wrecked. The woman and the baby lost. Gave us your number, so they must have tapped your phone, tracked your car. Besides, they now have tech that recognises your voice on any tracked lines, so they don't even need your number. He didn't give your surname, because he didn't ever ask you for it. Doesn't know where you live, which crew you run with, and it'll take them a while to track down your aliases. Christmas will delay them, but they'll do it. They've started on all their informants, those who deal and those who work for other crews, but I guess you told them even less. Or more bullshit. Either way, they can't even agree on what your first name is. I don't even fucking know. You exist, but not in any way we can configure. In some way, they admire that. In others, it makes them fucking mad. They feel impotent. You cut their dicks off and now they want them to grow back."

"What can you do for me?"

"All that I've already done," he says, flatly. "They started running their searches a day early, when that furniture magnate's dipshit son od'ed. His connections date back to Solidarity days, cast-iron loyalties, tough to sneak past. And the media, well, they put two and two together. Not coz they're smart, just coz of the coincidence. The timing. They love a bit of intrigue before the holidays start. They know you were at his place a day earlier, just before he died, and they had your description, had your number plates. Hence the recent heat."

"And now, what can you do? For me?" I repeat.

"Fucking hell, I dismissed some statements, told them to retest the blood samples, buying you time. They found plenty of shit in there, believe me. But a little time was the best I could buy. I ain't a party political shaker, for fuck's sake. I'm just a cop."

He stands there, but I sense him shaking. With my sixth sense. Trembling like a leaf. Like someone about to go down with a stroke or heart attack. Me, her, the ones who are breathing down his neck, his debtors, his kids. He's got himself into a position on the playing board which still offers hope, but with every move he makes, less and less of it. It's all generating friction, heat, shit that could explode in a fireball any time. The materials, the contents involved are just too explosive. Coke, fame, death, love. Dealing with all that takes plenty of fuel, more than we can sometimes supply – that's why I do what I do and make what I make doing it. It keeps the building from collapse, all this effort, but it won't last. It never does.

"I told you to vanish," he says, acting angry now, as if he was my father. "It's not gonna go and blow away overnight, is it? Vanish, and they'll lose interest eventually. Pin shit on someone closer to hand. You fucking know how it works, you have the money, the means, what the fuck are you still doing here? In my fucking family home?"

I say nothing, running my hand slowly across the marble surface of his kitchen worktop. My hand running over his property, or rather what he likes to think of as his property. Which it ain't. His house is smooth and cold and dead.

"You're fucking drowning in shit," he says, trying to sound like he cares about that fact. "Heavy shit. It's not about money any more. Not about freedom. People are gonna get angry when they smell you near. When they see you packing. They'll panic or shoot and mean it. When they find you. And find you they will. So go. Get away and let shit die down..."

I look at him. Right into his bloodshot, damp, permanently lying eyes.

"Your Christmas wish, Marek... it should be for you to never ever see me again."

I exit the kitchen without giving him a chance to come up with a riposte to that. His wife is slouched on the sofa, cuddling the kids protectively. Their minds distracted, hands full of freshly unwrapped toys. Her eyes remind me of big, black coins. As black as the gun I know she can sense, can see bulging beneath my blazer. I smile, raising my hand.

"Delicious. Never tasted better," I say, getting into this smiling thing. "Merry Christmas, kids!"

She says nothing. The kids look up, but they no longer have time for their new Uncle Piotr. Lego and Barbie have greater power than my charisma and cash and coke. I toy with the idea of sharing a spoon with her too, as a parting gift, but decide against it.

When I was little, I wondered what would happen if I could just magically wander into any home I walked past, any home I wanted. I wondered what would happen if I was ever caught. How people would react, having a ghost in their house. Or if the magic failed and I suddenly appeared, sitting there or crouching behind a sofa, touching their family photos, going through their books, their clothes. I always imagined what they would look like, their mouths hanging there in shock and shame and awe.

I wanted to play with that. To appear and then vanish again. Like a demon. Like the devils we find in all our kids' books, traditional fairytales, or rather folktales, of playful horny devils, making bets, scaring housewives, stealing children.

Before I get any more ideas, my phone pings again. Walking towards the front door, silence behind me, I check the screen: *Kuba, you're making me sorry. I don't like to feel sorry. Dario*

6:41pm

From this high up, Warsaw looks like a colourful board game, seen in negative. White dots, yellow lines, a drawing on the back of something rough and black, quick sketches with dirty lamps.

The hand which painted it doesn't clap, doesn't wave, doesn't give any thumbs up. The hand which painted it doesn't forgive. It is the hand of a crazed child.

The light at first gives the impression of a structure, a plan, a map, but keep looking and you soon realise that it's a mirage, the spots begin shifting, the colours changing, everything mobile, awkward, broken. From the 43rd floor of a luxury hotel, Warsaw looks like a void, like what it is – a toothless maw, all those lights down below the souls of those it's already swallowed. Afterglow.

A helicopter flies close by.

"It's all a question of perspective, dear Kuba," Piotrek says in his usual fashion.

Nothing is a question of perspective, Piotrek darling. Everything below is just a concrete ecosystem, one we're all trapped by, even if I could try living in a cloud over it. Forty-three floors beneath my feet there is asphalt, frozen solid, sprinkled with sand and salt by the lovely city authorities, littered with the shit left behind by its less than lovely residents, puked over, bled on. The black mass which lives beneath the black asphalt has me tied down with an invisible line which is attached to my neck.

"Not true," I say.

"You know fuck all, Kuba," Piotrek says, standing next to me, holding a cup of mineral water, wearing a perfectly white towelling bathrobe. He's looking down at the same thing as me. We're at the swimming pool in the Hotel Intercontinental. The space is lit with soft blue lamps, meant to give the impression of comfort and freshness; behind us the perfectly still pool glowing with deeply artificial azure, lit from down below. Jays, one of Piotrek's men, is lying on one of the sun loungers set up around the water. He's not listening to our conversation, ignoring the view, eyes closed, focused on the music playing through his headphones. Over us, at an upper level, we can see an almost completely empty fitness gym. Not many keen on keeping fit on Christmas Eve, except for a single middle-aged woman, sweating it out before piling on the holy calories later. She won't see us, or that view either, wouldn't notice if we started a gunfight around the swimming pool.

"I'm the one who is here and looking down, because I can afford it, to swim here any time I like, to drink my fucking plastic cups of flat water, pay my membership fees and not care. But if you were down there, Kuba, sweeping those streets, spreading sand to stop people sliding to their deaths all over town, and you looked up at this fucking hotel, up at this fucking window with its glowing water, and you wondered what the fucking fuck it was, that glow, you would notice a different perspective, wouldn't you?"

"You, me, that shit down there, we're all trapped. Warsaw our slave-master," I tell him without looking down. "Nothing changes that."

Piotrek is a simple guy. Checkers not chess. He thinks if you can look down at something, then it's already half yours. Piotrek likes to feel like he owns things, possesses them. Likes to roll things around his still-chubby fingers. He believes Warsaw is his, that he can fit it inside his fist, like a coin.

"You really have to change your attitude to life. I've never come across anyone quite like you. You got brains, I give you that, but they're slowly turning against you. You gotta ease off, boy, and ease off quick. My boys get sent on holidays. Martinique. Ibiza. They're given business cards for places they're not gonna catch anything I don't want them to bring back here. They fuck, they snort, they spend and they sleep. You can laugh, you can call them stupid, brainless cunts, but they come back good as new. Ready to take this city on again."

"I'm leaving tomorrow."

"Alone I bet. With a suitcase full of fucking books. Fucking romantic fucking novels. Historical thrillers. I've seen them at the airport. Or books about chess problems, for crying out loud."

"Or maybe," I think to myself, "He too senses this rain, this flood, which is coming, feels it in his cells, his bones, like a nasty case of rheumatism. Maybe he's already arranged some shelter, thinking that the rain will pass him by, that he will watch it from the safety of a 43rd floor swimming pool, floating about holding a fucking plastic cup everyone knew was full of vodka."

Bullshit. The water that will come will carry everything away, all of us, the rich and the fucking insanely poor. We'll all be last. None first. When the end comes, I will be ready. I am ready.

For a moment I feel a chill come over me, turning to ice. I close my eyes, realising the cold is a sign of impending death. I guess it shows, because Piotrek stops with his monologue and asks: "Is everything kosher, Kuba, lad?"

I nod. He laughs.

"Fuck, we recently went with the lads to the seaside, fucking Sopot, splashed out, spent stupid sums, ten of us, but then this group of thirteen young girls get close to us, and next thing we know fifty grand is gone, one weekend, unlucky thirteen. Champagne, cabs, hotel bar tabs, food, puff, blow... boy, once they were fed they fucked like locomotives, like evil little trains. Two of us on one girl, then three. I woke with a whole heap of them next to me, Kuba. Don't know how and don't fucking care. Don't have to care.

Shouldn't fucking care, and that's my point. Entertainment, Kuba. You have to remember to unwind. Else you'll fucking explode, like an overwound watch. Some of the boys are still sleeping it off. Or working off the substances in their private gyms. One way or another, you got to let go."

He tosses the cup into a bin. Stretches.

"Take some flip flops, speedos, they've got them all here for hire, and come to the sauna like a normal fucking gangster," he says.

Jays gets up without being told, takes the headphones off, approaches the pool. I see the words YOU PAY WITH RESPECT tattooed in giant, ugly letters all across the back of his shoulders. As I try to work out what the fuck that could mean, he dives in, not inelegantly for a guy his size.

"What if I'm not a fan of sweating?" I ask.

"You want to control everything, Kuba. Even your fucking natural processes. Want to be the lord of all you survey. In charge. A fucking dictator. A Stalin. You're holding on too tight. Remember what happens to all dictators when the music stops playing. When the marches end. You don't know how to release. It'll cost you your sanity, genius. Or the valves in your ticker."

"Maybe," I say.

"You are mental, a complete madman, but I like you."

I turn away from the view, from that gaping maw. The swimming pool is small, maybe twenty metres in length. Jays in it looks like an overgrown child playing in a paddling pool.

"Someone bust into my home. Stole cash and drugs. Which did not belong to me," I tell him.

"Who did they belong to?"

"Uncle said the lot was his. But it was not. It belonged to your buddy Dario." Piotrek looks down, sighing. "Uncle's made an awful fucking mistake. Tried to pull something on the side, but in the end he's just come to screw himself. Meanwhile, Dario is not best pleased. Angry and hungry."

"Did you talk to him?"

"By accident. I bumped into him while taking care of some other business."

"What about the missing gear?"

"No idea. Still trying to find out who took it. I don't know if it was the cops or one of the crews or somebody else again."

Piotrek looks me in the eye. He seems tired. He is tired, the tiredness of a typical working-class Polish male. Decades of hustling in a reality shaped by the fallout of Nazism and Stalinism, of doing business in a corrupt land, burdened by insane bureaucracies and an even more insane culture of aggression and mistrust, where everyone – fathers, husbands, all men – at a certain point in their lives quit fighting their alcohol intakes, quit going to the gym, grow moustaches and buy into the socks and sandals holiday beach wear combo. They start spending the weekends fishing, or watching football on their big-screen TVs. God forbid they should go to see an actual game or play one. Piotrek imports high grade cocaine from the other side of the world, but he could just as well be running a family-owned construction firm or pet food store.

"Do you know why I'm not home for Christmas?" he asks.

"Good question – why not?"

He sighs again. Looks back out at the city.

"Because I'm fucking sick and tired. Everybody wants something from me. Everybody."

"We have things to resolve," I tell him.

"I'm not talking about you... I'm gonna get home around 8pm, once that bitch has gone. I mean my mother in law. I can't even bear to look at the cow. She sits there, poisoning her daughter, constantly. That I don't give her enough to spend on the house. That the kids should be going to a private school. A private fucking what? What will they become then? Dyslexic fucking faggots? This and that, you know how it goes. Nothing ever right. That our villa in the mountains is falling apart. Endless, endless fucking complaints."

Jays emerges from the swimming pool, shaking his heavy body dry like a dog. He sticks a finger into his ear to unblock it, and then stares at its tip in the dim lights for a good few seconds.

"I have to go," he says to Piotrek.

"You're not going any-fucking-where. You're gonna drive me home." Jays drops back down onto his lounger and Piotrek continues his monologue. "And she will then replay everything back to me, even though the witch herself is gone, like she was recording it all, perfect playback. There's nothing else inside that skull. Just her mother's voice. Money. That's all she wants from me. She has a cleaning lady, a cook, so what the fuck am I paying her for? Raising the brats? Her brother keeps fucking up every business he tries, wanting me to rescue his ass every time, a complete, charmless moron. I don't even want to think about how much money I've pumped down that fucker's well. It keeps her quiet for a while, so there are advantages, but you know what I mean. There are limits. Their younger sister, now her husband's chased her out of the house and she's got herself a depression, hangs around the house, moping and dying and making everyone's life a fucking misery. That's why I'm not fucking home for Christmas. I told her I will build a monument to her depression, put it in our garden, with a Hollywood sign saying DEPRESSION, just so she'll shut up about it. Let everyone see. Why should we suffer alone?"

He stops himself, takes another deep breath, realising that he's gone too far. I don't mind. He needs to get it off his chest. He does this to me, every time I collect more powder from him. Maybe not every time, but often. As if wanting to signify that we have something of a business relationship, rather than just transactions. I don't know, though, if he only does it with me or with everyone else he comes across and wants to offload on.

"You understand, right? You ain't got this shit going on in your life, but you understand why I'm tired." I touch the reinforced plate-glass window with my hand, nodding. "I can't help you with those who took your property. Not in this case. You're gonna have to handle this one alone."

"The cops. The TV fucker who killed that girl with his car told them about me. They still don't know how to track me down. Or maybe they didn't but do now."

"Handle this alone. I can arrange for the best lawyers, but nothing more. For now, you're on your own."

"What about Uncle? And Dario?"

"Dario is my problem, not yours. Don't talk to him. Uncle?

The bastard can do what he wants. If he crosses lines, I'll be there waiting for him."

He tells me nothing I didn't know. I know I have to sort this mess out myself. I'm not yet at the stage when I need rescuing, and we both know it. I just want him to be informed. So he'll never have to say – *you should've told me* ...

"Things went wrong with the club, though, Kuba," he says, suddenly looking at me. "You were supposed be there, watching things."

"I could have shut him up straight away. He could have just talked to us. The kitchen equipment he had in there was worth two hundred grand alone. That would have cleared his debts. But there's no accounting for what stupid fucks will do."

"Did you not extend the offer?"

"His debt, his problem finding a solution to it."

"Yeah, but he's in your debt so it is your problem. Had you told him, we wouldn't be in the shit now. You got to sort this. Find him and fix it. We've not just lost heaps of investment and now income. What's worse, I have to keep answering questions. I don't like questions I don't ask myself, Kuba. I get enough of that shit at home."

Something flashes outside the window, like lightning, though the skies are clear. I blink my eyes to clear the afterglow. Everything back to normal. I notice the helicopter flying back towards us.

"I need to have that fucker Tiny brought to me on a plate," Piotrek states.

"I'll do what I can. You know I depart tomorrow."

"I do. Tomorrow. So do it tonight. A present, from you to me. Clean up the mess you made."

"I need powder. Is the delivery here?"

"What do you need it for if you're going away?"

"I want to make a few extra deliveries, so my best customers don't go wandering off while I'm away. Secondly, I'd rather have powder than money, because – for example – when I get back, there might be more supply problems. More interceptions."

"Shouldn't be," Piotrek says, semi-convincingly.

"I gotta manage the risk, though."

"You said they took your money."

"I have enough to cover what I need from you."

"The usual place then, two hours from now, I'll let them know to expect you."

I turn my back on Warsaw, and stare at the surface of the pool. At the gym above us. The woman has just stopped running and is standing there, as if paralysed by the view, the realization of what it means. I wonder about her. Where she's going on from here. Some fancy apartment, bought with an insanely expensive mortgage? Is the prick she's fucking at the office spending Christmas with his family? Of course he is. A good boy. He's never gonna leave them, no matter how many calories she burns trying to run towards him, how many luxury treadmills she wears out, how many gym memberships. How many marathons she runs for charity. She's just praying for a text message today, from him, one that isn't just standard wishes and crap.

"I know you'll sort it, Kuba. I know. Just do it now."

"Before departure," I say, nodding.

"I know about your departure. I'm more worried about you being intercepted upon your fucking return. If shit is left untidy." I shake the hot, sweaty hand he extends toward me. "Write me updates. Talk to no one. Especially not to Dario. And have a merry fucking Christmas."

I nod, walk over to shake Jays's hand, then head for the exit. Before I enter the corridor, I hear someone hit the water, the sound like a gunshot ricocheting around the place. I turn. Jays is still on the lounger. Piotrek is gone, only his bathrobe on the floor. Then he emerges and pauses on the surface of the water. His comfortable belly sticking up like a lonely island.

I know he's looking out at the stars. 43rd floor. The limit of his ambitions. He thinks he owns the place, owns the view, can tear it up any time he wants, like a postcard.

I know the view calms him. Makes him happy. Which makes me worry.

Walking down towards the lifts, I bump into the girl from the gym upstairs. I don't see the colour of her eyes, her phone glued to the side of her head as she stomps towards the changing rooms.

"Answer!" I hear her growl into the phone, a little prayer put up at Christmas, a little gift from someone who must right now be stuffing himself full of overcooked carp, his phone on silent, pretending to care, while she, sweating and furious, opens a door and still gripping that phone disappears inside the changing room.

9:00pm

These sorts of places are what most of our civilisation is made of. This is what the earth is made of. What Poland is composed of. City centres are small, segregated sections for the winners, the invisible rulers. The rest live elsewhere, shop elsewhere, where the warehouses, the landfills, the factories, the housing projects are. Some small villas, but not many. Not enough to go round. The real peripheries.

The air is cold and contaminated. I can taste rubber, rust and plastic, all on a fine bed of petrol fumes.

I'm about fifteen kilometres outside of town, heading for Gdansk, the suburb of Lomianki, the odd place where Poland becomes Warsaw, the border line, covered in ads for local shops selling timber, roofing tiles, jacuzzis and cheap insurance deals. The land here is all cut up with high fences and solid walls, houses all struggling to express how tasteless their owners can truly be.

This place is hard to define in terms of purpose, but it is above all else a storage space. There is no other reason why here, between the warehouses, the stacks of breeze blocks waiting to be collected, the second hand cars lined up, rusting in the cold light, the car washes and gas stations, someone opened up a hotel specialising in wedding receptions and called it Swan Lake.

When I visited it the first time, I was sure it was only set up for a film shoot, a comedy probably, that it was too crazy, too extreme to actually exist. I feel the same way now, and it's my umpteenth visit here. Swan Lake – a joke invented by someone completely lacking a sense of humour.

We're standing outside, surrounded by a two-metre tall hedge, a horrible, pre-cast concrete fence the other side of it. The garden is covered in snow which hasn't melted or been dirtied yet. It looks and sounds to walk on like crumbled up polystyrene. Nobody is talking. I have a bag hanging on my shoulder – it contains 100,000 zlotys in cash, the money I was keeping in my actual apartment, saved for a rainy day. There was more in dollars, but I left that for the holiday. I am keeping my hand on the bag, feeling the cash emanating warmth. Money always feels warm.

Argentina. When I think the word, I instantly see a whole host of images. The word has become a spell for me, opening up vistas, visions, possibilities.

He sees me staring at a huge, plastic bath which is covered with a large sheet of ugly blue plastic sheeting.

"They're all gone," says one of them, bald, fat, wearing the clothes expected of a construction worker.

"Who's gone?" I ask.

"The carp. We sold them all. People came here to buy them up. A good thing."

"Why do you keep carp?"

"And why do you drive around with all that shit?" the other one asks, a skinny, older guy, unshaved, dirt and concrete dust ingrained into his skin, in all his wrinkles. I've never seen him before.

Swan Lake is one of the many businesses Piotrek uses to launder his illegally gained cash. On paper, it belongs to the fat one here. That's why I've dealt with him before. I think he's a distant cousin. That's what they told me. Obviously.

The fat guy extinguishes his cigarette, stomping it into the snow. The wiry guy flicks his far off into the hedge, then nods and starts walking towards the ugly, grey building. I follow, with Fatso behind me.

Inside, we find a set of long wooden tables, pink walls, glass sculptures set about the place, dolphins, fat winged babies, wild horses – all the iconography of what people do to show how happy they are to have found the love of their lives living in the same village or housing estate. A plastic sculpture of a pair of swans sits dead centre, their necks intertwined, locking each other in some sort of death grip. A huge, red heart painted onto the wall, like an enormous stamp. Beneath it, the words: HEALTH, HAPPINESS, FORTUNE. We're not alone – two ageing women are on their knees, polishing the wooden floor with tiny cloths.

"Stop a moment," says one of the men. The women rise, heavily, slowly, and leave the hall, ignoring the wet, dark stains our shoes are leaving on the freshly polished floor. More work for them, I guess. More money, less problems. Maybe they don't even speak Polish... Ukrainian or Belarusian migrants, their hands wasted, skin broken by cheap detergents. Fatso notices me watching them leave.

"Belarusians. They work harder than any other old Russian scum."

"Ukrainians are getting fucking cheeky," says the wiry one. "They'll be setting up labour unions soon."

I can see he's high on something, eyes itching, mouth going like he was sucking on a sweet. He has a limp which he's trying his best to cover up. He smells of cheap booze, always taken first thing in the morning.

We cross the hall. Fatso opens a set of double doors the other side of it and we go to the back of the building. The smell hits me like a fist. Fried offal, old vegetable oils, pig fat, potato peelings. There is a kitchen the other side of the corridor we're in, the floor tiled with plastic, like in a hospital. The walls, at hip level, are brown with smudged fats.

"What is going on here today?" I enquire.

"A wedding in the morning," the wiry one says.

"People get married on Christmas Day?"

"Sure, a fancy date, innit? Good for us. Costs them extra... Merry Christmas!" he suddenly starts shouting and singing, "Here come the shepherds, come to see the newborn child, Merry Christmas!"

The fat one doesn't say anything, clearly used to this drunk's outbursts and essential rudeness. They know each other well, too well, like an old, rotting marriage.

We turn left, just before the steel kitchen doors, into something akin to an office, an ancient PC and empty ring binders on the shelves trying to give the appearance of a legitimate business.

There is a giant calendar on the wall, a totally naked woman draped over a long, metal drainpipe. The calendar dates back to 1988. Released by a firm which produces drainpipes. My eyes skim over another naked woman, a framed painting, the worst I've ever seen, along with a cheap electric fan, a fern plant and a litter basket full of empty energy drinks cans.

Poland – imagining that such a place is not just a bad dream – is all here, ready and present. This is where business is done, where people make their money, their essential living.

"Weddings are an awful joke," says Fatso, apropos of nothing.

I notice the wiry guy is still with us. Standing there, tense, his hands itchy, the rest of him twitching perceptibly. It's gone beyond the stage of silliness. The guy looks seriously ill.

"I don't know you," I say to him, making sure the fat bloke hears.

"Easy does it, that's Romek," he says. "Romek's alright."

"I don't know any Romeks," I repeat.

"He's my brother in law. Trusted."

"I don't know any brothers or other trusted fuckers called Romek. I've never been fishing or drinking with anyone by that name. I don't have his name or address. Up till now, his presence was OK. But now it's not OK."

Fatso stares at me, trying to work out why the hell I'm so irate all of a sudden. I'm not going to explain to him that you don't just handle kilos of coke or bundles of cash around jumpy motherfuckers you've never seen before. Or that I haven't slept much this week and anything that reeks of risk is making me itchy too.

"So, you two be friends and let's get to work," Fatso says, still not comprehending shit.

"I'm off," I tell him.

As I turn to walk back out the door, Fatso says: "OK. Romek, pop out for a second, will you. We'll talk this through later."

Romek stares at me, eyes blinking, and I return the stare, though his irises are colder in colour, like ice on a dirty lake. It is only now that I notice a small, black dot beneath his eye. Romek got angry once, too angry for someone else's good, and ended a human life. Romek ain't nobody's loving brother in law. Romek cannot be fucking trusted.

I watch him walk out, clearly unhappy, though he takes care closing the door quietly and firmly. Fatso sighs, though I'm not sure if it's hurt feelings or cardiovascular problems. I focus my listening on what might be happening the other side of that door, my mind on the gun still concealed under my blazer.

"Yeah, weddings. A fucking ball," he says again, taking the awful painting off the wall.

Behind it is a concealed safe. He spins the dial, and judging by the look on his face, it's not something he's expert at doing.

"We once had this wedding when the bride found her soon to be husband giving the best man a blow job, just before the ceremony. I was told they're still married. Five years now," he says, struggling with the dial. "People can get used to anything. Any fucking thing. Especially if it involves getting used to people who have money and nice houses and shit."

"I have a hundred on me," I tell him.

"Fine, fine," he replies, the safe popping open. He removes a large brick, wrapped in layers of shiny, black plastic. "Always something going down when people get married. The best one was when Conker, a guy from the Ochota gang, got married here. You know Conker?"

"No, I don't know Conker."

He carefully places the brick on his desk, as if the thing was filled with nitroglycerin, not coke, and then goes about unwrapping it carefully, his tongue sticking out of his fat lips like a button.

"I was a guest that time, helping out as well. I've known Conker for years. You must know him. It's a small town. Lovely guy, totally stand-up."

He unwraps the powder block and it lies there, compressed into smaller bricks, separated by transparent cling film. There are stickers on it, indicating the transport, date and place it was reloaded. I pick one up and hold it against the light. Then I place my bag on the table next to him and pull on the zip. He looks inside, scooping out the money, wrapped in batches of five thousands zlotys each. I check mine, he checks his. It is a ritual, essential, a sort of play where the actors know their lines very well – a form of mutual protection, like phones being visibly shut down before a conversation which is supposed to be confidential. Though I sense Fatso is taking his time, counting too slowly, too carefully, as if he was up to something. I take the coke and stuff it, carefully re-wrapped, into my bag. He puts the cash away, shuts the safe and replaces the painting over it.

He sighs again, rubbing his hands as if trying to shake them free of dirt.

"You know Conker. Well, there was a whole crowd of ex-prisoners sitting there all at one table. As you do. And there was this one guy, Waldek was his name, from the groom's side, and he really wanted to impress the crew. Acting all tough and mighty. Trying to sell them cars he was importing from the East. He's there with us, we all know each other, though no one knows Waldek, and we're drinking... I forgot, do you want to have a sip of something?"

"No, thanks," I shake my head, waiting for the punchline. I turn towards the door, hearing the sounds of frozen things being tossed into scalding hot oil, the noise of cutlery being tossed into industrial dishwashing machines, some shouts, though no footsteps.

"And so this Waldek, he was trying to impress them something rotten. Telling them what a tough guy he was, about how he was involved with gangs smuggling shit to Germany, that they had to get rid of some Turkish client, bury him by the border, that sort of bullshit... And he is talking and they are listening, watching him like he was a joke, a prick, and it's not helping that we're all drinking and snorting and the atmosphere is just getting more and more tense. And then this girl's voice comes a-calling across the hall: 'Oh, sparrow, my sparrow! Darling sunshine!' His bloody wife or girlfriend or whatever rushes towards our table, arrived late and sober, didn't she, her fucking leg wrapped in plaster. Sparrow! Fucking hell." Fatso chuckles to himself, while I keep an ear out for the corridor. Still nothing. "He gets up, escorts her to another table, waddling with her crutches. By the time he got back to our table, well, you can imagine. 'Sparrow! Sparrow!' We just couldn't stop laughing. He tries to dig his way out of it, chatting even more now, trying to explain, pointing at the bitch, sitting there now, giving us dirty looks, hearing us mocking her, and you know what that fucking little sparrow says to us?"

I shake my head, still waiting for something to happen.

"He says that he was the one who broke her leg," Fatso finally reveals, laughing all the harder. He doesn't seem to notice, or care, that I am not laughing at all. Not even smiling. "He broke her fucking leg."

I move towards the door, bag slung over my shoulder, not blocking access to the pistol. He must have noticed I'm moving, inching towards the exit. Then an idea occurs to me.

"Let him come in here," I ask Fatso.

"Let who come in here?" he asks, the laughter draining out of him slowly.

"Your man Romek. Your brother in law. Bring him back in here."

He stops, as if trying to recall something important but still beyond recollection.

"I don't get it. He's gone. You told him to fuck off, so he did. I don't know where he's wandered off to."

"He's the other side of that door."

He's silent again, still thinking. I'm starting to feel a chill. Fatso's awkward face is now no longer so cute. All this – his office, his artworks, his fucking funny anecdotes – are a cover for something, and it's something I do not like the look or the sound or the stink of.

"What are you talking about?"

I pull the door open with one hand, the other going for the gun. Romek is standing outside, holding something in his hand. As he turns to see me, I realise what that thing is. A spring-loaded knife, the kind that can be concealed in the palm of a hand and activated instantly.

"Get in here," I hiss. He freezes on the spot. Not moving. Looking at me, nostrils flared, like a wild animal, trying to figure out which one of us is more scared. "In here, now, else I fucking blow you away."

He notices the gun.

"Gents, wait, what the fuck?" Fatso pleads from behind his desk.

I stare at the wiry fucker, waiting. He finally gets the message, moves slowly inside. Watching me.

"Get behind that desk," I instruct, waving the gun in the desired direction. Fatso is just sitting there now, trying to work out how this all went so wrong and how many other ways it might fuck up now.

Romek doesn't do what he's told. Makes some kind of weird groan, his shoulders shaking with spasms. The guy is mental. His eyes are death, a dirty, useless death. As blunt as an old spoon, as dark as the waters which carry away the bodies of his victims, the earth he buries them in. Death which comes in the most ordinary of ways – a bottle, a length of wire, a knife. It's the knife for me today.

I hold out my hand, keeping my body at a clear arm's length from him.

"Hand it over."

He doesn't move.

"Let's not fuck around, lads," Fatso whines.

I smile and cock the hammer on the gun, trying to keep the heavy thing steady. After a long, long while, he closes his eyes and tosses the knife towards me. I don't take my eyes off him, let it fall to the carpet, keeping his head in my sights. His eyes opened the moment the knife was released. Maybe he was thinking of jumping me while I was busy trying to catch it. Maybe not.

"Go over there. Behind the fucking desk," I tell him.

I have no idea what their genius plan was, thought up last night over a menu of ten beers and left over wedding dishes, but I didn't come here to dance to their fucking moron tunes. Romek moves away, just takes the heat of that gun barrel off himself for a second, stands in the far corner of the room, thinking. I can tell he's thinking. Still looking at him, I bend down, pick up the knife, flash it at Fatso and then put it in the pocket of my coat. I bet his brother in law was looking forward to sticking that thing in between my ribs, as a little extra bonus for the pleasure of taking my money. How close was I to being carp food?

No one is ever going to pull anything over me ever again. I open my mouth, like a fish, soundless. Never ever. My mouth shuts.

"Yeah, let's not fuck around, lads," I echo.

"Merry fucking Christmas!" Romek suddenly shouts again. "Health, happiness, fortune!"

"Shut it," Fatso growls, not taking his eyes off me.

"Health, happiness, fortune!" his brother in law repeats.

"Now, here is a Christmas story worth pondering. Why was our man here standing outside that door? With a knife? Why did you bring him here in the first place?" I ask, nicely.

"Let's call Piotrek and talk this over. Sort it out," says Fatso.

"I don't think so. It won't be necessary. Now, get that naked aberration off the fucking wall and give me back my money."

"What?" he answers, confused.

"The fucking painting. The safe. Get my money out."

"Don't be doing this, brother. Don't be trying this. It's not gonna be nice. Nobody wants blood for Christmas," he says, in a voice filled with unexpected hardness and determination. I am impressed.

"Don't worry. The money will get to Piotrek. It ain't staying here, where any old piece of shit, any trusted member of any fucker's family could do something suspicious to it. Something I might then get the blame for. Do we understand each other? Romek? Are you receiving me?"

I address him politely, but he doesn't move. Doesn't have anything to add. Which is impolite of him, so I drop the gun, walk up to him and bring the barrel up so that it smashes into the side of his face. His head jerks sideways, while I keep my distance. He's trying to act tough, but I know how much one and a half kilos of military grade steel can hurt when suddenly applied to someone's skull. There is no blood, but I can hear the ringing in his head from here. The headache will last a week, and the teeth he's now chewing on inside that grizzled cheek are gonna cost an arm and a leg to replace. But boy, he's tough. Didn't go down, like most guys his size.

"Fucking hell! What was that for?" Fatso exclaims.

"My fucking money. Now!" I shout back.

"This is a misunderstanding. You've gone mad. Go home, brother. Go home and sleep on this. You'll see the light. Call Piotrek."

Colours. Colours. For a while. Yellow, brown, colours starting to appear on the side of Romek's face.

"My. Fucking. Money. Now. Or I execute."

Fatso jumps up, too sharp for my liking, but it's only to get at the safe. My gun is back on Romek's face. I have to hurry – the longer I spend in here, the greater the chance I might put a bullet between those cold, hateful eyes just for the sheer satisfaction of it. This time, Fatso is much quicker with the combination. He grabs the money and throws it on the floor, at my feet. More danger. I now train the gun on him, as I bend down to pick up the tightly packed wads of notes and shove them inside the holdall.

"This ain't gonna end happily," Fatso says.

"It will. I love happy endings. Christmas time, people only want to watch movies that end well. And that's your fucking job. To make people feel good, isn't it? To show them the time of their fucking lives?"

Fatso shakes his head, but he hears me well enough. I keep talking.

"You wanted to put that thing into me. Into my soft, vulnerable parts. Take my belongings. Feed me to your fucking fish. To your fucking guests. Then tell Piotrek that I never showed up. No idea why. No sign of me. You probably already know who you were gonna sell my car to as well, you fuck."

Fatso grimaces, but says nothing. I've got him and he knows it and has the good fucking grace to stop struggling. Romek is pent up tight like a fucking loaded knife, like a deadly spring. He won't last long, that boy, his heart working too much overtime. I take a step back towards the door. Open it. Keeping the gun trained on them both.

"Romek was watching my back. Didn't know who you were. Thought it was the right thing to do. I didn't fucking tell him to stand outside, playing with knives."

Sounds good, but a little too fresh. Too raw and unbaked to be true. Good try, though. I nod.

"You will soon have a visit, from an unannounced guest. Merry Christmas, lads," I say and vanish, leaving them to their naked fantasy babes and their fucking fantastically laid plans. The lino beneath my feet produces a nasty sound, the kind I associate with hospitals and police stations, not wedding receptions. Before I cross the corridor and get to the hall, the stink of all that overcooked food hits my nostrils. My stomach once again tries to bring things up via my mouth, but there's not enough there for actual vomit. Just water and a bit of bile. Remains of what Agnieszka had served up. I feel better to be rid of it, though sorry for the two Belarusian women who will now have to clean it up, along with the mud we've dragged in here.

To make myself better, I put my hand on the bag. It feels very warm now. Money emits heat. As do drugs. A fine and dandy kind of heat. A feelgood warmth.

Crossing the wooden floor of the hall, I see the two cleaning women in the corner, smoking.

"Sorry," I call out, then reach into my wallet and take out two hundred zloty-notes. I wave them so they see, and put the notes on the nearest table to me and shout "For the trouble! Spasiba."

It's the last bit of Russian I can still remember from high school. Forced on us when we were little, when this fucking country was young and ruled by our neighbours. Screwed by its big brothers, from the east and west. I whisper "Dasvidaniya, guten nacht" under my breath and leave, sharpish.

11:40pm

Violence is the most natural thing in the world.

It is everything, the essential engine of our species. I think it's rather funny that people spend their lives pretending they have no idea where it comes from. That they are shocked by it. Offended. Claiming to be immune, innocent, like pools of distilled water. They're helpful, engaged, well-intentioned, always there to listen to their friends, helping their parents, giving the odd bit of cash to charity every Christmas, happy for some of their taxes to go on hospital repairs and kids without kidneys.

Everything is violence, and that's the most comical thing of all. Everyone is in a state of permanent, everlasting war with so many other people. Our allies are only ever those we are looking after, because everything else is either taking possession or keeping possession of that which was already someone else's, taken and kept for a long time.

Warsaw is a cage filled with battery beasts, caged animals ready to give their souls to the cause of commerce. Warsaw is a diagram of violence itself. Everyone exists here in order to secure and keep what's theirs – positions, monies, properties, debts, wins, losses, things we reach for with all we have, that we walk through the darkest forests of the night to get to. Things we'd give up everything for, give up everyone, and when we get it, when it's caught in our slippery grasp, that little button, worth fuck all, that's when we wave that knife or gun around, screaming and shouting, growling and gnawing.

Everyone is a perpetrator. Every day. The only difference is in class, social standing, good taste. As in the way you handle your cutlery, the way you pronounce certain complex words. Everyone knows how and why to eat, but not everyone can keep their mouth shut and the noise down doing it.

Yet everyone is a killer. Everyone has this one day assigned to them, a day they are ready to commit blue murder. Like Michael Douglas in that film about an office worker trying to go postal and failing miserably. The guy who can no longer stand waiting in any lines.

Today is my day of murder. It is now well below zero. Touching minus twenty Celsius. Midnight mass will start soon. Church doors will be unlocked. Maybe someone will pray for rain, for an end to this divine comedy. Maybe I too should try prayer one day.

I'm outside Tiny's front door. I will stay here until he shows signs of life. Until the bug emerges.

I am sober, calm, cool, breathing steadily, trying to compress all my exhaustion into one part of my body, into my left foot which is moving fast, very fast, like the foot of a death metal percussionist. I'm trying to drink more water. Avoid taking any more coke. My stomach feels like something has ruptured or is rupturing, or maybe it's my throat, maybe a hernia of some sort. Not enough food down it. Too much acid coming up the other way. Sleep is good for everything, though. Even just thinking about it.

I've hidden the coke and the cash in my apartment. Taken a shower. Quick, ice cold. Took some pills for indigestion. In the morning, on the way to the airport, I'll take the money to Piotrek, and will stash the drugs somewhere, maybe in a locker. I could call Pazina, but Pazina is gone. She's out of order. Removed from the playing board. Removed herself. It doesn't matter which. She's missing. "My garage," I think. "But if they knew about the apartment in Goclaw, they could know about the garage. I rented it not far off, not close either, but it's too unsafe. The door old, commie-era wood. The lock a joke. Maybe Piotrek will suggest a solution. Yeah, he'll know. I'll hand over Tiny, and the cash, a double Christmas whammy."

Tamka is a wickedly steep street. Great views of the wild riverside on the other bank of the Vistula. Tiny chose his pad well. Or rather the girl whose place it is. Though it only occurs to me now that they might not be home, today being today. Or else he could have skipped town, packed off to visit the family of some new bird he's been seeing – she's gonna be from out of town, Lodz or Krakow or Wroclaw, they're easier to impress and undress. And tonight is a perfect excuse to visit, be introduced, charm them with gifts from the capital. Keeping well off my radar. Maybe he'll like it there. Spend a year looking round for premises, change nicknames, open another club. By the time word got round who and where he was, all would have been forgiven. Just about. Enough to let him live.

Nah. I bet he's not smart enough for that sort of play. Too freaked out, too fucking wired to think safe. He still thinks he's the man, that this is his turf, that we all deserve to be taught a lesson.

A light comes on in his flat. Bingo! I nod, key in the workmen's door code, and go inside. It won't have buzzed in this flat, giving him no warning I'm here. The lift is taking its time. A minute, two minutes go by and no sign of it. Fucking hell, at Christmas? Don't Polish lifts ever fucking work? Some fucking ancient tradition? I climb up the stairs, fourth floor, taking it easy, making sure the bile stays down this time.

It's very quiet. The air cold inside, the city having a jolly old time. Frozen fish, frozen vodka, frozen desserts. An explosive combination, but hell it tastes good. The city is going into its seasonal period of hibernation. Only now that everyone is indoors, the streets empty, the lanes and parks quiet, snow absorbing what little sounds there are left, can one feel the full force of its terror.

The freezing temperature is something which can be touched, which can touch back, which can kill. Inhaling it is as painful as inhaling coke laced with too much crushed glass.

The city is hollowed out, because the people who still believe they can escape its gravitational pull have left. Some gone to visit their family shit hole towns, take boring walks through greying landscapes, meet friends from school, from playschool even, drinking their favourite vodkas, looking at those who made it without leaving the country with envy. They are all busy seeing their parents fading, dying, the old traditions going down the toilet, no new classic films on television, so bored some of them might actually fuck, have an extra mouth to feed next year, a new line of credit with the bank open, forcibly, a new chapter in the art of coping with foreseeable and yet inevitable disasters.

The rest of us – those who were born here, though they are few, and those who cannot escape the gravitational pull of the dark heart of this country – might have deserted the place at the last minute, jumping on planes to Thailand, Costa Rica, Fuerteventura, anywhere that's warm, anywhere far, far from the ice of here. They are now away, exhausted by the journey, the kids screaming, the spouses bitching about the food and the prices and the lack of manners, about the locals, the Russians, the Poles still surrounding them, even a million miles from home. Cheap cocktails, crap kitesurfing lessons, trying to avoid looking at the world through the smartphone screen all the time. Trying to disconnect from news about accidents and assaults and conferences. They breathe in the kind air, massaging their insides, trying to relax, to stop stressing, stop being angry. Stop thinking about the dark heart of reality still waiting, patiently and very unkindly, for them back home. Waiting for them to set foot back in their fucking motherland.

I'm going to do the same thing, just a little bit further. A little bit wilder. No tour company sorted the tickets. No guides await me. All I need is a little sleep on the flight, someone to shake me awake when we land, a taxi to the hotel, and enough energy to turn up that air con and slide between those starched bedsheets.

Marta opens the 4th floor door. The tall, skinny rural beauty who remembers me for telling her to get out of her boyfriend's office.

"He's out," she says, holding the door half-closed, but before she can finish the short sentence I've already pushed past her, closed the door behind me and turned the locks.

I did this once already today. Locking someone else's door behind me.

"We know you're looking for him," she says, looking truly petrified. "That's why he's not here."

"So where is he?"

"Gone. He specifically didn't say where to."

"Interesting. What if I don't believe you?"

I look around the place. The same as every other temporary Warsaw home – wooden floors, no bed, a mattress covered with a pile of clothes, bare white walls, crap old chairs, some old records lying around. I see one by The Clash and am momentarily impressed.

"He broke up with me last night," she says quietly, voice deadened by what must have been a serious dose of antidepressants, judging by the state of her eyes. "We were meant to go visit my folks. A long drive. And now I can't go home. And he's not here."

"Oh, fuck me. He broke up with you last night?" I feign sympathy, worried I'm overdoing it, but she's so out of it she can't see I'm only trying to ridicule her.

I start looking around. Tiny kitchen. Even smaller bathroom. All the fittings cheap. She's right. He's not here. But I can wait.

"He said he doesn't want me to get hurt. That we shouldn't meet again. Told me to come here and pack and go home. Christmas Eve."

"So why are you still here, honey, and not spending Christmas with your folks? What's keeping you here, I wonder... "

"My mom... passed away." Her face is so grey and expressionless, I can finally tell she's not lying. "I told you I don't know what's happened to him. Said to leave the keys in the mail box. Said he'd call in a week or two."

"Do you have any clean glasses?"

She wanders over to the kitchen, swaying dreamily, takes a glass out from one of the cupboards. I pour some tap water, take a sip, but even that tiny amount turns into something disgusting, something sticky on the lips. My whole throat is jammed with bile.

"He's gone..." she drawls, meaning gone from her life as well as my affairs.

"Fine. I'm in no hurry."

"He won't come here. Not tonight."

"I can wait. He'll show eventually. I can afford to buy all the time in the world. People try to cheat me, but I get paid anyhow. I get my bonuses. Two weeks, you say? I can wait that long."

It's only now that some sort of recognition flickers in her eyes, some reaction. She's wondering if he lied to her now. Wondering if I'm right to wait.

"What will you people do to him?"

Her eyes go glassy again. She doesn't want me to answer. She loves him. Trying to cover his ass, for her own reasons. She's very young and a very poor actress.

"We're just gonna have a talk."

"He's impossible to talk to."

He loves her, probably, but there's something she's not telling me, something ugly, because what else is gonna arise between a young girl like this and a fucking loser like Tiny? Violence. Abortion. Kinky sex. Who the fuck cares.

"You were at Anastasia's last night. I know. They went to the cops," she tells me. "The whole town knows you're after him. He has his friends. Why do you think he would come back here? That's just stupid."

I put the glass down. The water's not helping. Even air is not going down smoothly, the pain going right down like a needle down the gullet.

Calm. Calm down. It will pass. It's passing already, slowly.

"All good," I tell her. "In a second, you'll have the chance to tell me about all your pals. And list for me all the places he might be hiding. And I will pay them all a visit. Tonight."

"I thought you were going to stay here and wait for him."

"Just talk to me. You know I'm in the mood for a little darkness tonight, don't be on the other end of that desire." She does a strange thing with her head, like she was shaking it and nodding at the same time. Unpleasant-looking, but I carry on. "In fact, I have a better idea. You will accompany me on our search. Pointing them out as we ride along. You will enter, and if we find him, you'll simply bring him to me. To my lovely, heated car."

"No," she whispers.

"Yes," I reply.

She looks frozen already. Says nothing more. I take the glass and another sip and then throw it against the wall, right by her head, not trying to hit or miss. She crouches by the floor, screaming, but I approach and bend down over her.

"Get up. Don't make me do things I don't want, but have to. Not if you don't want to be in the way of what's coming for him. Sometimes things are settled. All around the world. Like school. You can't just bow out, can you? You have to see it all the way through. Think of me as a teacher. You graduated not that long ago. You remember."

I extend my hand to help her up. She gets up without my assistance, scrabbling with her hands against the kitchen cupboards.

"I can't," she whispers.

"Gun, force, or your own free will. You choose. You get to keep your looks. Your health. Your family nice and safe. Choose wisely."

She looks like she wants to say something, but it gets lodged in her brain, her throat. Then she looks at me, having processed what I chose to say, with hate. The hate of a tiny child.

"You're all gonna rot in jail, or hell, I don't care which first."

I think I even smiled for a second. Brushing my own face to check.

"Could be, darling. Could be you're very much mistaken."

I take a step towards her, ready to grab her by the arm and start dragging. She braces, trembling. "The first address. Now," I demand.

"Most... most of them are not here. Outside of Warsaw. Lisbon," she says, struggling to get whole sentences out.

"Let's fly to Lisbon. Not a problem. The first address?"

She can't look at me, won't let me see the terror in her eyes.

"There's a squat, an arty shit hole, on Pulawska Street."

"I've heard of it. Let's go."

I watch as she slowly dresses for the season. A thick, quilted jacket, knee high boots. She looks like a kid who doesn't want to go to school, stretching once, then again, as if still not ready.

She opens the door. I look out, hand on the concealed pistol, then follow. She locks the door behind us while I scope the corridor. The apartments behind the doors we pass are quiet, like they really got the silent night message. American-looking Christmas wreaths attached to communist-era front doors, and one just opposite her place, with a picture of a Santa Claus pasted to it.

"Someone fucking broke the lift. They said they're coming to fix it tomorrow."

She walks down the stairs slowly, starting to get on my nerves. Costing me precious time. I feel like shoving her, or grabbing her arm and pulling her along, or else picking her up, throwing her over my shoulder and running forward. I can't wait for her to be rid of the fucking idiot ruining her Christmas. I'm doing her a favour, even though I don't have time to do people favours: for silly girls I'll never lay eyes on again, girls for whom what matters in life are bicycles with thin retro frames, coffee in paper cups, who they got likes off on Instagram recently, or who saw them in the right sort of place last night.

"He could be in there. With the mate he plays music with," she says about the squat. I think about the place, about the legends that surround it, then realise that she's talking too loud, louder than before, as if trying to be heard a little way off. That statement about the lift was unnecessary, but she said it aloud, too loud for my liking.

I should have noticed it earlier, but it's too late now. The flat opposite. The one with a paper Santa I noticed pasted over the peep hole. We're half-way down, and she stops, which is when I hear the fire door to the stairwell creak and then, far too late, see the relief in her eyes when the sound of a gun being cocked is all too clearly audible behind me.

A gun. Now I remember. That cop, the one we fired, the one working for Tiny, the one whose head ended up smashed into Tiny's office wall, the one who wore those dirty hiking boots, the fleece top. He mentioned something to Tiny about firearms. Back on Friday, a long, long time ago.

I quizzed him about guns. Asked why he needed them.

"First, take out the pistol and put it on the floor. I bet you have one on you," I hear Tiny say, his voice theatrical in the tall stairwell. "Marta, go inside. My place. Go."

I don't bother turning around. He sounds shaky enough as it is. In a bad way. Much worse than me. Crazed, as if someone has been torturing him, applying shock therapy to his balls. He's crazed and very much dead, and some part of that stupid head of his knows it too.

The girl runs past, trying not to look at me, not to come into any contact with me at all.

"The gun," he hisses. "The fucking gun! Out! On the floor. Now!"

I can hear him taking some steps towards me. Three short sounds. A safe distance. If he was closer, I could swivel, hope to smack the gun out his hands. Assuming his finger is not on the trigger. Which it's unlikely to be. He's such a fucking coward. Yet, today could be his day to murder. He sounds mad enough.

"Should I now finish you off? Would you like that?"

"First, tell me about the last two weeks of your life," I say, closing my eyes. I can now see something flashing beneath the lids, on fire, a picture made of light, a map, a sketch made looking from the top floor of an exclusive hotel – it's been there all along, travelling with me, embedded in my eyes.

"I'll fucking kill you, I swear," he says, who knows who to and why.

Just to kill time, I take out my gun and ever so slowly place it on the stairs.

"Turn around and toss me the piece. Now. Turn."

"Did you not at any point have the impression that you've spent the past fourteen days making some insanely stupid mistakes?"

He says nothing. I turn.

"Toss it over."

I stare at him. Pale, almost translucent, like a terminal cancer patient, dying of hunger, unable to digest anything, the body consuming itself. His hair greasier than usual. The whole of him stinking badly. It's not just my imagination – it really does seem washing has not been on his list of priorities.

"All this can only come to one sticky end," I tell him, arms

315

splayed out by my sides in a gesture of indifferent surrender. I then bend down, pick up my gun by the barrel, and place it without making a sound on the stairs a little ahead and above me, next to his feet. His hand is trembling. Guns are heavy things.

He looks like the living embodiment of total stupidity, like someone who delights in being condemned to death, in suicide.

"Move. Forward. Now."

I do as told. I'm dictating the speed. Moving fast. I could try and turn around at some point and try and grab the gun off him. Or else wait until we get to the bottom of the stairwell. Smash the door into his extended arm – chances are he won't shoot where there might be cameras, he'll stall, panic. I could wait until we're in the car, build up speed and then try something, a bit of fancy driving or some close-quarters combat.

Of all the things I could do, I choose to stop.

"Keep moving!" he hisses behind me. "Move it!"

I turn around. I was wrong – his finger is on the trigger. Can't see the safety catch from here. He barks, a little louder,

"Turn around! Fucking move. Now. Faster!"

I do as I'm told again. I could try all sorts of things, but I don't quite trust my reflexes, not enough sleep, too much blow, my head spinning slightly. Getting close to the ground floor, I'm having to grab the handrail to steady myself. The fact is, though I don't have a mirror to hand, I may not be looking or doing any better than Tiny tonight.

We go outside, onto the pavement. The air is stunningly cold, attacking every bit of bare skin, every nook and cranny in my clothes. I feel as if someone has applied a block of ice to the back of my neck. Tiny meanwhile no longer feels the cold – I can tell just by looking at him. He's wearing nothing more than a shirt and not trembling at all, immune to the heat or the cold. That gives me a faint bit of hope. A possible advantage.

This is the end of his line, but he's too scared to go it alone. He wants to take someone with him. Someone stupid enough to have embarrassed him in front of his friends, his employees, his girl. This is no longer about money. Money has long dropped off whatever's left of his radar. Advantages, wins are all beyond his comprehension. He wants to live, but he knows it's impossible. Hence the wild panic. The animal grief.

"Where's your car parked?" he asks. I point. He waves the gun, indicating I should go towards it. "Give me the keys!" he screams.

I turn around. Look him in the eyes. It feels as if he was covered in petrol from the inside, and then someone tossed in a lit match. As if he was about to fall apart. I try to get through to him before it's too late, before we both go up in flames.

"It's not about you, I told you that. Your kids too. I've never hurt anyone smaller than me. I'd never do that. But you messed with people who don't have such reservations. You gotta decide. Is it about this moment, or the rest of all your lives? Payments can be arranged. Shit undone. Think of the little ones."

"Give me the fucking keys before I blow you away!"

I toss the keys into the snow between us, then walk towards the car. He unlocks it remotely, goes round to the driver's side and gets in. I look around the cold, dark night, and decide there is nothing for it – the passenger's seat is mine.

I sit and stare dead ahead, unable to look at him. Since I bought this car, no one has ever driven it but me. No one's hands have been on its steering wheel. I should kill him just for that.

I hear the jangling of a set of cuffs.

"Put those on," he tells me.

"Did those come as a set with the gun? Christmas present?" I ask, trying not to sound ironic. I really am wondering if the off-duty cop working for him also gave him a badge to play with.

"Put the cuffs on, right fucking now," he says, struggling to speak and breathe at the same time.

He throws the cuffs in my lap. I put them on, feeling the cold metal against my skin. This is the first time in my life I've worn a pair of these.

"These aren't Marta's by any chance? You didn't sneak these out of your bedroom?" I tease. "Fine. I also hope she likes fucking with a plastic bag over her head. You're a musician. I'm told you guys are into this sort of kinky shit."

He throws my gun on the floor, between the pedals. Then, I hear him fumbling with a packet of cigarettes, struggling to light one.

"There's no smoking in this car," I tell him.

"Give me the address," he says, blowing smoke in my face.

"Don't smoke in my car, Tiny," I repeat, grimacing.

"Address."

We pull away, out of the estate car park and stop at the first set of lights. He pulls the gun out of his pocket and sticks it into my ribs.

"Lowicka Street," I say.

He puts the gun away.

He was meant to die in a civilised fashion. But for smoking in my car, handling the wheel with his filthy hands, filthy fucking dope head hands, for the ash he's not even bothering to tip into the ashtray, I will make sure something very bad will happen to him. There are rules. If rules are broken, they'll keep on being broken if the punishment is not severe enough. I close my eyes, begin to breathe in deeply, imagining what will happen to him, allowing me to sit there in the passenger seat of my own car, calm as hell, cuffed like a common criminal.

I will make sure he suffers. I will make sure he watches *120 Days of Sodom* on VHS while all the things on screen are done to him. Make sure a few of the lads get creative, once they've cut off his dick and his balls, ensuring they cut him open with a very blunt and very red-hot knife, his mouth full of sulphuric acid, same for the eyes, the ears. He's heard the stories. The bad old days of Warsaw's gang wars. He thinks they're long gone, legends, but somewhere deep down he knows all legends are based on facts.

I will do my best to ensure it happens before my departure.

By the time I board that plane tomorrow, my hands will have been scrubbed clean of his blood. Perfectly clean.

I should have smelt his presence in that stairwell, even going up. I should have focused and sensed his presence. Not so much his fear, as just his stink.

Could've. Should've. Must've. This and that and the other. I have this fleeting idea, this hint of an idea, that maybe I couldn't have done jack. That my story's up, my time wandering the dead corridors of this city, a city that is a vampire, so many times in the past having feasted on the blood of its inhabitants. That's how it is. Nothing any of us can do about it. Me, gone. By Tiny's hapless hand.

Everyone in the end gets his own punchline.

But on the other hand we're still here, and I'm doing a fine job of winding him up, because I believe he won't shoot me, not here and not now. There is a reason why he wants me to take him to my place. Some strange motive, some avenging spirit that burns in whatever's left of his guts.

My phone rings. A customer, I guess. My fault for being open 24/7. I can't reach because of the cuffs.

"How you liking it now? Still feeling like lord of the fucking manor? Kings of the fucking world, is it? Who elected you bastards? Who crowned you?"

"Why are you talking about me and some others?" I ask.

"You're now left holding nothing but your own dick. A fucking limp dick, not any sceptre, my royal fucking friend."

"What the fuck did you take before you left home?" I ask, honestly wondering about his state of mind.

He's driving fast now, jumping lights when there's a small delay. I watch his face, his body dehydrating, dribbling at the mouth a tiny bit.

"You think," he spits, "that you can come to my fucking club, my club, and put the frighteners on my people, my fucking family, threaten me in my own home, and I will just fucking roll over and take it? You think anyone can live like that? That I'm a sort of punk who'll take it up the ass and pay for the privilege?"

"I still don't know who you have me connected with."

He wants to talk, but it's costing him energy, focus. I suspect he may be close to fainting. It might be to my advantage. A weakness. An impending fit or heart attack. Lots and lots of ways to die in this damn town.

"But you think it's all fine and dandy. Well, let's see what you've got at home. Let's consider it compensation. What you owe me, fucker."

319

I look at him sideways. He looks like he's snorted all the coke in Warsaw this evening.

He says nothing, but his face suddenly changes, as if someone's poked his belly with something sharp. He's swallowing, not doing a good job of it, his body doing its best to cater to his need to keep going, to talk smart, but whatever it is he's trying to swallow down must be very bitter, something slimy seeping from his sinuses, because the look of pain doesn't leave his face as I see his Adam's apple doing its work.

"Ah, so you've not been given any insurance money?"

He's still not answering. We're now on Narbutta Street, not far. He's driving erratically, too slow or too fast, thank fuck the streets are so empty.

"You forgot to fill forms out. The formalities. So no money due to you after the fire... Oh what a shame." I keep talking just to keep him awake. "You're just letting everything burn. Everything that was still worth saving," I say, patiently, encouragingly even.

He stops the car and picks the gun up off the floor.

"Get out," he barks.

I don't move. Instead, I stare right at him. He's hyperventilating. I look up at my apartment window. It looks dark, but that doesn't mean it's empty. Anything could happen tonight. And nothing at all. This is why I am right now completely defenceless, like a small, naked child, like a real life Tiny, his twin, unable to control what happens next. My brain is starting to set, set hard, showing me Tiny, the insides of the car, the city outside, everything in one solid colour again, brown, and then blue, as if seen through a cheap photographic filter. I guess I must be feeling feverish and looking hellish to boot.

But I still want to be a decent host this Christmas Eve.

"Get out," he repeats. I do as I'm told, struggling with the door in the cuffs. "To your place. Now!"

"You want a shower? I wasn't gonna say nothing, Tiny, but you're not smelling your best. Not sure if my clothes will fit, but we'll find you some baggy running gear, maybe..."

"Move, you fuck!" he says, shouting now, making a scene, the gun out again, stabbing me in the lower back. We're like two lunatics, wandering through the deadly cold, on our last legs, ready to kill or be killed, does it matter which? Now, I'm the one slowing down, dragging my feet like his girl, Marta, on the staircase, trying to throw him off his rhythm. Trying to get him riled, to slip, to miss something I'm trying to pull. We get to the entry phone.

"I need to get the cuffs off to slide the entry card through."

"Where is it?"

"Put the piece away. I've seen enough of it already. There is a night watchman at the front desk. You want me to scream?"

He says nothing. Shaking more and more. I stick my arms out and, eventually, he sees the sense of it. He fumbles for the key, unlocks the mechanism, taking an instant step back with the gun trained on me again. I look for the card in my blazer pockets.

"I'll tell you one more thing," I say, unlocking the door. "This is no longer about our personal losses. About the money you could have salvaged, and which just kept piling up as debt. It's about how much money went up in smoke from what we could have sold through the club before you torched the place."

It then occurs to me, at the oddest of times, for the most mysterious of reasons, that I actually like living here. Maybe it's this deadly cold, maybe some dim awareness that everything could end at any moment, someone could jump out, another gun going 'pop!' That yeah, I like this place. I think 'like' is the right word.

"There are simply people who are more important than you or me. And they have lost substantial sums because of you. You didn't think that for the next ten years they were just going to let rich kids spend their parents' savings on illegal substances, did you? It was all supposed to be demolished and replaced with luxury flats. Offices. Shops. And now you have a police investigation into arson, and the death of an underage drug addict. Fucked, really. A nice deal truly fucked."

He gets close to me, the gun buried in my back to hide it from the closed circuit cameras and the doorman's prying eyes, indicating I should stop talking and lead us through the building.

I suddenly remember the situation I told Paz about – a musclebound ogre, speeding off his nut, who kept me in his house for fourteen straight hours, trying to get info on Piotrek. For all that time, I just kept repeating the same sentence: "We're wasting time and we're wasting money".

I've repeated it since a few more times to a few other troublemakers, some of whom were pointing firearms my way. Sooner or later, they got the message that blood is bad for business. And we're all in this for the money, first and foremost. The problem is, I worry that Tiny is now beyond reason. Not interested in his kids. His pride. In what he is owed. My words like a foreign language to him, like a tennis ball bouncing off a wall.

The lift opens. We ride up to my floor, then walk slowly up to my front door. It looks good, in fine fettle – dark, honest wood. Not some cheap, plastic reproduction. "I like it" – the phrase goes through my mind once again, as I think about my Philippe Starck sofa, about the hand-made furniture, the heated floor in the bathroom. About the scraps I've managed to extract from the world. My little, lightweight gold chain, worn so that nobody sees. Nobody, except a few women, especially that last one, the beast from the pink lagoon, the dirty aquarium queen, the wench I should never have looked at more than once, and even then fleetingly.

"Nice pad," Tiny nods. Then hits me in the face with the butt of the gun.

Pain, colours, and the first crunch of teeth today. That nasty, nasty dental taste of things in the mouth which should not be there.

Tiny stands over me as I sit on my sofa, in his sweat-soaked, stinking shirt , his beard stuck together with spit.

"All the money you've stolen from people, nicely invested. Very nice. Nice set up," he says, quietly, as if still unsure of what to do next.

"I've never taken anything from you that you didn't owe. I sold you things. You stopped paying, Tiny. You're the one who fucked up."

I touch the side of my face, my cheek already swelling. It's gonna look rotten during check in and passport control tomorrow.

"You're scum. A rotten, two-bit bandit. A fucking thief." He begins going through my drawers, throwing things on the floor, smashing plates, glasses. Searching for something. And we all know what for.

"Where is it?" he asks.

He walks up, waiting for an answer he knows is not going to come, bends down towards me, and punches me in the stomach. I retch again, the remains of the last real meal I ever had, which is still in my guts.

"This is not going to help you," I wheeze.

He goes up to the wardrobes in the hallway, starts throwing things from them, suits, shirts, dancing on them, dancing across the apartment, as if wanting to stamp his mark on the place.

"Where is it, Kuba? Where the fuck is the stuff?"

He vanishes in the bathroom. He's not going to find shit. He won't, and then if he shoots me in the leg, I will die, and I will die because the only thing keeping me alive right now, the only thing I actually have that's worth anything, is that aeroplane ticket, a pass for a flight I may not be able to board with a gunshot wound.

"He's not going to find shit," I think again, but I'm finally proven wrong. He finds it. The special panel, over the toilet, next to the gas meters. The bag which three hours ago I took possession of at the Swan Lake wedding hotel, from that suburban hell hole. The bag which contains the only capital I have left – half a kilo of my coke and a hundred thousand zlotys – which belongs to Piotrek. His Christmas gift – from me to him.

This is how the last chapter of my life ends. This is how it was meant to end.

Now that he has what it was he wanted, he will kill me. On orders from his rotting brain, his stinking instincts, the bawling child inside him, the voices in his head.

For the time being, he walks over and slams me in the stomach again. Almost falling over in the process.

"Everything can be fixed, all problems. You just need to be smart. And being smart is what I do," he says triumphantly, pointing to the side of his own skull.

"Not everything is fixable," I groan.

"You didn't think this was how it was going to roll, did you?

You're surprised? You must be fucking surprised. Fucking awfully surprised. You must now be thinking to yourself – at which point did I make that one key mistake? I'll tell you, you fucking piece of shit. The moment you walked into MY club and tried to take it from ME!" he screams, hitting me with the gun again and again about the head.

That which flows from my lips now, some kind of thick acid, is like something they keep locked up in hospitals. I think my stomach might be in need of a transplant now.

"I'm betting I win..." I say with infinite effort.

"What?!"

"I bet I win. Like in that film... the one you were in. Everything will end like in that shit movie you were in."

"That they find me and they kill me? Is that what you're saying? Right now?"

He holds the gun out, pointing it right at my head, as if I had just reminded him of something.

"You can be sure no one is going to find me," he says, a little too softly to be really convincing. "No one is going to even know it was me. No one is going to go searching for the perp. No one, pal, is gonna push for the police to do their fucking job. No one will even know who you were when they come to burn you and bury you in the ground. You're dead, because you threatened my kids. You wished them dead."

He closes one eye. I close both mine. So this is it. I try to feel something, something vivid. Hear a song, my dog day song. Or the *Goldberg Variations*. Maybe Stravinsky. *Movements for Piano and Orchestra*. Get lost in the music, dissolve.

Warsaw flows through me, in that final moment the black river rushes forward, the city pinning me down, condensed to a caustic, cancerous black ooze.

I am ready. Let it happen.

Of course I'm scared. But I also know the fear means nothing, won't speed or slow anything down. Things are as they are. As they are meant to be. How they turned out. I wanted it to be different.

You can do all the wanting you want in the world. It's just there's no future in it.

Somewhere, far off, I hear a siren. Maybe an ambulance. A heart attack following too much Christmas goodness. Or a tree on fire, shitty, deadly lights wrapped round a dried out pine. A single spark is all it takes. But maybe it's the cops. The cops, I think, for the first time ever in my life with something I could also call the opposite of "dislike".

"Fuck."

The voice is dead and dry, but it's Tiny still. I then hear the safety catch click. I open one eye. The pain instantly returns. The smashed jaw. The battered guts. Those always hurt the most. I open the other eye to see him throw his gun into my bag, throw it over his shoulder, slap it with his open palm, making sure it still exists.

He leaves my apartment, closes the door, and then waves of pain continue their dance. Along with tsunamis of relief. I close my eyes, feeling a giant, concrete duvet being pulled from over me. I see a small boy, standing next to the body which is now filling that whole room, smiling at me. He vanishes when I open my eyes. He's there when I close them again. Momentarily. Then vanishes altogether. I really have to lie down now, for just a second. Before I start packing.

Serotonin floods my brain. I hear more sirens, though it might just be my imagination. Which is now filled with early nightmares, or dreams rather... featuring Tiny captured, tortured, drawn and quartered. His entrails spread all over the city, dumped in all its canals, its parks, its squats.

Then he's also gone. All I see is light. A map made of light.

My heart still beating.

Fancy that.

As they force the door open, my lovely door made of imported oak, I can still feel it beating. Then I hear an explosion. Like someone threw a grenade out in the corridor.

"It's open!" I mumble, not sure if it's loud or not, and then start laughing, and then writhe in pain, laughing and writhing in turn.

"Everybody on the fucking ground, now!" I hear the call, opening my eyes to try and see, count them. Four officers, in nice, dark green uniforms, army issue, though the sewn on patches roar POLICE. Faces covered with commando masks, machine guns at the ready. Some other, less severe cops follow, guns at the ready, their badges dangling from their necks. Ooh... the anti-terrorist crew. Heavy. They always send them in when there could be cameras around. TV cameras. One of them pins me down to the sofa, watching me bleed, while the others scour the apartment.

"It's all gone," I tell my personal bodyguard, trying to smile with what's left of my facial muscles.

He just nods, keeping shtum behind that mask.

"The TV still works, I think. You can take that," I say, spitting blood and bone.

I hear them tossing about what's left of my home, which doesn't last long. Another crew will come in here and take it slower later. Where is Tiny?

"Is someone else here?" asks one of them, as if reading my mind.

"No, I fucking broke my own jaw... All alone. Poor me."

"Hands. Give 'em!" a humourless officer of the law screams. I hold them out, the second set of cuffs in my history clasped round my wrists in a single day. I can't be laughing. If I laugh, I will die. My stomach knows how bad it is down there.

"You're coming with us, fucker," one of the unmasked cops growls.

"Oh, do tell where?"

"Somewhere we can talk. In private. In total silence. With what's fucking left of you."

I want to speak. I want to say something, anything, but then I black out and everything goes blank.

THURSDAY

DREAM

"Go on, get up now. Go on," says the blonde woman in bed next to me, who I somehow know is my wife.

A strange feeling of comfort. Of having woken in a bed that's way too big for my body, in sheets that are just perfectly laundered, the duvet perfectly weighted. Like a womb, all of it.

"Up, up, up! School's not gonna wait for them, you know," she says.

The smell of bedsheets which have not been changed in a week. Soaked through with bodily odours. A smell which won't let you rise. I finally open my eyes. I see her for the first time ever, but I know her through and through, better than I know myself. I don't yet know her name, but I know she hates Polish home-cooked food, loves Italian cuisine, she does yoga, always changing styles, a little too easily bored, loves David Bowie, films by Wes Anderson (though she knows it's now unfashionable), the show *Girls*, especially the main character, the overweight fool who pierced her own ear drum with a cleaning bud one time. I know she meditates, but isn't very good at it, runs half-marathons and runs a media house with an old friend she met in school. I know she has one tattoo, on her left shoulder blade, a pretty, brightly coloured bird, a design taken from her favourite book of Russian folktales.

I know her younger brother lives in Australia, that her parents don't need our help to manage – that they managed to open the first ever McDonald's in Olsztyn. Now, they spend time travelling, then resting, then checking their investment portfolios, then travelling back again. She's on good terms with both of them, though the father is not an easy guy to like. They never are.

I know this is the eighth year we've been together. Seven since the wedding. It was in a church, mainly to avoid a battle with the elders, on both sides of the family. We got married just as soon as Justyna – yeah, that's her name, Justyna – discovered she was pregnant.

"I made you coffee," she says.

"Can't you take them today?" I ask, rising out of bed.

"We have that presentation at eleven. Have to get ready first."

She goes into the bathroom only wearing a pair of panties. I still like watching her walking around naked. She's slim, long-limbed. The kids have not taken her body, she's actually got rid of some of the puppy fat she always carried around. She stands in the door, looking at me for a second, then goes into the bathroom. I know we have two kids, twins. I already know I have half an hour to get them ready for school.

The apartment is spacious, overly bright, like something from a banking ad, a poster advertising mortgages. We met in the last year of art school. In Warsaw, but she too happened to be from Olsztyn. I remember the exact moment, at a bar which is not there now – The Philosophers' Dining Rooms.

"You look like you're thinking. Thinking long and hard about how to get the hell out of this place," were the first ever words she said to me.

"Yeah, I do want to go," I said. Never did like the place.

"Well, now there's two of us."

We kissed that first night, after we discovered we were born in the same hospital, which seemed very romantic at the time. Destiny grinning at us. Call it what you like. No one was innocent enough by then to go using such words with strangers, but that's how we felt.

We slept together a little while after. Later than we both wanted, but games have to be played with people you care about. And feel drawn towards more than you feel is safe.

I know it all now. The images stored in my memory banks, flashing up as I follow her into the bathroom, look in the mirror, start brushing my teeth. My face seems to be my face again, as I remember it also. Very clearly so.

We moved in together, saving money in our last year of studies. She was already doing bits and bobs for advertising agencies, and I had bagged a job as art director at Ogilvy, though I was soon to be promoted to chief of the creative section. I'd never really wanted to be an artist. Disgusted by the artifice everyone seemed to surround their school work with. In my heart of hearts, I couldn't give a damn about their dreams of shows and catalogues and sales consultants. Agents, managers, promotors. Their grant applications, their struggles with essays and dissertations, all the rest of their hysterical forms of self-expression and realisation. I was a nihilist, or as close to being one as I could imagine. Art was for nothing. It was only the markets which mattered. What was sold on them didn't matter to me in the least.

I realised long ago that I had nothing nice to say as an artist, and so chose to say nothing at all.

Back then, advertising was about rolling in cash. I loved earning bigger and bigger salaries. I still do, as head of creative at Barnaby & Partners. When I feel pangs of guilt about the sums I take home, compared to all the junior staff coming in on fuck all, I keep calm thinking they would be just as happy if roles were reversed.

Justyna was like me. She still paints, but it's a Polish female mothering instinct thing. Not wasting precious skills, potential, juices. Giving birth to all manner of things. She likes touching up and enlarging Polaroid shots of our kids, in abstract fashions.

"Dad," says my daughter, stepping inside the bathroom. I walk her back out, looking around at my home. The view of Saxon Marshes, the park, the smell of super-strong coffee wafting out of the kitchen – my morning shot of legal high. I never said a word about any of the furniture, fittings, colours I see before me. All the wife's work.

"Dad," I hear again from my waist level. My daughter is called Zuzia. I say to her, while pouring myself a hot black coffee: "Yes, dear? What is it?"

I then look round to see she has long, strawberry blonde hair, like her mother's, the shade of straw, and is dressed in a green onesie that makes her look like a little frog. She won't sleep in anything else, so we've had to buy several such onesies. Zuzia doesn't look like she'll be ready to go to school in the next ten minutes.

"I have to tell you something," she whispers in all seriousness.

Last year, she had a very severe bout of Crohn's disease. We spent a total of seventy-two sleepless nights in hospital with her. I know this. I can remember every single hour.

"What is it you want to tell me?"

"I dreamt I saw a ghost and when I told others about it, nobody believed me..."

"What did the ghost look like?"

"It was tall and pale. Had looooong hands. Down to his knees. Like this," she says, dropping her shoulders so her hands reach down past her knees.

Her brother is called Olaf. I know it seeing him standing there now, in the doorway to the kitchen. Olaf doesn't look anything like me. He reminds me of someone else I know. He looks at me, half-awake, as if we knew each other but not through blood, a totally different context. His dark eyes are huge, his head oddly perched atop a spindly body, skinnier than his sister's. He always walks round with a Transformers toy, they're inseparable. The toy has a name, something Latin-sounding, but I can't quite recall what it is now.

"My leg hurts," he announces whiningly.

"Every morning, you say the same thing. This hurts, that hurts," I say, shoving them both gently out of the kitchen. "Brush your teeth and let's get going. School isn't gonna wait forever."

I chew on a piece of a dried out baguette to build up some energy. I want another coffee, with sugar, pure white sugar, not the stuff we have in the house, which is brown and lumpy like cake dough.

"Ready? Guys? Girl?" Justyna shouts from the bedroom.

She comes into the kitchen, looking at me. For the first two years of our union, I kept on telling her how beautiful her eyes were. I should go back to that. It was a good habit to have. Her eyes contain tiredness and love.

"What are your plans for later?" she asks, sipping on some water.

Later? I remember that today I'm not going to work. I took a day off to spend a bit of time with the family.

"I finally found your passport," she says.

"And? Is it still valid?"

"Two more years. Enough to cover the trip."

"We'll be back in good time."

Now I remember. It's not just about quality time with the family. Monday, we fly out to South America. Starting in Buenos Aires. We've never been there, and always wanted to go. Uruguay, Paraguay, Bolivia, Chile, Peru. A wonderful, formative journey, for us all.

(I intend to sleep in the hotel. I mainly intend to sleep. That sense of spending time inside someone's belly, buried in warm fabrics. Of being untouchable).

It will be an incredible adventure.

"Make them get dressed, please, and I'll take them to school," I plead, taking out some very oily olives from the fridge, just to counter the texture of the dry bread roll. "Distribution of labour."

(*A stranger's hand on my arm*.)

She walks up to me, kisses my cheek, as warm as a fully ripened fruit, smelling of vanilla-flavoured cream cakes.

"Which car will you take?" she asks.

"The Saab, I guess. Weather like today, we can take the roof down."

She kisses my right eye and that is when the first cut occurs.

(*A voice saying something, telling me to wake up, but there is only more darkness, the voice slipping, evading me*.)

The kitchen dissolves, vanishes, we're now in the car. The kids in the back seat, talking about something, arguing really. Zuzia colouring a book. Olaf wants in on the action. Upset he left his own colouring book behind.

"Play with your stupid Transformer," Zuzia says, authoritatively.

"Optimus is not a toy," he barks back.

"Well, what is it then?"

"He's my protector, my guardian."

We've covered half the distance between home and school. Stuck in early morning school run traffic. The city air already superheated and insufferable. If I had taken the Volkswagen, I'd just turn up the air con and the music, but no – the kids love riding with the top down. They never sweat.

We're running late. Their form tutor, the one I will once again have to apologise to, hates parents, especially those she knows take home three or four times her silly salary. We should pay people like her more. Maybe they'd be nicer to our kids, no matter how ugly their hair, how bowlegged they might be, how miserable their lives.

"Why do you need a guardian, Olaf?" I ask. "You're in no danger."

"I don't think we're going to get to school today," Zuzia says, focused on her crayons.

"And why is that, young lady?" I ask and only then realise that her utterance is more of a magic spell than a kid being a smart ass.

Everything slows down. The world extends in all directions, stretching, like bubblegum. I hear horns blaring, the dust of dried out grass banks swirling slowly in the hot air. People walking past doing so ever more slowly, languidly, as if in a parody of slow motion effects.

"Turn right," my daughter instructs.

02:52am

Voices in the dark. Very soft, as if recorded a long time ago.

"Is it not better just to call an ambulance?"

"I don't think so, no."

"What if he checks out on us right here and now?"

"He won't. Leave him for another few minutes."

"That's what we tried before, and then we had fucking problems. I don't want to have fucking problems, because afterwards..."

"Shut up and leave him. Cover the asshole with a blanket, we're in no hurry. No one is going anywhere any time soon."

"Hey, you! Get up!"

I hear hands clap, one, two, then hear and feel them turn into slaps. But this makes no difference to me.

"Leave him, will you? Give it time."

I would like to try working out what their outlines might tell me, what identities they might reveal, but instead things dissolve again and I can't get hold of anything anymore.

DREAM

I turn towards her. Her hands empty, the colouring book gone somewhere. My son is still next to her, though they are now both sitting erect, stiff, pinned to their safety seats. The Transformers toy is perched on the seat between them.

"What are you talking about?" I ask her.

Then everything stretches and twists even more. Sounds drawn out, images smudged, cars ahead of us becoming one long mass of steel, as if the heat was melting them together.

"We have to go on a journey. Beyond the city. You will see what awaits there," she answers.

"We will show you," adds my son.

"Did you two watch some silly cartoons last night?" I ask, even though I am starting to understand.

My son is no longer my son. My daughter, Zuzia, not my daughter anymore. My son who is no longer my son looks familiar however – I know him from somewhere else. I now know where. He looks at me with those big, black eyes filled with calm, eyes belonging only to those who know that all the orders they issue will be followed to the letter.

I know him. He led me to that block of flats. Eating corn chips.

The skies over our head change, something covering the sky, something like clouds, but more akin to monochromatic steel plates. As if a giant cupola had appeared over the city.

"Turn around," the girl says. She appears transformed, more skinny, her features more severe. The boy is silent, though he watches me intently, the gaze of an animal studying a source of potential danger.

"I can't turn around, there is a traffic jam."

"You must. We have to go. We have to get to the end of this tale," the boy says.

I drive over the central grassy reservation, over to the opposite side of the two-lane road, no cars at all going the other way. The air is filled with shards of something and colours whirling over our heads, like confetti discarded over us from above by a giant hand.

"Make the first turning into the woods," he says.

"What woods?" I ask.

But then I see them. We're no longer in a city and the day is no longer sunny. We're now on a narrow, country lane, Warsaw long ago dissolved, the sun vanished – all that was just a moment ago swallowed up by some power. The car is floating slowly along, the gas pedal disconnected from the engine.

I take my hands off the steering wheel. Everything keeps on happening. The kids driving me, the car, everything forward.

"In order for everything to conclude and start over again, we have to get to the end," the boy says.

"This has always been the way," the girl adds.

"I bet you'd like to know what we are called. But we do not have names," says the boy.

"We know you want to run. To escape. Very much," says the girl.

"I do," I confirm, then turn round to look at them. The girl's mouth opens, releasing a pinkish, fleshy mass, which at first looks like a giant tongue, and keeps on growing and growing, the girl vomiting it all up, as if she had eaten tons of pink pudding, all of it sliding down her flowery dress, onto the floor of the car.

The boy pays her no attention.

"We'll take the first turning into the woods," he says.

I spot a turning in the wall of trees to the right – it's only when we get to within a certain distance that I notice a blank road sign, pointing us into the forest.

"You can't escape. Not a chance, unfortunately," says the boy.

We enter the woodland. I don't feel any fear. Everything I had just a moment ago, my wife, my kids, my home, work, is now just a chaotic sketch, manic doodles.

"Everything will now start over again, like it was before," the boy tells me. "There are no changes, only temporary melting away. Tectonic shifts. But nothing ever really changes. This is your great dream, but not just yours. In order for something to change. For a messiah to come, for everyone to perish. For a real rain to come."

"What can I do?" I ask.

The woods around us are dead, the trees giant, black hands. I suddenly realise what is guiding the car. It is being drawn by whatever it is we are travelling towards.

The girl who was my daughter is no longer in the back seat. There is only this pink, fleshy goo. An organism. I know it from the inside of that block of flats, from the top floor. I see the small holes appearing in its skin, moving mouths. It's developing, growing. The boy doesn't seem to be paying any attention to it, the Transformers toy still perched between them.

"You have no influence over anything. You can only pray and sing your songs," the boy says.

"So nothing will happen?"

"You've no idea how true that is."

The forest becomes more sparse, shorter, fading away. At the end of the road I can barely make out the shapes of some buildings.

(*More shoves, slaps, voices, echoes of voices, blotches of something which could be phrases, sentences, orders.*)

As we near the building, I see it is a church, one I recognise from before. An old, Evangelical church with grey, cracked walls, a drooping roof, a dead clock up on the tower, the hands long gone.

"Why are we going there?" I ask

"Why are we going back there?" the boy retorts.

"What is inside?"

"You wanted to pray."

"I wasn't actually being serious..."

I turn toward him, at the very moment the car stops outside the church, burying its wheels in soft, muddy grass. I know I won't be able to get it started again.

"Now, you have to go alone," he tells me.

"You're leaving me alone again," I remind him.

"Again? Nobody left you alone before. You've always been alone. Since the very start."

The pink mass now covers the whole back seat, covering the boy like a quilt, slowly creeping into his nostrils and mouth. The boy accepts it. Nodding his head.

I look up at the sky and notice scratches, blotches, marks – the sky is like a membrane, the skin of some unknown beast, being burnt from the other side with a blow torch. The boy smiles.

"Good luck," he says. "Though I know you will never get used to it. No one ever gets used to it."

I get out of the car, my feet instantly sinking in the muddy earth. I struggle through it towards the church, through the stink of shit, manure, rotting earth. I now know where I know the smell from. As well as that church.

When we were little, we took a trip to a small town in the Lake District, where my grandmother was born. The church was in the centre of a small town and was derelict, unused, abandoned. I kept hassling my parents for answers as to why no one had ever done anything with it, repaired it, looked to see what was inside.

Approaching the steps to the church, I look back. The car is gone, swallowed up by the earth within seconds.

My parents assured me there was nothing inside that church. That everything had been robbed. But I felt, I knew they were lying.

I watch great, brown bubbles appearing in the sky, only to then explode in blinding white light, announcing the arrival of someone.

Some lettering can be seen on the doors, etched in faint chalk, crooked and hard to read – BITCH, GIVE BACK WHAT YOU TOOK.

I know it is time, I just don't know if I should push on the door or if it opens by itself.

03:04am

"Enough of this," I hear.

Cold water, very cold, landing on my face. I swallow air, along with the water, coughing, choking on it.

"Nice. Good. Time to talk," the voice says.

Hands snatch, pick me up. Someone opens a door, shoves me through it. Everything spinning. The corridor we're in, the others. My eyes slowly focusing. Very slowly. I am pushed forward. Their hands stink of fags. Saturated with the stench, as if they only breathed cigarette fumes, as if they sweated nicotine.

I slowly begin to recognise one of the faces. The guy who made the joke about knocking teeth out. One of the cops who stopped me on the highway leading out of town.

"Slept well, princess?" he asks.

I don't even try testing my mouth out by trying to speak.

"Feeling better? Can you walk by yourself now?" he asks.

I stay silent.

"You can. You're fully recovered. A cute princess. Let's go get you some nice tights."

I don't react.

"The prosecutor's office will want to hold onto you, pretty princess."

All I want to do is drink. My insides are completely desiccated, as if all I've done the last few weeks is drink nasty grain spirits illegally smuggled over from Belarus or Ukraine. Let's. Keep. Going. Everything is spinning.

"You haven't found anything," I tell him.

They are silent. Everything buzzing. Speeding up, harder. I have to stop. I retch, but now there really is nothing there but noise. Nothing at all left to vomit.

"Boy, you're lucky there's nothing on that floor now, else you'd be licking it all back up again now, princess."

We're walking. They shove me inside a room, a sterile space, like a cubicle in a brand new corporate skyscraper. "They've changed," I think. "Refreshed." An Apple laptop, a fan, some plants, freshly painted walls. The MacBook is closed, separating me from a guy sitting in front of it, ready to interrogate me. I don't remember ever seeing him before. They toss me down into a plastic chair.

My brain is slowly but surely starting to regain composure. First, the body. Pain, the gut, the throat, hands. I massage the wrists. Blink my eyes. Desperately in need of some water.

He looks a little over fifty, but is a cop, so he could be ten years younger, his short hair half-grey, neatly shorn. No uniform, his blazer too tight, the shirt beneath it the same. He's swollen since the last time his wife went shopping for his clothes, and he can't afford to send her out for more. His face is sweating, his eyes like those of a giant, dumb dog. It's been a long time since he got any decent sleep, maybe just as long as I.

Then facts make themselves felt again. Tiny. The bag he took. The money. The drugs. Them. How did they know where to look for me? How did they find my apartment? Who ratted me out? Paz again? Revenge? Could be. She knew the address all too well. She went to the cops before the neighbours reported all the noise I was making. The gun I waved around at the neighbour. Told them I pushed her around. Threatened her. Insurance policy. Paz is vengeful. Is she vengeful?

"Good day, sir," the greying guy says to me. "I am an officer investigating a certain matter, my name is Darek Piechota."

"More like good evening," I answer.

"Let's not wind each other up this early on, shall we? Try to keep it smooth," he states calmly.

"I'm not too sure what could be thought of as 'smooth' in this whole set up," I tell him.

"Don't fucking wind me up, OK, pal?"

He turns round, towards a bare wall missing a clock. Then he turns back to me.

"How the hell do you know it's evening anyway?"

I look at my hands. Then notice they took my watch.

"You found nothing," I say.

"Easy. I will ask, and you will answer. From time to time, Officer Malczak will ask additional questions."

The Joker is still standing behind me, smiling his sour smile, the grin of a ruthless child. Is Paz a vengeful person? The question bothers me, I have to know, or maybe not, maybe I just have to forget all about her – human character has no influence over what is going to happen next.

Only she knew the address.

"And so – your name and surname?" he asks.

"I have the right to a phone call," I tell him.

"How did you come to meet a certain Mariusz F.?"

"Can I have something to drink?" The guy looks at me without any sort of expression on his face, like a cat staring at a TV screen. "I can't speak. Parched," I say, pointing to my cracked lips.

"Go make him a coffee," my interrogator says to the Joker, who leaves the room. We stare at each other for a while, then he jots something down on the papers in front of him.

"How did you come to meet a Mr Mariusz F.?"

"Can I have some sugar with that?" I ask.

"Was Mariusz F. a regular customer of yours?"

03:17am

"I've never had any dealings at all with anyone called Mariusz F. I didn't supply him with cocaine, didn't take coke with him, did not talk to him, in fact I don't think I've ever been in the same room as the guy. Never even queued for the same till in the same supermarket. Not once."

"Has Mariusz F. ever rung your telephone number? How many times a week?"

"I've never parked my car beside his. Or maybe this one time. I don't know what it is he drives. I don't watch TV."

"We have you on camera."

"You have many people on many cameras, I don't doubt that for a second."

"You're there, entering the building where he resides."

"Coffee. There was no sugar."

"Thanks. It will do... I don't even think I've ever crossed paths with that celebrity punk."

"So what were you doing in his home?"

"Did I make myself unclear somehow, talking about the room and the cars and the queues? I've never been in the same postal district as the guy."

"How's the coffee, you prick?"

"I see him on TV. And billboards. I don't really follow those forms of media broadcasting, but I know of him."

"What were you doing in his home?"

"Alright. When is it you suspect I visited this Mariusz F.?"

"Last Saturday night. There was a party. And then an accident. You might have heard about that."

"I was in Hong Kong last weekend. You can ask my mum."

"So the guy we have on that camera recording is your identical twin brother?"

03:52am

"Perhaps. Not that I would know."

"You'll just keep jabbering the same crap until we drag you in before a judge. You know how long we can keep you waiting behind bars for a hearing. Six months. Twelve."

"I don't know anything. I don't have any celebrity pals. I keep busy with other things."

"A year and a half. Two years."

"I don't think I've ever snorted coke. It's not my style. Unhygienic."

"Stop bullshitting us."

"I don't drink alcohol and I don't smoke cigarettes. It's only green tea for me, and the odd coffee," I say, taking a sip and wondering how much of it is that comedy cop's spit.

"Who is your wholesale supplier?"

"It's said our boy retails a very pure grade of shit," says the Joker. "The best. He only services real celebrities."

"Fine, but we're not interested in his clients."

"I don't know anything about any suppliers or any coke. I live from

342

online investments. My money circulates online all day, sometimes all night. You're detaining a totally innocent fellow."

"Mariusz F. has provided us with statements that in the past two years, you've supplied him cocaine to the tune of some 800,000 zlotys. We would like to now know where it came from."

04:37am

"I don't know where cocaine comes from. I've heard it is Central America."

"Do we have to have this conversation in a slightly less polite fashion?"

"I've no idea what you might mean by that."

"Formally, the owner of your apartment is a trading firm called Ampix, a limited company, based in..."

"I rent the place from them."

"The owner of said company, Michał Dubieszyński, where can we find him?"

"How should I know? I've never actually laid eyes on the guy."

"You've never actually met the owner of the apartment which happens to be your home?"

"There are leasing agencies. Companies that take care of such things. I can show you how it works, if you open up that laptop and connect it to the world wide web."

The greying cop chuckles, which feels kind of him.

"Your previous address was in the town of Olsztyn, Andersa St, the home of Ewa and Leszek Nitecki."

"Yeah, I'm a jam jar, that's me."

"A what?"

"A jam jar. The slang for those who move to Warsaw to find work. And happiness. That's me."

"I know what it means."

"So what is it that's baffling you?"

"A number of key things."

"Not sure I can help you anymore. Can I ask for another coffee?"

"Don't fucking try to annoy me, boy."

"I did not change my permanent address for Warsaw, nor bought a place here."

"You haven't bought property in Warsaw, but you rent a place that costs you 6,000 zlotys a month?!" he asks, incredulous.

"Many people do so."

"Not many people can afford to do so."

"Are you guys involved in conducting some sort of sociological research here? I prefer to rent. Banks don't like lending to guys like me. We make too much money in random spurts. It frightens them."

"And a good thing too. Very soon, you're not going to need a place of your own. The state will be providing for all your needs, princess. All except freedom of movement."

"Very soon, he's going to be dining on dick each night. The boys from Goclaw will love to pay him visits at night, once they find out he lived there and sang to us. Such a pretty princess song."

"You wouldn't do that to me, gents? Would you? Telling gangsters, real life gangsters, that me, a legitimate online stockbroker, was involved in illegitimate businesses? That I gave you information? Oh dear."

"Your personal ID card says your surname is Grajcar."

"Kuba Grajcar."

"Your parents have a different surname."

"It's my mother's maiden name."

"Why do you go by that name here, in the capital?"

"I changed it, legally."

"Any reason why?"

"A bit of beef between me and the old man."

"You're not as smart as you think you are, pal. You're just acting smart. Which is not the same thing as being smart. Or funny."

"I'm not acting smart."

"Mariusz F. testified that the cocaine he had consumed on the night of the 20th of December, just before he caused a fatal accident involving the death of one Anna Kabaszuk, and her unborn child, came from you. That you visited his home at around 1am. You sold him a total of thirty grams of the stuff."

"I don't know anything about that." The Joker kicks the chair out from under me. I fall to the concrete floor. It's cool. "I don't know anything about any of that. I've never met Mariusz F. or anybody he might have driven into. I don't watch the news. Bad for your health."

The Joker grabs my sleeves, pulls me up and perches me back on the plastic chair.

"I have the right to a phone call," I remind them again.

"You have the right to suck my fucking cock."

"Joker man, you sure have a lot of jokes about homosexuals in that repertoire of yours. Expressing something subtle there, buddy?"

"Shut your mouth, faggot."

"Listen to yourself. Really. It's the secret of happiness."

"Shut your gob, for fuck's sake, else things are about to turn nasty."

"Meanwhile, see how nice they are."

"We're taking you to our HQ. Criminal investigations. Right now."

"You can only hold me for forty-eight hours."

"The prosecutor has other ideas."

"Can I have something else to drink? Can you tell me if you found any illegal substances in my home?"

"We'll take our time with you. It's your opportunity. See it that way. A chance to think it through. Your last chance. I will ask the question, politely – where did the cocaine your delivered to Mariusz F. come from?"

"You don't even know what it is you want to ask me about."

Joker once again kicks my chair. Once again, I fall to the cold ground.

"You're out of ideas," I tell them from the floor, receiving a kick in the guts for my observation.

"Enough! Fucker!" he screams, while the other tries to hold him back.

"Go on, pick him up," he tells his colleague.

Once I am replaced in my seat, the interrogator restarts his work,

"From the top. Where did you get the cocaine you supplied to Mariusz F.?"

"Take him away."

The funny one drags me off my chair, standing me up straight. I don't resist. Resistance will only make him enjoy hurting me more. I can hear him breathing right into my ear. His breath smells, as if his diet consisted only of the cheapest kinds of meat, offal, sausages. I look at his colleague, whose face has changed colour since I entered his office. He has gone red around the neck and cheeks. Looking like a drunken heart attack victim. He's had enough. Exhausted. He knows full well that he's not going to get anything valuable out of this whole set up. That within thirty or so hours he will have to release me. I just have to call Piotrek who then has to set his best lawyers on these fuckers.

I have to get to Argentina. This evening. Check in closes at 10pm. I am not missing it for these pricks.

"Get him out of my sight," the greying cop tells the other one.

A corridor. Not whirling any more, allowing me to walk straight, even though I am still very much dehydrated. I will throw up once I get to my cell.

But before that can happen, as carefully as I try to walk, the Joker cop still has to keep on being funny – he puts his foot out, tripping me up and sending me down to the floor.

"Now we can fucking talk," he says.

He picks me up and throws me against a wall, as if he didn't really know how to go about beating me up. He grabs me by the lapels of my blazer and headbutts me, making no solid impact, nothing in my face giving way as his forehead connects with my nose. He then punches me in the guts, chaotically, no planning involved, as if he was only warming up for a proper bit of violence to come, testing to see what will bring him the most pleasure.

"Hey!" someone shouts from the other end of the corridor.

"You're such a clever lad? Always know the right thing to say? Well, let me show you what we do with smart asses like you round here. I will fucking personally show you, boy," he tells me.

"Give him a bit of a break," says another cop, the one I remember smoking a cigarette in my car.

"I'm going to smash his fucking face in," says the Joker.

"Take it easy," his colleague advises. "You have to calm down."

"You have to calm down, because you got less than nothing to pin on me, and tomorrow my lawyer will be doing my talking for me," I tell him, feeling blood trickling from my nose.

He grits his teeth, eyes desperate to rid this world of me right now, his bare hands all he would need to get that job accomplished. I sort of understand where he's coming from. He's probably been here for forty-eight hours now. Snorting speed only so as to still be able to function. Like a chaotic, yet well trained dog, he does what little he can: shoves me forward, hard, forcing me to move down the corridor, spilling blood as I do.

Soon enough, a lawyer will be here. Buying my freedom back. I will chat to Piotrek. Explain how all this came to be. Make all the money I owe when I get back. Quickly too. Maybe I could give him my apartment as part payment. But to come back, I have to first go. I have to leave to survive.

Tomorrow, I will be sleeping in a hotel room, slid in between cool bed sheets, concealed, curled into myself, on the other side of the world.

The overhead light in the corridor is cold and pierces the eyes like two blunt knives. Light that penetrates everywhere, covering the whole of Warsaw. I will finally get a break from it. Rest from the lights.

"For now, you'll have a nice lie down on us," says the one who lit a cigarette in my car. He opens the cell door. "Just don't start rearranging the furniture or any other fancy shit," he tells me.

"I wasn't planning to mess with your feng shui," I spit back, just as he shoves me inside, slamming the heavy steel door behind me.

I fall back on the bunk, shut my eyes against the light. Only now do I feel pain, flooding my face, dominating the guts, overwhelming the rest of the body – I curl up into a foetal position, as if trying to hug the hurt out of myself. It feels as if I've swallowed a plate full of razor blades.

Eyes shut, I can hear whispers down the corridor, as well as steps. Is there a point trying to get to sleep, if all they're going to do is wake me up again in half an hour to go over the same stupid questions? Why would they imagine I would risk giving up my wholesale supplier? Do they realise what sort of chain of command stands behind him? It is Piotrek I need to speak to, to actually sort out the lawyer, get me out of here long before that flight starts boarding.

I want to keep my eyes closed, keep my breathing steady, regular intervals, right up until they come back to wake me with the same stupid questions. Until they give me my phone call, and I finally get someone from Piotrek's legal team to come and look after me.

Close the eyes, breathe evenly, a steady tempo.

Check in closes at 10pm.

Regular, even, steady as you go.

Check in closes at 10pm.

DREAM

I knew I would go back there, that I would not end up anywhere else. The doors to the church slam shut behind me with a dull thud; I don't have to turn around in order to know that they have just stopped existing, and that there is nothing but a solid wall behind me. The thudding noise sounded final, something irreversible.

The church interior is all covered in gold, all of it. It looks like only moments ago all the gold had just been melted down, was liquid before being cooled and setting hard before me.

There are no pews here, only a long corridor, lined with red lino. No windows either. The walls uniform, the arched ceiling much higher than it might seem by looking at it from the outside. Golden columns rise up out of the floor, carved in leafy motifs, styled to look ancient, topped with fruit and human figures. An altar at the far end, majestic, massive, irregular in shape, a huge mound of melted-down gold, all the individual elements combining into an erratic whole, a giant mound, a golden clump.

A golden Christ hangs suspended over the altar, concealed in a cavity, his arms outstretched, nailed to an invisible cross.

Either side of his suffering body there are golden washbasins, the taps dripping water onto red satin cushions. The sound of all those drops striking the wet fabric sounds like a hammer, like the beating of a giant heart hidden somewhere in the basement.

The gold begins to move, to speak, mouths opening in the smooth surface of the altar.

I know the man standing at the other end of the corridor, beneath the altar. I know his face, which is round, as if glued to a completely round, shaved head. He's dressed all in black, as well as being barefoot. He's waiting for me.

"Come, Kuba," he asks. "Come. We were destined to meet. You don't reply to my text messages. Not nice of you."

I know who he is. I know his name.

I see various figures appearing out of the altar, as if flowing from it – cupids, saints and angels, as well as the writhing bodies of women who've sinned, the bodies of girls I've seen on the stages of this city: as well as those of Pazina, Uncle, Piotrek and Beata; cars, furniture, rooms, doors, windows, bathrooms – all of it locked in a single dance, in a blurred orgy. In the lump of this crazy gold chaos more mouths open up, black holes, face forming around the mouths – the barefoot man in black is conducting their song – it's enough for him to wave a hand for the mouths to fall silent and vanish.

I know his hand rules this space, that it has mastery over everything.

I approach him, which seems to take a long time, the red floor of the church as soft as grass, as the muddy grass we parked in, hard not to get stuck in. I know that all the gold is just an optical illusion, painted on, a shell covering processes of mutual consumption, devouring, digesting of all the matter within and without.

The man puts his hands on my shoulders.

"The rain I keep hearing you praying for," he tells me, "It is not going to be to anybody's benefit."

"So what now?" I ask.

"You're not the only one who would like to clean up, I swear to you... Not the only one."

"What next?"

He smiles, turns and approaches the altar, burying two fingers in the golden goo, which then drips down his wrist... Then, he turns back to me, grabbing me by the face, and when he does so, my body is shot through with a paralysing charge of electrical current, freezing me in place, unable to so much as blink.

"Try. Remember that this is your favourite taste. Understand that the judgement has already been cast and there is no one and nothing you can appeal to, Kuba."

He shoves his fingers in my mouth, which is when everything begins to drip down, his fingers no longer his own but a pink mass, shapeless, slippery, everything starting to turn dark, the world vanishing. The last thing I see is his face – grinning, so familiar, and yet so alien, a face which dominates everything, my mouth once again filling with the taste of vomit. I have the impression this taste will never leave me, that it has been injected into me for all time.

"Remember that this isn't a prison. Indeed, you cannot leave here, but you have total control over the interior designs. You have a lot of money, even if you don't really have any at the moment, in a short while you will make much more, twice as much, enough to buy the best, most luxurious bed, as well as the subtlest wallpaper," he tells me.

His face dissolves into a blur. I can only see colours: red, yellow, green, orange, brown, black. Irregular, weakening, turning to black.

"But you will never escape here, Kuba, it was so fucking childish of you to just want to come in and out. A silly fantasy. But I understand you – everyone has dreams..."

I can still hear his voice. I am being absorbed, and I now know by what, by whom.

"You just have to forget about all those fantasies. All the possible dreams you ever had," the man's voice sounds final, vanishing in mid-air.

For a few more moments, before darkness descends, I see the boy who once led me into an abandoned building, a boy emerging out of a lump of pink goo, the boy looking very serious, holding a Transformers toy in his hand, watching as I am devoured.

"She doesn't know any mercy, but that does not mean she is unjust. She devours everyone and everything. Don't feel hard done by."

I want to tell him that I am not feeling injured or cheated, that I know it is all happening according to plan. I would like to assure him of this, but I finally lose the ability to see or hear anything at all.

08:12am

I hear a conversation on the other side of the door. Quiet at first, then louder; the noise seeping through the wall. I open my eyes, feeling as if someone has slammed into me with a car. The conversation wakes me, along with a belly ache. My insides must be heavily damaged. In order to sit up on the bunk bed, I need the help of a giant hand, a hand to grab and lift me up, sit me up. The hand finally appears, but squeezes too hard, crushing my ribs. I sit up, feeling like all of my insides, all that is beneath my skin, has been ground down to a soft, weak pulp.

"Fucking hell," I say out loud, as if trying to reach the voices outside.

"There's no fucking question about it, we've got to let him go."

I hear the Joker's voice, swearing as always.

A moment's silence. I try breathing and spitting.

"What the fuck do you mean we have to let him go?" The Joker's voice does not sound happy with the original answer to his question.

"A guy's just arrived out front, claims to be his lawyer. He heard the sum, nodded his head and took the cash out of his briefcase," I hear the other voice say. "Two hundred grand bail money, officially set by the prosecutor's office."

"Don't be converting that sum into whatever it was you'd spend it on if you got your hands on it," Joker insists.

"We've nothing on him. Nothing found in his home. No camera

footage of any dealing activity. Nothing in the car either," says the serious cop.

Silence. More feet shuffling.

"Even so, if the car was clean," Joker's voice muses, "They probably made a deal with that lot upstairs, don't they always," he hypothesises. "And now the order from up above is that we release him. Just let me have him for fifteen minutes. No one has to know. Fucking hell, I will sort him right out."

"Orders from the top, Janek, can't let you play it any other way."

Janek Malczak – that is all the info I need to find him and make sure he comes to the right sort of harm. I'll find him easy enough, and when I do I will not be trying to be funny. The comedy will be very black. But now, first things first.

I rise up from the bunk, let them open the door, see me standing tall.

"Sorry, Janek, once again, no can do," the other cop says as the door opens. I feel the light sneaking in from the corridor stripping the skin from my tired face.

"Get on out," says the cop whose name I don't know, but I do remember him from that stop and search they put me through. The one who looks like his mother drank meths throughout her pregnancy. He stands in the doorway, his face ugly in resignation, the look of a tough and honest and tied public servant, defender of the streets, and the innocent heartbroken.

"Bye bye, princess. Till we meet again. On the streets of this mean town." Joker keeps on with the act. I put my hands out, in a gesture of surrender, though they hurt to be moved and held out. He could hit me again now, as I leave myself exposed, unable to move with the pain. "You've no idea how long we're going to put you away for, fucker. You really have no idea."

Maybe I am fucked, but it's not me but him who a year from now will be drawing his disability benefit payments, injured in the line of duty, caught out like a punk, made a joke of in front of his cop buddies. Caught with his pants down, not ready for this particular princess's revenge. He's the worst kind of cop – one who actually thinks he's decent, who watched too many 70s TV cop shows and movies with the likes of Eastwood, and Pacino, who still believes in the idea of good and evil. Right and wrong. Too bad Janek is just a dumb son of a bitch, so focused on sniffing mephedrone, drinking vodka and smashing detainees to a pulp, he no longer realises that his career has now become a dirty old rag.

"Lead me out of here, gents," I request. "I don't quite recall the way."

The other cop nods and escorts me down the corridor, slowly, dragging his feet, while I sense my body waking somehow, back straightening, head no longer drooping, hands under my control, my stomach settled, my steps steady and straight. I slowly begin to imagine what I need now to make a full recovery. I turn back to look at Janek the Joker, standing there by the entrance to my cell, staring at me with unchecked disgust. How unprofessional of him, I think to myself and imagine he can read my thoughts by staring into my eyes and now hates me all the more.

I stop looking back, trying to fight off the super strong and violent light.

09:45am

I only started to laugh once I saw myself in a mirror, the one on the reverse of the sun blind in my car, as I started driving home. I laughed a long, long time, almost until I fell to my own car floor. I had to prop myself against the steering wheel to stop.

When half an hour earlier I reached my Audi, I was in no laughing mood. A small baggie of coke was stuffed into the side of the passenger side seat – I had forgotten about that and it seemed implausible that the cops hadn't spotted it. That their dogs didn't pick up the scent, if they had bothered to use the animals. I pulled it out, the powder stuffed into a small, damp, crushed down plastic baggie. Then held it in my tightly clenched fist. I then pressed a concealed button beneath the dashboard, which released a motorised shelf, similar to a CD-loading tray, and grabbed the last of my cash hidden there, packed in metal sandwich foil. Twenty thousand

American bucks. I ran the tips of my fingers along the edge of the package, as if thanking the banknotes for still being there. Not a great sum of money, but enough to pay for clean bedsheets and an air-conditioned room.

I will fix everything when I get back. Easy does it, I thought to myself.

The interior still smelt of the cops who'd been in here not that long ago, doing a crap job of searching through it, so once back on my own street I got out of the car and sat down in the snow, back resting against the front passenger seat. The street was empty, all the apartment and office windows looking dead – "There is something noble about abandoned cities," I thought to myself.

Warsaw has the potential to be pretty, in its own way, if only all of its inhabitants were wasted by one of those neutron bombs that don't touch any of the buildings, only wipe out the human population.

That's the kind of Warsaw I could see myself strolling across.

I rub the remains of what was in the baggie into my gums. No point leaving it behind for the cops to find. I instantly feel a sharp, refreshing intake of breath, settling everything inside me like a long, calming wave washing over my flesh. All the mess of my insides once again arranging itself in a naturally preordained order. The liver, the spleen, my intestines, and finally the brain.

Getting out of the car I fall and it's only once I try and fail to get up off the snowy ground, using my hands to steady myself, that something comes to my attention. Something attached to the undercarriage of my car, next to the front wheel, a small black box the size of my old Nokia cell phone, with a simple digital display panel. I tear it away from where it had been glued to the metal with special adhesive. I then come to rest with my back against the front passenger door, without worrying about how the snow is starting to soak through my jeans. I take a closer look at what has to be a tracking device, and say out loud: "Now why did I not think of that myself? But who the fuck does it belong to?" Anyone could get hold of toys like this one these days. Not that using it on someone else's car without necessary papers was legal, but the people I had fallen foul of recently were not the kind to worry about crossing such subtle lines.

What troubles me more is that I had not thought about inspecting my car much earlier. The people who wanted a cut of what I had been making over the last few years wouldn't have any reservations about attaching something far more explosive to the undercarriage of my vehicle, and I was being a real fool forgetting that fact.

I held the black box in my hand so hard it felt like I was about to crush it with my bare hands, trying to work out at which point in the past few months had I become so bad at risk management.

I get up and go home, ripping the yellow "POLICE LINE" tape from over the smashed up front door. I made a call and half an hour later a slightly annoyed locksmith arrived to install a new lock.

I kept thinking about that naughty little box standing in my own bathroom, laughing again while staring at myself in the mirror, trying to shave my battered face, making it look presentable, like something that resembled the unbruised photo in my passport. Looking in the mirror this morning I was staring at someone who was the walking embodiment of stupidity, of carelessness, of not paying attention to details. Lifesaving details.

On the way back, I had bought a medical drip in an all-night drug store. Seeing the state of my face and confronted with a crisp 100 zloty note, the lady behind the counter sold it to me without a prescription. I now attach it to the wall using some surgical tape, and submerged in the bath I try to connect it to an appropriate vein, failing too many times, but getting the right spot eventually. I have to succeed – after so many days of not eating at all and not drinking enough my body's resources are dangerously depleted. The coke will not suffice. I'm likely to pass out at any point, a luxury I can only afford once I'm safely on board that plane. Having chosen my inflight movie, covered up with the complimentary blanket, my hands on the inflight meal I am highly unlikely to touch.

I lie back in the bath, listening to the bubbling electrolytes as they enter my bloodstream, drop after soothing drop. I want to stay in that bath for a whole hour, but my phone rings. Pazina – I pick up and simply say: "I'm sorry," but there is no reply, so I repeat the apology. "I'm sorry. I was wrong..."

"You promised you wouldn't hurt him," she says after a short silence.

"I'm sorry that I threatened you with a gun in your own home. It was unnecessary and unfair of me," I tell her, trying to sound convincingly serious, but I only end up sounding like a young priest, a breathless, uptight, decidedly unconvincing preacher.

"You fucking promised you wouldn't touch Tiny. Not a hair on his stupid head," she repeats, almost shouting down the line.

I draw my knees up to my chest, the water dark from all the dirt coming off my battered body. I am trying to keep the arm attached to the drip extended straight along the edge of the bath. There is a long, dark red trail of blood flowing into the water from where the needle pierced the skin.

"And I didn't. Though I also told you I had no influence on what the other people he had managed to annoy were going to do."

"They found him battered and lying in a park in Mokotow. Yesterday morning. He's in intensive care, fighting for his life," she says more loudly than usual, letting her anger off the leash, which in itself is an act – I know her well enough to sense it.

"I told you I had nothing at all to do with that. I've no idea who did. There are a lot of folks in this town who would be on my list of suspects."

"He's unlikely to come out of it. He's suffered serious concussion, a cracked spine, one of his eyeballs poking out. Heavy internal bleeding. Someone did a good job of trying to kill him."

I then remember when I saw him last. He'd been armed with several guns. I try to explain to Paz what little I can recall,

"I never touched him. In fact, he robbed me, taking several things that belonged to me, including my pistol. And a bag. Was a black sports bag found with him that you know of?"

Sitting up a little in the bath, the needle slips out of my arm, causing a sharp pang of pain I'm not quite braced for.

"Fuck you, Kuba," Pazina spits down the line.

"Just tell me if anyone found a black sports holdall next to him," I say patiently, gritting my teeth.

"I'm not going to the police, none of that. But I want you to know from now on that the only person who was close to you in this whole damn town, in this crazy world, now thinks you're just a common gangster, a nasty prick who should be doing time for all the things he's caused to happen of late, where he's likely to end up soon enough from what I hear anyway," she almost shouts at me down the line.

"How many times do I need to apologise to you, Paz?" I ask in all earnestness.

"Fuck off, Kuba," she answers.

"So no news about any bag being found. He robbed me at gunpoint in my own home," I tell her the crazy-sounding truth.

"This really is the last time I ever call you," she announces. Then really does cut the call.

I carefully climb out of the bath, take some cotton wool out of the cabinet, apply it to where the drip had been attached. "He had two guns on him all the time," I think to myself. "His own and my piece." Someone was still able to get close enough to put him in a coma. Maybe Uncle with Shady and someone else. Or Piotrek's other crew... could have been any pro not scared of a big kid waving firepower about in a suburban park at night. Leaving my place, I suspect he was already well past caring and the ability to think and plan straight. The dopamine had to have torched the last of his cerebrum. He might have forgotten how he'd come by the bag he was driving round town with, forgetting the scene at my place. All he knew was that the bag offered some way towards salvation. A small Christmas present for mistreated little Tiny – a blessing he wanted to cling onto, ignoring the noise of strangers approaching. Guys who might have been tracking him, or maybe came across him by chance.

If he gets lucky, he'll die in his sleep a few days from now. Before his family spend too much money on legal counsel. If he's less than lucky, it will take some weeks. Or if his luck really has run out, the doctors might manage to patch up his battered spine, soothe his concussed skull, stick the eyeballs back in their sockets, and send him back into the world in a cheap wheelchair.

The problem with Pazina is that, like the majority of regular folks, they don't realise people like Tiny bring all their problems upon themselves. That's not to say they deserve all that happens as a result of bad and stupid moves they end up making. None of us really deserve what happens to us. The problem is that we try to save other people from themselves, without first asking how they managed to get into trouble in the first place. It's sometimes possible to help people, if they are truly deserving and desiring of the gesture, but it's never possible to save folks from their own inherent weaknesses.

There is nothing unjust about what has happened to Tiny, same as there is nothing wrong about smokers getting lung cancer, alcoholics dying of liver failure, people who drive at well over the national speed limit smashing their company-owned family saloons into oncoming lorries or trees. There is actually nothing at all that's wrong about death, or disease, or the painful ways in which so many of us meet our ends.

It just has to happen. The way of the world. Most people fail to incorporate major tragedies into any sensible analysis of how effect follows cause. Instead, they ask crazy big philosophical questions about the cosmos.

I pick out some clean clothes from the pile Tiny threw out of my wardrobes and tossed all across my apartment. I choose a pair of comfortable sports shoes, almost unworn.

There is no mystery to how the world gives or takes away. It's all written in the black hearts to be found beating beneath the streets of large cities. A darkness which emits its own blinding form of light. A tangible sort of darkness.

I grab a leather travelling bag, stuff some underpants, socks, a few toiletries and also books into it, hoping to finally have some time for reading. Mann, Celine, Proust, things I haven't thought about since university. I grab my old MP3 player, loaded up with Bach, mainly fugues and cantatas, and the *Variations* of course, a little Schumann and a bit of Haydn.

I get the tickets from a chest of drawers in the lounge. Two plane tickets, one in my name, the other in Pazina's. I bought it on impulse, without asking her first, and now toss it in the bag just in case. I have no return ticket. I'll buy that once I am done sleeping and breathing in tropical air.

I check to make sure I have enough sleeping medication packed. I need nothing else really. The last thing to end up inside the travelling bag is a pair of brightly colored rubber sandals, something I picked up by chance when shopping for clothes last year.

Visible darkness. Black flames. Right beneath the city's concrete skin. That's all. Nothing more. Some people struggle on through their lives never knowing about their existence. Others get lost and fall into the darkness or burn themselves on the black flames. Tiny is a perfect example of someone who got too close. There are others, very few such folks, who know and understand the darkness, who are able to stand firm in the face of it, stare it down the way we stare at people we work with, people we don't feel we're able to fully trust, but who are unlikely to also become enemies. Those folks can stare at the darkness without being paralysed with fear, can listen to what it has to tell them. Arrive at some mutual understanding with it.

I zip up the travel bag and head out, taking one last look at my demolished apartment. I will have the energy to clean it all up, as good as new, when I get back. I hear a voice in my head telling me to: "Treat it all like a lesson in humility. A set of instructions as to what not to do in the future. A little lecture in carefulness. A presentation about the consequences of making careless mistakes."

I look at the apartment and realise that I no longer like it so much. I have to move out of here. I work the new locks and walk down to the car.

11:50am

He looks at me suspiciously, but it is the suspicion typical of a sixty-something, overweight man for whom the toughest conversation he's had to deal with in the past few years was when he asked his daughter over Christmas Eve supper about why she still hadn't given him a grandchild. Other than that, he appears as soft as any static desk worker – someone who keeps completely quiet even when watching his national football team playing away.

As usual, he instantly recognises me. He must have heard all about it, and so must be putting my face together with the data stored in his soft brain. Nobody has ever told him my surname.

"Mr Fajkowski is out, I'm afraid," he tells me.

"I know he told you to say that to everyone who shows up and tries to gain entry. I also know he is heartbroken about all that has happened. But this is an important matter. I'm from the management board of the TV station," I tell him.

"And your name is?"

"Dubieński," I answer.

"And you wish to see Mr Fajkowski regarding which matter?"

"A matter which is sure to improve his mood."

It's a good thing he's here alone. Sometimes there's another watchman at the desk with him, a young kid, head shaved, someone keeping a watch on the monitors while the older guy can have his fag and toilet breaks whenever necessary. He looks at me over the top of his reading glasses, then checks the guest book, then looks at me once again.

"Last night, I had to come to the defence of a certain lady," I say, pointing to all the bruises glowing all over my face. He nods, hands me a plastic door entry card. Walking up the stairs, I put on a baseball cap. He opens the door on the tenth knock. I hit him with all I've got, a fist to the cheek, he grabs his nose and takes a few steps back – I push my way inside and close the door behind us.

He's half-naked, his skinny chest is not particularly attractive. I notice a porn film playing on a large flat-screen TV fixed to the wall. Some lines of blow are neatly arranged on the coffee table in front of the TV, along with a generously filled glass of whisky.

His eyes are ringed with darkness. Now that his hair has not been prepped by a TV make-up professional, I realise just how thin it's getting.

"Good God," he moans. "Why the fuck did you come here? The police will be round like a flash."

"I've been to see them, don't worry. They told me so many interesting things."

I grab the bottle of single malt off the bar and smash it with all the strength I can muster into the table, bits of glass flying all over the place, alcohol seeping into the shag-pile carpet. I'm left holding the broken bottle neck, and he takes a few steps back. I move forward. Each one of my steps as far as two of his.

"They said that you had informed them all about me. This is something which we don't do in our line of business."

"I had no other way out. No choice at all," he says, calmly.

We move backwards into his bedroom and he sits on his king size bed, so I grab him by the throat and slap him again with the hand holding the bottle neck carefully so that it doesn't tear flesh. He slides off the bed down to the floor and I bend over him, applying the jagged end of the bottle neck to his cheek, making sure it is as close to his eye as possible.

"You know I can get myself out of such holes. It would be stupid if I didn't," I tell him calmly. "It's like you, broadcasting live, knowing what to do when an earpiece stops working, or some such fuck up. Part of the job."

"What was I supposed to tell them?" He pleads for a hint, almost shouting.

"You could have asked me that. I would have told you what not to fucking do. Do you think telling them everything you knew about me was going to improve our relationship in the future?"

"I know less than nothing about you. I know fuck all."

"Somehow or other they knew where I live. They even found my secret hiding place, and no one knew where that was. You must have told them at least some of the info, but how did you know? Where I live?"

He says nothing, just sits there, trembling. I worry he might piss himself in a minute. My battered face can't be filling him with confidence right now.

"So what was I to do?" he pleads, still fearing the broken bottle.

"Where did you grow up? In some convent? Did nobody ever teach any of you kids that you never tell the cops anything. No matter what?"

"How much money do you want?" he asks.

"How did you find out where I live?" I ask.

He's breathing fast and heavy now, like a trapped animal, his pupils contracting and expanding all the time. He smells as if he was long-term sick, someone ageing quickly too – stuffed with antibiotics like a farm animal.

"The girl," he finally says.

"What girl?" I ask.

"The model."

"What model?" I ask again.

He falls down on the thick carpet, stretching out alongside the bed, going into funny-looking spasms. The broken bottle neck now safely out of the range of his gaze. "What model? What is he talking about? Who could it be?" I ask myself in my thoughts, grabbing my stomach as it begins to hurt again.

"Get up off the floor," I order him.

"I don't know anything about your codes of criminal honour or loyalty. Or confidentiality codes. Honour among thieves. I'm of a different generation. When I see a kid wearing a pair of baggy jeans, I instantly worry he's going to try and pinch my wallet and phone, do you understand? My cars are a bit too flash for their likes."

He gets up and walks past me back into the salon.

"Which model? I need a name!" I call after him again.

"Do you understand what was on the line? Someone's life, and my career, and my freedom. They had a lot more on me than even I realised. Taxes which my accountant avoided paying. Unpaid parking tickets. Outstanding speeding fines. All my sources of income have been put on ice. Have you seen the papers? Pictures of me, captioned with words such as 'murderer' and 'drug fiend'? Right next to ads for Coca-Cola, featuring Santa bloody Claus. Not a good look ever, but especially not good this time of year. Shouldn't be like that, but that's the way the world works."

"Tell me her name," I ask.

He doesn't reply, instead turning off the porn film. Mariusz pours himself more whisky, resting against his mini bar. He once again looks confident, in charge, that he can still convince me of things, that his gob can get him out of any trouble and into any sort of opportunity. As he has been doing for the past ten years with everyone in this rapidly changing country.

He takes another large swig of the golden stuff, then a deep intake of breath.

"I had to prostrate myself before them – they're broadcasting an interview with me on Monday. Yeah, I'm a drug addict, a boozer, lost in my own head, the accident was a terrible mistake, one which can't really be atoned for. Forgive me. I really am kneeling before everyone watching, all those listening and reading. In spite of all my earnings, all the fame I've achieved, or maybe very much because of these things, I have hit rock bottom. Yes, Father Józef Tischner was right – a black convertible Lambo Murcielago will not fill the emptiness deep inside anyone's soul. I will try to make amends. I've already transferred half a million zlotys into the account of the children's hospital that tried to save the lives of that woman and her foetus. Do you see the bind I'm in? In time, all of this disaster can be turned round and made up for, but the lovely gentlemen working for the prosecutor's office have already threatened to rip apart all my bank accounts, all my savings schemes, all my credit agreements and so on... I gave half a million in cash to that hospital, do you understand? I had to spend all day yesterday authorising all the answers with my agents so they can publish the interview on Monday as damage limitation. And apart from the accident, the cops are now digging up more funny stuff my accountants got up to. Off shore investments, buying up properties recovered after the war, from dead Jews here and there... and that airport for cheapo airlines, on the outskirts of town, had to buy up a lot of plots of land for that, you can imagine, and it seems some things were not done legit. You know how it is. Every time you make a little extra, someone out there loses that same amount off their profit margin, right?"

I still wait for him to say her name. Watching his face, I can see these unhealthy blotches appearing across his cheeks and neck, stuff that can be covered up in front of the cameras, but which still looks awful. He keeps on talking, "You know how it is with Poles, don't you? They'll forgive you for being violent with the old wife, for snorting high-end drugs with prostitutes, for getting some young nymphet pregnant and then paying for the illegal abortion. That you went hunting and accidentally shot and killed the last silver moose stag in the whole of Poland, and someone put a picture of you with that beautiful beast covered in blood on Instagram – they'll forgive all that. What they won't forgive, however, is if you ruin the life of an ordinary person, a young mother for example, leaving her kids orphaned, and then get off scot free, avoiding jail time by coughing up lots of money, or appearing in some safety film or advertising campaign for the police, warning people about the dangers of drink driving. Do you understand any of that, my man with no name and permanent address?"

Instead of answering, I walk up to him and once again launch my fist straight at his nose, and once again, something cracks in the middle of it as he falls backwards, across the coffee table and onto the floor behind it, taking a pile of remote controls with him. Trying to gather them all up, he scrabbles to stand up again.

"Name," I demand. "Which bitch told you where I live?"

"I don't remember. Do you recall all the names of all the girls you've ever slept with?"

"This one you would."

"Beata," he finally says.

I take a step back and he sees me flinch. Watching me carefully now, trying to scan my movements for signs of impending violence or else weakness he can use to his advantage. He's now standing tall again, but less than steady, as if he was about to fall over. There's something fragile, unpredictable about him, like looking at a freshly laid egg.

And so, it doesn't actually hurt. Nor does it surprise. Another thing which should have been obvious to me a long time ago, but which I've missed, to my own detriment.

"Yeah, I went round with her for a while, that girl of yours, the past few months," he says slowly. "I took her on a short holiday.

Nothing outrageous. Snorkelling in the Maldives. Though it was instantly clear she was no Madame Bovary. But you know her better than me. She told me she had an 'affair' with you, whatever that means. Mentioned the two of you had bumped into each other recently. She said she was in love with you. But then again, you know those kinds of girls don't ever allow themselves to fall in love," he states, leaning against his bar, blood running down his chin, trickling out of both nostrils – he does nothing to stem the flow, just keeps on talking, "you asked me to be honest, so here I am. A slight confession. The cops and the gentlemen from the prosecutor's office didn't know how to find your apartment. You've been very clever covering your tracks thus far. And I like that. I can't stand stupid folks," he states, then smiles, I guess to counter the severe seriousness he can see on my battered face. "You told her yourself," he adds.

I don't respond to that, simply take another step in his direction.

"She said she would hook up with you and ask about your place of residence. I gave her ten grand for that info. Do you think that is too little?"

I say nothing, only now remembering how Beata kept pressing to see my ID card or my driving license. My hands hanging loose by the sides of my thighs. It's only now I can feel just how cool it is in this apartment, the air con blowing loudly. I realise he's keeping himself as cool as he can, for health and longevity reasons, a sort of early application of cryogenic processes for preserving the flesh.

When I approach again, something in him changes. Some hidden defence mechanism is activated. He freezes, then raises both arms out to stop me coming near and says: "There, there now, dear. Let's tone things down a little. You had to get things off your chest, I get it. Never trust a woman, and other such truisms. You had to unleash and so I took it. But if you hit me again, I will have security hand you over to the cops before you get to your car. I assume your associates have already posted bail for you once today."

I feel as if there are hidden cameras recording this – he seems in such total control all of a sudden. The blood flowing down his chin has now dripped down to his chest. He knows he's won. Won the moment I walked in here.

"Ask yourself if they would be willing to stump up more cash for your release so soon after," he says.

I come even closer, close enough to headbutt him, watching him tremble gently, a completely natural reaction.

"I just have all these guilty feelings when it comes to you, buddy," he tells me, carefully watching my moves. "That's why I let you in here – I have certain guilty feelings, which are there because I happen to like you as a person. And I don't want you to be losing out because of me."

He already knows I'm no longer thinking about what he is saying. That I'm back in that pink aquarium of her bedroom, all that dirty water filling it, filling the lips and the nose and drowning the lungs.

Hands up in the air, as if I was packing a gun, he walks forward and opens a cupboard. I watch him searching for something inside it, slowly, methodically. He pulls out a pile of glossy rectangular cards made of stiff card, goes through them one by one, looking for something specific.

"Here we are," he exclaims. Approaching me, he finally wipes the blood from his nose with the back of his hand. He hands me a black and white piece of card, a photo of three heavily made up women advertising some sort of fashion event, in the centre of Warsaw.

"She'll be there tonight, if you want to talk to her before leaving town."

It's only now he mentions me meeting Beata that I realise she is one of the three women in the photograph. The makeup, along with the studio lights, have essentially deformed her features. Once I realise who it is I am looking at, a dagger once again guts me open like a freshly caught fish.

"She bored me in the end, you know – she's past it, twenty-four years old, and lacking a little imagination. You know what I mean, I think. And she rarely shaves down there, ahem."

I take the invite from him, crumple it into a solid ball and toss it on the floor. I can tell he knows he's taken control of this encounter. Knows I'm powerless to do anything to him. Knows he's grabbed a firm hold of the reins and is back in charge. The boss again.

"Well, too bad. I'm told the food will be remarkable. And you can't now say that I didn't give you what it was you came here to get."

Now, he's the one forcing my hand, though I have no intention of being forced to play.

I look at my watch. I don't have any more time to waste here. Can't take the risk. If he says anything else to wind me up and I unleash again, it's going to be heavy this time, the damage potentially serious. I want to hurt him. Or maybe more.

"I'll tell you something else. That girl, that Saturday night, I saw her from far off. I could have braked in time," he tells me, shrugging.

"I don't care much about that," I tell him.

"But I didn't brake. On purpose. It was, you could say, a certain notion I had."

I start walking towards the front door, without waiting for him to explain himself.

"Of course I regret it now. But I'll tell you what I had in mind. I wanted to..." I hear him raising his voice, trying to slow my departure, but I interrupt his monologue by slamming the front door. I head out through the lobby, throw the entry card at the doorman, without so much as looking at him.

Mariusz is right – I told her where my place was. She asked when we were resting in that pink aquarium, and I wanted to feel that there was somewhere else on this planet I could actually call mine. All because I felt the need to go back and fuck an ex-lover, to touch and smell someone whose texture and aroma I had become addicted to.

"Never mind. You got yourself into this mess," I repeat under my own breath. The day is grey and relatively fresh out. The air clear, suspiciously so for Warsaw in the middle of winter. Maybe it's because everyone has decided to take their gas guzzlers to visit families far away from here, wherever it is they have to take their washed and dried jam jars back to.

I don't even notice the pin drilling its way through my guts, the aftershocks spreading throughout the whole body, tiring me out, ageing me rapidly. My phone rings – Pazina. I answer.

"Our last conversation was meant to be our last one ever," I tell her.

There is someone standing next to my car.

"It's Bubbles," she tells me.

"What about Bubbles?" I ask.

"His girlfriend was a witness. Thankfully, they never did anything to her. But she saw everything. I talked to her a moment ago. It was Bubbles and a couple of other thugs who did the damage to Tiny."

I keep walking closer to the car and recognise them straight away. Shady and Gobby.

"Paz, what about a bag? Did she say anything about a sports bag?" I ask.

"Yeah, she did. Mentioned he had a black holdall with him, though she had no idea what was in it. Those who jumped him took the bag."

Seeing me approach, Shady smiles, placing a hand on the back doors of my Audi.

"She said they had to snap his wrist in half in order to get him to let go of that bag – whatever was in it."

I wave my hand, indicating I want them to wait while I finish my call. Shady nods. I hear an ambulance racing past a few blocks away.

"Who was it exactly? Who was there with Tiny?" I ask.

"He's no longer in the country, Kuba," she tells me. "Bubbles apparently popped into a bar on Saviour Square, a place he actually co-owns. While there, he told people he was leaving town, back in a couple of months, left enough cash to cover the rent, in cash. They said he was absolutely loaded. The manager who works for him told me. I tried to get him to contact you, but there's no need now."

"There's always a need for fresh information, Paz," I say.

"There really is no need. Tiny died twenty minutes ago. When Bubbles finds out, and he probably already has, I doubt we'll ever see him round these parts again."

Shady is grinning at me, indicating with his hand across his neck that I should cut the call.

"I have to say sorry to you too," she says to me.

"At half past nine this evening, I want you to meet me at the airport," I tell Paz.

"Where?" she asks.

"Listen, fucker, you're starting to behave a bit rude," Gobby says to me.

"Pack a few travelling light essentials and bring them with you. Nine-thirty, Okęcie Chopin Airport, bring a passport." I tell her, cutting the call without waiting for her response.

I put the phone away – Shady stretches his back, using my car to help prop up his tired back.

"We're off," he says.

"I imagine we are," I tell him.

"If you do, then let's get inside, warm up a little... do you have any blow on you perhaps?" he asks.

"Nothing at all," I say, raising my hands in a gesture of defeat.

"Are we taking your car our ours?" he asks.

"Mine."

Shady smiles, nods and then opens the door.

"Please, get in," he says to me, calm as anything.

1:50pm

"We have a huge problem, so you're going to have to explain it to Piotrek. Right now," Shady explains helpfully.

He sits next to me, in the passenger seat. No need for him to flash his piece – I can see the pistol stuck into the waistband of his trousers as he belts up.

"He's still not answering," Gobby says from the back seat. "What's taking him so long in that whorehouse? Is he handing out free condoms for Christmas?"

"Keep trying," Shady orders.

"Who's not picking up?" I ask them.

"Piotrek's in a foul mood. Very foul. That's why it would be best if you could give him back the cash you took from his brother in law. I've no idea if he's ever going to forgive you for this stunt. But if you wave a bag full of readies in his face, his mood might improve, coz for now it really is fucking rotten," he says, taking his phone out of his pocket.

"He's still not answering," Gobby whines from the back seat.

"Can you at least tell me which way you want me to drive?" I ask Shady, my voice as calm as it can be under the circumstances.

"Let me try," Shady says to Gobby, though out of the corner of my eye I see as he selects and dials Uncle's number instead.

"Has Uncle done a vanishing act?" I ask.

"I am assuming you're now driving to pick up Piotrek's money?" Shady says to me. The streets are ghostly and suspiciously empty, even for Christmas.

"No, we're not going to get Piotrek's cash right now," I tell him.

I hear the line go dead and the sound of Uncle's voicemail message being activated.

"I don't understand then," Shady says to me.

"I no longer have the money. I was robbed."

Shady bursts out laughing, my words seemingly amusing him profoundly. Gobby also starts to laugh, my car filled with the sound of merriment I can't quite understand.

"You've been robbed a lot of times of late, haven't you?" he says, still giggling. "Maybe you should hire some protection," Shady quips, amused with his own observation.

In fact, I can see he's laughing so hard, tears are welling up in the corners of his eyes.

"A bad week, has to be said," I tell him.

"You're not quite following me," he says, taking the gun out from behind his belt and placing the business end of the barrel, cocked and ready to fire, next to my ear. I try not to flinch as we approach a red light. "Piotrek said that instead of bringing you to him without the money we might as well drive you down to the river and throw you in for a bit of winter diving."

"I can talk to Piotrek," I assure Shady, but he shakes his head.

"You don't get it. Try to understand – not this time. Piotrek is in no mood for your fancy words and charming excuses, not after all that's been happening of late."

"Just tell me where to find him. Let's drive straight there," I say.

"No fucking way. Try to get the message, will you? For your own bloody good. Let's go anyplace where there is money that you know of."

He puts the gun away, as if suddenly convinced I've got the point. Once again, he pulls his phone out and dials Uncle's number.

"Where is Piotrek?" I ask again.

"At his brother in law's, attending a wedding party. Right where you happened to be last night. I've got to tell you that the Swan Lake people are mighty mad with you. They're mad about having to be mad at someone like you, while there's a wedding party going on."

I look round to take a quick glance at Gobby, but he's not busy with anything other than the views rolling past. He looks as entertained as a baby being driven round in a car for the first time in its life. Busy massaging his fists.

"So you better make some calls, quick, to whoever can serve up some cash for you this Christmas time, and let's go there, else we're going to find ourselves walking into a very unpleasant situation," Shady suggests.

I grit my teeth, then grab my phone. This isn't how it was supposed to play out.

"I'll say it again – this is for your own good," he says, dialling Uncle's number again.

"I don't have any rich siblings or wildly generous friends," I tell him.

"I bet you do. And I suggest you try and think of who they might be, and quick," Shady retorts.

2:20pm

I'm outside your house, and I need to chat, I text her.

"Without a minimum of fifty grand I wouldn't bother troubling

Piotrek's front door today," Shady states, yawning and stretching in the passenger seat. In the cool light of day, her suburban villa looks even more miserable than usual. I listen to all the joints in Shady's back crackling like static in a broken radio aerial.

"Is that a Gallardo?" Gobby asks from the back seat, pointing to the car parked in her driveway.

She's not going to come out. Highly unlikely. But we're here so at least I can say I tried, proving a point to the other two.

"Fuck, I overdid the squats yesterday, strained my calf muscles," Shady complains, his face frowning as the static stretches he's doing release lactic acids from his most recent workout.

"What about the new supplements?" Gobby asks. "Those fire-starters, any good?"

"Shit, Gobby. They just roast the muscles. I told you before – just eat a healthy diet, stop taking the synthetic stuff. None of them can be any good for you."

"Can't you go over and knock like normal people do?" Gobby asks me.

"Her husband is home," I explain.

"And you're poking her, huh?" Shady guffaws.

"No. She wanted some, but I turned her down. This is more a domestic budgets going missing for a few weeks sort of a problem. He wouldn't understand. Too nice a guy."

"Right, clear as crystal." Shady nods, smiling to himself. When he tries ringing Uncle again, the call goes to answering machine three times. There might not be anyone inside, even though alongside the Gallardo I notice a flash BMW sports coupe and a black Jaguar XF parked in the driveway. The Jag looks like Santa delivered it this morning. Standing well out from all the grey snow, the grey trees and grey concrete all around us. A shiny alien spaceship from a different fairytale. A different dimension.

Come out in 5mins, please I text once again. Maybe they've gone out for a walk?

"How did things work out with that idiot Tiny from the club?" Shady asks, still waiting for Uncle to pick up.

"Not all that well. He's dead," I tell him calmly.

"As of when?" Shady asks.

"Did you finish him off?" Gobby asks from the back seat.

"Someone caught up with him, though I still don't know who it was. The queue was long, but whoever got there first has my drugs and my money – the stuff I took from Swan Lake yesterday. The stuff I was planning to deliver to Piotrek this morning – before Tiny decided to rob me at gunpoint and I was then arrested by the goddamn anti-terrorist squad."

"Boy, you do attract a lot of trouble, don't you pal, almost as if you were intentionally trying to stir things up in our town," Shady says disapprovingly. "I think she's coming out. Some older girl... older and in a foul mood."

She's dressed elegantly, and does indeed look furious. Opening the gate to the front yard wide, and then tugging it hard, letting it slam loudly. She's put her hair up, nails freshly painted, high-heeled boots on – I imagine there's some sort of Christmas do going on inside right now – she looks most festive. I'm sure her nice-guy husband knows how to make himself look festive too. Which fork to eat the fish with. Which glass to pour the right colour wine into.

She approaches my window, and I suddenly realise that the people I normally see at night, handing over cash for drugs, really do have normal lives when the sun is up. "Maybe I just belong to a specific sort of world," I think to myself, a world which is separate from the world of all those other minor actors. She knocks on my window and I lower it, letting some very sickly sweet perfume waft inside.

"Get the fuck out of here," she says loud enough for everyone in the car to hear.

"I have a huge favour to ask of you," I say to her, feeling the sentence to come getting stuck in my throat, struggling to actually get it down my tongue and out past my teeth.

"Get the fuck off my street and as far away from my house as you can," she says.

"See?" I ask Shady. "See how easy it is to magic money out of nowhere at this time of year? Let's get out of here."

"Wait a minute," Shady asks, leaning across my lap, looking up at her face, "We have a slight problem here. You might be able to help us resolve it. You look like a wise and generous sort. Cute too."

"Do I look like a witch that waves wands around and does favours for rough, battered-looking men who pull up outside her house without being invited at Christmas?"

"Three minutes, please. Come with us. I wouldn't be here if it wasn't important," I say as she looks at me with the kind of concern mothers reserve for their youngest children, the ones most likely to get into scrapes. She then takes a step back and pulls the rear passenger side door open, Gobby instantly sliding sideways to make room for her. She then orders me to move my seat forward a little, give them both more legroom. I do as I'm told, Shady laughing to himself, while opening his own window and spitting out onto the sidewalk.

"There's this little matter we have to resolve," I say to her, turning round in my seat, but she cuts me off with a single hand gesture.

"Now, you lot, stop spitting on my drive, and just drive on out of here right this minute. We can talk this over a little way from my actual front door. All the neighbours are home. And you all know how mighty curious neighbours can be when mean-looking cars start driving up and down the street... Let's hit the road, jacks. You can bring me back in five, just don't park right outside my front door again."

I realise that she is a very different person when drunk, which is how I mostly see her, and when sober, like right now. Her ability to control her emotions is mighty impressive, attractive even. I drive forward, following her pointers.

"Two hundred metres up the road, drive now. I'm eating lunch with the kids and my husband's family. I've made two soups, cream of mushroom, a lamb casserole. Two desserts," she announces loudly.

I drive forward slowly, and she indicates I should pull into a bus stop.

"Nice talk of food. I'm feeling hungry all of a sudden," Shady announces.

"So go get a hot dog from the nearest gas station. That's the only thing which will be open round here today. Now, let's get back to the point. What do you boys need?"

"I'm so sorry we interrupted right in the middle of your Christmas lunch," I tell her.

"The point, Kuba. The actual point of why you three kings are here is?"

I see in the rearview mirror how Gobby is shuffling round uncomfortably next to her, evidently unused to being around such assertive, truly gobby women.

"The point is that I need fifty grand in cash right now. I can give it back to you a month from now – in cash or in blow."

"Otherwise your friend will have problems," Shady informs her.

"What sort of problems?" she asks disoriented, confused and bothered by the scale of the request – especially this time of year, when banks tend to be all out of cash, if they're open at all.

"Fifty grand, you say?" she turns to me.

"I need a quick loan," I confirm, my body all tense, struggling to say the words, feeling as if I was trying to cough up mucus filled with ground glass and sand.

She bursts out laughing, in all honesty, and soon enough the other two are laughing heartily along with her.

"Now I understand," Shady says to me knowingly.

"Understand what?"

"Why you have so many problems. Your friends seem to find it hard becoming solutions."

"Don't ever come back here again, OK?" she says to me loudly. "I mean it. It really was worth a laugh, I will keep laughing the rest of this Christmas, but please, realise there is nothing else for you to seek here."

"Your pal is in a lot of trouble," Shady says to her.

"Which is none of my business," she replies. "My son is in a lot of trouble. They've just thrown him out of Oxford, interrupting his degree."

I perform a rapid U-turn, head back in the direction of her home. She is of course aware of what might happen to me if I don't find the cash, that there is some likelihood, regardless of how faint, that I will be dead come midnight, or at least an invalid. Considering our most recent chats, her refusal to get involved doesn't surprise me at all. In fact, I should respect her for it. It is a wise and sane reaction.

"Do you know what is really entertaining?" she asks me. "After the new year, I start attending my therapy sessions. I think I'll share some of this with my therapist. How my dealer paid me a visit at Christmas, asking to borrow a pile of money. No explanations, just asking for cold, hard cash."

"Your friend could be in a lot of pain and in a lot of hospitals for a lot of complex treatments if someone doesn't come to his rescue right now."

I pull up, keeping away from her front door. She opens the back door of my car and jumps out. Before slamming it shut again, she looks in and tells me: "You should be pleased I didn't call the cops."

"I am grateful, indeed," I confirm.

"Farewell," she says to Shady, then "See you," to Gobby, whom she can tell is nobody's ring leader. Both of them respond politely, watching as she sways her hips down the sidewalk back toward her own front door.

"You should have fucked it," Shady says once she's far away enough not to hear. "Then you might have got her to help."

"Let's go see Piotrek. I told you, all this driving round is a waste of time," I tell him.

"You don't know how to treat people so they feel you need them – that's the best way to get them to help."

"Bullshit. People never help people unless there's something in it for them."

I wonder what she'll tell her family about who she's been with just now. I check my watch. I have a little time in reserve, not much, running down quickly.

"Maja just sent a message out, saying Uncle didn't collect his wage packet this morning, which never happens," Gobby announces from the back seat.

"That's odd," Shady comments, stating the bleeding obvious.

"Uncle without any cash on him. A suspicious proposition," Gobby adds.

"Odd," Shady repeats unhelpfully.

I see at a distance, as someone opens her front door, a man appearing in the open doorway, though I can't see what he looks like, whether he is young or old, if it is the husband or the son. He looks in our direction, probably trying to check if she told the truth about our visit.

"Alright, let's move it," Shady demands. "This is none of my business anyway."

2:59pm

I can't find a single place to park outside the Swan Lake. Cars lined up in tight rows along the muddy roads, women emerging from them wearing high heels that look like weapons and long, heavy dresses that look like chainmail covered in glitter, their faces and hair also sprinkled with sparkly stuff. They stand, their shiny stilettos sinking in the snowy mud, smoking slim menthol cigarettes, watching their men squeezed into ill-fitting suits also sneaking past, trying not to get their polished brogues too dirty. We finally stop a little way past the local bus service stop, a long way from the building.

We leave the car behind and walk to find Piotrek, hopefully not too drunk yet, all sorts of stupid conversations reaching our ears as we wander past: "I think we didn't give enough cash... where are the flowers.... can you call the nanny... she's five months pregnant already, with nothing showing yet... wow!"

"Come along," Shady says to me, seeing me listening in to the conversations as we pass all the smokers by. He seems nervous, maybe too much so. I've known Piotrek for a very long time. We've never had beef between us ever before. I wasn't the one trying to pull a fast one last night. And he knows all about Tiny and the others, the cops on my tail. This should be cool. Maybe not so much with Dario, but Piotrek knows I'll be good for the money soon enough. He just needs to make sure no more shipments get lost in transit.

That's his damn job. Paying the right people. Hiring the right staff in all the right transit points and junctions.

The other guests look at me and my blazer approvingly – not so much at Shady and Gobby's joggers and T-shirts worn beneath heavy black leather jackets, the official uniform of the local mafiosi. Shady says to me: "Give me the keys."

Then he shows me the gun still tucked into his drawstring waistband. I sigh, pull my car keys from my jean pocket and hand them over to Gobby. He puts them in a zippered side pocket of his leather blouson. I see the newly married couple shivering in the cold on the steps of the reception ballroom. They really do look young, early twenties at best. He looks like a comedy puppet – as if the designer suit he's invested in was topped not with a human head, but a loaf of freshly baked white bread. The features ill-defined to say the least. The girl cannot be described as either plain or pretty. She looks odd, the makeup totally wrong for her features.

She's trying to smile, her white teeth shining fiercely behind very narrow lips. Her belly is very much showing. Shady gestures at me with his right hand, suggesting I should stop. A waiter passes us by with a tray covered in fine crystal flutes topped up with champagne. The guests approaching the steps to the porch form an orderly queue in front of the young couple. I spot Piotrek among them. A photographer is trying to sneak about and get everyone's picture without offending anyone.

Piotrek tells him to move the crowd indoors, else they'll all catch colds. He spots us approaching. I make eye contact with him. His face turns a little red, maybe from the bubbly. Or the cold. A rotund blonde next to him whispers something into his ear. I guess that must be his wife. I've never met her before.

He clearly nods his head in the direction of the plastic pond full of carp, as if answering her query. Shady shoves me forward from behind. Out of the corner of my eyes I see him nodding to Piotrek or his wife. He keeps shoving me in their direction. We go around the side of the reception hall room. Past all those fish floating in all that freezing water covered with plastic sheeting. Shady keeps winking at Piotrek as if sending out secret coded signals.

He then shoves me from behind. I can now smell all those fish-farming activities, the plastic pond. We go round the back of the building to a gated entrance – Shady knows the door code, types it in to release the gate and get us inside via the rear.

"You know the place inside and out," I tell him.

"And why shouldn't we? Many people pass through here. And I've been best man at many a wedding here."

"Including that infamous one when the bride caught her fiancée giving the best man a blow job?" I ask.

"You what?"

"Never mind." I wave the topic away.

We go into the same courtyard I remember from last night. I now see all those creepy plastic Christmas decorations, flowing Santa sculptures, reindeer with bright red noses, utterly creepy little elves, chubby gnome types. We go inside the building via a corridor lined with hundreds of white and pink balloons, leading to a table crowned with a plastic sculpture of those two lovebird swans, their necks intertwined.

At the back of the hall, there is now a stage, occupied by a band made up of four very slim-looking men, their necks topped with rabbit-like faces, hair gelled just the way their fathers and grandfathers would have styled theirs. The women from Belarus are long gone, the band discussing the set list requested by the guests. The smell of boiling cabbage is still firmly in place, not adding any charm to the proceedings or the décor.

We go into the same office as last night, or rather I am shoved into it by Shady. Nothing has changed since yesterday. The same ancient nudie calendar and the same terrible painting over the safe. Fatso is perched behind his desk, his upper lip held together with a plaster, hunched over a plate of potatoes with a pork cutlet in breadcrumbs, served with boiled cabbage. Romek doesn't seem to be around today. Seeing me, Fatso starts to laugh.

"You found your way back here quickly, didn't you pal," he comments over his plate. "Do you have something for me? Something of mine? Or else what are you doing here? Looking for that blade again, or a couple of tough boys to show you a good time round the back of the kitchen?"

"I came over to straighten things out with Piotrek. He'll tell you what his thoughts are on the situation between us."

"I guess we should all have that conversation together." Fatso says what he thinks will be best.

The office door opens. The father of the bride enters. I note the huge gold signet ring on his chubby hand. The gold is old and tarnished, the man's hands and nails could also do with a proper clean.

"We have a little problem," he says to Fatso. "A delicate matter. Can I bother you for a minute?"

"You're doing so already, buddy," Fatso replies, pushing his plate away. His gaze then turns upon me, looking carefully at Gobby and Shady too, as they grin from ear to ear.

"The heating isn't working," says the father of the bride. "People don't want to sit around in their coats and scarves."

"But the heating is working. It's been on for an hour, but this time of year, as people wander in and out for cigarettes, looking for top-ups of bubbly, it takes a long time for these old concrete walls to retain the heat. Ask your friends and families to be patient. It will warm up in a minute. And get the band playing... once people start dancing and quit bitching they'll warm right up."

Fatso gets up from behind his desk to assure the man footing the bill for today's festivities that warmth is forthcoming with a big bear hug. I close my eyes, inhaling the smell of office paper glue and dust which is permanently suspended over his desk. No Belarusian babushka could ever shift it, no matter how steely their muscles imported from the former USSR might be. I really do not want to be here. At 10pm all of this grimness will be falling away beneath the wheels of my plane. And in another twenty-four hours the lights I will be blinded by will be Vegas, Rio-style lights, not this old communist-era neon which has become so trendy of late, outside shops, inside cafes and bars and shoe stores. I wonder whether there is any point in me coming back here at all. Considering I still haven't got a return ticket, maybe I should just stay far, far away from places like this.

"No, I need to you to sort the heat for us right now, not later," says the bald guy. "Later, I won't be your customer any more, like I am now. And it's now I need my daughter to have a great time during her wedding. So go down to that boiler room and stoke it up, seeing as I'm paying your wages."

Fatso sighs, trying to work out what to say to that, but then the office door opens and Piotrek enters, closing it behind him. His face looks grey, the colour of frozen fruit.

Fatso says to him: "Piotrek, you know my mother in law is out there, she's got a lung condition – can you do something about the photographer leaving the doors wide open, the guests are freezing inside. We need to keep the heat in."

"Wisiek," Piotrek says addressing Fatso. "Give us fifteen minutes, alright?"

Piotrek goes behind the desk and places his hands gently on Wisiek's shoulders, as gently as only those who can use their hands to wreak terrible damage are capable of doing.

"Patience, Wisiek. The secret of making money and keeping money. Give your mother in law some ibu-fucking-profen, stop her going weak at the knees. Now go find her some painkillers, spike her drink with them and hope for the best. Your attitude is spoiling the party for the rest of us. Ease off on the whining and bitching." Piotrek removes the threat of his hands from Wisiek's shoulders.

Wisiek nods his wrinkled head and leaves the office in search of the mother of his betrothed. He closes the office door behind him, Piotrek huffing and puffing in the stuffy air of the old office.

The father of the bride leaves behind him.

"This tragicomedy is just the last thing you have to survive before your holiday comes," I say to myself. Then I look at Piotrek's displeased face. "It's like having to straighten things out with a parent."

My father was a volatile kind of madman when I was small – a man boxed in by a whole spectrum of frustration and insecurities – I remember all too well how I learnt not to fear his outbursts, realising quickly that his fury couldn't really do much damage, and that he did not mean harm to any of the other people in his home. That the worst he could do would be to smack me with his hand or whip me with his belt. Talking to my old man, I was aware I was staring right through him, as if he were transparent, nothing more than empty air.

I then realise I could do with something to eat before heading off for the airport. Some wedding chicken broth. Something soothing for my troubled guts. But then Piotrek hisses at me: "That's my brother in law, for fuck's sake!" he says as Wisiek re-enters the office.

"Well, your brother in law tried to rob me yesterday," I say to him.

"He was as high as a kite, God knows what he took before he came in here," Wisiek says, looking at me, sitting back down behind his desk and toying with his pork cutlet. "He took the cash, took our gear, threatened us with a gun and left."

"This guy and his pal, this skinny fucker who looked like he'd spent his childhood drinking Russian moonshine and had just killed his own mother with a penknife for vodka money, tried to pull a fast one first – what was I to do? The skinny fucker was waiting for me outside this office as I was leaving with a knife pulled out," I say calmly to Piotrek. Gobby laughs out loud. "Anyway Piotrek, thanks for posting bail for me. I will pay it all back. I only need a couple of months. I know it's a lot of money you put up for me. I just need a few months, easy."

Piotrek pulls some pills from his pocket, swallows the meds and shakes his head.

"I never coughed up any bail for you, Kuba," he says flatly. "What the hell are you talking about?"

"I don't get it," I tell him – someone had to have told him, one of the cops he pays for information, that I'd been arrested. He must have sent a lawyer to bail me out, because that was always the deal between us – if I got into trouble, Piotrek would send his best people to get me back on the streets again. "I thought we had a deal."

"What fucking deal? What bail money? What the fuck are you talking about?" Piotrek asks, again.

"I was robbed – someone broke into my apartment and took all my savings and my drugs. Then the cops arrested me and took me in for questioning. I didn't tell them anything. They threatened me, locked me up without charges, muscled me about, but released me eventually, once a lawyer showed up and paid the bail money, in cash."

Someone is knocking on the office door, but no one reacts.

"Damn it," Piotrek says to me, looking most displeased. "I always knew you would trip me up one day. Like taking a young pup on a leash sliding across an ice-skating rink. Someone's ass is gonna hurt. And the damn pup is likely to trip up everyone else who slides along. You're that dog. Getting in my way of late. Making far too many wrong moves. I knew it. Instinctively. My intuition warned days like today would come eventually."

I shake my head, disappointed to hear the boss saying such belittling things about me. I have to tell him more though, about how they broke into my apartment, tossed it, but found fuck all, because that Tiny prick from Bethlehem got to me first with a pistol at the ready, concealed behind a cute femme fatale.

More people are now knocking on the other side of the office door. Fatso is still cutting up and gnawing on his pork cutlet. Piotrek screams "Enter" and the door opens and a chubby teenage lad enters.

"Uncle Jackie," the boy addresses Piotrek by his real first name, "Aunt Sylwia says that your jeep blocked her car in the car park." His voice suggests his balls are still a long way from dropping.

"Aunt Sylwia can't see shit and can't drive shit because of the meds that vet prescribes her, the one she goes to see about her lungs," Piotrek firmly states, ending the subject. The lad doesn't seem to get this point.

"Uncle Jackie, I had a good look outside, and she has to go drive now to get some more meds. She can't get her car out."

Piotrek nods and says, "Damian, so why don't you do something about it and move the car for me?" He takes out the keys from his trouser pocket and tosses them to Damian who does not appear keen on doing this favour for his wealthy uncle. "Get to it!" Piotrek barks at him.

"She has to get to the drug store before it closes for the weekend. Can't be without her horse tranquilisers, not over the holiday season.

It would kill her," Damian says, jangling the keys merrily, and walking straight back out the office door.

Fatso says from behind the desk to no one in particular: "My little brother... how will he ever finish high school? Can he actually read?" he muses, darkly. It's only now I notice the striking resemblance between balding Fatso and this younger sibling. The same face-to-fat content ratio. Hard not to spot.

Piotrek walks up to me and grabs me by the elbow. "You were detained by detectives, and you never called to let me know?"

"They wouldn't let me. Because of the accident last week. That TV chat show host. It looked bad, so they wanted to pin the drugs in his bloodstream on someone – they tried me, but they got nothing, in my car or my apartment. They're going to keep on sniffing all around me, which is why I am leaving. I'll be back in three weeks' time, a month max, I'll pay you back then. Then everything will be right between us."

Piotrek looks at me harshly. "One of your customers?" he asks.

"One of my best. A big time celebrity. That's why I had to watch my step. The cops wanted blood. But it's going to be fine, you'll see."

"Shut that fucking door," Piotrek says to Fatso.

I take a step back, but Shady pushes me the other way, towards Piotrek who stares at me from behind half-closed eyelids.

"Give me that pistol," he says to Shady.

Shady does as he's told – hands over his own gun.

"Big time celebrity. Everything will be right between us. Three weeks? Kuba, you're not going on any jet plane, we're having you taken away in a straitjacket, son. Get your head straight in a sanatorium. That's where you need to go, but first you need to pay me what you owe me. Not in a month or two, but in a day or two, you hear me?!" he exclaims.

"I had a run of bad luck," I tell him calmly.

"You didn't have no bad luck – what you did was try to fuck me up the ass, boy. You fucking tried to con me, like a little fucking weasel. Coming to me with some story about how someone burgled your hiding place, poor you!" He screams the last few words, foaming at the mouth, cheeks burning red, though the hand holding the gun is still not pointing at me but hanging limply by his side. "When I first met you I gave you a chance. Do you know why I did that?"

"No, I do not."

He wipes his sweating face, still staring me straight in the eyes.

"In every line of work there comes a moment when the boss is approached by some hungry young kid, someone so keen they will do anything and everything to climb up the ladder. So damn desperate they would chop up their own mother's corpse and feed it to hungry dogs, just to get rid of the evidence, get rid of the stink. And as the boss you appreciate that ruthlessness, that ice cold hunger."

His words sound cutely pre-rehearsed, but I know Piotrek well enough now to tell when he's lying. I also remember how we started working together – there was no fucking job interview, I just bought drugs off him and then sold them to have more money to buy more drugs. A very simple deal. Nothing personal about it. Nevertheless, I let him speak, my eyes shutting a little, his outline blurring a little as he leans against Fatso's desk and keeps on speaking: "And you give the young kid the work for one more reason..." His breathing sounds heavy tonight, like the diet and the swimming pool have not really made any difference to his fitness levels. He takes some pills out of his pocket, pops a few, washing them down from a plastic bottle of water he finds on the desk. "As the boss you fall into a certain mental trap, when you see this skinny hungry kid appear, ridiculous to look at, this kid from a good home trying to make it on the mean streets of this ugly city. It can't possibly work, but it's just ridiculous enough for a smart kid from a good home to pull off, if he has the right instincts. Because you see the kid is so very determined, so keen to survive, so far out of his depth, he'll never get too smart, too cocky, never try to pull any fucking stunts, any little tricks. His fear will make him loyal, like a puppy raised all the way to a faithful guard dog."

"I wasn't scared," I tell him, which happens to be the truth.

The fact that he is here, holding a loaded gun, telling me all

these fairytales, is starting to get on my nerves. I turn around –
Shady is looking at us with a big smile on his face. Gobby is
inspecting his fingernails like he was the one about to be signing
that marriage register.

"You were, Kuba, and you wanted to be so very different,"
Piotrek continues his psychoanalytical tale, "These are the best sorts
of motives. It's like going to the gym – people can stand the hardest
training regime as long as they want others to see how much they
want to change, to improve, to grow new muscle. But it's not in the
arms or the legs, Kuba, no – it's all up here in your head."

I can see he's growing calmer, the pills helping bring his blood
pressure down, his face growing a healthier shade of pale. Someone
knocks on the office door.

"I have to attend to that bloody boiler," says Fatso.

"Go take care of business," Piotrek says with a patient nod.

"But I want my money tonight," Fatso responds.

"That money is mostly my fucking cash, don't you forget who
bankrolled this shit hole. So get working on that boiler, keep the
punters happy. We'll talk money later. You're not kept round here
to give orders, but to make sure the soup is hot, and that the names
are spelled right on the cakes... do we understand each other?"

Fatso gets up, visibly offended, but heads for the office door just
as the father of the bride opens it and looks in.

"I'm coming, no stress," Fatso says to him. As he leaves, I
approach Piotrek, mindful of the gun in his hand. His face is as
hard set as it was when we first met Dario at Piotrek's restaurant.
Most of it is exhaustion.

"I'm telling you they tried to cheat me. His brother in law was
standing outside that door, holding a goddamn switchblade. Waiting
for me to come out with the money and the drugs." I paint the scene
for Piotrek.

"He's my brother in law. Are you trying to suggest that my own
brother in law tried to rob me of my own cash and my own drugs?"
He starts coughing. "It doesn't matter. I don't believe you either way.
What I do believe, Kuba, is that people will do anything for money.
Up until this point in time you've been sensible, but all of a sudden

you've got a whiff of easy money – thinking tonight you can just take off for some sunny shores without first paying what you owe."

I look straight at him, shaking my head in disagreement, then say: "If I tried a move like that then I would lose and not make money, we both know that." My eyes are showing him how disappointed I am with his interpretation. If he really thinks that was the move I was trying to pull then he really must take me for a fool. But maybe he's simply incapable of imagining someone as smart if not actually smarter than he is.

"You have three days in which to bring me back my money. And my drugs. If you don't, I'll kill you myself. Then you go round, trying to find yourself a new wholesaler."

As he says so, a crack of what sounds like thunder explodes outside the window, as if a giant fist had smashed into the earth.

I then hear Shady's voice screaming "Fuck, fuck, fuck!" Just as the window turns into a swarm of shattered smithereens. I fall to the floor, Piotrek doing the same right next to me. Everything seems to go into slow motion.

"What the fucking fuck just happened?!" Gobby screams behind us. Instead of an answer to his question we hear numerous other screams, female voices howling outside, grown women as well as young girls, just as the office fills with the smell of burning rubber and melting steel.

Piotrek gets to his feet, runs towards the office door. Shady follows him, which is when I notice that Piotrek has left Shady's pistol on the glass-covered carpet. Gobby is the slowest to react, so I reach for the weapon, then point it at Gobby.

"My car keys," I order. He starts to look for them in the numerous pockets of his leather overcoat, eventually finding and handing them over. I receive them with my left hand, then smash the barrel of the gun into the side of his face and watch as he slumps to the floor, out like a light, not mindful of the smashed glass all around us. I then go out the door into the corridor, brushing the shards of glass off my jacket. Running along towards the exit, I hear more female voices lamenting – running through the dining hall, I notice the long table is set up with lots of food but everyone seems to have gone somewhere else – everyone except the bride, who is being hugged by another girl, dressed in white, her face covered in coarse makeup, lips covered in glitter repeating the mantra: "Damian, little Damian was in there, oh dear God, he was in the car," the words spilling from her hard-drawn lips.

I walk past her, moving towards the main exit – outside I notice smoke, snow and dust swirling about in the air, stinking of burnt rubber and hot metal. All the guests are gathered on the patio, huddling in a panicked crowd, voices howling, some making calls, though most frozen still, staring at what is left of Piotrek's car, the musicians, the waiters, the guests. Whatever happened to it also smashed the windows in most of the other cars parked along the lane, alarms going off wildly, Piotrek's car sat there, a crumpled wreck of its former self, billowing black clouds of dirty, foul-smelling smoke, its emergency lights flashing a warning. One of the guests runs up to the wreck, trying to wrench the driver's door open, but the father of the bride pulls him back. I see Piotrek in the crowd, trying to call someone, staring at what is left of his luxury four wheel drive Nissan.

"Damian!!!" a woman calls out from the crush of guests. I sprint towards my Audi, which appears to be unscathed. Looking back, I notice Shady emerging from the dining hall – I raise the gun into the air, making sure he sees it. Piotrek is also looking at me as I do so, and I feel a sense of satisfaction at how things are turning out. As much as I would like to pay him back today, before my flight takes off, I know I can't, so I might as well just take off and vanish. As I open the door to my own car, I hear metal crunching – it's Fatso, who has got hold of a set of heavy-duty metal cutters and is trying to prize open the doors to Piotrek's Nissan. Once he's got them wedged open, the women's howling rises in volume and pitch, like something from a war film.

I get into the Audi, drive back the opposite way while my phone starts ringing. I recognise the number, but don't pick up. It's half past four, giving me five hours left – the thought that I still have some time left is soothing, though there is much left to be done in that time. The phone rings again, but I let it ring, hunting round the glovebox instead, searching for the folded knife, heavy, rusty, rough to the touch. That is when a strange sensation makes itself felt in the pit of my stomach.

It was by Three Crosses Square – I think – in fact I'm sure.

4:45pm (Threnus)

Once it becomes completely dark, at the tail end of dusk, as dark purple turns into a definite blackness, that is when everything feels real to me once more. Once the day is over, so is the dream – everything becoming visible for what it really is, all metaphors and adornments falling away, all the dirty foam of winter daylight vanishing.

I'm on the roundabout where Jerusalem Avenue and Marshall Street intersect, and I am once again reminded somehow of the fact that police closed circuit cameras record all registration number plates which go round this junction more than once or twice an hour. Strange things come to mind at a time like this – like: who was it that placed the explosive device on Piotrek's car? Who installed the GPS tracking device on my car? Who broke into my hiding place? Who robbed all my precious goods?

I know one thing now – how the police discovered where I live. That knowledge is enough for the time being – I need no other leads, no more hints or informants working for me.

Time to sing. The night is as clean as a freshly washed window – a hospital window. I am alone, finally alone to the end. No one can hear us anyway, not inside this soundproofed car. I am sated. My guts at ease. A block of ice beneath the lungs. Warming my song of the dog.

People don't matter one bit. As much as the shadows they are, haunting the streets of this dark city. The darkness has no end. All sounds swallowed up. Everything appearing to be a joke. Everything that lives within it laughing at everything else, all its neighbours.

This is my dog song.

People only ever last for moments, in total silence – leaving behind no traces. While they last they try to eat as much as they can, rubbing up against each other. From a distance they look like foam which tries to devour everything it rolls over, as effective as worms that are nourished by everything that lives or has lived. Those who are most effective devour more than the rest of their own kind, are cannibalistic... they thrive, multiply with the greatest effectiveness; some of their offspring will perish, but some of them will keep on replicating, increasing their shared wealth, capital their parents can make use of. Those who do not think or watch or listen then think that someone will come along who will want to help them in times of need, of trouble – their kind die in the stupidest and fastest of ways.

All it is, all of it, is wriggling beneath a microscope lens. Bacteria jiggling along. Useless data gathered. Nothing which could not be simulated by a cheap computer program.

People love their fantasies. Writhing with joy when they entertain them. Referring to them as their senses. These "senses" dissolve in mid-air the moment they are mentioned. They are the collective fantasy of those worms who still believe the weak are not destined for destruction, but can survive, cohabit, instead of feasting on each other, amassed into one wriggling mass, one happy colony... a happy colony of those too weak to do what needs to be done – cannibalism, no other choice.

Most of us worms harbour this fantasy that our wriggling has some sort of shape, some sense, some purpose even. That someone greater than us is using a metaphorical microscope to watch our development, our so called progress. That this being has a gift for us, something hidden – designed to reward us for all our wriggling.

These are profoundly misleading and harmful fantasies – just think of your own philosophies, how little of what you think you know you know. The words you live by: happiness, trust, joy, support, love, hope, meaning, health, harmony, goodness, wellbeing, truth, destiny.

Meanwhile, these are nothing more than hollow phrases, words invented by busy little bugs, microbes who want to live another day, want to wriggle some more.

The dog song lingers; it's obvious, it's painfully banal, I hum it as I go round and round the Charles de Gaulle Roundabout, then drive down to the Silesian-Dabrowski Bridge and off the ramp to the riverbank, cruising slowly and then back up the ramp to the bridge, singing all along, screaming, my voice reminiscent of an old, stupid ape.

All that you do each day, all the tasks you work so hard to remember to complete, are all in the name of some unclear purpose. The idea of God has become painfully unfashionable, so that each fantasy just feeds another, like bugs feed on other bugs, pretending no one can see, no one knows, no one is keeping score. You keep on listening to ancient fairytales, repeating them for each other.

This is my dog song.

You don't have to hear me out, in fact you can't, because in the deep space of my soundproofed car no one can hear me sing or scream, but just think for a minute about how much evil it is you do, holding onto things you know damn well are fantasies. You waste your energies and this is the evil that most men do and it is evil because it is a lie and a waste of perfectly good energy, energy and truth which belongs to all of us, and ought not be wasted.

Your happiness, your dreams, the hopes you and your dear ones hold dear, the things you love, your families, your parents and your kids, your friends and successes, your altruistic tendencies, your plans, your houses, your hopes, your holidays, your youthful years, your adulthoods, your joys and depressions, your flights of joy and downward spirals, the essential fabric of your lives; screw your cultured tendencies, your books, films, favourite records, your laws and your value systems, your heritage, your architecture, your codes, morality, your sense of good and evil, your little beliefs, your anecdotes, your associations, your identities, your struggles to survive, your silent prayers for eternal life, whispered while you think no one is listening, no one save some big guy in the sky – none of those things matter. They never did.

Almost all of us are in some way religious. None of us are capable of facing the reality that we are nothing more than writhing scum upon the surface of a ruthless planet, nothing more than bugs, creatures too scared to be honest about what they know. We need religion to fight off the despair that comes with such clarity of thought, with such enlightenment. That is my dog song.

And it would all be amusing if there really was someone out there who could comprehend and do something about the future of this bug-filled aquarium, this city and thousands of others like it, swarming with blind and brainless bugs, billions of us, not knowing the hour or the cause of why fate might pour a vast vat of boiling water all over our colonies. Wiping us from the face of this complex planet.

If there is a God, that is how he operates – that is my dog song.

I stop at Three Crosses Square, hiding my face in my hands, my forehead feeling awfully icy cold. My body feels only marginally warmer than that of a cadaver, which is perfect for a long and healthy life.

In this mingle of bugs, I have been assigned the role of a ghost. Most people do not see me, do not know I exist, do not know what it is I do, and why it is necessary.

I hide the switchblade in my pocket, right where it belongs.

My biggest mistake was that I assumed that I would not get caught up in things which were always coming to get me. That I had assumed people would feel a sense of goodwill and loyalty towards me. That there would be worms out there who would have my best interests at heart – when bugs clearly do not possess such vulnerable muscles.

He gave her ten thousand zlotys. That's a lot, because she's not worth that much. Not even half that.

Once I get to the entrance, I remember to close my mouth, to stop speaking aloud, stop singing.

She's not worth spitting on, in fact. Once I get to the entrance, I remember to start walking in a steady fashion, refrain from swaying like someone who's taken far too many hits and lost far too many hours of sleep in the past twenty-four hours or so.

All the people milling about the entrance – I smile at them. It softens slightly the scars and the swellings on my face. I now remember I forgot to take my invitation. He gave me an invite, but I didn't take it with me. I remember crumpling it up and tossing it away. I now recall other things. My body on the floor of my own apartment. My body in the pink room, on a folding bed, damp with liquids it produced all by itself. Somebody else's body next to mine. The people I see milling about me now are very nicely dressed – which seems to be the only thing their lives revolve around – being seen to be nicely dressed. They huddle round gas-burning heaters, smoking their designer cigarettes, drinking free booze out of paper cups, exchanging observations, stroking each other's arms – some of them recognise me and beam smiles which look decidedly unnatural beneath the UV lights. I happen to know for a fact that their teeth are black. As black as everything else they possess.

Everyone looks so damn jolly, though the night is only just getting into its stride. Showbiz personalities, most of them gay, surrounded by their forty-something girlfriends, mothers busy looking round to see if they can spot their daughters, spot and stop them from disappearing in the toilets with the wrong sort of 'friend'. Their twenty-something offspring, hopefully focused on their smartphones, surrounded by clouds of bitter sweet perfume – neither that nor the highly artificial makeup helping make them any less unattractive. No longer girls, not women yet, making some sort of living from blogging or other online activities, smoking slim cigarettes, drinking cocktails strong enough to make sure everyone gets wasted quickly and that the bar staff can knock off early and get some sleep. I hear a quiet sound, a sort of metallic shimmer. It is the sound of reality turning to profit. Everyone I see hanging around is busy cutting this city up like a cake. Cocaine. Listen, watch. Who brought them their coke this evening, if it wasn't me?

"Are you out working tonight, buddy?" I hear a male voice behind me, followed by a friendly pat on the back. I turn to see Xavery – the gas lit lamps reflecting in his eyeballs, making it seem like there are flames inside them. He's swapped his designer jeans for a casual suit, in tasteful black. He looks no different to most of the company CEOs, lawyers, investors, consultants, and the like.

"Changing your product line?" I ask politely.

"I heard you had some mishaps," he answers politely.

"You heard wrong. Everything is fine my end. People will always make up stories, all too easily bored, buddy," I explain. We step aside, his smile as bright as ever, the grin of a reptile which has had its fill of blood for the night. It seems everyone in here has already had their dose of blood, and they seem sated; the blood must have tasted good.

"Well, I don't know. I hope you're doing OK. Listen, either someone called someone to report you to the authorities, or else it was an accident, either way I am making a little on the side here tonight," he explains. "I got some good Colombian as a bonus from someone, and I'm selling it onto trusted clients."

"Keep up the hard work, Xavery. Poland depends on your courage."

"You know I don't mean to get in on your deals. Just so that things between us are clear, alright?"

"I'm not working tonight, just a social call. Trying to protect the honour of a certain dame."

I notice him looking all across my battered face and finally see the fear in his eyes, realising he's scared of me – he wasn't expecting to see me here today, and right now he sees me like some ex-girlfriend he wasn't expecting to see, someone who can still disrupt his sense of wellbeing.

"You said it yourself," I tell him, "The market is far from saturated. People can't take the pressure. We can all get paid, pal, enough for everyone to go round."

I pat him on the shoulder and leave him confused, moving on into the crowd, finally crossing the courtyard of this post- or even maybe pre-World War II block of apartments, by the magic of capitalist desire and drive now turned into a bar open for special occasions, like the fashion show this evening. There's fresh snow on my shoes by the time I reach the actual entrance. A couple of bouncers block my way.

"I need to see an invite," one of them says to me.

"I don't have mine," I tell him, smiling confidently.

"Then fuck right off," one of them says.

I close my eyes. Maybe happiness is the sensation of a specific sort of iciness in the blood. I open my eyes again and announce: "I have to get in and speak to someone."

"And I really have to screw Adriana Lima, but guess what – it ain't happening, no matter how many text messages I send her. She just won't write back," says the bouncer on the left.

I then hear another familiar voice behind me.

"Kuba!" it calls out.

"Yeah, hi there," I reply, turning round.

"Kuba, so good to see you here. Come, we need to talk." I recognise Lukasz, the friendly, cynical, gay socialite, once again sporting a bowtie, along with a pair of skinny black pants held up with a pair of suspenders. He now reminds me of someone I last saw at a high school camping trip – someone from a completely different kind of reality. Lukasz is a pleasant enough person, and generous with the cash when it comes to coke, not to mention that the same is true of his circle of friends – as long as they know they're getting their parents' money's worth.

"In a few years' time he's going to be a proper coke head," I think to myself with a smile. Maybe he'll still be pleasant enough. He's sure to keep on smiling. Even more so than now – that smile of his will take on the whole world.

"Nothing doing, Lukasz," I tell him, smiling back.

"What with?" he asks, clearly confused.

"I have to get inside, but I didn't bring my invite," I explain, pointing at the two ogres guarding the entrance.

"Did you bring some stuff?" he asks me. "The other guy is trying to sell some real shit. He claims it's some Colombian wonder drug, but all he's done is grind up some aspirin pills. Those who can't go without will take that shit, but you know... I wouldn't mind having a whiff of some quality. This is not exactly a rocking party. In fact, it's as stiff as a busy morgue. This whole event will be death by boredom, between you and me, if I don't get high on some decent supply... by that I mean you, of course."

"Sure, Lukasz, but first I have to take care of some business inside," I tell him, nodding at the barred door again.

"There's a break between shows right now," he explains. "The next set is in thirty minutes or so. The DJ's killing time for now."

"I have some business to attend to inside there," I tell him.

"Alright, man, anything for you, right? We're friends. As well as business associates," he says, patting me on the shoulder. I somehow find this amusing, to be standing there in that dirty snow, powder which all over this town is equally dirty and equally unpleasant – as unpleasant as the rusty flick knife in my pocket.

Lukasz makes eye contact with the bouncers, points at me then gives them the thumbs up, and I smile at him.

"Lukasz, I'll go in – give me fifteen minutes max," I tell him, then go through the swinging doors which try to keep some of the heat inside, the two ogres not saying a word this time. The club is like a deep hole inside, the dance floor down some steps, though today it serves as a catwalk, various ramps leading off to the back – one of these ramps will lead me to the person I seek, though which one – that is my quest for today.

I feel an easy sense of excitement. The air inside this courtyard is very still, no air con in operation – if a fire broke out right now, everyone in here would be toast, no signs pointing towards non-existent fire exits. It's odd, but I feel a thirst for some alcohol. I have to celebrate something, and I suspect I know what it is. I approach the bar, which is already loaded down with free glasses of champagne, and heavy cut-glass tumblers of whisky. I take one of these and swallow a gulp, no one paying me any attention – not the bored waitress, nor the two barmen occupied by swiping their smartphone screens. The alcohol is pleasant on the tongue, sweet, heavy, burning, reminding me that I still haven't eaten anything of late, but the high this gives me is not unpleasant. The booze flows along my veins, like lubricating oil through a car engine. I stretch and smile at the world.

Everything falls apart, crumbling into bits, in its own natural way and tempo – everything is as it ought to be.

"*Kuba, welcome back on our show – we have to be honest and tell you that you're not exactly the sort of guest we have on here every day, or week even. Though we do have many other guests who*

*do jobs that are not exactly typical career choices, this is the first
time we've ever had someone on who not only does a very unusual
sort of work, but the sort of work which is not only not quite legal,
but is actually very much illegal. I have to admit as the host to being
very much excited to have you back live on our show. What do you
feel now, after these past few days, Kuba? How have they affected
you? I have to admit that I listened to a lot of what you said about
this city and its residents with trepidation. Would you like a tissue?
No? OK then. For a moment there I had the impression you needed...
never mind. As if over these last few days you had lived through
more than some people experience in their whole lives. I will ask a
question we ask of all our guests: How is it when life slips loose of
your control, I mean completely, in the flash of an eye? Have you
asked yourself that? Do you feel you now have control regained?
Do you feel back on the right track?"*

Yeah, I just have to keep on going. To cross this dance floor,
covered in slippery lino, waiting to welcome all the people mingling
outside. I have this one final thing to take care of, and then everything
will be back to normal.

*"You know, I will tell you that the key thing is to focus on what
is the real aim of your life, what is the essence of everything you do,
every move you make. What is the source of your determination?*

*In every life there is trouble – no one ever has it all their way, no
one has it easy – but what really matters is the salvation you achieve
at the end, the light at the end of the tunnel – that's if I haven't said
too much and gone a bit too far for your listeners.*

*I've experienced many different misfortunes, but above all I
wanted to make that flight, tonight at 10pm. I have to go now, just
for a moment, I'll be back in a second or so."*

The door behind the stage is small, like the door to a toilet. Once
I open it, the sound guys, dragging cables around, don't even notice
I am there – if I am there it must mean I should be there for some
official reason.

The other side of that door there is a corridor, long and narrow,
the walls white, doors either side, and I wonder if there is any other
way out of here – or only through this little door. I go down the

corridor, hearing voices, male and female, confident, loud, like they're trying to sell something on the radio or TV.

I move softly, quickly, quietly. When I put my hand in my pocket, it touches steel, rough, heavy, rusty metal. It brings things back into focus. My reason for being here, my motivation.

"It would be dishonest of me to say that I have not been surprised by things over the last few days. I have to be honest with your audience. None of us are perfect. I don't feel responsible for the death of that young mother-to-be – Mariusz F. seems to have had something on his mind when he drove into that poor girl – what did he mean when he said he could have stopped in time but didn't?

How long am I going away for? I don't know yet. Until things calm down. Would I like to keep away forever? It's not possible to want things which are totally unrealistic. Why unrealistic? Ha ha ha!!! Ha, ha, Ha!!!"

Yes, that was meant to be my most brilliant, my most vivid laughter. I have the right to respond with laughter. But let's call things by their name. It's just not possible to escape this place. Dreams are just that – fantasies, fancies, flights of the human imagination.

There is a door at the end of the corridor, covered in steel, displaying a fluorescent sign. Good – I could simply walk out of here, be gone, quickly, smoothly, but why be indiscreet? Why when another way is possible.

"Our viewers have heard that you like singing."

"Oh yes I do, indeed. I practice a form of soundless singing. Unvoiced. I just open the lips and make the necessary movements with my muscles, but I don't actually exhale to produce sounds."

"What is it like to now be heading towards this critical meeting? Tell us, Kuba, how does it feel? Our audience is expecting something terrible to occur, although I imagine the knife is only there as a symbolic prop – you're not actually going to make use of it, right?"

I approach the last set of doors on the right, tuning into the sound of voices on the other side of it – picking out that one voice I came here to hear.

"What is it like, Kuba, to be moving towards such an encounter? Tell us how it feels?"

"It feels wonderful," I reply. "You know, I talked about bugs, but bugs have their little pleasures also. We should not forget that, but remember to delight in those tiny joys as often as possible."

I stand with my back against the wall just as the door opens, two girls emerging, tall, leggy blondes, their clothes hanging off of their bony bodies.

"We're going for a smoke, we'll be back in ten or fifteen," they say to whoever is still inside that room.

"Sure, I'll stay here, fix my makeup and hair," says a voice I know all too well. A voice which feels to me now like poisoned honey.

Worms have their own little pleasures – for example, they can punish those among them who transgress. Who do things which are unjust.

"Could you say that in a way which is easier to understand?"

"But it is all very simple. There is ice inside my body, things which are me and which are now frozen solid."

I open the door and go inside – closing and resting my back against it, blocking it from being opened from the outside. The room is long and narrow, lined with mirrors, and low shelves covered with all sorts of makeup gadgets – brushes, powders, paints, curlers, driers and such. At the far end there are clothes rails, a whole assortment of colourful clothes, coats and accessories. Once she sees it's me, her face freezes solid, covered in thick makeup – I probably wouldn't recognise her in the street, her hair piled up on top of her head, her body wrapped in a retro-looking asymmetrical shiny silver dress, one which looks laughably futuristic. Without advance warning I would need to compose myself and work out where the strange stabbing sensation I feel in my heart was coming from. I would need a while to realise it was her, just looking oh so different.

But here and now she is perfectly vivid, instantly recognisable.

"What are you doing here?" she asks, a question I was ready for. There is a key inside the door lock – I look down at it, trying to work out what it is I should do. Meanwhile, she speaks again: "You cannot be here, Kuba. I'm going to get security if you don't leave." She gets up in order to regain some control over the space around us. Again, she speaks, trying to shape our reality. "You frighten me, I feel distressed seeing you here – I don't want you to be here with me alone."

"Oh yes, indeed, that's what everything comes down to – the things which please or displease us, right?"

I take the knife out of my pocket.

"Get out of here," she insists, eyes focused on the knife. Her lips trembling.

"It's my fault, not yours," I tell her.

"What do you mean? I don't get it..." she says, taking a few steps back. I take a step forward.

"It's my fault I let myself be fooled. I came over that time, wanting you to cheat me."

"What the fuck are you talking about?"

"Couldn't he at least take you on holiday? Send you to Ibiza or some other resort? You'd be having champagne on the sand now, not on snow. Looking round for Russians or some other guys to fuck around with," I say, shrugging my shoulders.

"You have no right to say such things about me. As to what happened, that was... a misunderstanding," she blurts out without conviction.

"He just gave you ten thousand, right?" I say.

She turns a paler shade of white. It's visible, even beneath all the layers of makeup. I tell her: "I've had a lot of trouble because of you. Which is in some way my own fault. I chose to let things turn out the way they did."

"Get the fuck out of here," she demands, grabbing something from the desk in front of her. I dash towards her, grab her wrist and wrestle the set of hairdressing scissors from her – they fall to the floor with a metallic clatter. Then I draw her closer to me. Grab her by the neck. Apply the knife blade to her cheek – the hand which was wrapped round her neck is now covering her mouth, grasping her lips hard. Tears begin rolling down her cheeks, along the edge of the blade. I don't lessen the pressure, quite the opposite – I push the very sharp blade until it draws blood, the red mixing with her tears.

"Just look at yourself, you fucking bitch," I tell her calmly.

"Kuba, hello son. No, nothing is wrong. Kuba? Will you join us for some reheated supper leftovers? No? Listen to what I will tell you now son. I just want you to never forget – no matter what happens, never raise your hand against any woman, OK?"

"Sure, mum, but why are you crying, did anything happen, did Dad do anything to you?"

I clamp my hand around her face as hard as if I was trying to squeeze the lying life out of it. It feels like a large piece of fruit in my hand. She's trying to speak, but the words become lodged against the palm of my hand, becoming nothing more than spit which slides against the inside of my hand.

"You fucking stupid girl," I tell her straight. Then I grab the back of her neck and shove her towards the door – she bounces off it like a rag doll.

"Help! Security! I need help!" she screams, smashing her little fists against the back of the door, but I reach her in a flash, gag her with my hand, then draw her close to me, opening the door with my free hand.

"You just have to accept whatever is happening – take your punishment," I tell her as she tries to scream, bite the inside of my hand, kick my shins too.

"I also have a gun, keep that in mind, will you?" I warn her.

She tries to wrestle free of my embrace, so I apply the knife blade to the other cheek, the cut on the previous cheek still crying red tears.

"I'm punishing myself in this way, just so you know," I whisper in her ear. "And now be quiet – you know now that I can kill you any time I like, and get the hell out of this shit hole before anyone stops or catches me. Clear?"

"Kuba, this seems to be very important. You're not always going to be able to do the right thing. The noble thing. You might try, but you'll never succeed."

(Cut – memory from childhood, our old kitchen, before the refit, our old Soviet-made fridge covered with stickers featuring characters from Czechoslovak and Polish and Soviet cartoons – the walls lined with cheap pistachio green tiles, the cupboards made from the cheapest materials, which was all that was available in state run shops of the time – Mum sitting on the floor, trying to compress herself down, holding her face, Dad no longer at home. He was angry that day, because the poem he was working on was not coming out right. Something for him was wrong with it, and wouldn't go right.)

"You'll do your best, Kuba, but you won't succeed. Still, the one thing you must never ever do is raise your hand against a woman. Never strike anyone smaller and weaker than you. No matter what happens, such an act can never be justified. If you do so, you'll be condemned forever."

I look out into the corridor – it is empty, her girlfriends still outside smoking. All the stylists must be snorting their last lines before the show begins, while the audience assembles inside. I push her towards the emergency exit. She's stopped screaming and spitting and biting. Her breathing is fast though. Her heart beating like that of a bird which has been caught in a trap. The emergency door is unlocked. There is a metal staircase the other side of it. I sincerely hope it will lead us down to street level, more or less where I parked my car.

I shut the door behind us. She's breathing heavily – I can tell she's terrified.

"Are you afraid I'm going to kill you, once and for all?" I ask.

She swallows hard. Without saying anything. It's quiet, and when snowy nights are really silent, that absence of sound speaks for itself. The city's music bouncing off the walls clearly audible, water running along ancient pipes, electricity buzzing along outdated cables.

"You do, don't you?" I ask her. "You think I'm never letting you go."

"I've no idea what you're going to do," she answers honestly.

There is a key in the lock of the door which leads out onto the street. I hear voices from a long time ago in this odd, nighttime winter silence.

"But what's happened, Mum?"

"Nothing, son. Go outside. Go play with your friends."

"What time will he come home? Tell me, what time is he coming home?"

"Kuba, are you still there? You seem to have drifted off into some deep area of your own past."

"Well, it's Christmas – a time for remembering things. And somehow this one scene from my childhood seems to have come back to me, all by itself."

"Was your childhood a happy one?"

"I don't know how to answer that question."

"How can you not know? Did you feel loved? Looked after?"

"I was fed. I was raised. I was not left alone for any extended periods of time. I wasn't really beaten on a regular basis. There might have been a few times when my father flew into a rage. But why are we talking about this now? What does it matter?"

"Considering what is happening here, it might have a serious impact on the present."

"Am I being psychoanalysed right now? I hate psychoanalysts, sorry. They're terrible con artists. The worst of the worst. They get paid to tell people that they're special, that there's always someone out there who cares about them."

"He didn't give me any money. If he told you that, he's lying," she hisses, staring deep into my eyes.

"When do you plan to stop acting the total whore?" I ask her.

"He lied. I didn't get anything from him. He came to me with some guy – I think he was a cop, a detective, plain clothes, who said he knew you. They put pressure on me, the fuckers – they said they could just perform some blood tests and if there was anything illegal in the results, they would send them to my parents... what the fuck was I to do, Kuba?".

She starts to cry, but it's not working on me – I ask her: "In ten years' time? By the time you hit your mid-thirties – what is it you want to have by then? A husband? Kids?"

"That cop – I think his name was Marek. He said you were working together. My brother is twenty, and recently got a suspended sentence. This Marek cop knew about him and said it would be no problem to have him rearrested on some trumped up charge and have the suspended sentence actioned – my baby brother behind bars, and you know what those prisons are like. It would be hell. Might kill my mother stone dead. Do you understand? I might have slept with Mariusz once or twice, but then he started to get things into his head, things about me, about the two of us... He started to text and call me all the time. And I mean all the time – like a thousand times a day. He said I'd be finished in Warsaw. That he would kill this town for me. If I didn't answer when he called, if I didn't meet him any time he wanted..."

She starts to choke on her tears, acting her heart right out.

"You'll want a husband who won't ask too many questions about all those men, all the guys who lost their minds over you, wanting to leave their ageing wrinkly wives for you, taking you out to all the hot spots, wanting to be seen with you on their arms. You'll be wanting a husband who won't ask about the good old days, when your face still looked cute without makeup, the skin so natural, so young..." I drive the point home.

"I had no other choice. No other chance. I didn't take anything from him though. Not a penny, not a cent. Do you understand? I beg you, Kuba," she starts to plead.

"You want kids, right? How many? A boy and a girl? Twins maybe? And a house in the suburbs? Weekends doing yoga, filling your face full of botox? Killing time reading all the latest advice handbooks, how to lead a successful life, how to transfer happily into middle age, how to be a successful woman in today's mixed up world?"

"Kuba, please. Believe me when I tell you I took nothing from him. Nothing at all."

"Maybe I can increase your chances of finding such a guy. Such a wonderful guy. Other than money, he has to also be kind and merciful. A kind of philanthropist."

"A what? What are you talking about?"

"Do you know what I think is sad about the times we live in? Once upon a time to be a whore meant something specific. To be a whore was a question of necessity, not of choice. At times, it meant the only weapon some women had against the world. Now, for many it's just a game."

"Nobody gave me any money," she says over again. "They forced me to cooperate."

"Girls like you think being a prostitute is a game. The way little kids play hide and seek," I tell her.

I can feel her trembling, see tears starting to flow down her cheeks, her lips opening in order to scream, and that is when I grab her face with one hand and force her against the wall. Hard. With all my strength. Her body is now completely alien to me. Once upon a time it was precious to me, something I desired to have and hold, to lie down next to, to inhale its smells, but now it feels to me like a box containing things I no longer care for, items I have no desire to handle any more, things I want to be rid of, as quickly as possible.

It feels tepid to the touch – and horrible – things should either be cold or hot, but not in between.

"This really matters, Kuba. It sort of helps us answer the question of who you might be. But there is no such thing as a question of who we are. We're all the product of a range of reactions to external stimuli, reactions which occur under the influence of various factors, factors shaped when we are very young at times. Specific mechanisms. But many of the things we decide to do are merely pleasures, nothing more. Cleaning up, in my opinion, is the greatest such pleasure. Anyone who cannot derive satisfaction from cleaning and making things tidy is a negative kind of person, their influence on the world taking away rather than adding anything of value."

The knife slices into her cheek, quite deep, from cheekbone to earlobe, blood flowing freely from her face, all the way down her neck – her eyes open wide, I close the knife, hiding the blade inside the rusty handle, then deposit it back in my pocket. Some voice deep inside me says I haven't gone far enough, but I don't listen to it. Her eyes tell me she thinks I have and then some.

"When will he come back? Whatever time that might be, I will kill him, Mummy, I swear."

"No. You're not going to do anything of the sort. Calm down.

Look, I am calm already. Look at me. Your father is still on edge, no matter what happens."

She is still bleeding profusely – now trying to scream.

"Do you want a matching cut on the other side of your darling face?" I ask her.

She shakes her head. I can then feel a sudden burst of warmth emanating from her hips. She's pissed herself, it seems.

"Then shut your mouth," I demand. "Until I am gone down these stairs. Then afterwards you can whine all you want."

She falls back against the wall, then slides down to the floor, resting on her knees.

"If you ever tell anyone I cut you," I tell her straight, "I will find and I will kill you. Do you understand?" I ask her.

When my father gets home, I will jump him with a knife, trying to stick it in his thigh, right where his main artery is. He will hit my head, very hard, throwing me against the door, smashing the pane of frosted glass which all the doors in our home are fitted with. He will stink the same as he always does, seeing as my father always stank of digested alcohol, cheap cigarettes, of an unhealthily ageing body, clothes that needed washing more often.

"Do you hear me? Do you understand?" I ask her again.

She doesn't answer, so I climb the fire escape slowly, leaving her sitting on the floor down below, like a bleeding rag doll, arms and legs askew at unnatural angles. Blood staining her designer clothes. Her face paralysed, eyes blank, clearly not comprehending whatever might be happening here tonight.

It's only once I have climbed up some stairs that she begins to howl terribly. Someone runs out once I am another floor up, right by the actual exit.

The person running is not after me. The fire exit doors are unlocked. I close them behind me, exiting behind some rubbish bins on the other side of the building. I then find a gate and exit calmly onto the street. I throw the knife down a sewer grating, as if it was a murder weapon, even though I haven't really done her any lasting harm.

I approach my car, floating along like a discarded piece of trash, like a plastic bag tossed about by the winds. My legs seem to float above the snow, I can't feel them at all. I can hear some sort of commotion starting up in the courtyard I have just climbed out of, but then I am inside my car and no more noise reaches me from the outside. Perhaps I should go back in there, as if nothing had happened, but none of them will do anything to me anyway. They have no idea how to handle such instances of violence. They've not been taught or trained how to do so. Meanwhile, the girl bleeding all over their dance floor is just some hired model, possibly an actual prostitute. I pick up some snow from the relatively clean pile on the ground next to the car, rub it into my face. It tastes bitter. "This is what dirt tastes like," I think to myself.

I have another four hours before takeoff. Enough time to drop the car off at home, then grab a taxi.

"You're acting ruthlessly and brutally, Kuba. It's horrible to watch..."

"Actually, I'm doing neither. What I'm doing is not ruthless or brutal. It just is, rather ordinary actions. All related to how people will allow others to get away with crazy things. Allowing themselves to play the role of the weaker sort. Becoming slaves of their own weak choices. Allowing their lives to become tainted with mistakes, losing their own territory, their money, even the air they breathe. We all have the right to hurt those who do us harm. Acting like the weaker sort of worm is a choice, therefore is it true that I have just got my revenge? In some ways, yes, but then again I simply did what had to be done according to the rules of the game. I made sure the world could see what happens to those who cross me, who get in my way, who try to weaken me and leave me vulnerable."

"You talked about hurting women, Kuba. You talked about how unacceptable it is, always, and yet you just maimed a woman by cutting open her face."

"She did that to herself. She asked to be treated that way. A long time ago. This is what she was driving towards. Her actions inevitably caused this sort of action and reaction. No one told her to behave in the way she did recently. But the fact that she chose to do so resulted in her getting hurt."

"You're a terrible person, Kuba, I'm sorry to have to tell you, but I have to say it while we're live on air – I don't believe what I've just heard you say..."

"Sorry to interrupt, but all of us are horrible deep down inside. In our own different ways."

"We're all very much the same."

"Oh son, you've grown up to become a horrible person."

"No thanks, mum, I don't want any sandwiches, the dinner was enough."

"Did you hear what I just said to you? You've grown into a horrible sort of man."

"You sound artificial, mum, like a bad actress. A bad actress from a badly scripted soap opera."

I get inside the car. Once I start the engine, I have the impression of an odd sort of smell inside it, one which is totally alien. As if I had made a mistake and got into someone else's Audi. As if all those who had recently been inside it had taken it over somehow. And this was no longer my car. I lower the windows, trying to air the cabin, reclaim something of it back for myself.

No, it's not the car. It's the city outside which has begun to smell differently. An odd sort of aroma. As if I was already on my way, leaving town. As if I was already elsewhere.

I have four more hours to go before departure. Which means I still have time for a slow cruise along the streets of Warsaw. I can still wave goodbye to it.

Before driving away, my eyes catch some movement in the rearview mirrors, someone rushing out of the fire escape exit behind me – though I cannot tell if it is a woman, a man, or a ghost, maybe.

7:10pm (Excoriator)

I get out, shut the door and lean against the side of the car. Nothing around is visible, no lights have come on automatically, but I know this garage, I could walk around it happily even blindfolded. I can sense the outlines of other cars – in the dark, they remind me of sculptures.

This is the end. I've checked about a dozen times if the car is clean, if I've locked and double locked my own front door. This is the beginning of a long and beautiful break for me – I want to be ready for it.

I've already made so many mistakes. Still, I tried to make choices. Or if not choices, then at least to exert some influence wherever it was possible.

There are things which stop us being effective. Things that cause us to become feverish, to lose contact with reality, to see things from the wrong angles. Things we should always try to identify and neutralise as quickly as we can. Things such as unchecked emotions, certain desires – such as the need to feel safe and close to others. They're the things which make us miss things, or take the wrong turns, or make the wrong decisions. Such as the ones I've been making over the past few days. Mistakes which can prove catastrophic, though potentially salvageable.

Text message: *I'm on my way. I packed light. I will need to buy some things once we get there. I don't know why I'm going with you, you stupid son of a bitch. Don't ask me why. I am coming with you to Argentina.* I smile with the last of my good cheer and will, reading it over and over again.

The garage is cool, not cold, just cool, the right sort of cool, a specific kind of caress which soothes better than any human touch ever could. It's an early taste of the calm and peace I will be feeling in ten or so hours. If I was a person in the general sense of the word, I would think something along the lines of, "I can't wait to get there".

I touch the door to my car. It's cold. Which feels good. As good as I've felt in a long while. As long as I can remember. My travelling bag slung across my shoulder, I walk towards the exit of the garage.

That's when the movement sensor reacts to my presence, lights going on all around me. I wonder why this didn't happen earlier, then I hear his voice behind me – and my heart skips a beat, such a potent beat, it almost gives me a heart attack.

"Kuba, my dear boy, wait a second. No need to hurry – rushing makes no sense now, lad."

I could never mistake that voice for anyone else's.

I turn round – he's there, next to my car. Wearing the most awful leather jacket, like something pulled from some communist-era sofa, patchwork leather no good for anything other than the cheapest sorts of products. He's smoking one of his cinnamon cigarettes. The lights over our heads bounce brightly off his shaven skull. He lifts his tinted glasses, then lowers them back onto his nose. He's wearing a pair of cheap moccasins on his feet, covered in mud, and generally looks like the kind of street peddler of pirated VHS tapes or DVDs from the early years after communism collapsed, when the question of taste in the way people dressed didn't come into anything, the only thing which mattered was how many dollars you had rolled up in the socks stuffed into those horrid moccasins or the pockets of that patchwork leather jacket. The kind of guy who could be selling all sorts of things from those VHS or DVD boxes – imported cigarettes or bullet clips for Kalashnikovs or other contraband.

"Good evening, Kuba. You didn't write back to the text messages I sent you," Dario complains.

I glance down at my phone. There is one new message: *I am coming because you happen to be my one and only friend, and this is factual proof that my life is a total mess. I am coming. Unfortunately. On my way.*

"I'm leaving for a while," I tell Dario, pointing to the exit from the garage.

"I know," he replies.

We stand there for a moment, facing off. Dario pulls a hand out of his jacket pocket and makes a sweeping gesture with it, as if he were casting some sort of abstract spell.

"Get in the car," he says.

"I have a cab coming in ten minutes time. We'll have plenty of time to talk when I return," I inform him and turn around, so as not to have to look at his ugly face and the rest of him – then start slowly walking towards the exit. Even though I know I'm about to hear that familiar clicking sound, a click which is now becoming so familiar that it's starting to bore me with its inevitability.

And right on time – there it is, along with his voice, announcing: "You know all too well that you have no control, Kuba, none."

I place my travelling bag on the ground.

"I'm leaving, Dario," I repeat for all the good it's worth.

"I want to help you, Kuba. I want to help, because you've really no idea how badly you've screwed up."

I turn to see him holding the same small automatic pistol he had with him in Piotrek's restaurant. He's smiling – then drops the hand holding the gun, starts laughing.

"Do we really have to play these games, sonny? These idiotic formalities? You're such a smart lad, Kuba. I liked you the moment we met. To be honest, though, I wasn't really ready to take to you all that readily. Still, all the disasters which have befallen you of late, I could see them hanging over you like a dark cloud. Do you believe in destiny, Kuba? In auras? Everyone has theirs, you see."

I'm listening to him, trying to keep my heartbeat steady. Dario is the last thing I have to take care of before leaving. He was bound to be waiting here. I knew that. No point being spooked.

"We'll go for a ride in my car," he tells me. I pick up my bag and head towards his wheels – slowly. I still have three hours left. Looking at his ugly mug I realise I'm capable of killing tonight, murdering in cold blood anyone who tries to stop me getting on that plane. "Throw your luggage on the back seat, son," he tells me.

He drives a brand new, black BMW X5. Considering what he makes from all his little deals, it's a humble ride, even though the inside of the car looks and smells older than it should – stinking of his cheap cigarettes, the floor littered with fag packets, food wrappers, plastic bottles, etc. Dario stretches, something in his spine cracking, something hissing.

"I have another offer to make you," he says, getting in behind the wheel. I watch him turn the key in the ignition. The radio comes on automatically, some horrid song from the 1980s. The sort of song my father still listens to any time he's had too much, or not enough, to drink.

"I have to be at the airport at 10pm." I tell him.

"Oh really, Kuba? As far as I know nobody has to do anything or be anywhere. That includes you."

I notice an odd sort of dampness in his eyes. He reaches out a hand towards me,

"No, Kuba – give me your gun." Instead of doing any such thing, I smile. "What is so funny, lad?"

"Did you think I would be taking a firearm with me to an international airport? No. I left it upstairs."

He puts his pistol back in the pocket of his jacket. Laughing along with me now.

"Of course. How right of you. Kuba, you are a smart lad."

"How did you manage to drive in here?" I ask him.

"What do you mean how? I just turned the steering wheel in the right direction, that's how you drive most places you want to drive into."

I feel calm. It's true to say that I still fear him – small animals are always going to be afraid of bigger beasts. Having said that, my breathing seems to be holding steady – it's important to feel fear, but also not to show too much of it. I've no idea what else might happen tonight, but all that depends on how I play things now – how he reads my moves, my mood, my instincts. I have to focus on the block of ice I can still feel in the pit of my stomach. That's what's going to help me get from here to that airport, any which way. I once again remind myself that I'm ready to off this fat fuck if he does decide to come between me and that airport. I realise I have to focus on that thought and be mindful of any opportunity which might present itself. He has the only gun in this car, and that is a major sort of advantage. Sitting in the passenger seat beside him, I notice some pens lying in the pocket of the door, pens sturdy enough to pierce a jugular or his actual throat, should I consider that to be necessary. I am now certain he wants his drugs back – the bag someone whose identity is still a mystery to me stole from my hiding place in Goclaw. What really isn't all that good is that I can't offer him anything in exchange for the bag someone stole from him and then stole from me. I don't have anything like enough cash. No inside information on anybody he might be interested in. Nothing other than the twenty thousand dollars I intend to take with me to Argentina. For Dario, that sort of sum is nothing, no great shakes. Twenty grand is decidedly not enough to get out of the obligation to kill or torture some unfortunate bodies. Meanwhile, I suspect these are the designs he has on me.

"Where are you driving us to?" I ask.

"Do you remember what I told you the last time we met?" he asks.

The doors to the underground garage lift slowly. We exit the building, though I have the sensation of being swallowed by the city instead of exiting its throat.

"I do not, Dario. You said a lot of things. Hard to keep up with it all." I tell him exactly what I think.

He lights another cigarette that stinks of cinnamon. More maudlin songs come on the radio. Decades old, Polish, sang by some woman whose name I can't recall, even though everyone of my parents' generation would remember it even if you woke them in the middle of the night by playing this damn song and demanded they tell you her name.

Dario seems to smell my confusion and says: "Izka, now she was a gorgeous girl, I tell you. The first occasion I did time in the prison in Wałcz, all the lads in my cell beat off to pictures of her we cut out from magazines. Then this one time they were turning this one idiot into a cell whore – they cut out a poster of Izka's face and made a mask of it for him to wear while the more experienced prisoners fucked the kid – the rule was if you let them, then you deserved it. If you were a man, you fought back so hard they would never come near you with their cocks."

"You were saying something about a bag of cash which was left behind on a gondola somewhere," I remind him.

Looking out the window, I realise he's leaving my district and not driving towards the airport, but in the opposite direction. I see him scratching his head.

"No, Kuba. Not that story. That wasn't the point. I was talking about making amends for mistakes made. That was the point. How we all have to stand up for our own interests, not let anyone fuck us around, whether it's sex or money or anything else." I nod, realising that what is worst and most dangerous about Dario is that he really does have sensible things to say at times. "But there are situations in life when the mess really is horrendous – this is the kind of situation you find yourself in tonight. And someone will have to help you tidy up."

"I don't understand," I reply, watching the city roll on by the window.

"That means you're ever so slightly crazy, Kuba. But that is not a problem."

I feel the BMW speed up – we are now crossing over a bridge, heading in the totally opposite direction from the airport. Still, I feel remarkably calm, cooling down somehow, straightening up. I feel the same way I did a week ago, before all the colours started to appear everywhere, before I started to have problems with my sense of balance, with keeping to a regular diet or sleeping partner. All those ailments are gone – I feel like they're gone for good.

"Why beat about the bush? Let's start at the beginning," Dario says, driving his heavy Beemer crazy fast, ignoring traffic lights, making some wild overtaking manoeuvres. All he cares about is getting to his destination as quickly as possible. Nothing else matters. This city is his personal property, like something he built of Lego, and he has every right to use it, including its streets and junctions, as he sees fit.

"I like you," he says to me. "I do. I have this rare tendency to like those who are smarter than me, or at least as smart as I think I am. Most people tend to prefer those weaker than them, those who do not represent a threat. Right? I like those I can learn from. Those I can chat with. Those I can learn from the same way as I learn by reading books. Maybe a bit of that I took out with me from those jail cells. The need to keep the mind active, and not to grow weak by surrounding myself with people who are slower and dumber than I am."

As he says that, I once again look down at the pen in the passenger door side pocket.

"Where are you driving us?" I ask.

"I want to show you something back at my place. This is not something I do for just anyone, you understand. I like you, Kuba, and I want to help you out of a nasty bind."

"What sort of bind?"

I'm not just curious about what he thinks, but also about what he will actually tell me. I'm also curious about him. I've no idea what he's planning to do next. What sort of logic is guiding his moves right now.

"You've not had much luck of late. I want to help change that, Kuba. I want you to be happy. Or at least happier than you feel right now. That's what really matters in life, you know."

We drive into this district of old villas, not that expensive, mostly home to retired, not particularly wealthy folks. Piles of snow swept aside off the sidewalks, but not actually cleared away. Not many modern Christmas lights blinking in the gardens or the windows. Those American traditions haven't caught on round here yet. He stops at the end of one side road. I take a good look around, making sure he hasn't set up an ambush for me.

"I know this place is a long way from the centre. But far from the centre means less hassle. Less noise and trouble. No one bothers no one round here."

"I have to be at the airport in three, maybe less hours." I repeat my mantra. Dario doesn't seem to have heard me. Instead, he turns and puts his hand on my knee. I swipe it away.

"Easy does it, lad," he says trying to calm me down. "I'm no queer," he says with a stupid grin.

"I don't care. I just don't want you to touch me, that's all."

"Let yourself be helped just a little, Kuba," he whines.

"Helped with what, specifically speaking? Be clear, will you?"

"That's why I like you. You like to talk straight."

He gets out of the car, and I watch him going through his pockets in search of something. He eventually finds a small remote control for the gate to one of the driveways. He pushes the button and the gate slides aside. The house looks abandoned, shapeless, painted a rusty sort of red – nothing here fits – not the columns supporting the roof, the porch they're propped up against, nor the bushes and trees which surround the house – right now they're still covered in snow, but in the summer when covered in leaves they must do a good job of hiding the house from prying eyes in neighbouring houses or the street.

He comes around to my side of the car and opens the passenger side door.

"An ugly son of a bitch, isn't it?" He says, reading my mind again. "Anyway, come follow me." He waves his arm in the direction of the driveway.

I grab the bag from the back seat, not wanting to leave it back here at night, then get out and follow him across the snowy, muddy drive towards the house. It doesn't actually feel like snow, more like some sort of marshland, or a bog, trying to suck my boots down and the rest of me with them. He opens the front door and we go inside. The house reeks of old people, their medications, their cooking, their toiletries. My stomach does a little leap, not a happy one of course, but I manage to steady it. Feeling that everything will be OK.

He turns on some lights in the hallway, and I see we're in a narrow corridor, decorated with a large dress-length mirror, framed with dark wood – we keep going through to the kitchen which is next, a kitchen and dining room combined.

There are houses and apartments that when you enter them you instantly have the overwhelming sense that the owner died, died right there, and the place has never been gutted or redecorated or even aired out since. This house must have belonged to Dario's parents or grandparents. The very heavy, very old furniture doesn't appear to be his style. The television set is ancient, the screen round, clearly not a machine which sees regular use. The antique-looking furniture is not really antique – upon closer inspection I realise it is all reproduction stuff dating back to the days of communism – it would have been expensive at the time, but now in the cold light of day it would look just as shoddy and tasteless as it really in fact is. The walls are decorated with old family photos and religious icons – along with a calendar from a porn magazine from a decade ago, featuring a girl that looks like she belongs writhing on stage with Bon Jovi.

I have the overwhelming impression that Dario doesn't live here. The house was left to him by some ancient and now very much dead relatives, and serves as a hiding place as well as a hideaway.

"I actually live in Wilanow," he says, reading my thoughts once again.

"So why are we here?" I ask.

"What will you have to drink, Kuba? Some tea?" Waiting for me to answer, he observes, "I think you'd better go wash that blood out from underneath your fingernails. The passport control people might take an interest in that. Blood is always best washed out using cold water, Kuba."

I put my travelling bag on the floor, then go over to the kitchen sink and start scrubbing.

"And so you see, Kuba, you do have problems, a whole heap of new problems. They want to kill you. They do and they will, unless you and I remain the best of friends. We're fine pals already, I hope you agree with me on that, but we now have to establish a real friendship," he states.

"Who wants to kill me?" I ask, then grab a kitchen towel to dry my hands with, sitting down in one of the heavy dining chairs – they prove to be heavy to look at and heavy to move, as well as being uncomfortable.

I then hear a noise coming up from the basement, something slow moving around, nothing dramatic. I look up at Dario to see if he noticed, and he sure has, grinning at the floor and then at me and then back at the floor. He then fills up a plastic electric kettle and puts it on to boil.

"Many of Piotrek's associates. But not only them. A lot of the crews around town have taken a dislike to your style of doing business. They get it into their heads from time to time to off someone – just to be seen flexing a bit of muscle, you understand that. Nothing personal, doesn't always have to be, but motives aren't really the most important thing when the guns are pointing your way, right? You've lost a lot of money... money that belonged to someone else. Some people think it is a sign that you are losing touch with reality. People know you were interviewed by detectives, and they would like to find out exactly what it is you did and said while behind those closed doors. They'll be coming back for you soon too, once that girl you just cut open in that nightclub reports the assault. Kuba, I myself might be inclined to think you've already lost the plot. It happens to the best of us. The work we do is not about bean counting or selling groceries. It's more complex than that. The hardest sort of work anyone can imagine. Stressful. And a girl like that can confuse even the most professional mind. You didn't just lose your mind, you lost your ability to see things for what they actually are."

"How do you know about her?" I ask, rising off the awfully uncomfortable chair – Dario motions for me to sit back down again but I don't do as I'm told.

"I know about everyone, Kuba. I know all there is to know about all that is going on. That way I can have a say in what happens next. Let's get this straight between us once and for all. It's been a while now that nothing in this dark city happens without my say so. You may not know how that happened or like it much, but you're young, a kid from out of town, so you don't remember the bad old days. When communism collapsed, sonny, this was the wild, wild east. Anything and everything went. This is also the reason why they want to get rid of you. No one respects the likes of you – an unknown quantity, with no roots locally, no firm friends. No one to vouch for you. No one to connect you with. This is why they want you out of the way. Before now, drugs used to be dirty things, but you represent the creative, clean industries, those who snort fancy drugs, not dirty things like meth or speed or heroin or ketamine or whatever else. You were a way into those with serious disposable incomes, the world of celebs, but that has now all gone sour."

I end up sitting down, suddenly sensing how soft my knees have gone.

"I don't have your drugs," I tell him. "I had your bag, but someone lifted it from me."

"I know. I also happen to know who stole it from you. Don't you worry about a thing, son. Not a thing, right?"

As he says that, I feel cold and hot shivers running up and down my spine. Dario walks over to the boiled kettle, makes me a tea and then brings it over. I am both flattered and frightened. I realise I could take the boiling hot tea, fill it full of sugar and then scald Dario with the super sweet tea – the high sugar content makes the mixture stick to clothes and skin, causing maximum pain and long-lasting disfigurement – an old prison trick I heard about. And while Dario was trying to rinse the scalding, sticky mix off his flesh, I'd have enough time to find a knife and put him out of his misery. I could, I think to myself, but I do no such thing.

Now I get it. We both get it. Me sitting down and Dario standing over me. We both know our paths were always going to converge like this. This is where it was meant to end. Only now is it starting to dawn on me what it means to be denied any sort of control. Dario has stripped me of all freedom. Some of which is a blessing, and some a curse.

When Tiny was walking me down those stairs, a gun pointed at my back, when those fucking cops were dragging me down the corridor to be interrogated, I could have made some other moves, could have said something else, could have retained my dignity, my honour, even if I had been smacked in the face again, or even shot in the back. Regardless of what the reaction would have been to my action, it was still the last time in recent days that I still had any say in what was going to happen next.

Currently, I no longer have any control over what happens next. Dario can do whatever he likes. He can decide he wants to be the one who will from now on be known as the one who killed that pesky coke dealer, the smart ass from out of town, and if he pulls the trigger I will be able to do nothing about it. I suddenly realise my mouth is full of spit. Fear is making my throat tighten up – I can't seem to be able to swallow my own saliva. I then realise this whole bungalow is heated to some insane degree, must be a wood-fired furnace downstairs or some gas boiler – whatever it is, the whole house is like a sauna.

"So, they could try it tonight. They could be waiting for you outside the airport. Unlikely, but it's Christmas, so they might chance most of the high-end security guys, the ones toting Navy SEALs-style submachine guns, their anti-terrorist squad, are off duty, maybe on call or actually a long way from work, enjoying their holiday season without worrying about having to keep away from the vodka, because of the reduced Christmas air traffic."

He bends down and opens the hip-height fridge, looking for something within it. I see on one of the shelves inside it two more guns, medicines, a surgical drip and some surgical tools – scalpels, clamps, saws and hammers – along with some other items wrapped in tin foil. The only standard thing in that fridge is a bottle of vodka and a solitary can of Red Bull. He finally closes the door, without taking anything from it, as if whatever it was he'd been looking for was not in there.

"Why would they try tonight?" I ask, unable to move, wondering how long this whole ordeal is going to last. I put my tea down on the floor without touching it. Eventually, I move my legs just to get some circulation back into them. They both feel like I've been lying here, tied up, for hours.

"You know, Kuba. You're an interesting, creative, unpredictable kind of guy. That's what makes me like you, but it frightens others. They don't know how to read you."

He finally pulls his leather jacket off and tosses it onto an equally ghastly leather sofa. The chequered shirt he's wearing underneath it looks like the exact same shirt he was wearing when I first met him at Piotrek's restaurant. He rolls up both sleeves, carefully studying his hands as he does so.

"You're a completely unknown quantity. That is your brand, Kuba, and now your biggest problem. It's good to stand out sometimes, but you have to make sure not to stick out like a sore thumb. You earn far too much money for those watching you from the side, without actually getting your hands dirty – many think you're just too fucking soft to deserve respect, or maybe they just want what they think you have – that would be obvious. Piotrek told me straight – he said you're the highest earner of all his retail dealers, no wonder you've made an enemy or two if such words are out doing the rounds about you."

"You're right, I do have a problem with Piotrek now."

"You sure do. Or did – Piotrek is no longer a problem."

I stand up slowly, not trusting my knees or Dario's reflexes. I pick up the tea from the floor and close my eyes – bright red flashes are now exploding behind shut eyelids.

"A week from now, Piotrek will be gone. Maybe two, at most. Once I get tired of him running around town, leaving a mess all over the place, that's when his luck will run out... If it hasn't already – that bomb planted beneath his car, that really was unheard of – that he wasn't the one driving just as it was primed to go off, but some idiot kid, his fat nephew in this case, who is now going to have problems shitting and pissing for the rest of his life after he decided to do something nice for his uncle and repark his fucking Japanese jeep, was a stroke of undeserved good fortune. I don't find such coincidences funny, so very, very soon my patience with his lot might run out. And when it does, I won't hesitate to pull the trigger," he says, looking straight at me.

Dario's eyes are suddenly very clear and frighteningly glassy, his mouth drawn in a tight grimace. I realise Dario doesn't just have the one face for everyone, but has a whole set of different masks – and every time he decides he wants to change shape, he does so very effectively – in fact it's hard to say it's still him standing there before me, the face is so thoroughly transformed. He's emotionally unstable, but that doesn't mean he's logically unpredictable – he's not that hard to read in fact. Everyone who knows him is scared of what he's thinking and going to do next, but that is only because they allow themselves to be overwhelmed by his moody act, instead of trying to read between the lines of his performances, trying to peek behind his masks, to see the true nature of his monstrosity.

This is maybe why he needs me. To see just how much a guy like me is able to read of his act. To test the limits of his performance. This man we keep calling Dario, even though no one really knows what his true name is, has killed many men, men who died slowly when he wanted them to suffer, men whose bodies were still being nibbled on by the fish in the Vistula by the time he was already driving his latest luxury car to some warm resort in Croatia or Italy or maybe even Crimea. A few days in the tropics was probably always enough to improve his mood.

"It's only business, Kuba," he says to me, snapping his fingers. "Me and my boys. This whole town owes us something in one way or another. The fucking mayor, the president of this goddamn town owes us. You see, ten years ago, when the present order was settling in, and everyone was looking at the old maps of Warsaw, trying to work out which plot of land belonged to whom, we were the ones who helped people agree and sign the right documents, either paying sweeteners or just cracking heads together. And then afterwards, many people thought I would be sitting behind bars for a lot longer than I did, or that I would take the coward's way out and tie a belt round my neck and the other end of it around the top of a bunk bed while no one was looking. Or that a shank would find a way into the side of my stomach, piercing a kidney or the liver – why? Because I know things about people they would rather I didn't, you see. Knowledge, oh yes Kuba, it is power indeed, and not everyone feels comfortable around real power. Still, I know how to deal and how to turn a profit off the things I have or know. Unlike a certain Piotrek we both happen to know. Don't you go worrying about that associate of ours. His days are fucking numbered. He's a loser that fat fucker, and like all losers he'll end up out back on the rubbish heap. I might even say that I'm sorry about that, but I won't because I'm not."

More noises from below, scraping, banging, voices perhaps, low growls.

"Are you keeping dogs down there, Dario?" I ask.

"No. I hate animals. They all stink like hell," he answers, grimacing.

I put my hands in my pockets – trying to do all I can to speed up this conversation. I have to get the hell out of this horror steam house as soon as I can.

"What are you offering me?" I ask Dario.

He smiles again, turns and stares at me, unhurried. Then he reaches over, putting his hand on my shoulder. I let it lie there. He uses the other hand to remove his glasses and place them on the kitchen worktop. When he starts speaking, I have the impression someone is spreading some form of edible oil in mid-air. He speaks softly, his voice floating out like an oily, warm liquid.

"Offering... Not sure if 'offering' is the right choice of word," he tells me. "You're just too valuable to kill. You can make a lot of money for me, it's that simple. Besides, I like watching you work. No joke. A great pleasure. It's like watching an action movie develop, a crime thriller. In real life, I would deal with the likes of you differently – I would grab you by the scruff of the neck, punch your teeth out, chase you right out of town. But watching you I feel we're just actors in a movie. I would never have said that someone like you could actually thrive in our dirty old town. But you've made up your mind to be a tough guy. It seems you were a talented little lad when you were little, am I right? Always chosen for the school plays, right? Able to act whatever was called for. Always quick on the uptake. One of the first to learn how to read and then write. My sister has a kid like that. A boy called Adam – show him all those Jap cartoons about all those scientist kids, bionics or whatever, he can pick it all up straight away, no explaining needed. He can recite whole sections of plot from every episode. Rather scary, Kuba, I have to tell you. Gifted kids are always going to spook people. Being so quick to count, to read, to analyse and assess. They quickly work out that the future for the likes of them is wide open, unlimited. That they can be whatever they like in life. You, my lad, at some point decided you were going to be making a living from working in the criminal underworld, am I right? You didn't want to be a doctor or a lawyer, or whatever else your parents wanted you to be, or maybe even become a real life actor, starring in actual movies, rather than like now acting a certain role but in real life. You wanted respect, didn't you? Money and power and fancy clothes. And for people to fear you, because you worked out a long time ago that this emotion offers the greatest guarantee of security. Though you were a gifted kid, Kuba, you were no playground boxing champ, am I right? You wanted to live a life where you would no longer have to live in fear ever again. Not of the other kids, nor of your own father, who

I imagine did like the odd drink, and when he came home he liked breaking things – your toys? Your school things? Maybe even liked to crack you over the head. And now you don't have to depend on the old man for anything, not money, not acceptance, and you now know how to handle the old man, how to neutralise the original ogre. I had the same sort of monster in my home. I liked building plastic Airfix and Matchbox kits, you know the old war planes, Spitfires, Lancasters. And this one time he called for me to come have my supper but I was so absorbed in building this plane that I didn't hear him. Then he came to find me, and when he entered my bedroom, he picked up the biplane, I remember it had two layers of wings, some World War I aeroplane – picked it up, smashed it into smithereens, then ordered me to eat those plastic shards. Do you understand, Kuba? According to my father, if I was more interested in plastic toys than in the food my mother had prepared for me, then I would fucking eat the fucking biplane. And eat it I did, with all the toxic glue and paints, while my papa stood over me, laughing as I cried to have to say goodbye to a precious model. I cried crunching all those plastic parts, and later that night an ambulance took me to hospital to have my stomach pumped, all those chemicals clearly not doing my young entrails any good. That's how afraid I was of the old man. So I get where you're coming from. But others were scared of me too, Kuba. Because I was always slightly different than most of the other kids. Not that I remember myself, you understand, but they said I was – like this one time when I was four years old and I strangled all the geese on my aunt's farm. Fifty fucking geese killed with these bare hands. When my aunt came to check on the birds, she found me in the pen holding a finger to my lips, telling her to be quiet because 'Shush, shush now, don't wake the geese, because they're all sleeping now'. And so others were scared of me too. I know what it is like to feel fear and to be feared. I had this pal in high school, this loser, a bit of a camp lad, not exactly a tough guy, and every day he'd sit in the school corridor between lessons, reading up on his homework. And every day I would walk up and kick those books from his hands, send them flying down the corridor, while he scrabbled to pick them and all his papers up off the floor. He probably still has daydreams about killing me. If anyone ever does kill me, it's not going to be any cop or any of the lads from the city crews, no gangster, it'll be that guy. I know it. One day he will show up at my house, holding a knife, and I will open the door... he will just stroll in here and he'll fucking stab me, and I won't do a thing, because I'll be powerless to do anything, that fucking spineless kid holding all the cards for once, just because he's tired of living in fear of me."

I let him talk on and on, then I check my watch. He approaches and touches me again, sticking his index finger right into my solar plexus.

"You, you, Kuba," he says. "You're no tough sort, no bad guy. You like acting the tough, heartless, soulless type, dressed in the finest, most subtle designer clothes, like some psychopath, not a street thug, no gangster. That's how you want them to fear you. You think if you put on the right kind of act it will work the right sort of magic for you. Always busy scripting events, always nurturing new thoughts, new visions for your own personal movie. Because the world around us is simple – your friends are the most important things in that world, there's no such thing as dirty money – and you'd best remember that all women are only interested in the same few things, all of them except your own Ma. Simple, see, Kuba, but you don't want to accept these ancient truths. They're too simple for you, and you don't like things too simple. You're too creative to do that. Simple thugs don't get that – when they see you they imagine you must be gay or some sort of deranged freak, others yet think you might be mentally unhinged, seeing as no one has yet come after you, no one has put a bullet in the back of your skull... that if you fuck around, then it must be weird kinky shit. I tell you this to make you aware that it's not just you watching and analysing people, they're doing the same to you too. They say all sorts of things about you, and you know why suddenly everything in your life went crazy of late? Because someone managed to work out you're not really insane, you're just acting, that you're just an ordinary kid trying to get paid without getting your hands too dirty or putting your neck too close to the line. That you're no tough guy, not really. That at night you cry into your pillow, that you've been having recurring nightmares since school. That you do like to cuddle up to girls not to fuck wild but just to cuddle, to suck on their little nipples. And now I have you here and I can look right into your eyes, I can see it's all true and there's not a thing you can do to disprove that. Why did you waste time going to see that cold bitch – just to cut up her face? Because you love her, right, Kuba? While she was cheating on you, and if you didn't love her then you wouldn't have felt the stinging, the burning, your brain wouldn't have boiled over and put you in that compromising position with her."

I get my breath back, still saying nothing in reply. More sounds of movement rise up from the basement.

"You were living in a fairytale of your own making, Kuba. Time to start walking on solid ground. I will help you find your way there. More than that, I can finally help you become who you've always wanted to be. I will do that because I like you somehow. Because I want you to work for me, making a lot of very nice, clean cash. Then once we're done running the streets of this town, we can have interesting chats about all sorts of things. I will have you, smart ass, to advise me on a range of matters. Then once we're done establishing our rule over this city, we can go on holiday, somewhere cheap and sunny, to go fucking local girls in the surf. Maybe go as far as Thailand, those girls with dicks, they are fine I tell you. The best in some ways. Anyway, whatever it is you fancy, you'll buy it and have it all for yourself. We'll make a lot of lovely dollars. You can go on holidays wherever you like. You'll buy yourself a house. Open some legit businesses. Ten years from now you'll be fully legit. You'll be able to piss and shit all over people if you feel like it. Fuckers like Piotrek – they'll be the ones working for you. They'll be kneeling before you just to catch all of your golden piss. I will help you and you will let me help you too. Otherwise they'll find you one of these days and kill you on the spot – they've already worked out your secrets, how your mind works, that you're just an ordinary mummy's boy, teacher's pet. You studied fine fucking arts and that was where you got your start dealing. As soon as they find you, they'll use your fucking blood and brains to paint a picture. And you can imagine what that's going to be of. What it will look like."

I glance down at my watch.

"Stop looking at that thing," Dario tells me, smiling. "You've got all the time in the world."

I look up into his eyes, which glow like there was some kind of inner torch lighting them from within.

"Come with me to the basement," he says. "I want to show you something. Don't be scared," he appeals, reaching his hand out to me.

"Visible darkness," the phrase runs through my thoughts again. He is darkness made visible. He wants to take me to his house, the bit of it which is below the surface of this city. Beneath the sidewalks, the streets themselves. And there he will make me an offer...

"Leave your tea up here – come, I want to show you something special, lad."

We leave his kitchen and salon combined and go deeper into the house, which is filled with more objects and smells, the stink of dry rot, of rising damp, of vinegar.

I see objects piled up in huge plastic sacks resting against the walls: clothes bought decades ago, raincoats, summer jackets, books, broken pottery and plates, rubble.

"I'm removing my grandma who passed on," he says. "She lived here for the past fifteen years. She passed in the spring. Managed to make it almost to a full century. Wonderful woman."

"I don't have much time," I remind him.

"Didn't I tell you just a moment ago that you have all the time in the world?" Dario asks, turning before a shiny white door, apparently the entrance to the basement.

He opens the door outwards and enters the doorway.

For a moment we remain in the darkness, then Dario lights the overhead lamp. The basement is filthy – dirt on the walls, on the bare concrete steps – dirt rising up from the ground, mixed in with dust, set in layers upon the walls. A solitary bare lightbulb hangs from the ceiling, revealing more useless objects – old wellington boots, boxes of imported washing powder, rolls of electric cable, rope and wire.

Before he descends all the way, Dario turns and stops to look at me and say: "I will help you become the person you want to be. That is when we will be happy, Kuba."

I descend once he walks all the way down, and we walk along a narrow corridor, lined with doors to some cupboards. The space is dark and oddly silent. Then I can hear those noises again, things growling and shuffling about. Someone is at the end of the corridor.

"Treat this as a fortunate beginning to our partnership," Dario tells me.

"And so we're partners already," I say to clarify the point, staring at the door at the end of the corridor. The person or thing which is on the other side of it was making those noises, the ones I could hear from upstairs.

"Yes, we are," Dario confirms.

"But I am leaving," I remind him.

He begins to laugh.

"Yes, I've always liked travelling. Me and the lads from the Pruszkow gang did like to jump on a plane to Tenerife, to Greece, charter some yachts, go sailing, this was before all the fucking last minute deals everyone goes mental over nowadays, back in the days when people who had money and class flew out to those places, not the peasants we get now, with neither money to spend nor class to show off."

"I'm going somewhere none of the local crews will bother trying to find me," I tell Dario, with the uncertainty of a five-year-old, a dissonance I can't seem to be able to swallow down and remove from my voice.

"Everyone can be found, Kuba," Dario assures me.

In a moment of sudden realisation, when all the coolness of the block of ice lodged in my guts rises to my head, a change of inner dynamic my body crowned with a deep sigh, I suddenly realise for certain that I will never be coming back from Argentina – that which was originally planned as a holiday has now turned into a permanent escape. That things I had to come back to are now gone, that Dario is right once again, that I will be shot, drowned in the Vistula, or if I'm actually lucky I'll just get arrested a day or so after I get off that return flight.

That's the end. The only way out. The dark heart which beats beneath the surface of this city releases a long, slippery thread, a thread which has lodged itself in my stomach, my heart, and the time has finally come to cut that thread. That is why I have been driven here, that is why Dario has brought me down to stand in front of the door at the end of the corridor in his basement.

I don't yet know what is expected of me. I have twenty thousand bucks in cash. It's not much, but something to go on. Me and Pazina will rent an apartment. She can get a job working behind a bar. I can get some stupid job managing a place to start with, or maybe just clean up after others, or look after someone, helping out in a kitchen, chopping salads, prepping fish, all that sort of jazz. We'll be happy, saying less than ever. She knows talking doesn't always help. One of her best qualities. We will probably start sleeping with one another. That far from home, it would not be an unhealthy thing to do. I can find some better work soon enough, if I manage to pick up some of the local lingo.

It will be a strange, impoverished sort of life. Short of many things, but it will be far from here, that's what matters.

Or maybe I'll just keep doing there what I've been doing here. In order to do what I've been doing here I just need to meet a few of the right faces. If I pull the same trick out there, I could be making real money again real fast.

How much coke can 15,000 dollars buy in Argentina? And what's the profit margin on wholesale prices? Hell, I can get that sort of info in the first nightclub I come across. Tomorrow really is the start of something very new. Not totally new, but very new all the same.

"Kuba, now then. Let's get down to some solid facts. You'll rent a different apartment, I've already sorted you out with some new documents, a new identity," he says, looking at me with his watery fish-eyed gaze. Only now he looks authoritative, like a teacher.

"Dario, I don't think we're really connecting here. I haven't agreed to anything yet."

"It's a nice pad, in the suburbs, the classy end of town, a new block of luxury flats, a friend of mine just had it built and it's still mostly unoccupied. As for supplies of coke for you to sell, forget all the troubles you've been having with Piotrek. I have my own supply lines, and we've just taken delivery of a few kilos of really top notch, pure grade coke, via the Black Sea, you might say. Crimea is wide open right now, I can tell you that much. I have the first kilo here for you to test and make sure you approve of the quality. You just tell me what price you think I can sell it at wholesale, and then we can be in business, as long as we get the lawyer business sorted first, of course."

"What lawyer business, Dario ?"

The thing which is on the other side of that door can hear us – it hears and thus begins to howl. Meanwhile, Dario begins to explain.

"Who do you think got you released from the interrogation? It was my guy, a certain barrister, we've been friends a very long time – he helped me deliver 200,000 zlotys to their door, seeing as that was the bail amount they were setting. If he hadn't delivered the money on my behalf, we would not be here right now having this little chat. They wouldn't be letting you see the streets until next Christmas, at best, if not for his little handout. But when you get back I'm sure you'll be keen to sell one of those apartments you've been using for your nefarious activities, thereby making your debt to me good real quick."

"Wait a moment," I interrupt his train of thought. "So you sent the lawyer who paid my bail? But how did you know I'd been taken in for questioning?"

"Kuba? Do you never listen to anyone other than yourself? I told you already – nothing happens in this city without my knowing about it, even if I can't always exercise early approval." He then places his hand on the handle of the door at the end of the corridor.

The person the other side of it is still howling, even though it seems a little muted, as if it was escaping a pair of lips which had been sewn together. Dario pushes down on the door handle, but doesn't yet open the door itself. I hear him talking: "Kuba, I will tell you one more thing. Your biggest mistake was to believe you really are living inside an action movie – filled with rich zombies who only come alive when you show up with your little baggies of magic powder. Driving your fancy car it's easy to believe that you're some kind of superhero. Well, there's more to real life than such silly fantasies," he says, opening the last door in the corridor.

I see through the open door a room the size of a small bathroom – in the centre of it, I instantly recognise Uncle, tied to a heavy old chair with gaffer tape and several tie clips – although considering how covered in blood he is, recognising him is not that easy. His face is swollen, his limbs are too, wrapped and tied together to the chair, the rest of him looking exhausted – not from doing anything, only from battling pain. I look down at his knees, which have been drilled through with a cordless electric drill lying on the floor between us. Someone has taken his socks off in order to pull his toenails out using the set of pliers lying next to the drill. His face has been cut into with something sharp, like some crazy kid was trying to etch some tribal shapes into his cheeks, forehead and chin. His toenails have been torn loose and tossed into a bucket which is set next to his chair. I don't know what else is in that bucket. I look at Uncle, able to recognise the man only because of the shape of his body – his facial features are now all over the place, mutilated by pain, the rest of him soaked in streams of blood, dirt, tears and grease.

"You have to prove yourself of being able to respond to new circumstances, Kuba," Dario says to me and finally stops smiling.

Some sort of noise is coming from the other side of one of the walls, like the beating of a giant heart.

Dario approaches a wooden shelf, roughly constructed with simple nails, holding up some tools, screwdrivers, pliers, buckets. There's also a gun lying up there. Dario picks it up.

"I'm the most generous person you've ever met in your life, Kuba," he tells me. "With the possible exception of your mum."

Uncle begins to howl. Dario approaches him, grabs the rag which has been stuffed into his mouth with two fingers, carefully pulling it loose and tossing it into the bucket on the floor. A pained howl flies loose of Uncle's lips, followed by a whole load of spit, dripping down his chest.

They must have really taken their time working on him, and it seems they enjoyed the torture. There's no way Dario could have overpowered and dragged and tied Uncle up all by himself. He must have had help.

"This gentleman had my drugs," Dario says. "And he gave them to you to keep safe, Kuba... and when he realised the drugs were stolen, he then stole them back from you, am I right? And not just that, but he took all the other precious items you had stashed away, correct?"

I don't get it, looking first at Uncle then at Dario.

"You explain it to him," Dario instructs Uncle, seeing the confusion on my face. "You explain how you left him holding some stolen cash and gear, and then you robbed him of it. Tell it straight."

"This is why you've done this to him? Just because he stole something from me?"

"Nope, not just because of that. In our line of work it is sometimes necessary to take off a head or two, just to make a valid point."

"Fucking hell, have mercy..." Uncle blurts out. "I didn't... We attached the tracker device to your car, yes. Back in that Russian restaurant. That's how we found your second apartment. How we knew about your stash."

He looks at me with a tired but hard gaze. His eyes don't know how to ask or plead, even if his lips utter the pleas. I still have respect for him. In some ways I feel sorry for the man.

"We planned to steal the bag with the drugs and the cash back from you even before we gave it to you to look after," he mumbles with some effort, battered lips and missing teeth not helping either.

The beating of a black heart. I feel it somewhere nearby. Over us or next to us, in some corner of this basement, which seems to me an endless labyrinth, which must extend beneath all of Warsaw, as far as that damned Bethlehem, maybe even Swan Lake, or even further than that, maybe it really does never end and can be used to disappear in for as long as anybody would want to live in it, indefinitely, in the darkness which replaces everything, including air to breathe.

That is the final stage. This is how it was supposed to look. How it must look.

Maybe Paz and I will find an apartment in some old house by the sea, just like that. On the coast or on some island. I don't know why I'm all the time thinking of moving in with her. Some place where the night is not the full story, where the nights are light and refreshing like a cool, fizzy soft drink, where they go by fast because they're always followed by a satiated, burning hot day, a day wild enough to spin anyone's head. I will only have one pair of trousers, will eat only fresh fruit, will not have to speak to anyone, will not have to be confronted with tortured gangsters, won't have to deal with the consequences of small and major crimes, be interrogated by violent detectives.

There are people out there who live free of such miseries. There are many people out there in the world who do not live in Warsaw.

"You're mine, Kuba," Dario says, handing me the pistol.

I don't want to accept the gift. I don't even want to touch it, but my hand reaches out and wraps itself round the grip, like it was a totally natural thing for it to do. The gun feels like a tool, not a deadly weapon, something which has over the years evolved, warped shape to better fulfill its purpose, to fit the human hand – Dario stands with his back to Uncle, then places his hands on my shoulders.

"First, you will take care of those clients you already have. And then we can think about expanding your customer base. We won't take over any more clubs, that is always going to mean trouble, strong arm tactics – it's better to open our own – make a profit on everything, booze, a whole range of snorting powders, girls, restaurants that will be known for the quality of the food and the service. You know what all the bloggers are looking for now, what's in and what's out. This city will soon belong to us, Kuba. I could sure use a smart alec like you, Kuba."

"Yes, Dario, but do you remember my flight is taking off soon?" I ask sternly.

He takes out the gun he has hidden in his pocket and puts the muzzle to the side of my head.

"First, Kuba, we have to make a man of you. And then we can get to work. You know what you have to do when someone wants to kill you, and is trying to catch you in an ambush?" he asks.

"No, for fuck's sake, lads, we can sort this out," Uncle mumbles.

His body makes one more strained attempt to break free of his binds, but it's too tired and the tape and the zip ties too strong.

"I'm leaving and you'll have to kill me if you want to stop me going," I tell Dario, but too softly and quietly for the words to really hit home.

"Kill the motherfucker," Dario orders me. "Kills the scumbag, the one who set you up and then stole what was yours. Go on, do it!"

I have a gun in my hand and another pointed at my head. In front of me there is Uncle in the kind of state when a human being no longer looks like a member of their species. Dario's lizard eyes are unreadable, the light behind them furious.

"Kill the fucker. Now, Kuba. Do it."

"I'm leaving. I need a break. You understand."

This is the end. I will never see Warsaw again. A good thing too. The best sort of solution. All I need now is to get to that airport and cut that slippery black thread.

"I know, Kuba. You keep on telling me about it over and over. I told you I get why. Do it. Do what you have to do and then you can get to your airport, and from there wherever it is you chose on the map to get your richly deserved rest," he says kindly without lowering the gun.

Cut the thread. Tonight might be my last chance to do it.

"You should never pretend to be something you're not, lad. Lying is wrong. You have to face the true music. The truth is this giant, welcoming, beautiful door, at least it is to me. Before you step through it your feet are mired in all kinds of bull crap, but the other side of the door there is a treasury. Filled with gold," Dario muses.

"No! For fuck's sake, don't!" Uncle growls. "Please, no! Not now!"

"If not him, then you die tonight, Kuba," Dario announces. "This I can guarantee you, personally. Without me on your side, you won't get far. And if you ever get back from your foreign holiday, you'll be dead the very same day you land, guaranteed," he whispers, his mouth moist, the words slithering out.

Cut the thread. Run far from here. If he tells me not to breathe, I will stop doing that. Dario can do anything he likes. I can only do what he lets me. But then he will let me leave this hell hole. I will make good my escape. Leave, finally. My heart beating fast.

"Kuba, we don't have time for deep thoughts. I thought you were in a hurry to catch a flight," Dario presses.

Although he's standing next to me, his voice sounds like it's coming from a long way off.

The escape. To cut loose.

Bang!

This is an ordinary, simple moment, the pushing of a button on a complex remote control, nothing major, a moment and it's done, when my hand raises the pistol and pulls the trigger, and Uncle's head stops existing with a sound which is just as banal as the sound of a hand bursting open a plastic bag which has been inflated like a balloon for a joke.

"Good boy," Dario says and I smell his stink as he kisses me on the cheek.

Fuck.

In my thoughts, I apologise to him for what I was forced to do, in order to get out of this basement, because I have to do that in order to get further away. The thread has been cut. Suddenly, I realise I am shaking, and only now see that intense red colour everywhere, flooding all the surfaces around me, becoming more and more vivid with every beat of that black heart. A slight delay has crept into all that which exists. A lack of synchronisation. I can no longer keep on standing in one place.

I start to cry, my head hurting terribly.

"It's done, Kuba. You've changed. You're no longer a liar, a fake. Good boy. Don't worry about it."

I take a step. Something crunches under my shoe. Bits of brain and skull. I crouch down over whatever is left of Uncle, as if I was going to tie a shoelace. I pause there for only a second.

I can't kneel – too much risk of getting blood on my trousers.

Somewhere far from here there are nights that are refreshing.

"Now go home, get changed, get some rest," Dario says. "Take a shower. Have a short nap. Tomorrow, at twelve noon, you'll come back here. I will give you new ID, new number plates, keys to your new apartment, and that kilo I promised you."

He grunts like a pig.

"It's just like working in any big firm," he tells me. "I'm always on the lookout for good employees, simple, right? And when you find such people, you try to grab them and get them working for you as soon as possible."

"But I'm leaving. I told you I'm leaving for a while."

"You're not going any-fucking-where, kid. We start as of tomorrow," Dario whispers moistly. His voice is now very close, right by the side of my head.

Dario opens the door. I look down at Uncle. There's little left of his head. Something black is beating loudly and evenly like a bell the other side of the wall.

"Do please finally realise that you're not going anywhere, not going to do anything, not even to take a dump without me saying the words 'shit now' first, Kuba my boy," Dario announces.

I still can't keep my hands from shaking. Something has altered, something permanently rearranged in the world.

"You're going home now," Dario explains. "You're coming back here tomorrow at noon."

I want to once again tell him that I'm flying tonight, but I don't have what it takes to keep driving that point home.

"I don't give a fuck about you, lad. But in a way which is different to others. I don't give a fuck about you, not because I don't care, but because I know I can trust you to do the right thing."

And again his laughter fills this underground hell hole.

9:45pm (Diluvium)

I see them from the back seat of the cab slowing as they overtake us.

Maybe they're slowing down, or maybe everything has changed tempo. Maybe time has become stretched, the tape on which we're all recorded chewed up by the machine of the world and soon enough everything will stop full stop.

They are riding in a V-shaped formation, as if on parade – angels on parade. Their white overalls blend right in with their white motorcycles, only their faces covered with multicoloured masks, souvenirs from a strange carnival which took place a long time ago, on a different planet. They pull all sorts of strange moves on their machines, standing the bikes up on the rear wheels, standing up on the saddles while still holding on to the handlebars.

Each one of them passes close to my cab and looks me in the eyes. "They're angels," I think to myself for some reason. Maybe because I cannot tell what sex they are in those over-suits. Angels riding in formation through this hell, soon to sail away, for there is no room for the likes of them round here, not that they have any intention of asking to be allowed to stay.

"Fucking crazies," the cab driver says, and it's the only thing he says all the way to the airport.

I can't remember the last time I was in a taxi cab. My leather travelling bag is in my lap – in it I have some money, documents and tickets. I hold on to it tightly. Dario could have kept hold of it, all he needed to do was to point one of those handguns at my head again. He didn't, the thought didn't even seem to cross his mind. Then again, I was still holding the other pistol. Maybe he wanted to put himself in a safer position. Or maybe he wanted to see if he could trust me.

Some go down beneath the concrete, to the lowest level of the city, coming face to face with darkness, and listen to what it claims to have to offer them. But they always lose. When you start doing deals with the darkness, there is no room for negotiation when it comes to the conditions of the deal.

Warsaw is a desert. Made of blood and cement, its residents are Bedouins, and can die any time of any day – they claw at the blood and the cement with their fingernails, just to find a little water.

I am a resident of a desert. About to leave it behind. I don't feel sorry for whatever it is I'm leaving behind. I don't give a damn about Uncle, not worried about whatever's happened to Beata. All I need to do is wink to make all those things just vanish in the blink of an eye, to make everything vanish. To turn everything that happens in this city into a faint dream.

The route out is covered with advertising billboards on both sides – dedicated to petrol stations, care repair garages, stations of the cross. It's a tunnel which leads outside. We are cruising along it slowly, the road iced over and slippery. I feel neither calm nor frightened. I feel no sense of joy, nor the block of ice which has been lodged in my belly for the past few days. The ice has melted, nothing of it left. I cling onto the bag, the radio dripping distant tunes, almost inaudibly quietly – but eventually I recognise those subtle sounds, the *Goldberg Variations*. But I don't bother trying to read anything into the coincidence.

I close my eyes but can't keep it up for long; the inside of my lids seem permanently covered with bright red paint. Was Dario right? I don't know, I've no idea.

I didn't want to be anyone else – because it's not possible to be someone you're not – if you're a nobody, then a zero multiplied by any given number is still a zero. All I am is a worm. A bug. I wanted to move around without hindrance. Deal with as few other bugs as possible.

The fact that I've just had to kill someone is impacting on my body, but that's all. We're driving down a tunnel beneath the airport terminal, and I start to get the right amount of money in cash for the driver.

"Did you not have anything in the trunk?" the guy asks.

I shake my head and, once we've stopped, hand over the banknotes then exit, clutching my precious bag. It's awfully, bitingly cold outside – I'm only wearing my blazer. It might have spots of blood on it, but I hope the artificial lights in the airport buildings won't let it show. Maybe no one will look closely at my fingernails, nor ask any questions about the blood still lodged beneath them.

I'll have a shower and get changed once we land.

The taxi drives off. I see Pazina standing nearby, smoking, watching over a pile of suitcases. I recognise her straight away by the odd sort of dance she always performs when waiting for someone and feeling impatient.

I have a moment in which to approach and greet her. I turn,

wanting to look back at the city, now barely visible, black blurring into blackness.

Nothing will change here. Everything will live on forever the way it is now. Small, blind beings will keep on bumping into each other in all that darkness, falling asleep sometimes, dreaming and fantasising about something happening, a sign appearing in the sky, a golden light that will appear at the end of the labyrinth.

But none of that shall pass. Nothing more will change. It won't even deteriorate. Perhaps this city has exhausted its fair share of apocalypses – the wars, the uprisings, the occupations, partitions, etc. What else could go wrong in the middle of such a desert?

I now notice other people standing about – a man in a suit, bald but bearded, staring at his smartphone; a middle-aged woman wearing sunglasses at night, hanging around with a younger woman, maybe a daughter, both silent; then there's another guy standing not far from Pazina.

They don't seem to have noticed me or to care that I'm here.

I don't know who they might be, where they're going to, and if they would ever be capable of believing me if I told them all the things I had to do in order to make it to this terminal this evening. Maybe they'd just shrug their shoulders, because in spite of what Dario said, we all live in separate voids.

I don't know who they are, but I do know I am a drug dealer and now a killer – this was what I wanted and maybe in a moment I will have to change again, or maybe it's enough transformations for one night. Maybe this is a kind of truth about the lives we lead, that the dreams we get to have for real are a cross to bear, a burden we then have to drag around with us until our dying days.

Pazina waves to me, which is the very moment Dario chooses to ring me. I take the phone out of my pocket, but don't answer. Instead, I keep on walking – that's another thing I like about Paz: she will never come to you, instead she always has to be approached. I feel strangely light walking towards her. Everything that was weighing me down is now being left behind. Nothing else can happen now to interfere with our plans.

"Come here, Kuba, now!" she shouts at me.

I smile at her, though I know she can't see it. Dario rings again and for some strange reason I choose to answer.

"Kuba, I forgot to tell you one thing," he says.

I say nothing, watching Pazina waving at me. I keep walking towards her, the phone glued to my ear, the heavy bag weighting me down, putting me off my balance.

"If you did after all go to that airport," Dario says, "Then you really do have to listen to me."

"Speak," I reply.

"You know, it's damn annoying when someone agrees to work with me and then fails to do what they're asked to. The conditions of our partnership were made clear, weren't they? I give the orders round here, right? You're meant to be at my place at noon tomorrow."

"This is now behind me," I say to myself in my thoughts. *"It is all done and dusted. All that was is now behind me. See you."*

But then I find myself actually speaking into the handset: "Fuck off, Dario," I tell the boss, still getting closer to Pazina.

"Ha ha! Fuck off me, how clever of you, Kuba, listen, I know you're probably at the airport, I understand that, I would have gone myself if I was in your shoes. But give me two minutes, and let me find my glasses."

I'm now just a couple of steps away from Paz. She's wearing some comfortable joggers, a T-shirt and a warm hiking jacket. On her face I see the usual expression of irritation and impatience. She doesn't like long introductions and small talk – always has to get straight to the point. And in some way I have missed that about her.

"Bloody hell, Kuba, I thought for a minute there that you weren't gonna show," she tells me.

I point to the phone, indicating to her that I'm talking to someone.

"And so, Kuba," Dario continues. "Andersa Street number 41, apartment number 29. Ewa Nitecka and Leszek Nitecki. Olsztyn, that's where your folks live, is that right? Your father works as literary director at the Stefan Jaracz Theatre, right? Hours of work – from 10am to 3pm. Mother already retired, right? Either sits at home or does little hobbies – yoga, knitting circle, all the things elderly ladies feel becomes them, right? Or else she'll go visit Aunt

Marlena. Marlena Dogmańska, Station Street number 30, apartment number 7. Right? Or do you not remember, because you've not been there for so long?"

"Shove it," I say firmly.

Pazina's eyes squint.

"Not you, Paz," I tell her, first covering the mouthpiece of the phone.

"But I think she's probably home. And can be found there most days. Olsztyn is not far, isn't that right, Kuba? Won't cost my boys a lot in petrol to drive there and back. I might go with them, take some cakes for mum and auntie."

My back becomes stiff. I look back at Warsaw, at what is visible of its rooftops from this spot outside the terminal. I see it changing colour.

"Does your Ma know how to drink boiling hot water? Well then, maybe she'll find out. What else? Paulina Nitecka, soon to be Kuczyńska, the wedding booked for the spring. Did they tell you? If not, they will soon. They have to have the wedding soon, because there is a second little Kacper on the way. They didn't tell you? You're not very close to your family, right? But family is what is most important in life, isn't that right?"

Something rumbles down beneath the sidewalk, some underground train taking airline passengers straight into the heart of the city, but I hear it as if a giant beast was rolling about in its cave.

"They live on Warminska Street number 8, apartment 11, and their little stationery shop is on Artillery Street number 15. So you see, we could stop off and pay your sister a visit too while we're there. Maybe they're not making that much money and she doesn't really want another little baby in the house. We could help her out. There and then, do what's necessary to stop new life forming – while Michal watches – that's her husband's name, right? Michal? We don't foresee him putting up much of a resistance, what do you think?"

My hand starts shaking. I lean against a column stood outside the terminal. Looking up into the sky, I see black clouds upon a black sky, forming the shape of a smile.

"That's all from me, Kuba. You start working for me tomorrow.

I will make sure the conditions of your employment are suitable. You can submit an application for a holiday later. Hugs and kisses from me," Dario hisses.

I put my phone away, without checking to see if he cut the call or if I did it first.

"You look as pale as a ghost," Paz comments. "What's wrong?"

"What's up with you?" I ask, turning towards her.

"You first."

"What's up with me?"

"Yeah. No change in my life. He went back to his wife – for the sake of the kids of course. But I'm sure the fact that his girlfriend's apartment was visited by an armed thug also made him reconsider his position. And so I am here now, and he can go fuck himself, and you can do the same – because I still haven't forgiven you. I'm considering giving you the chance to make amends once we get there. You'll have to buy me some very fine dinners for the next three weeks, Kuba. You'll have to treat me like a real life fucking princess, boy."

And so this is the way it's going to go. I signed this contract not today, but many years ago. Possibly in that out of town car park, picking up my first kilo of coke, when that girl – I still don't know who she was and what happened to her – escaped into the darkness. When I was left all alone, totally alone next to my car, with a bag of powder outside a closed McDonald's.

Or maybe I signed it earlier, at some party packed full of people working in the media, in fashion magazines and those sorts of things, which at the time were a money-printing machine – I don't even remember who invited me there – scared, shy and curious I asked how much someone would pay for a bag of powder a jolly group of them was right at that moment going to snort in a bathroom.

"Four hundred," someone said. "But we've just won a new bid for a project. So when you have the money, who'll tell a rich man: 'No?'"

Four hundred zlotys. During that rather odd party, which then became something of a timid orgy, people starting to get undressed, having sex, wrestling each other, dancing – another five such bags of powder were ordered. And there I was watching people completely off their heads blowing their hard-earned cash, trying to get away from their orderly, hygienic, nicely designed lives, sweating, dirty, loud, tearing off each other's clothes in full view of everyone else. I wasn't paying them the least bit of attention. Instead, I was doing basic maths – four hundred times five, times ten, times three hundred and fifty six. I did the sums and felt a sense of freedom, felt as if someone had opened a window inside of me and let in a gust of fresh air.

Before me there is asphalt. A wide river, a great asphalt desert. I am affixed to it permanently.

I unzip my bag and pull out an aeroplane ticket which I then give to Pazina. She takes it, puts it away inside her pocket, then lights another cigarette.

"So this is all I have left. I am going to Argentina with a coke dealer, because that's all I have left to live for, the only bit of fun coming my way. But that's how these things work out. We take what we're given," she says.

I look at her, smiling as honestly as I can. Then I come closer, lean into her and kiss her on the lips. They taste of cigarettes, bubblegum, something else that's sweet – lip gloss, probably. She leaps away as if she'd been struck by a bolt of electricity.

"Have you lost your fucking mind?" she asks.

"You're flying alone," I tell her.

It's clear she's having trouble comprehending what it is I've just said to her.

"Have you gone completely fucking crazy?" she asks me again.

"Go alone. Don't come back. Of course, if you contact me, I will buy your return ticket, but don't ask. Don't come back here, Paz. Promise me you won't. I'm asking you," I say, but it's not coming out as speech, more like coughing up rubble.

Her eyes open very wide. The cigarette falls from her hand. I pick it up, put it back between her fingers. I then open the bag, take out the last of my money and hand it over.

"This should be enough to start with, to get settled in. Put some money down on an apartment, rent for a few months, once the hotel bill comes up for renewal (but the hotel I chose and paid for up front really is something special). Then maybe you'll find some work for yourself. Maybe not. But don't come back here," I plead.

"What the hell are you going on about? Why aren't you coming? I'm not going alone. Fuck you. No way, Jose."

"You're going alone. Just so that I can really know it's possible to get away from here, Paz, to cut the black thread." My voice cracks when I say the words.

She says nothing then, just comes close, puts the money in one of her suitcases, then starts crying.

"You have to do it. You've always dreamt about this sort of trip. Consider it payback for all the horrible things I've done to you."

"You've always known, right? You knew you weren't going to go?"

"Maybe I did."

She could be right. Something beneath the surface of this city is hungry, mouth whetted with awoken appetite, ready to be fed again.

Maybe she is right, because not counting certain kinds of cancer, everything that happens to people is always what they serve up for themselves.

"Something terrible has happened," she says quietly.

She brushes my cheek with her fingertips.

"Terrible things happen all the time. I'm a fucking bandit, Paz," I say, instinctively checking my fingernails.

"We're all bandits," she replies and kisses me on the cheek.

Then she hugs me. She feels warm, or maybe it's just me suddenly realising how bloody cold I feel tonight.

"I really did like you a lot. You're the only person I met and got to really like," I say, my mouth right next to her naked neck.

She once again whispers in my ear, a soothing "shh", and starts stroking my head. She stops soon enough, as if she realised it was somehow inappropriate for us, while I realise I am sorry she stopped. But that it is also too late.

"As I said, your hotel is paid for up front for the next three weeks. Then you rent an apartment. You can go travel around from there."

"I'll write you. You have to know that places others than this really do exist," she says.

"If we ever come to talk about this, don't ever ask me why I didn't go with you," I ask her.

"Thank you," she replies.

"Don't thank me."

A woman's voice announces something over the speaker system, mentioning the start of check in, but I don't hear the details – the loud hum inside my body is too loud for me to hear anything else. It might have something to do with the cold, maybe not.

"I guess I have to go catch a plane," Pazina says.

She sniffles a little, rubs her eyes once more.

"Go on," I tell her.

"Look after yourself, Kuba," she says.

I nod and say nothing more. I will never get the chance to say anything to her again, I know that now. I do hope the life she finds on the other side of the planet is one which will somehow be to her liking.

She waves to me and slowly, without turning around, vanishes inside the terminal building.

I turn back towards the city. Warsaw too is quiet tonight and I exhale, rubbing my hands for warmth. It knows what I might have to say to it tonight, so my lips remain sealed. No point wasting words. I lift my head up. A cloud overhead, a shapeless, ill-defined growth upon the sky. Then something hits my face. And the skin of my hands.

Drops of water.

Rain.

I reach my hands out, letting some drops land on my palms, and then look at them in the light of the terminal.

The drops dirty my hands, leaving long trails of dark water, as if someone had emptied a vat of ink into that cloud.

The sky is dripping black, warm water.

I smile to myself.

It's started at last.

My phone rings a symphony.

If you enjoyed what you read, don't keep it a secret.

Review the book online and tell anyone who will listen.

Thanks for your support spreading the word about Legend Press!

Follow us on Twitter
@legend_press

Follow us on Instagram
@legendpress